The
MILE HIGH
CLUB

Indigo Publishing Group, LLC

Publisher	Henry S. Beers
Associate Publisher	Rick L. Nolte
Executive VP	Robert G. Aldrich
Editor-in-Chief	Joni Woolf
Designer	Scott Baber
Print Studio Manager	Gary G. Pulliam
Print Studio Assistant	Nick Malloy

©2009 William Rawlings

Disclaimer: Indigo Publishing Group, LLC does not assume any legal liability or responsibility for the accuracy of any information or content in this publication.

Library of Congress Control Number: 2009937762

ISBN: (13 digit) 978-1-934144-76-3
       (10 digit) 1-934144-76-2

Indigo Publishing Group books are available at quantity discounts with bulk purchase for educational, business, or sales promotional use. For information, please write to: Indigo Publishing Group, LLC, 451 Second Street, Macon, GA 31201, or call 866-311-9578.

The

MILE HIGH
C L U B

a novel by
William Rawlings

For Tommye Cashin,
My most loyal fan.

CHAPTER One

Laura McIntosh looked almost as beautiful in death as she had in life. She lay in repose on a large mound of fragrant green pine boughs, her eyes closed, her arms spread comfortably at her sides. Were it not for the fact that she was totally naked, and the ugly stump of a tree branch protruding from a ragged wound in her right upper thigh, one might have assumed that she'd chosen this shady spot for a brief nap before continuing with whatever plans she had for the day.

The clearing was deep in the forest at the base of a small pine-covered rise in the otherwise flat terrain, miles from the nearest paved road. The morning sun inched its way into the cloudless May sky, daubing the scene with splotches of yellow light. The logging foreman flicked his cigarette down and ground it out with a scuffed boot saying, "Shit." Then, "What the hell happened here?"

"I have no idea," I replied.

"You say you know her?"

"Yeah. Her parents live down the street from me. I had a couple of dates with her last summer." I took a deep breath. "Who found her?"

"They did," the foreman said, nodding toward two Mexican laborers standing to his side.

"You called the sheriff yet?" I asked.

"No. It's your property. I figured I'd better wait on you."

"What'd your guys say? How did they find her?"

"They got here a little after seven," he said, glancing at his watch. "About half an hour ago. I pulled up few minutes later, took one look at the situation and called you first thing."

"But how...?"

"Damned if I can figure it out," he continued, not waiting for me to finish my sentence. "A rainstorm blew through yesterday afternoon 'bout time we were knocking off. There was a good little shower, but when we got here this morning there weren't any fresh tracks leading in or out—least any that I could see. And the gate on the road was locked anyway—whoever left her here had to have a key."

"But...." I started again and was interrupted a second time.

"She don't look to me like she's been dead that long. Look at her," he said, gesturing with his right hand while fumbling with his left in his breast pocket for another cigarette. He was right. She appeared more asleep than dead.

"And where's her clothes?" the foreman continued. "I looked around before you got here. There ain't nothing. Just a naked girl laying up there on a bunch of pine tops." He fished in his pants pocket, extracting a Zippo to light his cigarette.

"We need to call the sheriff," I said, taking advantage of the foreman's distraction.

He inhaled deeply and replied, "Yeah. I know. I think...."

"Mr. Charlie?" He was interrupted by one of the Mexicans standing behind him.

The foreman turned his head. "Yeah, Mario. Whatcha think?"

"I am not sure, but I think this *chica* flew here from the heavens."

CHAPTER Two

It occurred to me that from the perspective of one of the vultures circling lazily above on the morning thermals, the scene would have appeared to be some sort of a religious ritual. A glade deep in the middle of thousands of acres of pines, a sacrificial pyre with the body of a beautiful young woman on top, and before it, groups of reverent pilgrims come to witness the ceremony.

As it were, though, the truth was more mundane. The glade was nothing more than a clearing bulldozed in the midst of a pine plantation for the loading of logs onto trucks for shipment to the mill. The "pilgrims," who now numbered more than two dozen, were an assortment of law enforcement officials, technicians from the State Crime Lab, and a gaggle of morbidly curious loggers hovering on the periphery watching the investigation. As for the dead girl, only the happenstance of my recognizing her gave her a name. Otherwise, her presence there and how she had arrived remained a complete mystery.

The possibility of a religious connection did not seem lost on the sheriff, who paced back and forth as he spoke. "Well, it don't make sense," he said. "No fresh tire marks leading in or out by the road so the victim—and whoever was with her—had to get here cross country, through the woods." I watched him carefully. He was about my age, just past thirty, and had been in office less than six months. I didn't really know him that well.

"Looks to me like it could be one of those satanic things, you know. Pile of brush, naked woman, that sort of business. They were probably planning to burn her as a sacrifice to the Devil. I read about something like that happening a few years ago in north Georgia. Couple of dopers...."

"I doubt it, Ben." The voice came from Wayne Guillard, one of the local physicians who served as Adams County's Medical Examiner. He stood watching as the crime lab techs examined and photographed the body. Nodding his head in their direction he said, "Those fellows' take on the situation is that nobody brought her here—they think she landed here."

"What...?" The idea clearly caught the sheriff off guard.

"It's not a bad theory. Think about it. Here we are in the middle of nowhere with a dead girl up on top of a pile of discarded pine tops." He pointed at her leg. "Look there, see the branch that looks like it's poked through her leg from beneath? That kind of injury would have required a tremendous amount of force. And the guys up there examining her say she's got a bunch more branches stuck in her back. They're thinking it looks like she may have fallen up there. The pile's soft enough to cushion..."

"Wayne, that's the craziest bit of bullshit I have ever...," the sheriff snorted.

One of the deputies who'd been assisting the crime lab team tapped on my shoulder. "Mr. Rutherford, the GBI is ready to take your statement now."

I was a little surprised. "I don't have a statement to make. I don't know any more about the situation than anyone else."

"I'm sorry. Capt. Moore said he wanted to talk with you. I'm just delivering the message."

"Sure," I said, and followed him over to where the captain had established a make-shift desk on the extended tailgate of a pickup. He appeared to be studying his notes.

The officer looked up and extended his hand, "You're Mr. Rutherford?"

"Call me Matt."

"Okay, Matt. I have a few questions for you if you don't mind."

"Not at all," I replied, wondering why he wanted to talk with me.

Moore flipped to a clean page in his notebook and scribbled "Rutherford" and the date across the top. "First, a few formalities," he began. "Your name is Matthew Rutherford, correct?"

4

"Right. Matthew Rutherford, no middle name."

"And I understand you own this piece of property."

"I do."

"And I was told the loggers discovered the body this morning, but it was you who identified her, is that right?"

"I recognized Laura, yes. But I haven't seen her in nearly a year."

"Hmm," he replied and scratched a note. "And exactly what was your relationship with the deceased?"

"We had a couple of dates, in May or June of last year if I remember correctly. At the time she was a graduate student in Atlanta. It didn't work out, so we haven't been in touch."

"No contact at all?" I shook my head. He continued, "You're not married, is that correct?"

"I'm not."

"Mr. Rutherford, how is it that the body of a woman you say you know and dated ends up in the middle of a piece of your property? Sort of a strange coincidence, isn't it?"

It dawned on me that I was on the suspect list. "I have no idea."

"Okay." Moore wrote a few more words in his notebook, then said, "Can you account for your whereabouts last night?"

"Up until about ten, yeah. After that I was at home alone."

"Did you talk with anyone? Make or receive any phone calls?"

"Not as I recall."

He flipped his notebook shut and said, "I'm sure we'll have more questions once we've finished here. I just wanted to get a gut feeling about you."

"Suspicious of me?"

"I have to be. It's my job."

"And...?"

"I think you're telling the truth, but I'm going to need documentation."

I breathed a silent sigh of relief. "So what are you thinking?"

"Don't really know. The techs think she was alive at least for a short while when she was placed on that pile. Had some bleeding from her wounds. Right now I'd say she was drugged; someone brought her here early this morning and threw her body up there. Probably intended to set fire to it to cover up some forensic evidence. In all likelihood they didn't count on the loggers showing up so early—scared 'em and they hightailed it off through the woods. 'Course you don't ever know about these things. We'll need the autopsy report, drug screens, and...."

"Capt. Moore," the sheriff yelled across the clearing.

"Yeah?"

"I think you better come here. There's someone you need to talk to."

Moore walked over and grabbed the cell phone from the sheriff's extended hand. He listened in silence for a moment then said, "You've got to be kidding me." Then, "How long ago?" A pause. "You're sure about that? Women's clothes? And...?" Another pause. "No shit? We'll wrap it up here and be on our way." He handed the phone back to the sheriff.

"You never know...," the sheriff began, his voice trailing off.

"What happened?" I asked.

"A plane crash, thirty miles north of here in Hancock County. No fire. Looks like it ran out of gas."

"What does that...?" I started.

"There was a body in the wreckage, apparently the only one in the plane. Male, late twenties. Naked. And a pile of clothes, including a bra and panties."

"And one more thing," Capt. Moore said.

"Yeah, one more thing," the sheriff echoed. "A purse with a driver's license in the name of Laura Anne McIntosh."

CHAPTER Three

The general assumption seemed to be that Laura McIntosh had fallen from the sky. The fact that she was naked, and the fact that her clothes, identification, and a naked male body were found in the wreckage of an airplane in a neighboring county implied her final flight involved more than staring at the stars. But at this point, it was all speculation.

A violent death is never a routine event, particularly one that snatches the life of a beautiful young woman. Even more so in a small town, where everyone seems to know at least *something* about everyone else. Rumors of the bizarre demise of Laura Anne McIntosh swept through Walkerville like wildfire in a June wheat field. I had scarcely been home ten minutes before the phone calls started. I politely pled ignorance to the first few callers, then took the receiver off the hook.

I couldn't say I'd known much about Laura's personal life. As I'd told the investigator, we'd had a couple of dates nearly a year earlier. She was in graduate school at Georgia Tech in Atlanta, working on her PhD in applied biochemistry as I recalled. We'd had dinner, went to a movie, drank some wine and made idle conversation. Nothing more. I hadn't heard from her since. The discovery of her body on some property I owned had to be a freakish whim of fate.

Laura's parents lived several blocks from me up Main Street. I didn't know them well. As a child growing up in a town the size of Walkerville, you have a vague idea where adults fit in the general scheme of life. I was dimly aware that Laura's father had once owned the local Ace Hardware franchise, and that her mother had been a school teacher. They were an older couple and both now retired. Laura was their only child, conceived unexpectedly when her mother was in her mid-forties. Protocol dictated I needed to pay them a courtesy call.

I called the local funeral home to find out if there were any plans as yet for services. They told me they expected the State Crime Lab to release the body the next day. Laura's parents had requested she be cremated. There were possible plans for a memorial service "at a later time," but nothing definite. The receptionist did say the family would be receiving callers at their home today from six to eight if I wanted to go by and pay my respects.

I left for Laura's parents' house shortly after six, thinking I could be in and out in less than ten minutes. I dressed conservatively in a dark sport coat, white shirt and somber tie, walking instead of driving the short distance. The McIntosh home was a nondescript red-brick ranch with white trim, set back behind a meticulously groomed yard landscaped with late-blooming pink azaleas. It looked more or less like most of the other houses on the block, built in the late fifties and early sixties during one of Walkerville's rare housing booms fueled by Korean War veterans with low-interest government loans. Dozens of cars and pickups lined the street for several blocks in each direction, with a queue of visitors awaiting entry snaking down the front stoop and across the grass.

I saw my Uncle Jack and Aunt Margie standing in line near the steps. I cut ahead and joined them. Jack shook my hand; Margie gave me a hug and a peck on the cheek. "I hear they found the body out on the Brooks tract," Jack said by way of greeting. Several nearby conversations suddenly stopped and half a dozen pairs of eyes turned our way.

"Yeah."

"What do you think happened?" Jack asked.

"I really don't know, but maybe we should talk about it later."

He nodded and changed the subject.

The line inched its way up the walk, across the porch and into the front parlor. Through the door I could see Laura's parents, alternately hugging, smiling grimly or looking very exhausted as the crowd filed past. Her mother, hair drawn back in a tight bun and face heavily made up to hide the dark circles under her eyes, intermittently daubed at her tears with a crumpled tissue. I didn't know her exact age, but guessed her to be in her early seventies. Laura's father appeared to be a good decade older. He was thin, slightly stooped, and stoically thanked each visitor, shaking their hand with a mechanical regularity as if in a daze.

I followed behind Jack and Margie who passed through with softspoken condolences and words of encouragement. I wasn't sure if the McIntoshes would remember me, having met them only once. To my surprise, Laura's mother hugged me and said, "Matt, thank you so much for coming. I keep thinking about last year when you and Laura...." She stopped suddenly in mid-sentence and swiped at her eyes with the tissue. She didn't finish, biting her lower lip and saying, "Thank you," then turning to the next person in line.

Laura's father brightened a bit when I shook his hand and mumbled something about, "She really liked you, you know," before thanking me for coming. I caught a strong whiff of bourbon on his breath.

I moved on to the tiny dining room with its heaping plates of fried chicken and cheese straws supervised by the Senior Women's Sunday School Class of the First Baptist Church. A cup of punch and a paper plate were thrust at me, which I politely refused. I cut through the kitchen, shook hands with half a dozen acquaintances, and ducked out the side door, through the carport and onto the street. I'd made an appearance. I'd done my duty. It was a tragedy, yes, but such things happen. I was as curious as anyone as to what the final story would be, but at this point I had no need for further involvement.

The following morning's *Atlanta Journal-Constitution* had a small item on page D4 of the Metro & State section mentioning "2 Fatalities Connected to Small Plane Crash in Hancock County." The single paragraph was filled with phrases such as "continuing investigation" and "believed to be an accident," and noted the names of those killed were being withheld "pending notification of the next of kin." No reference was made to the fact the bodies of the two victims were found some thirty miles apart, and that both were naked.

The afternoon's local *Adams County Sentinel* was scarcely more revealing in terms of details, focusing instead on the untimely accidental death of Laura McIntosh. It featured what appeared to be a photo of her taken from a high school yearbook. Her obituary stated she had recently been awarded a doctorate and "was living in Atlanta where she was engaged in ongoing research for the Southeastern Division of American Timber Holdings Company." The only survivors listed were her parents.

The news of Laura's death was the main topic of gossip and raunchy conjecture in the cafes and coffee shops for the next few days, but by the end of the week Walkerville was settling back to its usual leisurely pace. I half-expected to hear from the Georgia Bureau of Investigation for the promised follow-up interview, but by the end of following week no one had called. I did receive a handwritten thank you note from Laura's mother, acknowledging the flowers I'd had the florist deliver to the house.

For practical purposes the short life and tragic death of Laura Anne McIntosh seemed to be fading into memory.

CHAPTER Four

It wasn't that I was being callous, or that I didn't care about Laura's death. It was just one more event in what had become my joyless world.

I'd lost control of my life and was drifting. It was the start of my third year back in Walkerville. This was not where I had intended to be, but the twin events of losing my job in Silicon Valley and the unexpected inheritance from my great aunt of a rambling old house and several square miles of timberland had changed my mind. I'd traded my Jag for a Ford pickup, and my Starbucks and sushi for coffee served in white porcelain mugs in restaurants featuring fatback and grits for breakfast.

It was a comfortable, even easy existence. The one thing I didn't like was living alone. I'd been seeing, and thought I was in love with, a girl named Lisa. We'd split up during the winter, and I'd wandered aimlessly into spring. Somewhere in the back of my mind I expected a sign, an undeniable signal from the gods that would give me a sense of purpose and direction. In the meantime, I muddled on, living day to day, managing my inheritance and wondering if life was in fact this meaningless.

I kept a small upstairs office with a part-time secretary in a building on the City Square, dropping in for an hour or so every day to sign checks and return emails. Otherwise I read or hung out at the local coffee shop. With Lisa gone, my life was empty. I tried writing, but could find nothing of interest to say.

I'm not close to my family. My father died when I was young, and my mother has spent the intervening decades in and out of an alcoholic haze. My only consistent friends and confidants have been my father's brother, Jack, and Eula Mae, my aunt's housekeeper who stayed on to work for me after I moved into Rutherford Hall. Uncle Jack keeps his distance, checking in every now and then to see how I'm doing. Eula Mae, on the other hand, considers herself my surrogate mother and resident expert on all things pertaining to my life, especially relationships.

The next few days trudged past with slow deliberation. I saw nothing more about the accident in the newspapers, and local gossip moved on to juicier items. The talk on the street was that the body of the man found in the wreckage had been identified as that of David Hargrove, Laura's fellow employee at American Timber Holdings, someone she'd recently been dating. Details of the accident washed up in bits and pieces from various sources.

According to one of the sheriff's officers with whom I'd shared lunch at The Country Buffet, Hargrove was a licensed pilot and avid skydiver. Based on some video surveillance footage gleaned from an airport camera, he and Laura had "borrowed" his skydiving club's plane, apparently for the purpose of high-altitude sex. The deputy was quick to point out—between mouthfuls of okra and turnips—that the seats in the back of the plane had been removed in order to hold more passengers who intended to jump out of the plane, anyway. "Just the perfect spot for that sort of thing," he concluded. "They just put that sucker on autopilot and were going at it in the back seat. Just like in high school."

I ran into Dr. Guillard while filling up my truck at the corner convenience store. He said he'd been told by the techs at the State Crime Lab that both victims had carboxyhemoglobin levels between 40 and 50 percent. When I told him I had no idea what that meant, he explained the working theory was the plane must have developed a small exhaust manifold leak. It probably hadn't been detected before because most of the time it was used for short flights, and even then the door would be left open after the divers jumped.

"But this time the door stayed shut because they were..." he paused, with a sly grin, "...distracted. Probably fell asleep on the blankets in the back of the plane. The guys at the Crime Lab figure Laura woke up and realized what was happening. She had to have been pretty groggy and in her confusion pulled the door open to try to get some air. She tumbled right out. Even if she hadn't, though, they were both doomed. It was night. The plane was about out of gas with no place to land. Anyway you look at it, they both were going to die. Sad."

The thought of it all, the terror, what must have been going through Laura's mind as she fell, made my flesh crawl. I paid for my gas, bought a six-pack of beer and went home, trying to purge the images from my thoughts.

✈ ✈ ✈ ✈

The next day I was standing in the checkout line at the grocery store with a cart full of microwave dinners and junk food when I noticed a headline on the front of one of the tabloids: PROM QUEEN KILLED IN "MILE HIGH CLUB" INITIATION. I jerked it out of the rack and stared at a candid shot of Laura McIntosh posing in a bikini on a white sand beach, her arm around a tanned, muscular guy in his late twenties. They were both grinning and waving at the camera.

I threw it in my cart and shuffled through the selection of soap opera weeklies and glossy magazines featuring advice on weight loss, sex, child rearing and quick ways to disguise hamburger hash. I found two more. The *National News* featured a photo of Laura in a formal gown and tiara wearing a ribbon proclaiming her as "Miss Adams County," under the bold black headline "MILE HIGH CLUB LEADS TO BIZARRE DEATH." The *East Coast Post* ran a small item on the front referring readers to page six inside, and another headline proclaiming, "NAKED BEAUTY PLUNGES TO DEATH FROM AIRPLANE."

I got home, opened a beer, stuffed a dinner in the microwave and spread the tabloids out in front of me on the kitchen table. Despite the difference in headlines and the varying photos, the stories were basically the same. It was easy to see they had all been adapted from the same source. The facts were sketchy and none were bylined, most being attributed to "local authorities," whatever that meant. The theme was the same: Small town girl moves to the big city, is corrupted by the evils of urban life, dies horribly as a direct result of engaging in kinky sex. I felt sorry for Laura. I felt sorry for her family. I wondered how the hell they'd gotten the photos.

As usual, Eula Mae had her own take on the situation. "If you axe me, it be that dope they smokin' up there in Atlanta. My sister's husband's niece, she moved up there after she finished school, say she was gonna get outta this here small town and find herself a decent job and make some big money. Well, she ain't been there no three months before she be smokin' that crack, and next thing you know, she wavin' down mens on the street..."

"I really don't think Laura was into drugs..."

"But that's jes' it. You don't know 'bout nobody these days. Look what all *you* been through with the people you thought was yo' friends."

She was right. "You may have a point. I don't think you can ever truly predict what a person's going to do, but from what I remember of Laura, I just can't see that side of her."

Eula Mae frowned and began rattling pots in the cabinet. Her face turned away, she muttered, "Miss Lisa's gone. You never thought she'd do that, did you?" She was opening old wounds.

✈ ✈ ✈ ✈

I spent most of the next couple of days checking on the logging operation and working on the old stables behind the house. Part of them had already been converted for use as a garage. The rest, mainly the old tack rooms with their shelving and storage racks for saddles and harnesses, would make a good workshop, I'd decided. And it gave me something to do. I had no basic knowledge of carpentry, but figured I could learn on the job. For the last couple of months I'd been ripping things out and was now in the process of putting them back together.

I quit about five-thirty and walked back across the yard to the house. I grabbed a beer out of the 'fridge and noticed the light on the answering machine was blinking. I hadn't heard the phone ring, but I'd been sawing and hammering so I could have easily missed it. I pressed the message button and heard an unfamiliar voice say, "Matt, this is Carl McIntosh, Laura's father." There was a slight pause. "I, er, rather we, my wife and I, would like to talk with you. I know you're probably real busy, but when you get a chance, we'd like you to come over to the house. We're here pretty much all the time. You don't have to call, just come over—tonight will be fine. We'll be expecting you." There was a click and the machine announced, "End of messages."

It was more of a command than an invitation. I had no idea what they wanted. I finished my beer and headed upstairs to take a shower.

CHAPTER Five

It was just after eight when I arrived at the McIntosh house. The sun had sunk below the treeline, bathing the yard in soft twilight. I could see the grass needed cutting, and the few remaining azalea blooms were wilting on the plants. The front porch glowed from a single overhead lantern, but the windows were otherwise dark. I rang the doorbell and waited, watching the candleflies fluttering around the glowing orb of the light.

Inside the house there was a shuffling, then the tinkling of a chain being unlatched followed by the creaking of a turning deadbolt. Laura's mother opened the door cautiously and peered through the crack. Confirming that I was alone, she turned on the lights in the small foyer and invited me in. "Matt, thank you so much for coming. Things have been...." She paused, not knowing what to say. "Come on back to the den. Carl's been wanting to talk with you." Taking one last glance around the yard, she shut the door and turned the bolt.

I followed her down a narrow hall toward a dimly lit doorway at the end. The house exuded an old-people-musty smell, as if its inhabitants rarely ventured into the outside world. We stepped into a large den illuminated only by the silent flickering of a small television and a single reading lamp next to a worn recliner. I ventured a quick glance around the room as my eyes adjusted to the relative darkness. The walls were lined with cheap plywood paneling. It was sparsely furnished for a room its size, just the recliner, a worn matching sofa, a single wing chair, plus an assortment of small tables, one of which supported the television. A set of large windows looking out on the back yard was covered with tightly drawn drapes. A mismatched assortment of frames holding photographs and certificates hung over the sofa. I could make out Laura's face and name in several of them.

There was a stirring in the recliner. A boney arm reached out as Carl McIntosh slowly pushed himself up. His plaid shirt was buttoned to the top, and he wore both a belt and suspenders. This was not the sort of man who took chances. Gripping my hand firmly he said, "We really appreciate you sparing us some time." His wife leaned over and turned on another lamp near the end of the sofa. His already thin frame had lost even more weight since Laura's death. "This has been real hard on us, you know."

"Of course," I replied, unsure of what they wanted.

"Sit down, please," Mrs. McIntosh said, pointing me toward the sofa. She sat in the wing chair while her husband eased himself back into his recliner. "Can we get you something to drink?" She appeared nervous.

"No, thanks."

There was a moment of awkward silence, then Carl McIntosh spoke. "I know you're wondering why we wanted to speak with you." He hesitated, then said, "We really appreciate your being here," for a second time.

"I'll have to admit that I am curious. Can I be of help to you in some way?"

With that suggestion they both seemed to brighten a bit. Audibly taking a deep breath, Laura's mother said in her best schoolteacher voice, "Yes. Perhaps. We don't really know." She bit her lip. "We need some, er..., guidance, direction." She unconsciously gripped the armrest of the chair, her knuckles turning white. "You know about Laura, of course...? The circumstances? How she was found?"

"Yes. I was there."

"Oh, I know that! It's so stupid of me to ask. It's just that..."

Her husband interrupted her. "Agnes, let me do the talking. Matt needs to know why we asked him here. We don't want to waste his time." Turning to me, he continued, "My wife's very embarrassed about this, and rightfully so, but this is no time to stand on formality. We need some advice, some help. We didn't have any idea who to turn to, but we talked it over and since you already know some of the details, we called you."

"Okay." I had no idea where this was going.

"We just...," Agnes started.

"Honey, let me do the talking," her husband repeated softly.

She nodded assent. He reached over the side of his recliner and picked up a small pile of newspapers. Holding one up under the reading lamp he said, "I guess you've seen this?" It was a copy of the *National News* with its MILE HIGH CLUB headline in bold 2-inch letters.

"I have."

"And these?" He held up successively half a dozen other tabloid-style papers from around the country with similar headlines. Most of them featured candid—almost sexy—photographs of Laura. Several showed her in swimsuits or on the beach, others appeared to have been snapped at parties. A couple were semi-formal portraits taken at her Senior Prom and as a member of the Adams County High School Homecoming Court. He passed the newspapers over to me one by one. Like the ones I'd seen at the grocery store, the basic story was the same with varying degrees of speculation and detail: Small town beauty queen moves to the city, falls in with evil companions, and dies while having sex in an airplane.

I looked them over silently then said, "That was not the Laura I knew."

"That was not our Laura," her mother replied.

"How did they get these photos, though?" I asked. "They had to have come from one of her friends—or at least someone who knew her very well."

"That's exactly correct, Matt," Carl McIntosh said. "They got them from us. We signed a release for them to use every single one of them." My head jerked up. "Let me explain. If you don't mind listening, I'm going to tell you the whole story."

CHAPTER Six

"We never thought we'd have children," Carl McIntosh began. "We both married late—I'd spent twelve years in the army and was nearly thirty-five. Agnes is eleven years younger than me. Back in those days you married young and had most of your kids by the time you were thirty. We tried and tried to get pregnant. When nothing happened after several years we began to look for help—went to half a dozen doctors all over the southeast. Every one of them gave us the same story. Said I had a low sperm count or something like that. Said we'd never be able to conceive on our own and suggested we either use a sperm donor or consider adoption.

"Well, we talked about it and prayed about it. We finally reached the conclusion that if the good Lord wanted us to have children we would have, and we just accepted our fate. We were pretty well surprised when Agnes turned up pregnant when she was forty-four and I was fifty-five. She had the baby just after her forty-fifth birthday. We named her Laura Anne, after both of our mothers.

"Matt, you don't know what Laura meant to us. She changed everything. She gave us a new reason to live, to make life something special for our darling little girl. And even though we were older, it didn't seem to matter. Heck, I was the same age as the grandparents of most of Laura's classmates. She was a perfect child. She was beautiful and well-mannered. She did well in school. She...." He hesitated, snuffling and wiping a tear from his eye. I looked at his wife. Tears were streaming down her face.

"Anyway," Carl continued after a pause, "as we got older, our whole life, everything we did, focused on her. Laura got this idea she wanted to go to medical school. To do research on cancer or something—I don't really know. She was accepted at several colleges, but finally settled on Georgia Tech. She said they had a real good pre-med curriculum and so on. To make a long story short, somewhere along the way she decided that rather than see patients, she wanted to do research, something about helping the environment and all that. Laura was always idealistic. Thought if she worked hard enough she could do some real good. Maybe change the world. So she got her PhD instead.

"When she was at Tech, she started working part time for this company, American Timber Holdings. She finished her dissertation and got her doctorate last December and they gave her a job right off. Good starting salary, she said. And it was right there in Atlanta so she didn't have to move and could be back here to see us in a couple of hours on the weekends. In fact, they've even got a research lab right here in Adams County on one of their timber plantations up near Warthen. Laura thought there was good chance she might get to work down here full time. Seemed like the perfect opportunity for her."

I couldn't figure where McIntosh was going with this. He was clearly devastated by his daughter's death, but he seemed to be rambling. I decided to speed things up by getting him back on track. "So how did the photos end up in those newspaper articles?"

"I'm getting to that," he said. "I guess I was trying to make two points. First, our daughter meant everything to us. She was our world, our whole existence. The sun rose and set in her eyes. The second thing was that she couldn't have done what they said she did. Agnes and I just can't believe our daughter, our precious baby, would be involved in something like this." He waved one of the tabloids, his voice cracking. "They say she was up in some plane in the middle of the night having sex with this boy, Hargrove. That was not her. She couldn't...."

"Mr. McIntosh," I gently broke in, "the world's a different place than it was a few years ago. People Laura's age—my age—have different values and ways of expressing them than they did in years past. It may be hard to believe...."

"No, no, *no!*" Agnes interjected. "We were very close. I'm her mother. She would have told me if she were involved with someone. We could talk about things like that. I think she was still a virgin."

Mentally, I rolled my eyes. These people were totally out of touch.

"She was seeing a boy here locally—Roger Barmore. Runs a heating and air-conditioning place. They'd dated some in high school and had started going out again last year. She wouldn't. She couldn't...."

"But the photographs?" I asked again.

"Those," Mr. McIntosh said. "Yes, those." He paused. "It's probably my fault. I...."

"No it's not, Carl," his wife said firmly. "We were both fooled. That man Rizzoli just suckered us both right in. Let me finish telling Matt what happened." Her husband nodded and hung his head.

"You remember they found Laura's body on a Tuesday morning?" she said.

"Yes."

"Well, we had a lot of people over here at the house, helping out, doing what they could to console us. But those ugly rumors about Laura just wouldn't stop. I know she didn't have any clothes on when she was found, but there *has* to be another explanation. Whomever I saw that week, or whoever saw me, I knew what they were thinking. It was so embarrassing, so disgusting. I just wanted to scream that it didn't happen the way they thought it did. But I couldn't. I couldn't because I..., I didn't know what to say.

"And we got phone calls—a lot of them—from newspaper and television people wanting to hear our side of what happened. I talked to a few of them—the first ones that called—but then I started hanging up on them. They didn't really care about Laura, about how smart she was and about all her accomplishments, they just wanted to know what she was doing up in that airplane and how we as her parents felt about it. The very idea! A beautiful twenty-five year-old girl who died tragically, and that's *all* she's going to be remembered for?"

Agnes McIntosh blotted her tears, blew her nose in the tissue and continued. "Well, on the following Monday morning—that was six days after

Laura's death—we got a phone call from this man from Atlanta named Tony Rizzoli. He said he was a freelance writer and photographer for newspapers and magazines, and he'd heard about what happened to Laura. He wanted to interview us. Of course, the first thing I thought about doing was slamming the phone down, but he had a nice voice and he sounded sympathetic and wanted to listen to what *I* had to say instead of just asking me questions. I told him about all the ugly rumors and all, and he said maybe he could do something about them. Rather than having our daughter remembered as this…," she searched for a word, "…*slut…,*" spitting it out, "…that folks were making her out to be, he could write something saying how smart she was, and about all the good things she'd done. He was very polite. I told him we'd think about it and he said he needed to know quickly because if he was going to get a newspaper to take an article he needed to have it quickly while Laura's death was still fresh on everyone's mind. He said he'd call me back in an hour.

"So, Carl and I talked it over and agreed to meet with Mr. Rizzoli to at least see what he had to say. He called us back and we told him we'd talk with him. He said he had some free time, and he could come right on down that afternoon."

"He was a kind, sensitive man," Carl McIntosh said. "Or he seemed to be. He told me he was a Yankee and he'd grown up in Boston, but had been living in Atlanta for about five years. Said he made his living writing. He was Catholic, and said he'd sent articles to *Today's Christian Woman* and some other magazines we'd heard of—I guess looking back at it he didn't say he'd had anything published in them, just that he'd 'sent' them articles."

"We talked with him for a while, and he seemed like the nicest man," his wife continued. "He wanted do an article memorializing Laura, focusing on all her achievements in high school and at Georgia Tech. We must have gone on for three hours. He said he wanted to get some photographs, especially ones that showed Laura smiling and having fun with her friends—told us newspapers and magazines were much more likely to print an article if it had illustrations. So we got out Laura's old scrapbooks and photo albums and let him pick out about two dozen of the best ones."

"Did you give him the photos?" I asked.

"Oh, no," Mrs. McIntosh replied. "He had this little portable scanner with him. He just plugged it in and scanned them right there on the kitchen table."

Her husband resumed the story. "He told us anywhere he might send the article and photos would require a release, so we signed one for him. And that was it. He said we'd probably see something in print within two weeks. And we did. *This* garbage." He waved the stack of newspapers. "I want to know if we can do anything about this? We want to demand a retraction—or an apology—or something."

"Do you have a copy of the release form you signed?"

"Yes, of course. Get it for him, honey." Agnes scurried off toward the kitchen. I still had no idea what they wanted from me. After a moment she returned with a large manila envelope from which she withdrew a single sheet. A business card was paperclipped to the top.

The card read "Anthony M. Rizzoli," and under it "Freelance Author and Photographer." The address given was in midtown Atlanta, with phone number and email address below. I perused the release form. It granted Rizzoli Media Services rights to publish, syndicate and/or sell "any and all photographs" supplied by the McIntoshes, in whatever form of print or electronic media he saw fit. Worse, by signing the form, the McIntoshes had agreed to "indemnify and hold harmless" Anthony M. Rizzoli and Rizzoli Media Services from "all forms of civil liability" for the use and publication of information relating to Laura Anne McIntosh, her family and acquaintances.

The McIntoshes watched intently as I read the document. After a moment, Carl McIntosh said, "What do you think?"

I tried to choose my words carefully. "Mr. McIntosh, I think if you want an apology or a retraction, you've got problems." In the dim light I could see their faces go pale.

CHAPTER Seven

There was a moment of silence, then Agnes McIntosh said quietly, "We feared as much."

"The problem is trust," her husband continued for her. "You know, Agnes and me, we've lived here in Walkerville all of our lives. I was in business, she taught school. I suppose you could say we've both seen our share of bad folks, people who'll lie to you or steal from you in a minute, but for the most part I think we both believe in the goodness of human nature." Agnes nodded slightly, signaling her agreement. "Of all the good and bad things that have happened to us in the course of a lifetime, this has to be among the worst. That fellow Rizzoli, taking advantage of our trust just so he could sell a story—a pack of lies—and a few pictures."

"I'm not a lawyer," I said, "but I suppose you could sue him. Just from my brief look at the release, though, I think it might be an uphill battle."

"No," Carl said, "it'd not be worth it. I can imagine that sort of thing being tied up in court for years. I don't have long on this earth, and by then Laura's life would be nothing but a faded memory to most people." He paused, "No, the harm's been done."

I presumed their questions had been answered, but still couldn't quite figure out how I fit into the picture. Anyone could have told them. I sat up, preparing to leave. "I'm sorry I couldn't be of more help. Laura was a wonderful person, and I know there's nothing I can say that...."

"Matt." He stopped me. "We realize we were foolish to get involved with Mr. Rizzoli. To tell you the truth, after we saw the newspaper articles and read the release carefully, we knew we'd shot ourselves in the foot. No, I'll have to admit we sort of expected you to say what you did. We just wanted to hear it from someone else...."

"....Someone who has a more objective view of the situation than we do," his wife continued for him. "But that's not the main reason we asked you to come over tonight."

I sat back on the sofa, a bit curious, a bit annoyed. Carl resumed speaking. "We want to ask you for a favor, a very large favor. We know you knew Laura, and we hope you recognized what a fine person she was. We don't want to go to our graves not knowing what happened. Yes, we've talked with the authorities, the folks from the sheriff's office, the Georgia Bureau of Investigation people, and even the federal man in charge of looking into the plane crash, Mr. Newman..."

"Noonan," his wife corrected him.

"That's right, Mr. Noonan from the National Transportation something."

"National Transportation Safety Board, the NTSB," she said.

"Right," he said, giving her a slightly bothered glance. "What we need," he continued, "is someone to help us find out what really happened the night Laura died. We've talked about it a long time. We've prayed about it—even spoke with Brother Cason, our minister. He said—and I think he's right—that we need to close things...."

"He said we need closure," Agnes interrupted again.

"Hell! The truth is I want to know what happened," Carl exploded. "We sacrificed everything for Laura. We scrimped and saved and did without so she could have the best. The best education, the best clothes, an expensive apartment, a good car. Her mother has one idea about her. I'd like to say that I feel the same way, but I'm not a damned fool. I'm getting tired of apologizing, covering up our embarrassment, smoothing over things. I want to know if she was up there screwing some...."

"Carl!" his wife gasped and rose from her chair, heading toward the kitchen.

"Agnes, come back here and sit down," he commanded. She complied, reluctantly.

"You try to do the right thing, to raise your children the way they should be raised, as hard-working, God-fearing people who will be grateful for all they've been given. For all we know, she could have gotten into drugs...."

I tried to stop him. "I don't think Laura could have accomplished all that she..."

"Let me finish, please," he said. Then, having lost his train of thought said simply, "We want to ask you to do something for us."

I didn't reply, waiting for his request. Agnes sat quietly, cowed by her husband's outburst.

"We'd like you to go to Atlanta, to speak to a few of Laura's friends, to find out what sort of girl she'd turned into..."

"...to find out the truth about what happened that night," his wife tried to correct him.

He ignored her, continuing, "...and how she got into the situation that ended up killing her." Agnes winced at the sound of the word.

I took a deep breath, trying to think of a polite way to say no. "Mr. McIntosh, Mrs. McIntosh, I understand how you feel, the sadness, the uncertainty, even the embarrassment—to use your word—but I'm not the person you should talk to. You need a lawyer, or a private investigator, or both. I'm just a guy who...."

"....who knew Laura," Carl finished my sentence. "And who is about her age and can run with the same crowd, and who has enough time to spend a day or two on something like this."

"Mr. McIntosh...,"

"Call me Carl, please."

"Mr. McIntosh, I know you're been through a lot, and I'm honored that you'd have enough confidence in me to ask me to help you, but I am absolutely sure that this is the sort of thing you should hire someone to do. Or even check into things yourselves. I have no doubt if you wanted to talk with...."

He waved his hands with an agitated look. "I'm eighty-two years old. I'm not in the best of health, and while I do drive my old pickup down to the post office to check the mail or to the café to have coffee with the other old men, I don't even dare drive out of town. And Agnes has never driven on an expressway in her life. She...."

"I'm afraid," she said by way of explanation. "Too many cars coming up on all sides of you. I just know I'd have a wreck. The only time we ever went to Atlanta to see Laura was when she'd come down and pick us up."

"For something this important to you," I said, "I'm sure there is someone who…"

"We didn't even go to Atlanta after the break-in," Agnes said. "It was right after Laura's death. The police wanted us to come up and see what was missing, but we just couldn't. We got on the telephone and finally got the apartment manager to fix the door and repair the lock. He said he'd keep an eye on Laura's things until we could make…," she hesitated again, "…arrangements."

"What break-in?" I asked.

"At Laura's apartment," Agnes replied. "You didn't know? But I guess you wouldn't have any reason to. Apparently someone broke in her place a day or two after her death—they're not sure. We called the manager to ask him to check on things and he found someone had jimmied the lock on the sliding glass door opening onto a little patio. You couldn't see it unless you were looking for it—that's why they're not sure when it happened."

Carl spoke. "The police said it goes on all the time. There're thieves who do nothing but read the obituaries and specialize in robbing homes when the family's away at the funeral. It's a travesty. Just shows you what this country's coming to. 'Course, if Laura had gotten involved with some drug dealers, I wouldn't be sur…."

"Carl! That's enough," his wife said.

"I'm so sorry," I said, and meant it. Carl and Agnes McIntosh were suffering. I waited for them to continue. They sat there, not speaking either, apparently waiting for me to respond. Finally I said, "Let me do this, I'll make some phone calls for you, see if I can't find a good private investigator to look into things. I've still got a few friends from my days in the hi-tech industry. They should be able to give me some reliable names."

"I appreciate your offer, but we can't afford it," Carl said flatly.

"I'm not sure, but I don't think it would be that much. I'm guessing, of course, but I would say that for a couple of hundred dollars a day plus expenses you could…."

"We can't afford it," Carl repeated.

I noticed Agnes wringing her hands. "We really can't," she confirmed. "We don't have the money. We've had some problems. Financial problems. We don't...."

"We're goddamn broke, Agnes. Just tell the truth. Quit trying to hide it. We can barely afford to pay the water and light bill. If things get any worse, we'll be living on the street. And if you want to know why we're broke, it's because we spent everything we had on Laura."

"Carl, it's not like that. We had a daughter whom we loved, and we made the commitment to let her have the best possible life we could provide. It's just that there were some problems...."

"Stupidity," Carl said, looking at his wife. "That was the problem. And I'll have to take the blame for this one. Why try to hide it?" Turning to me he continued. "I had a very successful hardware business. I didn't get rich, but over the years I made a pretty good income and managed to salt away enough to pay for Laura's education and to tide us over in our old age. I retired when I was seventy. Laura was still in junior high. I sold the business—got a good price for it, too—and put it away in some fairly conservative investments. Well, that was in the nineties, and every time you turned around you were hearing about all the money folks were making in the stock market. Heck, there was a guy in my coffee club who kept talking about all the money he was making—five thousand here, ten thousand there. Sort of made me feel stupid that I had tied up all my money in blue chip stocks and corporate bonds.

"I asked the fellow who he'd recommend to give me some advice about the market. Gave me the name of a broker in Atlanta that he used. The guy's name was Lewis, Merritt Lewis. I called him to see what he had to offer. He was a little iffy until I told him how much we had saved in our various retirement accounts. When he heard that, he offered to drive down here to Walkerville so he could make his pitch. He was about like Rizzoli, seemed to be just the finest gentleman, but he was a snake in disguise. Showed us all these charts that said if we'd put our money in the stock market instead of mutual funds and bonds we would have done so much better. We listened to him and it sounded good, but Agnes told him right off the bat that neither one of us knew how to use a computer, and had no idea about buying and selling...."

Agnes chimed in. "Carl is right. Mr. Lewis made it all sound so easy. We felt like we were getting left behind when everybody else was making money in the market."

"He said it wasn't a problem," Carl continued, "that there were lots of retired folks just like us and that his firm acted as what he called 'investment advisors.' He said all we had to do was to tell him about our goals and where we wanted to be in, say five or ten years. We told him we wanted to be comfortable ourselves, but also that we wanted to leave a nice nest egg for Laura. We talked numbers, and he figured that we needed what he called an 'aggressive'—I just cringe when I hear that word now—trading strategy. Told us his firm could handle it for a small yearly fee.

"So we signed the forms giving him the right to buy and sell based on our investment goals. He had all of our accounts transferred over. He liquidated our old portfolio and started buying and selling what he called 'technology stocks,' and he did well at it for a while. It got to where I was so proud of things that I looked forward to the first of the month when I'd get my statements. He'd made us a whole lot of money, but of course it was all on paper. I didn't feel like such a fool when I went to the coffee club in the morning.

"Anyway, sometime in late 1999 or early 2000 or around that time, things began to cool off, and there was a time there when the value of my stocks started to drop. I got concerned and called Merritt several times. He said it was all what they called a 'normal market correction' and called the fact stock prices were going down 'a buying opportunity.' Even sent me some literature about how folks who'd bought when the market was down in '72 and '87 had come out smelling like a rose two or three years later. So, like the gambler I'd become..."

"*We'd* become, honey," his wife corrected him.

He shot her another annoyed look and rephrased his sentence. "So like the gamblers *we'd* become, we doubled up, started buying on margin so we could cash in when the market went back up. It went on and on. Then came the margin calls..."

"Carl, I think Matt has heard enough to get the picture," Agnes said. "We lost everything. We felt like such fools. By this time Laura was in college and we just *couldn't* tell her that we couldn't afford to support her any more. So we ended up mortgaging the house. We were just hoping that once we got her through school and all we could start paying back some of what we owed. We both have social security and I get a good teachers' pension check every month, but we have to watch every penny." She bit her lip, then said, "Matt, even if we could drive to Atlanta to talk with Laura's friends, I don't think we could afford the gas."

I wasn't sure what to say.

CHAPTER Eight

This was getting out of hand. The McIntoshes were two very unfortunate old people. Sure, I'd been on a couple of dates with their daughter, and certainly they found themselves in a bad situation, but from my perspective it didn't give them any right to ask me to look into the circumstances of Laura's death.

I stood up to leave. "I wish I could be of more help to you, but honestly I don't think I'm the right person for the job. I will make a few calls, though. Maybe I can...."

Carl cut me off. "Thanks anyway, Matt. We knew it was a lot to ask, but we thought we'd give it a shot." He slowly pushed himself out of his recliner and extended his hand. "Just don't say 'no' quite yet. Think about it for a day or two."

"Yes, please," his wife echoed and trailed me as I inched toward the door and the hall. Following me to the foyer, she turned the deadbolt and cracked the door open a few inches. After peering out into the now-dusky front yard, she opened it wide for my exit, thanked me again and extended her hand with a forced smile. I was only a few steps down the front walk when the porch light went dark. Walking in pools of light from one streetlamp to the next, I strolled home turning things over in my mind.

The next morning I was finishing my cereal and reading the newspaper when my uncle Jack appeared on my back doorstep. I invited him in for a cup of coffee. "Just wanted to come by and see how you're doing." Jack was lying. He rarely shows up without a reason.

"Fine," I said, "How's Margie?"

"Good." He sipped his coffee and looked out at the stables. "I see you've been keeping busy."

"Some, yeah." I kept waiting for him to tell me why he was there. In the South, conversations and negotiations are rarely done directly. There are the necessary inquiries about one's family, comments about the weather, and other pleasantries that must be exchanged before getting to the point of any matter.

"I tried calling you last night," Jack said. "No one answered. I didn't leave a message."

"Sorry, I went out for a while."

"Oh." He took another sip of coffee and pretended to stare out the window. He seemed to be waiting for me to volunteer where I'd been. After a moment he said, "Did you talk with the McIntoshes?"

"How'd you know?"

"They called me after you left their house."

"Did they tell you what they wanted with me?"

"They did," he said.

"Why did they call you?"

"To see if I could convince you to help them out." He set his mug on the table and gave me a serious look. "What do you think?"

"They're a pitiful old couple. They've had a terrible tragedy, and if losing their daughter were not bad enough, all this crap in the tabloids is beyond belief. I honestly feel sorry for them—I really do. But the idea of my going up to Atlanta and talking to Laura's friends to try to find out what happened is just crazy. There was an accident. She's dead. Nothing's going to change that. If they are so...."

"They want to know, Matt. They need to know."

"Why?"

"Closure."

"That's psychobabble bullshit."

"She was all they had. She was their reason for living, and the only one that might have remembered them after they're gone. They're hurting."

"I don't deny that, but why the hell did they call me? I don't...."

"I told them to."

"You *what*?"

"I told them to call you. I told them you were a nice guy. That you liked to help people and that you had some time on you hands. That you...."

"Now that is *real* bullshit, Jack." I slammed my mug down on the table and stood up. "What gives you the right...?"

"Calm down, Matt. Just listen to me for a minute." I sat down.

Jack got up and poured himself another cup of coffee, adding a slug of milk and stirring it slowly with an oversized spoon. He took a deep breath, leaned against the counter and said, "You know, for all that's been given to you, it seems to me that you're a pretty arrogant fellow." He waited for me to respond. I was silent.

He continued. "Look around you. This house, the land, the timber, those gardens out there, just how do you think you got them? Did you earn them? Did you work your ass off for years so you could have the opportunity to sit here and manage your money? Hell, no, you didn't. It was given to you, every bit of it. Between what you inherited from your father and Aunt Lillie, you're fixed. You'll never have to lift a finger. You don't have to get out of bed in the morning. Doesn't that ever bother you? Don't you ever feel just a bit guilty?"

I didn't answer.

"Look," he continued, his voice a bit softer, "I know you've had a lot going on in your life these past couple of years since you've been back in Walkerville. I know how much you miss Lisa. You're probably depressed, thinking life is pretty meaningless. Am I right?"

He was. I kept silent.

"Matt, I think you're what the kids call a 'slacker.' You're intelligent, you've got a good education, and yet you just spend your days killing time as if you're waiting for something to happen. Is that the way it's going to be for the rest of your life? You need to quit feeling sorry for yourself. Get involved. Quit thinking about Matt Rutherford for a change and do something for somebody else. It'll give you a different perspective on life."

I opened my mouth to speak, but thinking better of it, shut it.

"You remember how it was a couple of years ago when my son Lance was killed? I know firsthand how it feels to lose your only child. I guess I tried to hide my emotions, but it was *so* very hard. There is a huge hole in your soul that you just can't fill. I had this horrible sense of guilt about what I could have done or should have done or might have done to prevent it. And nothing—*nothing*—seemed to help. If I hadn't had a good wife and friends to pull me through it all, I don't know how I could have made it.

"Think how it must be for Carl and Agnes. They're old, and so many of their friends and contemporaries are either dead or in the nursing home. Laura was the one bright spot in their life, and now she's gone. Yeah, their desire to know the details of her death may be crazy, but it's what they want—maybe what they need—to accept the reality of it. Carl called me a couple of days ago. Just wanted to talk. Basically, he said they were confused and couldn't understand how someone they thought was the perfect daughter could end up dying like she did. He said they needed to know what happened. It won't change anything, but it may give them some peace.

"Carl asked for my advice. I suggested they call you. It was my idea. They wouldn't have thought of it on their own. They asked for your help only because I told them to. Matt, everything that you'll ever need has been laid on your doorstep. You've done nothing to deserve it—your good fortune is merely an accident of your birth. You owe somebody—I don't know who. And helping these old people is a good way to start repaying your debt."

My sign from the gods had arrived.

CHAPTER Nine

Twenty-four hours later I was on my way to Atlanta. As much as I hated to admit it, Jack was right. I needed something to get my mind off Lisa and all that was going on in my life. It took him shaming me into agreeing to help the McIntoshes to prod me out of my funk. And, too, it was an excuse to get out of town for a few days, maybe meet some of Laura's female friends. No matter how pure and altruistic my motivations, I was certain there were fringe benefits to be had.

Jack had stood over me while I called Carl and Agnes. I think he wanted to make certain that I wasn't going to back out. I spent another two hours sitting in their den, listening and taking notes. The curtains were open this time, looking out on a small back yard with its wilting flowers. Carl wore the same plaid shirt and faded khakis. Agnes's hair was heaped on her head in a toned-down version of a mid-twentieth century beehive, adding another set of curves to her already ample frame.

I was amazed at how little they actually knew about their daughter's lifestyle. Laura had been living alone in an apartment in Buckhead, one of Atlanta's tonier districts. She had a roommate at one time, someone named Sandra—last name unknown—who also worked at ATH. The McIntoshes didn't know much about her except that she'd moved out several months before their daughter's death. There were friends, again mostly first names, but no one person they could identify with whom Laura was close or confided in. They said they'd never heard of David Hargrove, the man whose body had been found in the aircraft wreckage along with her clothes and IDs.

"You probably should talk first with the manager of the apartment complex," Carl said. "His last name's Thigpen. He's been keeping an eye on her place until we can get her things moved out."

"Didn't she have a car?" I asked.

"Yes, of course," Agnes replied. "She left it parked at her apartment. It's a Honda Civic we bought her when she finished college. The police impounded it right after they found the bodies—before they realized this was all a terrible accident. The sweetest lady called and said they'd keep it for us until we could pick it up. They were very sympathetic." She smiled. Just a little out of touch with reality, I thought.

I remembered they'd said Laura was dating someone locally. "Yes, Roger Barmore," Agnes said. She lowered her voice slightly and continued, "I think they were getting serious," as if this were a secret that still might have some importance.

"Think it would be all right if I talked with him?" I asked. "Get his perspective on things?"

Agnes hesitated before saying, "Let me speak with him first. As I guess you can imagine, he's taking this pretty hard. I'll call him tomorrow."

I told them I planned to leave for Atlanta the next morning. Agnes handed me a large manila envelope and a small cardboard box held shut by a red rubber band. "Laura's key chain is in the box," she explained. "The man from the Georgia Bureau of Investigation brought it back to us along with her other personal things they found in the plane wreckage. I see her car key's on there. I guess some of the others are keys to her apartment and office, but I don't know." She tapped the envelope with her forefinger. "We made you up a letter of introduction signed by both Carl and me. We wanted you to have something official, so folks won't think you're snooping or just being curious. I even had it notarized. And I put in a few photos of Laura in case you need to show them to anyone."

As if any of this mattered, I thought.

I left Carl and Agnes standing on their front porch, his arm around her waist. I couldn't decide if it was a gesture of closeness or if he simply needed someone to support him. Perhaps both. "You'll let us know right away if you find out anything, won't you?" Agnes yelled. I nodded, smiled, waved and walked on home.

Eula Mae was pushing a carpet sweeper across the hall rug when I opened the back door. She'd obviously been waiting for me. "You gon' do it, ain't you?"

"Do what?" I was annoyed.

"Hep them ol' folks out."

"How did you know about that?"

"Ain't much I don't know 'bout you, Mr. Matt."

"Have you been talking to Uncle Jack?"

"Yo' uncle's got yo' number. He know you ain't been yo'self since Miss Lisa left. Yep, we talked 'bout it and I'm s'pose to call him iffin' you make like you ain't goin' to Atlanta to find out 'bout them folk's daughter."

"Eula Mae, this is really none of your business, okay?"

"Mr. Jack's a good man, and he's thinkin' 'bout you." She crossed her arms, cradling the handle of the carpet sweeper against her bosom. "And he's right about one other thing. You spendin' too much time studyin' Matt Rutherford's problems when a man of yo' upbringin' should be thinkin' 'bout all the good he could be doin' for other folks what ain't got as much as he has. I was watchin' this preacher on television last night, and he say that...."

"Okay, enough said. I got your point. You don't have to worry. I'm going to do what they want."

"But is you gon' do it out of the goodness of yo' heart, or 'cause we be tellin' you it's the thing you s'pose to do?"

I didn't answer. I didn't answer because I didn't know.

CHAPTER Ten

I went in my study and shut the door, leaving Eula Mae standing in the hall waiting for my reply. She meant well. Jack meant well. They were both trying to do what they thought was the right thing, but sometimes I wished like hell that they'd stay out of my life.

I flipped on the computer and googled "Laura McIntosh." I got more than three hundred hits, about half from genealogy websites and most of the rest from references to the recent series of articles in the tabloids. The name was surprisingly common. I narrowed the search by adding "Walkerville" and "American Timber Holdings." This time I came up with 14, of which five were obituary notices. There were a couple of short pieces from the *Atlanta Journal-Constitution* and the *Atlanta Business Chronicle* noting Laura's appointment as "Associate Research Scientist" with ATH. The only one of any interest was a feature piece in the current issue of the *Georgia Tech Alumni Magazine*. I downloaded the file and printed it out.

The first page of the article was basically a large photo with a title across the top reading, "Recent Tech Grad Helps Free America From Dependence On Foreign Oil." Below it to the left side, Laura stood in a long white lab coat, arms crossed and looking as if she'd just won the lottery. She was as beautiful as I remembered her. The shot had evidently been taken on some of ATH's timberland. Behind her, rows of planted pines stretched off into the distance under a clear blue sky.

The first paragraph began at the lower right of the page in oversized type, "When Laura McIntosh was a little girl growing up in rural Adams County, Georgia, she had no idea that the pine trees covering the landscape there could one day be the key to America's energy independence. A recent Tech PhD graduate in applied biochemistry, McIntosh did her doctoral research and dissertation on ways to extract the potential energy locked inside...." The article continued on the next page in smaller type.

There were a couple of other photos of Laura. One was taken in a laboratory of some sort with her posed in front of a shelf filled with multicolored vials and beakers. The other showed her wearing a hard hat and standing in front of a large hopper-like structure into which a loader was dumping what appeared to be wood chips.

I quickly scanned the text. The point seemed to be that graduates of the Georgia Institute of Technology were doing good things for the environment. Typical public relations spin from a university that turns out math geeks, industrial engineers, and rocket scientists. There were a few paragraphs from an interview with Cranston Gray, ATH's CEO. I put it aside, thinking I might want to read it later.

I unfolded the clasp on the envelope Agnes gave me and shook out the contents on the desk. There were half a dozen copies of the same letter, each typed in duplicate on an old-fashioned typewriter. The paper was cheap, and there was a random assortment of whited-out and typed-over corrections. It read, in overly formal schoolteacher verbiage, "This document is to introduce Mr. Matthew Rutherford V, who has been empowered by the undersigned...," *et cetera*. Below the text were Carl's and Agnes's signatures, his small and shaky, hers rounded and flowing. At the bottom was a notary's signature and seal, dated and timed the afternoon before my first visit to their house. They were confident, I thought. I wondered what Jack had said to them.

I picked up the photos of Laura and studied them. Judging from the date stamped on the back, they'd been taken the preceding December. In one view she was standing in front of a scraggly Christmas tree, smiling and holding up a sweater. An opened box and crumpled wrapping paper lay at her feet. In the background I recognized the plain brown paneling of the

McIntosh den. The flash had painted her face a ghostly white. In another, apparently taken in their back yard, she was posing with a brown-haired man in a police officer's uniform. I didn't recognize him. He wore a small brass name tag above his right pocket, but I couldn't make out the letters. Most of the shots provided a good view of Laura's face, but I wasn't sure they'd be of much use.

Putting everything back in the envelope, I turned my attention to the box. It was wider than it was deep and made of plain white cardboard, the kind that might have come as a gift container from a jewelry store. Scribbled on the top in a girlish script were the words, "Gift from Daddy and Mommy, Christmas 1989." Laura would have been nine years old. I slipped off the rubber band and examined the set of keys inside. The Honda key and its attached remote were evident; the six or eight others were nondescript. Only one, a thin key to a warded lock stamped "Ultimate Fitness Gym & Spa" was identifiable. Probably opened a locker.

I threw the keys, letters and photos in my briefcase. I figured I'd need two or three days in Atlanta to poke around, so I got back on-line and booked a couple of nights at the Grand Hyatt on Peachtree. It was only a few blocks from Laura's apartment and fairly close to some good restaurants and nightlife. Not a bad place to end up with a date, should I be so lucky. I didn't intend to spend much time in my room.

I arrived at the Hyatt shortly before eleven. The valet looked suspiciously at my pickup and wondered out loud if it would fit in the underground parking lot. I gave him a ten and told him to do his best. I checked in, asked the bellman to take my bags to the room and ate a leisurely lunch in the restaurant before setting out to find Laura's apartment.

According to the address and the map I'd printed out, she'd lived in an upscale, roughly triangular area bounded on the west by Peachtree, the east by Piedmont and on the south by East Wesley Road. At one time it had been a solid middle-class suburban bedroom community, but the edges were now being gnawed upon by commercial development. Most of the homes were built in the 1940s and '50s, but here and there small apartment complexes dating from the '70s and '80s dotted the otherwise shady single-family streets. Atlanta's population boom of the 1990s had sent home prices skyrocketing, so those who could afford to buy there now were usually either fairly well-heeled or deep in mortgage debt. Or both.

Laura's apartment was in an unassuming twenty-four unit complex incongruously named Chateau South, apparently in honor of the attempted mansard roofs on the second stories of the buildings. The sign next to the driveway said "Private" and "Waiting List Only." It occurred to me if you couldn't afford to buy in the neighborhood, perhaps renting there was the next best thing.

I turned in and cruised slowly to the end of the parking lot, mostly empty this time of day. There were five buildings, a mixture of townhouse units and flats. Laura's building was in the back, a ground floor apartment in a four-unit architectural bad dream with Williamsburg-style doors and filigreed cast iron balcony rails. According to a faded sign, the manager lived in the townhouse nearest the street.

After double-checking the address to be sure I had the right place I drove back and parked in front of the manager's unit. I walked slowly up the short sidewalk, trying to decide what I was going to say. I really didn't have a plan. The sounds of a television game show filtered through the thin metal of the door. I rang the bell and waited. A balding man in his late sixties cracked the door and looked out, a bit cautious. "Can I help you?"

"I'm Matt Rutherford from Walkerville. I was…."

The door opened widely and the man stuck out his hand, "Of course. Mr. Rutherford. I'm Theo Thigpen. I've been expecting you. Agnes McIntosh called, told me you'd be coming around to check on things. Come on in and sit down. Let me cut this television off so we can talk." He motioned me in, shooed a cat out of an overstuffed chair and pointed to it. "Have a seat," he said while digging through a pile of newspapers on the sofa looking for the TV remote. He found it and pressed the mute button. The room smelled of stale cigar smoke and cat box. As my sight adjusted to the dim light I saw several of the long-tailed creatures slinking around the periphery of the room eyeing me warily.

"I hope you like cats," Thigpen said. He was wearing a yellowed V-neck tee shirt, plaid shorts and flip flops. His hairy belly bulged out over his shorts, giving the impression of a furry smile.

41

"They're fine," I replied. I hate cats.

"So, you've come to check on Laura's things?" he asked.

"Is that what Mrs. McIntosh said?"

"In so many words, yes. But I'm pretty good at reading between the lines. What she really wants to know is what kind of mess her daughter had gotten into."

I wasn't sure how to start. "They just can't understand how she died..." I tried to think of a polite way to put things, "...the way she did. They asked me to talk with a few people who might be familiar with what was going on in her life these past few months."

Thigpen picked a half-smoked cigar out of an ashtray next to the sofa. He clamped it in one side of his mouth and said, "I'll tell you right now, she was a saint. One of the finest people I've ever known." He dug around in the clutter of the end table, apparently looking for a match.

"I know her parents will be glad to hear that. How well did you know her?"

"I've been the manager here for fifteen years. Laura moved in about,... what? Three and a half, four years ago? Not long after she started work on her PhD. She and my wife got to be good friends—they both grew up in small towns. Me, I'm from New Jersey. Moved here in the sixties to work in the construction business. Got married and stayed on."

"Is your wife here?"

"Oh, no. Sorry I didn't make myself clear. She's dead. Ovarian cancer."

"I'm sorry."

"Don't be. She'd lived a good life and was ready to go. She survived with it for nearly ten years—died this past February. I don't think I could have made it in the end without Laura."

"How so?"

"She was Florence Nightingale and Mother Teresa rolled into one. Even when Evie—that's my wife, Evelyn—came home from the hospital to die, she'd come over every day, just to be with her. She'd sit there, talking, keeping her company, holding her hand. A regular saint she was."

I wasn't sure how to respond. "I didn't know Laura that well, but people have said nice things about her."

"Rightfully so," Thigpen said. He flicked a kitchen match against his thumbnail and sucked on his cigar until the tip glowed. Exhaling a cloud of blue smoke, he continued, "She was as beautiful as she was smart. A real caring person, but...." He stopped, glanced at the silent television for a second, then continued, "...but you never really know people sometimes, now do you?"

I sensed he'd almost slipped and said something he'd not intended to say. "How do you mean?"

He needlessly flicked the cigar over the ashtray and stared at the television for a few more seconds without answering. The contestant must have given the wrong answer. The camera panned close-ups across the studio audience. I could read "Oh, no!" on several lips. "Well, sometimes folks disappoint you, you know?" Thigpen said.

"Laura's dead. She doesn't have any secrets now. Her parents want to know what happened. They want to know the truth. If there's something that might help them understand it all, that's okay."

He studied my face for a moment then said, "There're no police in this, right? No cops?"

"None."

"She was so smart, so precise and hard-working. I just can't understand how a girl like her got on drugs."

CHAPTER Eleven

"rugs?"

"Yeah. You know, dope. When you do what I do here, you run across all types. I know how kids are these days, but she just didn't seem to be the kind who would get into that crap."

"That's the first time I've heard anyone mention drugs. From what I knew of her...."

"You were friends?" Thigpen interrupted.

"I had a couple of dates with her last summer. Nothing more. How do you know she was using?"

He didn't reply, but instead propped his cigar on the side of the ashtray and stood up, easing two cats out of the way with his foot as he disappeared toward the back of the apartment. The losing contestant on the television game show was silently crying despite what appeared to be the offer of a generous consolation prize. I heard a cabinet slam shut. Thigpen returned with a rumpled brown paper grocery bag. He swept a pile of newspapers off the coffee table to clear a spot and placed the bag in the middle of it. "Agnes told you I found the break-in?"

"She did."

"I was doing a walk-about. Routine thing I do every couple of days, just a look-see, you know, making sure there're no problems."

He seemed to be waiting for me to reply. "Right," I said.

"I'd heard about Laura. Guess I was in some kind of state of shock—I don't know. So I'm checking out her back patio and I find that some sonofabitch has pried the lock open. I hadn't really looked that close before, but I was guessing it'd happened in the last day or two—it was right after they'd found her body, see."

"Okay."

"So I got my key, let myself in. You could tell there'd been a robbery, drawers open, things strewn on the floor, that sort of thing, you with me?"

I nodded.

He tapped the bag. "So I see this stuff, sitting right there on her kitchen table and I say to myself, hey, the cops are gonna come and when they do, they're gonna find this. I thought about all Laura had done for Evie, and I said, Theo, you can't let things go down this way. The girl's dead, but you owe her a favor. So I found a sack, scooped everything in it, made sure there was nothing else around, went home and called the cops."

He reached in the sack and pulled out a plastic baggie containing about an ounce of a fine white powder. "I found this," he said. "There was a ceramic cutting board, a razor blade and some straws. I think it's cocaine. I washed the cutting board and ditched the straws and razor blade in the dumpster. I don't know why I saved this—probably should have gotten rid of it, too."

I picked up the bag and turned it over in my hand. I'd seen plenty of cocaine during my California days. "Why would she leave it out on the kitchen table?"

"Who knows?" Thigpen said. "I guess she and whoever she was with were getting high—why the hell else would they get into such crazy shit as stealing a plane to go on a joy ride? I know she was home that evening. The police questioned me after the robbery, and I remembered seeing her car here late that Monday afternoon before they found her body the next morning."

"Did you find anything else?"

"I didn't really look. You gotta understand, I was upset. I mean…, I'd sorta started thinking of her as a daughter, the child we never had. If you want to know the truth, it's been a rough year, first losing Evie, then Laura." He took a deep hit on the cigar.

I wasn't sure where to start. "If you don't mind, I've got a few questions, and I guess I should take a look at her apartment."

"Sure," Thigpen said. "Why don't we have a look at her place first, then we can come back over here and talk for a while." I nodded. He stood up and rummaged through the jumble of newspapers until he found a dingy white guayabera that he pulled on over his tee shirt. Retrieving a large key ring from the end table, he headed for the door.

I walked slowly as Thigpen puffed his way up the slight incline toward Laura's building. "I understand she had a roommate at one time, someone named Sandra?"

"Yeah, Sandra Williams. I didn't know much about her but she seemed like a nice girl. We have a policy that all the residents of the complex register with us, even if their name's not on the lease. I met her when she moved in and then talked with her maybe a couple of times before she moved out."

"When was that?"

"I don't know—a couple or three months ago. It wasn't too long after Evie died. I was in kind of a fog, I guess. All I remember is that Sandra had been living with some guy, her boyfriend, I guess. They were having troubles and she wanted out. She needed a place to stay so Laura offered her the spare bedroom. They both worked at the same place, what is it? Some timber company?"

"ATH—American Timber Holdings."

"Yeah, that's it." We'd reached the door to the apartment. Thigpen picked through his keys. I noticed a tattered shred of yellow and black plastic tape hanging from the wrought iron railing. I could make out a "CRI..." on it and guessed it had read "Crime Scene."

He found the right key and inserted it in the lock. Opening the door, he gestured for me to enter first. The room smelled musty. "The power's still on." Thigpen said. "I've been forwarding the utility bills and the rest of the mail to the McIntoshes." He paused by the door. "Have a look around. I'm going back over to my place and wait for you. I..., uh, I..., get a bad feeling..., being here, you know. Things are just like the cops left them. The only thing that's missing is a little jewelry box I found and took back to my place for safekeeping. I told Agnes I'd send it home with you. Take your time. I'll be waiting. I ain't got nothing else to do. Just lock the door on your way out." With that he headed back to his apartment.

I shut the door, opened the blinds and flipped on an overhead light.

CHAPTER Twelve

I stood in the entryway and studied the apartment. The front door opened into an L-shaped space, a sort of living room that flowed into a dining area. A worn leather sofa and a couple of overstuffed chairs pointed toward a large-screen TV with sound system and DVD player set against one wall. Toward the rear, a small round dining table with four chairs sat in front of a sliding glass door adjacent to the kitchen.

I walked back and inspected the glass door. The aluminum frame near the handle had been bent back to force it open. Dark splotches in the area indicated the cops had dusted it for fingerprints. The door was wedged shut with a two-by-four forced in the frame. A simple but effective solution from Thigpen, the ex-construction worker.

A short hall opening off the living area led to a larger bedroom with a private bath in the back, and two smaller bedrooms sharing a second bathroom in the front. The back bedroom must have been Laura's. Closet doors were open with clothes tossed haphazardly on the floor. The drawers of a dresser and a smaller chest had been removed, their contents dumped on the floor. More dark smudges of fingerprint dust were evident around the drawer pulls and door handles.

One of the front bedrooms was furnished only with a bed, a night table and lamp, and a mirror-topped dresser. The closet door was ajar, revealing empty racks. This must have been Sandra's bedroom.

I eased my way through the tiny shared bath into the third bedroom. Laura had used it as a study. A long scuffed table took up one wall, with a comfortable office chair tipped over on the carpet in front of it. On the adjacent wall a crude bookcase made of plastic milk crates and boards strained under the weight of books and stacks of journals. A flatbed scanner and a high-speed laser printer occupied one end of the table. A wireless keyboard and mouse had been tossed in the corner, but there was no sign of a computer. Two filing cabinets stood near the door, their drawers open and some of the contents scattered on the floor. I picked up a manila folder and read the title inked on the tab: "Enzymatic catalyses." I had no idea what it meant.

I decided to start my search in Laura's bedroom, not at all sure what I was looking for. The queen-size bed was unmade, its dark green bedspread thrown haphazardly back to reveal celadon sheets. Stepping carefully around the contents of the drawers and closets scattered on the floor I looked for some revealing clue about Laura's life. There was nothing. In contrast to the rest of the room, her brushes and makeup were still neatly laid out on top of the dresser. Clothes and underwear from the drawers were still folded, just as they'd been dumped.

In the bathroom, an expensive blow-dryer hung on a small hook next to the sink and mirror. An electric curling iron, its cord carefully wrapped around it, lay to one side. A louvered door above a towel bar opened on shallow shelves filled with mascara, jars of powder and flat cases with eye shadow in half the colors of the rainbow.

Several plastic prescription medicine bottles filled part of the bottom shelf. There were a couple half-taken bottles of antibiotics with dates more than two years old, a bottle of Ambien prescribed six months earlier and still containing 8 of the original 12 tablets dispensed, and a bottle of Lexapro, an antidepressant. I looked at the refill date and counted the remaining capsules. Laura had been taking these regularly. I half-expected to find birth control pills, but saw nothing. I opened the drawers, looked under the sink cabinet, and searched the linen closet. There was the usual assortment of bathroom things ranging from Tampax to drain cleaner, but no surprises.

In the bedroom, I rifled through a stack of magazines under the bedside table. Laura's reading habits stretched from *Cosmopolitan* on one extreme to the *Journal of Applied Biochemistry* on the other. The table drawer contained a well-worn leather-covered Bible with "Laura Anne McIntosh" embossed in gold letters, and a sleek plastic vibrator tucked discreetly in a satin pouch. No condoms. No contraceptive foam.

Back in the study-bedroom I sifted through the folders still in the filing cabinets and those tossed in heaps on the floor. Most of what I could understand seemed to be notes and research related to Laura's PhD thesis. A series of file folders labeled "ATH Biofuels" contained schematic drawings of some type of production facility, but no notes or other correspondence. I presumed this was the same project mentioned in the Georgia Tech magazine article.

In the bottom drawer of one file cabinet I found a checkbook with an expandable folder full of bank statements for the past two years. Other folders contained paycheck stubs, credit card receipts and bills, each of the latter neatly labeled "Paid" with a date and check number. I picked up the chair, cleared a place on the table and sat down to study them. It didn't take long to figure out that Laura had no particular financial worries. Based on a quick review of her paycheck stubs, I estimated she made roughly seventy-eight thousand a year—not bad at all for a first job.

There were no unusual expenses. She'd been paying $1,150 per month for the apartment, and about $250 a month for utilities. A savings account contained a little over ten thousand dollars. Most of her fixed expenses—her rent, utilities, etc.—were paid by check. Others were generally paid by debit card, so I could get a pretty good idea of where the money went. Her salary was transferred to her account by direct deposit, but she withdrew only about a hundred-fifty to two hundred a month in cash from ATMs. No unexplained expenditures. Nothing to suggest a drug habit.

I picked up the folders scattered on the office floor and stacked them next to the filing cabinet before turning my attention to the kitchen and living room. For the most part, this area of the apartment appeared undisturbed. The thieves had evidently focused on the bedrooms and office, not illogically so, based on the assumption that things of value were most likely to be found there.

A coffee table in front of the sofa displayed several dust-covered copies of *Veranda* and *Southern Accents*—Laura kept her issues of *Cosmo* in the bedroom. A forlorn ficus tree near the window, unwatered for weeks, had shed most of its leaves on the carpet. I picked up the TV remote and pressed the power button. Oprah appeared, vigorously praising a thirty-somethingish woman who had overcome the ravages of single-motherhood by writing romance novels featuring single mothers who found true love and happiness with the Fabio-like characters portrayed on the dust jackets. I cut it off.

The kitchen in the rear of the unit was dark, illuminated only by a single small window over the sink. I flipped on an overhead fluorescent strip, bathing the space in white light. A sink, dishwasher and microwave were on one side, a stove and refrigerator on the other. A small table with two chairs was pressed against the wall in the back. The sink contained a few dirty dishes, now growing fuzzy grey mold. A clean ceramic cutting board was propped in the dish rack. I presumed it to be the one Thigpen washed.

The trashcan under the sink was empty except for a few crumpled paper towels. The refrigerator shelves held a corked half-empty bottle of chardonnay, a few Cokes and some bottled water. Thigpen had cleaned out the rest.

Taking one last look around, I cut off the lights and left, locking the door on my way out. I took my time walking back to Thigpen's apartment. Everything I'd seen was perfectly mundane. Nothing out of the ordinary. No red flags. It appeared that perhaps a computer was missing, but I couldn't be sure without knowing one was there in the first place. The TV, stereo, DVD player, etc. were untouched. I remembered there'd been a jewelry box of some sort, but Thigpen said he'd taken it to his place for safekeeping.

The one thing that was totally out of place was the cocaine. It didn't seem to fit with Laura's lifestyle. And, too, considering the high probability the burglary was drug-related, it seemed improbable that the thief or thieves would ignore a bag of nose candy sitting in plain view on the kitchen table. On the other hand, if it were a typical smash-and-grab robbery, they'd try to snatch something that could be easily fenced and get out as soon as possible. They probably didn't even look in the kitchen.

I knocked on Thigpen's door, letting myself in to his call of "It's open." He was once again ensconced on the sofa, chewing on an unlit cigar and absorbed in a fishing show on TV. He glanced up and said, "You ever go fishing?"

"Not recently. Not since I was in high school."

"You oughta take it back up. It looks like fun." He pressed the mute button, carefully laid his stogie in the ashtray and said, "Find what you needed?"

"I don't know. I'm not sure what I was looking for. Does anyone have any idea what was taken in the break-in?"

Thigpen took a deep breath. "Not really. The detective in charge said he thought it looked like a computer was missing—probably one of them small ones you hold in your lap..."

"A laptop."

"Yeah, that's it. It looked like somebody had gone through her jewelry box, but they left a lot of little things—cheap earrings, bracelets and the like. Laura wasn't one to wear fancy stuff, and her parents said they'd never bought her any. About the only thing of value she had was a gold thing you wear on a necklace. Her boyfriend gave it to her when she finished her PhD. She showed it to me right after she got it, and I know she wore it most of the time. It was in the shape of a small pine tree with a diamond set in the middle. He'd had it specially made for her. Her mother mentioned that they didn't find it on her body or with the things in the plane and asked me to look for it. I guess they took it from the jewelry box."

"So not a lot was missing?"

"Who knows?" A large calico cat leapt into Thigpen's lap. He stroked it gently, then said, "Think you know Laura any better now than you did before?"

I hesitated, thinking, then said, "How can you ever really know anybody?"

Thigpen raised his eyebrows, shrugged and picked up the cigar, his attention distracted by the silent struggle of a bass at the end of a taut fishing line on the television screen.

CHAPTER Thirteen

"Do you have time to tell me about the roommate, Sandra?"

Thigpen shot his eyes toward me, then back to the television screen. "Sure," he said, a hint of reluctance in his voice. "I made a copy of some things for you. Let me get them." He raised himself slowly off the couch and padded to the back of the apartment, followed by two cats. I used the remote to cut off the TV, then hid it on the coffee table under a pile of newspapers.

Momentarily he returned clutching several sheets of paper and a small fabric-covered jewelry box. "I made copies of these for you," he said, handing me the papers. "The one on top there is Sandra's info sheet. It's the one she had to fill out when she moved in with Laura. I see she didn't give a work number, but you shouldn't have trouble finding one in the book. I really don't know that much about her." He cleared his throat and picked his cigar out of the ashtray. "Why don't you just go see her in person? She can probably tell you a lot more than I can about Laura.

"The other thing—it's those papers stapled together—is a copy of the police report. I had to get it to file the insurance on the door. I told Agnes I'd send her a copy just in case Laura carried any insurance on her stuff."

He leaned over and handed me the jewelry box. It had smudges of dark fingerprint dust on the shiny brass of the latch. "I picked this up in Laura's bedroom after the cops finished with everything. When I first found the break-in, it was on top of the bed where they'd dumped the stuff and dug through it. There are a few earrings and bracelets and chains and things, but it's what's left after they picked it over. I guess they took anything they thought they could pawn."

I thanked him and told him I'd get the police report and jewelry box back to Laura's parents. Laying them on the table, I asked, "Tell me what you know about Laura's personal life. Did she go out much? Was she dating anybody?"

"I may not be the best person to ask. I mean, Evie and I used to go to bed kinda early, and I don't keep close tabs on the tenants if they don't cause no trouble. Far as I know, though, she wasn't seeing anybody—at least not here in Atlanta. I say that because she spent a lot of time over here when Evie was so sick. They'd talk for hours. I remember her saying something about a boyfriend back home—the guy who gave her the neck jewelry thing—but no one else. And she and Evie were so close that I think I'd know if she had something going on."

"What about this guy Hargrove whose body they found in the plane? Ever meet him?"

"Hell, I never heard of him. The fact is," Thigpen continued, "Laura sorta kept to herself. I remember her talking about her new job, and about how they wanted her to figure a way to make gasoline from pine trees, or something like that. Evie used to call it 'making gold from dross.'" He paused, his eyes a little misty. "You know, I never asked her what that meant. Evie had an education. I didn't. She'd use them big words like that and I'd just pretend I knew what she was talking about. What does 'dross' mean, anyway?"

"Something worthless."

"Like people's lives sometimes." Thigpen eyed the blank TV screen.

"I suppose you could say that."

"Yeah," he said, and began digging in the newspapers for the remote. He found it, flicked on the TV, and quickly pressed the mute button. The baseball-capped angler was holding up a huge bass for viewers to admire.

I rose to leave. "I really appreciate your time, Theo. I'll see if I can get in touch with Sandra. Maybe she can shed some light on things."

Thigpen smiled and nodded, but made no effort to get up. I headed for the door. The television's sound came back on. It occurred to me there was one question I hadn't asked. Turning back, I said, "There is one more thing I'd like to know."

He looked up, a bit annoyed. "Yeah?"

"The cocaine. Why didn't you throw it in the dumpster with everything else?"

Thigpen's head flew around, and his eyes locked on mine. Fumbling to find the remote, he hit the power button and the TV screen went dark. "You really want to know?"

"I guess I'm just curious."

He waved his arm around the room, "See all this? It's my world, it's all I have now that Evie's gone." He pointed to the television. "See that? That's the world I want to live in. You know, I'm sixty-eight years old. I'm kind of on life's downhill slide. It ain't gonna get no better, and I know it. I see these big people on TV using the stuff—movie stars, football players, those kind. So I said, Theo, before you check out you gotta see what you've been missing. I guess I'm just saving it until the time is right."

With that, he pressed the power button on the remote and turned his attention back to the screen. I let myself out.

It was just after five when I got back on Peachtree heading north toward the hotel. The traffic was the usual Atlanta bumper-to-bumper now hardened into gridlock by the five o'clock rush. It took me forty-five minutes to drive less than two miles. I considered trying to contact Sandra Williams, but realized I didn't have her new home address. It would be too late to try her at work, assuming she was still employed by ATH. I handed the truck keys to the valet—who said nothing this time—and headed for the hotel bar.

I awoke at seven the next morning, mouth dry and half hung-over from about three too many Wild Turkeys. I'd spent most of the evening trying to pick up a female lawyer from Chicago in town for some depositions. She was interested, but after a couple of drinks started missing her boyfriend back home. I ended up with a white parchment business card and the promise of cheap legal work should I ever get in trouble in Illinois.

By nine, after a long hot shower, a room service breakfast washed down with a carafe of coffee, a liter of ice water and two Tylenol, I was back to some semblance of my usual self. I found Thigpen's information sheet on Sandra Williams. She'd completed it in a flowing girlish script, the sort where you'd expect to see curlicues and smiley faces at the end of sentences. Her middle name was Marie. Assuming she didn't lie about her age—why would she?—she'd be twenty-seven. She'd listed Jesup, a small railroad and timber town in south Georgia, as her home and Mr. and Mrs. Henry C. Williams as her next of kin. Under "Occupation" and "Place of Employment" she'd written "Research Assistant" and "R & D Lab, American Timber Holdings." The address given was an office park in north Atlanta. No work contact number was listed.

I found a phonebook in one of the bedside cabinets and looked up "American Timber Holdings, Inc." There was one listing for "Corporate Offices" with an address on lower Peachtree. An efficient-sounding operator told me Ms. Williams now worked in Administration and it was her pleasure to connect me to her office. A secretary picked up on the first ring, "Ms. Williams's office."

I introduced myself, spelling my name at her request, and told her I was trying to reach Sandra Marie Williams who formerly worked in the R & D lab. "You've got the correct office," she said. "Ms. Williams is now the Assistant to Mr. Gray, our CEO." She'd moved up rapidly, I thought.

"I know it's short notice," I said, "but I was wondering if it might be possible to arrange a meeting with her today? I'm from out of town and hadn't planned on being in Atlanta that long."

"Do you know Ms. Williams?" I read suspicion in the voice.

"No. I was a friend of Laura McIntosh."

I thought I heard the secretary catch her breath, then, "Just a moment, please."

There was a pause and a click, followed by another female voice, "This is Sandra Williams. How can I help you?"

"Ms. Williams, I'm Matt Rutherford. You don't know me. I apologize for bothering you at work, but I was wondering if it would be possible to speak with you in person for a few minutes later today?"

"I understand this is about Laura."

"Yes, her parents asked me to check on a few things for them."

"Are you an attorney?" I sensed something in her voice; I wasn't sure what. Why would she ask?

"No, just a friend."

The voice softened. "It was such a tragedy. About Laura, I mean. You know we lost two of our best employees in that accident." It was more of a statement than a question. She paused. "Hold on a second. I need to check my schedule."

Her reaction seemed a bit odd, but I didn't know her at all. In a moment she picked back up saying, "I've moved some things around and can meet with you at three today. Will that work?"

"Sure. I don't know where your offices are located."

"We're in the ATH Tower. It's on Peachtree near Five Points—you can't miss it. There's a parking garage in the building. We have the top six floors. Just sign in at the desk in the lobby. There'll be a visitor's badge waiting for you."

I thanked her and hung the phone up. Laura had taken her in when she had no place else to go. Why was she so matter-of-fact? Maybe corporate protocol required it. I figured I'd find out sooner or later.

CHAPTER Fourteen

I glanced at the bedside clock. I had more than five hours before my appointment with Sandra Williams. I lay back on the bed and turned the preceding day's events over in my mind. I couldn't say I'd learned a lot about Laura. She was as much a mystery to me as she'd been before, perhaps more so. Thigpen confirmed what everyone seemed to be hinting at—that she'd somehow gotten into drugs. If I'd listed it all out on paper, the one obvious blank would be David Hargrove.

I searched the white pages in the phone book under "Hargrove." There was only one listing that might be a match, a "D. Hargrove" in Decatur. After three rings an answering machine announced, "Hi, this is Debbie. I can't come to the phone…." I hung up, making a mental note to question Sandra Williams about him. I considered getting dressed, but still felt like crap from too much bourbon. I hung the "Do Not Disturb" sign on the doorknob, closed the curtains and went back to bed.

If I lived in Atlanta, or perhaps paid more attention to it, I'd have recognized the ATH Tower. It's a downtown landmark that shows up prominently in every photo of the city's skyline. I realized that as the cab dropped me off in front of the forty-two story granite and glass monument to the excesses of the American business ego. I'd taken a taxi instead of trying to drive; extended cab pickups don't do well in municipal parking garages.

The security desk seemed lost under the soaring forty-foot ceiling of the lobby. The walls were sheathed in pink Georgia marble, contrasting sharply with woodwork of darkly stained oak. The guard handed me a bright green badge and directed me to a bank of elevators that would carry me to the forty-second floor.

The elevator doors opened onto a reception area with raised paneling carved from tight-grained longleaf pine. Brass accents and furniture upholstered in muted burgundy leather exuded tradition and stability. I told the receptionist I had an appointment with Sandra Williams, picked up a copy of *Forest Landowner* magazine and sank into one of the sofas to wait.

I'd scarcely finished perusing the cover when the most strikingly beautiful woman I've seen in years emerged from one of the paneled doorways. She walked directly toward me and extended her hand as I stood up. "I'm Sandra Williams," she announced. "I'm pleased to meet you, Mr. Rutherford." There was something about her, the way she moved, the turn of her features, her flawless body, that hit me on a subliminal level.

"Thank you for making time to see me," I said, a bit taken aback.

"We'll meet in my office," she said, turning and heading back the way she came without waiting for my reply. I followed, meekly.

Her office was more of a suite within a suite, guarded by a severe middle-aged secretary and reached after passing through a secondary reception area. This, too, was paneled but with cherry wood stained a deep red color to match the hues of the antique oriental rugs covering the floors. Sandra's desk was a slab of dark granite supported by a chrome base. A floor-to-ceiling window peered toward the northeast and the massive dome of Stone Mountain in the distant afternoon haze. She motioned for me to sit on a damask-covered couch. She settled into a comfortable lounge chair on the other side of a small coffee table, crossing her legs and saying, "So, you'd like to know about Laura?"

"Yes. I'm really here on behalf of her parents. She was an only child, you know, and they've been devastated by her death..."

"I would imagine so...," Sandra interjected.

"They just can't understand how someone they thought was so perfect could end up dying the way she did. They saw her as the child who could do no wrong. Now,..., well, they're confused. I think they simply want to know the truth."

Sandra nodded, her long blond hair bobbing slightly above her shoulders. She was wearing a dark blue linen suit with an open-necked white silk blouse that hinted at delights below. "I can understand that, but how do *you* come into the picture? You said you were a friend. Did they hire you, or what?"

I smiled, "Oh, no. If you want to know the truth, I got talked into it. I did know Laura, at least superficially. We had a couple of dates last summer. I suppose you'd say I'm here as a favor to her family."

"Oh." She appeared to be thinking. "I understand you live in Walkerville?"

"I was born and raised there. I've been back now for a couple of years." I hadn't told her where I lived.

"Now, are you the same Matt Rutherford who's in the timber business?" She'd obviously checked me out.

"I've inherited some timberland, yes, from my family. Not a lot."

"Quite a bit, according to my sources." I was beginning to pick up a subtle southeast Georgia accent, with long "i's" and dropped "g's." It was something Yankees would find charming but educated Southerners would consider a little country.

"I see you've been checking on me."

"I think it's what they refer to in the corporate world as 'due diligence.' It was a strange request, Matt—you don't mind if I call you Matt?—your wanting to know about Laura. As I said, it was a tragedy, but from what we've heard, the cause of her death was quite obvious."

"Oh, I don't think there's any doubt about that, but you'll have to admit the circumstances were strange, to say the least. Falling naked out of a plane...."

"We were told the autopsies showed high levels of carbon monoxide in both Laura's and David's blood."

"Yes. Did you see the coverage in the tabloids?"

"I did. I stand in grocery store check-out lines like everyone else. How could you miss it?"

"Did you ever meet Laura's parents?" Sandra shook her head. "They're both elderly and quite naïve about the big world out there. They've lived their entire lives in a small town and probably think people haven't changed much since the 1950s. I think they might have been able to accept Laura's death as a terrible accident, but the embarrassment of seeing her name and

photo splashed on the national news was just too much. They want closure."
I hated the word, but this seemed like a good time to use it.

"I see," Sandra said. "Then, how can I help you?" Apparently I'd
satisfied whatever concerns she'd had.

"Tell me about Laura."

Sandra looked out the window and took a deep breath. "Do you want the
unvarnished truth, or a sanitized version?"

"Just the truth as you understand it. I don't know yet what I'll end up
telling her parents."

"Let me start at the beginning. I've been living in Atlanta for about five
years now—I moved up here right after college. About two and a half years
ago I got a job here at ATH, starting off as an assistant in our research and
development lab just north of town. I met Laura about a year and a half ago,
when she was working on her doctorate. When she finished and was hired
full time here, I was assigned as her research assistant. We got to be pretty
good friends, at least on a social level."

Sandra bit her lip and looked out the window again before continuing.
"Anyway, I'd been seeing this guy. We got involved, and one thing led to
another. I ended up moving in with him. After a few months, I realized it
was a mistake. I felt trapped. Things got ugly and I knew I had to leave.
Laura offered me a place to stay until I could get my life back on track. I
guess that's it in a nutshell."

"You knew her well then."

Sandra pursed her lips slightly before replying. "I thought I did, but it
was only after living with her that I got to know the real Laura McIntosh."

"And...?"

"Do you really want to hear this? She's dead. It's not important now."

"Perhaps not, but I promised her parents I'd try to discover the truth—
good or bad."

"Okay, but it's not what you might think."

CHAPTER Fifteen

"Not what I might think? What do you mean by that?"

Sandra sighed and bit her lower lip again. "It's just that Laura was—how should I put this?—a complicated person. In some respects, she was everything you thought she might be: a talented researcher, a brilliant intellect, and a loving, caring person, not to mention the fact she was drop-dead gorgeous. But she had a dark side to her."

"How so?"

"My daddy said you should never talk bad about the dead," the south Georgia accent slipping through.

"All I'm looking for is the truth."

"Well, she was a good roommate, but there were problems."

"What kind of problems?" She was making me pick out each kernel bit by bit.

"Guys." Sandra did not appear to be the kind of individual who embarrassed easily. She looked embarrassed.

"Guys?"

"Yeah. She was into cruising the bars late at night. I don't want you to think I'm being prudish, Matt. I've had my share of fun at one time or another, but Laura, now there's a different story. She had guys at the apartment three or four nights a week. And they'd call her at all hours. We slept in separate bedrooms, of course, but still, the walls were really thin...." She looked down at her lap then raised her head and asked, "Need I say more?"

"No. Of course not. That's…, that's just a side of Laura I didn't know."

"Me, either. Otherwise I never would have moved in. It took me several months to save up enough for a deposit on a new place, but I moved out as soon as I could."

"How about drugs? Was there ever any evidence she was using?"

Sandra took a deep breath again and looked out the window again before turning her face back toward me. "I can't say for certain, but I was suspicious. A lot of the guys she'd bring home were…., how should I say this? They were…, no they *looked like*—that's the phrase—cokeheads. Or maybe meth. You know how it is, Matt. There's a lot of stuff out there, particularly with people our age. But Laura, she was Jekyll and Hyde. I was as shocked as anyone to hear of the circumstances of her death, but when I think about it, I guess I shouldn't be surprised."

Sandra paused. "Maybe I've said too much. There's no need in anyone knowing any of this now that she's…, she's dead."

"I understand. What about David Hargrove? Laura's parents said they'd never heard of him."

"David was a different story. Looking back on things, I don't know how he got mixed up with Laura. He was a graduate of Cal Tech with a Master's in something, I'm not sure what. He'd been with ATH about five years. He and Laura were both working on the same project. Not long after she came on full time they started dating. I saw them together at a lot of company events. He was such a great guy. I really wanted to go out with him, but no luck. I can't see what he saw in Laura."

"Sex?"

"Probably. Especially considering how they died." I caught a hint of sarcasm in her voice.

"Tell me about him. What was he like?"

"About thirty, single, California-handsome. He was into a lot of outdoorsy, macho kinds of things, you know, sky-diving, mountain biking, that sort of stuff. He was a licensed pilot, of course. You know the plane they died in was stolen from his sky-diving club."

"So I heard. Did he have any family? Anyone I could talk to?"

"So far as I know, none nearby. I remember him telling me one time his parents divorced when he was an infant and his mother died when he was in college. I think he was an only child."

"Where did he live?"

"I don't know. Somewhere in the area, I'm sure. I don't recall him talking about a roommate." She stopped, a slight mechanical smile on her face as she waited for my next question.

"I guess that's it, then," I said. "Risky lifestyle, bad outcome."

"It certainly looks that way," Sandra replied. "Can I be of any further help to you?"

"No, thanks." I looked around her office. I was curious enough to want to know how she'd moved directly from a research assistant to the company executive suite in a matter of months. There were a few papers in a neat stack on the credenza behind her desk, a multi-line phone, and keyboard with a flat panel screen on the desk, but little if any evidence of what she actually did. I decided to take the direct route and ask. "Ms. Williams, what....?"

"You don't have to be formal with me, Matt. It's Sandra."

"Sandra, then. What exactly do you do here?"

She smiled. "You're probably thinking nothing, right? I wish. Actually, my official title is Executive Assistant, which means I do everything from arranging meetings to picking up laundry and everything in between. I suppose the best way to describe my duties is to say I take care of the routine little things so the CEO can do what he does best, making money for ATH's shareholders. But on days like today when Bill—I guess I should say *Mr. Gray*—is out of town, I get a little break. Have you ever met him?"

"I can't say that I have."

"He's been to Walkerville quite a few times. The biofuel project is his special baby. We moved the main part of the research to our lab and test plots there more than a year ago. In fact, the plans were for Laura to move back to her hometown and head up the whole project. Have you ever seen our operation down there?"

"No. I've heard of it." The news of the biofuel test plant had been splashed on the front page of the *Adams Sentinel* for three weeks running.

"It's really exciting, all that's going on. It could change the future of the timber industry. If things work out like they're supposed to, this company stands to make billions in profits. And a lot of it is going to be based on the work that Laura was doing. It's so sad that she won't be here to see it through." Sandra paused. "I'm sorry. I guess I get too enthusiastic about things." She glanced at her watch. "Are you driving back this afternoon?"

"No. I was planning to spend the night and leave in the morning."

"Do you have any plans for the evening?"

"None that I can't change," I lied.

"Why don't we get together for a drink later? I'd like to continue our conversation."

"I'd like that," I said. A lightheaded feeling swept over me. I couldn't decide if it was the hangover or the thought of Sandra naked.

CHAPTER Sixteen

We agreed to meet at nine at The Pearl, a new Asian-themed bar in Buckhead that was the watering spot *du jour* for Atlanta's nighthawks. I'd never heard of the place. The concierge at the hotel said it was "fancy," whatever that meant, suggesting I wear a sport coat "to fit in with the crowd." He said it had been a strip club in a former incarnation, reborn now as an upscale nightspot while its former owner served a long prison sentence for cocaine trafficking. The cabbie knew the place immediately and got me there in less than ten minutes without asking for the address.

The taxi pulled in the *porte-cochère* with its *faux*-Chinese roof and oversized foo dogs just behind a silver-grey BMW Z4 coupé. I watched Sandra slide out from the driver's seat and exchange greetings with the valet, who acknowledged her arrival with a deep bow. She was apparently well-known here, or at the least, remembered as a big tipper.

By the time I'd paid the fare and passed the scrutiny of the heavyset oriental doorman who bore a striking resemblance to Oddjob, she was inside. I found her standing by the bar laughing with a group of thirty-somethingish lawyer types. Her face brightened with a smile when she spied me walking in. She waved me over with a cheery, "Matt, come meet some of my friends."

I was introduced as another "friend" from Walkerville. The dark-suited crew were all aspiring partners at one of Atlanta's more prominent law firms. We played a few rounds of who-do-you-know before Sandra took my hand

and led me to a quiet booth in one of the back rooms. I could sense their envy as we walked away.

We ordered drinks, bourbon and water for me, an Absolut and cranberry juice for her. The waitress brought a small dish of assorted Japanese crackers and left us alone. The flickering glow of a candle inside a paper lantern bathed the table in soft light. "I'm glad you could make it," she said, sipping her drink. She wore a bright red embroidered silk jacket with a high Chinese-style collar over a plain black skirt.

"I'm glad to be here," I replied. For the first time in a long while I felt awkward, unsure of what to say. "Thank you for inviting me." I thought it sounded stupid.

"I hope you don't think I was being too forward in asking you out. It's just that I find you interesting. I didn't think there was much chance of our getting to know one another sitting in my office. Too many eyes, too much formality."

"True." I hesitated. "But why do you find me interesting?"

Sandra smiled and brushed a strand of hair away from her eyes. "I think we have a lot in common. We both grew up in small towns and both ended up in the big city. I stayed; you didn't."

"You know my whole life story don't you?"

"Not really. It's just that we—ATH, I mean—have a number of employees in Walkerville. After we first talked this morning, I made a few phone calls. Your family's well known and well respected. The word I got was that you'd been a big-time executive with some software company in California, and you'd made a fortune and moved back to Walkerville."

I laughed. "So that's what they're saying? I wish. Looking back on everything, the truth is that I lucked into a position for which I was grossly overpaid and totally under-qualified. And as far as making any money, when the company was bought out, the deal was structured in such a way that my stock options became worthless. I was broke. I came home."

"And inherited well."

"I suppose you could say that." I wanted to change the subject. "But tell me more about you."

"What is there to know? I was born and raised in Jesup. My father works in the lumber mill and my mother's a nurse. I was the Homecoming

Queen. I got to ride on the float in the Christmas Parade. Boring, really."

"But how did you end up in the executive suite of American Timber Holdings?"

Sandra gave a faint smile and said, "Like you, I guess. Luck. I went to college at Valdosta State and moved up here when I finished. I started off as a secretary for a distribution firm in Marietta. I did that for a couple of years and then saw an ad for a position at ATH's R & D lab. They called it 'research assistant,' but really it was just another secretarial job. The guy who I ended up moving in with was doing some contract work for ATH, so that's how I met him. And you know the rest of the story."

"Not all of it. It seems like a big jump from the lab to the executive suite. How'd that happen?"

"The pay's lots better, but the job's not really all that different. I guess the main thing is that my new boss is not some PhD with bad hair and a pocket protector."

"But how did you meet Cranston Gray?"

"Bill? You know his full name is William Cranston Gray? For 'official' purposes he's 'W. Cranston Gray,' but to his friends, he's 'Bill.'"

"And you get to call him Bill?"

I thought I saw her blush. It was hard to tell in the dim light. "No..., well..., yes, but it's not what you might think. We work closely together and he likes to keep things somewhat informal." She paused and took a sip of her drink. "But to answer your question, I met him at the R & D lab. He's there at least twice a week to monitor the progress of several projects, especially the biofuel thing. His previous assistant had gotten pregnant and decided to stay home with the baby. He had an opening; I interviewed for it and he hired me. Again, luck."

"Or skill."

"I think the only edge I had was the fact that I'd worked in the lab for several years and knew who to talk with to get things done. You see, about five years ago the company was in trouble. The stock price was in the dumpster and the shareholders were about to revolt. The previous CEO wanted to take things in one direction, but the Board wanted to go in another. So they canned him and brought in Bill to turn things around. His focus has been on…." Sandra stopped suddenly in mid-sentence. "This is work talk. Let's change the subject."

"Okay." I tried to think of something intelligent to say. "It's good to be here with you, but I thought you might be involved with someone."

She peered at me over the rim of her glass. "Who said I'm not? And if I were, he'd have enough sense not to try to keep me on a short leash. Otherwise I couldn't be here with you." She gently set her drink on the table, positioning it precisely to cover the Chinese pictograph imprinted on the napkin. "But let's talk about you, not me."

"What more do you need to know about me? You've got the advantage; you've done your homework."

"There are some things you have to discover for yourself."

"Like boxers or briefs?"

She almost giggled. "Yeah. But we'll save that for later." Her eyes gleamed. "No, tell me how you got involved with this crazy quest to find out about Laura?"

"Exactly what I told you this afternoon. I got talked into it. I'd met her, and knew her parents in a superficial way. The circumstances of how she died were so bizarre, so out of character for the daughter they thought they knew. They decided they had to know who—or what—she'd become after she left home. They spoke with my uncle who put some pressure on me. I had the time, so I'm here. It's that simple."

"Really?" I couldn't decide if she believed me or not. "No hidden agendas?"

"Okay, I'll admit it. There is one."

"Which is…?"

"It gave me an excuse to get out of town. Maybe meet somebody. Have some fun."

"Are you succeeding?"

"I don't know. Ask me tomorrow morning."

"Confident, aren't you?" She reached out and drew a circle with her finger on the back of my hand.

"Foolishly so, sometimes."

"Well then, we should…." The muffled buzzing of a cell phone distracted her. Reaching in her purse, she pulled it out, looked at the caller ID and grimaced. "I'm sorry. I need to take this call." She stood up and walked out of earshot. She listened, then spoke, shaking her head, listening again.

With a look of disgust, she flipped her phone shut and walked back to the table. "Matt, I'm sorry, but I've got to go. Business. I can't get out of it." She put her hand on top of mine and said again, "I'm sorry."

I felt like I'd been kicked in the gut. "Can I call you?"

She looked at me, surprised. "Of course. Don't be silly. Uh…, what about tomorrow? Hey, how would you like a tour of the ATH offices? Maybe meet Bill Gray? He's back in town and will be in the office tomorrow. I think you'll find him interesting."

"Sure. I'd like that." Any excuse, I thought.

"Good. Call me at ten tomorrow. I'll arrange lunch." With that she handed me her card and headed for the exit. I finished my drink in one long gulp and sat staring at the patterns on the Japanese lantern.

CHAPTER Seventeen

I arrived at the ATH Tower at the appointed hour of 11:30 a.m. Sandra said she'd arranged for an early lunch with Bill Gray, followed by a tour of ATH's offices "unless you think that sounds too boring." I think I would have agreed to any suggestion she could have made short of holding hands and jumping off the roof.

This time she was waiting for me in the lobby, heel-clicking her way across the granite floor to give me a hug and a quick air-kiss. "I apologize for last night," she said. "I really hated to leave just when things were getting interesting."

"I know."

"It was business. A little after-hours crisis in our Denver office. I needed to come back down here and fax some files out to one of our VPs. Like I said, the pay's good, but they expect me to be available twenty-four hours a day."

I followed her to a private elevator and watched as she inserted a brass key in a polished lock. The door silently slid open. "Straight shot to the top floor," she explained. "The former CEO had it designed into the building. It let him avoid the riff-raff going to and from his little world up there. But Bill Gray's different. He's much more of a hands-on manager. We have more than twelve thousand employees nationwide, and I think he knows the names of everyone on the organizational chart down to the second assistant vice presidents. He's quite a guy."

"I'm looking forward to meeting him."

The door slid open onto the secondary reception area outside Sandra's office. The stone-faced bulldog of a secretary looked up and flashed a brief (and disapproving?) smile. I imagined she'd worked there for thirty years and deeply resented Sandra's leap to the top. "You remember Margaret, of course?" Sandra said.

I nodded. "We weren't formally introduced yesterday, but it's nice to see you again."

"Likewise," Margaret said and turned her attention to a stack of file folders on the desk in front of her.

I followed Sandra into her office and resumed my place on the damask sofa. She looked at her watch. "They're setting up lunch in the private dining room. We've got a few minutes. Would you like to see our roof garden?"

"Sure." She led me through a wide, indirectly-lighted passageway toward a blank wall. Pressing a small button on one side, the wall slid open revealing what appeared to be a path disappearing into a forest. For a brief moment I was confused. I knew we were on the forty-second story of a building, yet...

"Amazing, isn't it?" Sandra asked, stepping through the door and onto the path. "You'd think you were in a mixed pine and hardwood forest in south Georgia."

"It's.., it's unbelievable." I *was* at a loss for words this time.

"And it's probably one of the things that got the last CEO fired. I haven't seen the numbers, but they say it cost more than ten million dollars to create all this. We're standing on something like ten feet of topsoil under us. There is nearly three-quarters of an acre here under a glass roof in a totally self-contained environment."

I looked around in wonder. She continued, "Some of the trees here are almost half a century old. They were brought in by helicopter and lowered down on cables. Maintenance alone takes four full-time employees, not to mention all the upkeep on the mechanical equipment. It's wildly expensive. Come here, let me show you something."

I followed her for a dozen yards down the winding path toward a patch of sunlight ahead. It ended at a small clearing bordered by a floor-to-ceiling window facing north over the city. Four rustic benches were roughly arranged in a circle. "This is where Bill's predecessor would hold his daily staff meetings. The way he said it, ATH is in the business of growing trees, and he wanted his managers and department heads to be 'close to our work.' Strange, eh?"

"I take it he was kind of a nut? Or can I say that about a captain of industry? Poor folks are crazy; the rich and powerful are merely eccentric."

Sandra laughed and sat down on one of the benches. I sat down next to her. "It's a different world here. A long way from Jesup," I observed.

She smiled, "I know, but I love it. The excitement, the action. Don't you ever get bored living in Walkerville?"

"When I do, I come to Atlanta."

"Touché," she said, laughing again. She turned and looked at me, her face serious. "You interest me. You know that." Half-statement, half-question.

"That's good, I hope."

She looked at her watch. "We need to go. But let me say one thing first." Without waiting for me to reply she leaned over and kissed me on the cheek, gently pressing her palm against my chest. Pulling back slightly she said, "Again, I'm sorry about last night."

The Executive Dining Room of American Timber Holdings occupied a corner suite overlooking Peachtree and the skyscraper forest to the north. Like the rest of the top floor it, too, was ornately paneled, this time with wormy chestnut salvaged from North Carolina forests, or so said Sandra who had become the expert on the fineries of corporate life at the top. The table, which looked like it would easily seat twenty-four, was set for three at one end with crystal, sterling and neatly folded linen napkins. Margaret poked her head in to say, "Mr. Gray is on the phone and asked me to tell you he'll be here presently." Sandra thanked her and she withdrew with the same brief smile.

William Cranston Gray burst in like a locomotive from one of the side doors. He was physically impressive. At least six-two, dressed in a tailored blue suit and pinstripe shirt, he appeared to be exactly what he was, the head of a multi-billion dollar corporation. His hair was dark, grey-streaked at the temples. He sported a late-summer tan in June and a physique honed by daily workouts with his trainer. I judged him to be in his early fifties. He extended his hand with a genuine smile and said, "Hi. I'm Bill Gray. You must be Matt Rutherford." It was a statement, not a question.

I smiled back, shook his hand and we exchanged the usual pleasantries. A white-coated black waiter appeared with a rolling cart covered with a white cloth. He silently laid out salad, bread and a finely done trout meunière. Leaving a selection of desserts on the cart, he disappeared as quietly as he'd come.

We started with the salad. "So, Matt," Gray began, "Sandra tells me you live in Walkerville and that you're in the timber business." He definitely had a way of making questions into statements.

"I do live in Walkerville, but I'm hardly in the timber business. I inherited some timberland from my family. Actually, my degree is in anthropology. I suppose you could say I've been between jobs for a while."

"Don't be modest, please," he said, stuffing a sprig of arugula into his mouth. "If it weren't for private landowners like you, we'd be out of business. We have quite a bit of property, but nearly three-quarters of the timber we process in our mills is purchased from people like you. I'm really glad to meet you." He seemed sincere.

"And the other thing," he continued, "is that we've made a very large financial commitment to Walkerville and Adams County. We haven't made a public announcement as yet, but we're planning to build our first full-scale biofuel plant there. It'll be the working prototype for a dozen or more we intend to build in the southeastern states over the next decade. If things work out as planned, the net effect is going to be that the price paid for your timber will go up by fifteen to twenty percent almost overnight. Quite a potential windfall."

He definitely had my attention.

"Of course, all of this depends on our working the bugs out of our technology. That's why we were saddened to lose two of our best people, Laura McIntosh and David Hargrove. They were both so talented. They would have had a great future with the company." He paused and began to pick at his fish. "Sandra tells me you knew Laura." Another statement requiring an answer.

"Yes, but not well. In a small town you tend to know everyone." Sandra nodded agreement.

"It's certainly going to be a loss, but we'll pull through." He stabbed a spear of asparagus. "She was telling me Laura's parents asked you to look into her death."

"More or less, yes."

"Why?" Finally a question.

"You are familiar with the circumstances of how she died?" Gray nodded, chewing. "They are having trouble accepting how their daughter, whom they perceived as being as pristine as the driven snow, would—how should I put it?—die like she did."

Gray swallowed and glanced at Sandra. "They could have hired an investigator, a detective."

"They can't afford it."

"Hmm," he said, again digging into the fish. "So what have you learned and what are you going to tell her parents?"

"I don't know. Probably a gentle version of the truth. No details."

"Probably a good idea. I understand she had what our folks in Human Resources politely refer to as 'lifestyle issues.' Let the dead rest, I say."

"I think it's best," I replied, distracted by Sandra's foot stroking my leg under the table.

CHAPTER Eighteen

The same waiter appeared with fine dark-roast coffee in a silver pot, filling our cups after he'd rolled the cart around for our dessert selection. I had the key lime pie, Gray the crème brûlée. Sandra declined, taking only some pink packet of chemical sweetener for her coffee.

Gray said, "Good meal." He looked at his watch. "My next appointment is not until two. Matt, Sandra said something about giving you a tour of our operations here, but quite frankly, I think seeing folks in cubicles shuffling paper is something you've probably already had enough of."

I laughed, "You may be right."

"Instead let me give you a brief overview of our company. We're going to be playing a big part in the economy of Adams County in years to come and we need local people like you on our team. We've got to be realistic these days. We live in a world full of tree-huggers and city folks who think our forest resources should be subject to a lot of politically correct regulations and environmental red tape. I'm sure they mean well, but what they don't realize—or admit—is that forestry is just another form of agriculture where harvests take place every decade instead of every autumn. Do you have time to talk?"

I looked at Sandra. "Mr. Gray's right, Matt," she said. "Whenever you two are finished, I'll be in my office. See you then."

"Good," Gray said. "Let's go sit somewhere that's more comfortable." I followed him back through a short hall toward the other corner of the building. His private office was the same size as the dining room but finished in walnut with book-matched veneers centered in elaborate panels. In one corner, a massive English partner's desk was cluttered with papers and stacks of files. In the other, which was faced on two sides by walls of glass, an informal seating area of two small couches and three comfortable chairs was arranged around a freeform coffee table whose top had been sliced from a boulder of green malachite. A stack of newspapers was scattered haphazardly by one chair.

"I hope you'll pardon the mess," Gray said. "I usually come in early every morning to read the business news and get caught up before most of the staff arrives. You know, a huge part of being a CEO is keeping up the company's image. These days a lot of the major decisions are made by the Board of Directors, but I'm the one charged with making them work, and I'm also the one who takes the heat when they don't." He paused and motioned for me to sit down. He shed his coat and loosened his tie before flopping into the chair next to the stack of newspapers.

"How much do you know about American Timber Holdings?"

"Very little."

"Then let me give you some background. In fact I just got in from New York last night after spending the day meeting with financial analysts. We're a publicly traded company, you know, and those are the guys—and gals— who can make or break our stock price. A big part of my job is keeping those people up to date, pumping out the good news and explaining the bad. It's pretty stressful sometimes."

"I can imagine."

"I suppose you don't know our history, but we're one of the half-dozen largest forest resources companies in the world, rating up there with Weyerhaeuser, International Paper and that ilk. The company was actually started in the 1920s by a young fellow named Cashin from north Florida who inherited the family sawmill after his father was killed in an accident. During the Depression of the 1930s he began buying up land, some as cheap as a dollar an acre. By 1940 he owned close to two hundred thousand acres in Georgia, Florida, Alabama and Mississippi and ran a string of about three dozen small sawmills. After Pearl Harbor, Cashin Land and Timber became one of the major suppliers of structural timber for the war effort. Cashin died in 1953 a very rich man.

"Well, his family tried running the business for several years and failed pretty miserably. They were about to go bankrupt when a group of investors from New York and Florida made them an offer which they snapped up immediately—I don't think they had much choice. Those fellows built up the business for several years, acquiring a number of small producers here and there, and eventually renamed the company and took it public in 1965. And as they say, we lived happily ever after, up until about six or eight years ago, that is.

"Like everybody else, we were caught up in the market boom of the '90s. Our stock price tripled, and the company took on a lot of debt to buy more land and expand operations. Like most of the big forest resource companies, the goal was to run a vertical operation. The plan was that we'd own everything from the land that produced the trees to the trucks that distributed our finished products and anything in between. So we had one division that managed the forests, one that cut the timber, one that ran the lumber mills, one that ran the paper mills, and so on. It had gotten pretty big and pretty damned profitable. That's when they built this monument of a building. I think it was designed as more of a statement than a practical investment.

"As I'm sure you know, the market went bad several years ago. Forest products have always been a cyclical industry, and our stock tanked with everyone else's. We had a lot of debt, and to be perfectly honest, we were in trouble. Not to mention a lot of economic competition from places with vast forests like China and Brazil.

"About that time somebody in the industry got the bright idea to sell off the timberland assets. It really wasn't such a bad solution when you think about it. We were carrying land on our books at cost, averaging less than a couple of hundred dollars an acre, when in fact it could be worth a couple of thousand on the open market. And if we controlled the marketing and distribution through our ownership of the mills and plants, we'd still have the power to dictate the price we'd pay for timber. We could pay down debt, pump up the value of our assets and come out smelling like a rose, or so the thinking went. You're with me thus far." Gray was back to his statement-question mode.

"I am."

"So now we arrive at how I was picked for this job. My predecessor was a good guy. He'd been here for nearly fifteen years. The Board and the analysts all loved him, and the stockholders thought he could do no wrong as long as the trading price of our shares continued to soar. But when things began to go south, he suddenly became the skunk at the picnic. Trying to figure a way out of the slump, he reached the conclusion that ATH should start shedding its timberland. Matt, we own nearly three million acres in fifteen states. If we'd sold our holdings even at the bargain price of fifteen hundred dollars an acre, we could have raised more than four *billion* dollars. That's cold hard cash that could have been used to pay down debt and tide us over until things improved.

"He made his plans and brought them before the Board. They went ballistic. There are several major shareholders who just couldn't understand why we had to sell assets that we'd never be able to afford to buy back. So they killed the deal. They put him on notice and started looking for his replacement. They ended up hiring me. My background is in the paper industry, but the main thing they were after is someone who could come up with a winning strategy that didn't involve the company having a fire sale of its most valuable assets.

"Look, any way you slice it, wood products are a commodity. We're in market competition with half the countries in the world, most of whom have lower labor costs and laxer environmental regs. How can our unionized work force compete against some two-buck a day coolie in China? My strategy has been to capitalize on what Americans do best—innovate. Sure we're continuing to compete in the old standard markets, but we're pinning our future hope on making what we refer to as 'value-added products.' Rather than looking at pine trees as being full of two-by-fours, for example, we see them as a ready source of cellulose, something that is used in everything from fiber cereals to feminine hygiene products.

"And the star of the whole show is going to be our biofuel business. When we go in the forest to harvest a tree, do you have any idea how much of it is wasted?"

"A lot, I'd guess. The tops and limbs are left to rot."

"Exactly. My guys estimate that with current practices we lose on average between eighteen and twenty-two percent of the above-ground biomass of the tree. If we could perfect and patent a way to use that lost material, we'd be unstoppable. Which brings me full circle back to Laura and Adams County. Her work, the basis of her PhD thesis, has given us the answer. The Board has committed up to four hundred million dollars to building what's going to be one of the world's largest biofuel production facilities near Walkerville. That's why I was in New York yesterday. I was giving a select group of analysts the inside scoop. We plan to make the formal public announcement within the next few days. It's still on the drawing board, and of course I can't predict the markets, but I'd suspect ATH's stock will take a substantial leap when the news is made public."

"Making gold out of dross," I murmured.

CHAPTER Nineteen

It would occur to me sometime later that W. Cranston Gray was offering me a bribe. Or at the very least he had to be in violation of some SEC rule regarding the dissemination of confidential insider information that would have a material effect on the price of a publicly traded stock. Either way, I didn't take the bait. While I have a rather hefty portfolio—again mostly inherited—I couldn't care less about the whole concept of gambling in the market. No doubt Carl McIntosh would have agreed.

Instead I asked, "When do you plan to break ground?" thinking it would be a great excuse to get Sandra to spend a few days in Walkerville.

"Sometime within the next sixty days. We've been running a small demonstration plant there for about three months and it looks like we've got most of the kinks worked out. The plans are drawn, and we estimate that construction will take about nine months. By this time next year we should be up and running. We'll start out small, but within a couple of years we hope to be up to several hundred employees. That's going to be a lot of money dumped into the local economy." Gray looked out the window for a moment and then said, "I'm really sorry Laura is not going to be here to see it."

We talked for another half hour about nothing in particular. Gray had grown up in the suburbs of Chicago, and had spent much of his career in the upper mid-west, mainly Michigan and Minnesota. He'd been married for twenty-plus years, had a kid in college and another in her first year of medical school. He and his wife lived on West Paces Ferry Road, and were active in supporting the Atlanta Symphony.

He wanted to know all about me, where I'd gone to school, why I'd majored in anthropology, how I'd liked working in California. He seemed to be a nice enough guy and generally gave me the impression that he was happy to be having an informal conversation with someone who wasn't going to parse his words to get the "true" story about ATH's business outlook. At a quarter of two he said he needed to go over some papers for his next appointment and walked me back over to Sandra's office.

She was on the phone apparently arranging a Directors' meeting for the following week in the San Francisco office. She signaled she'd be just a minute more and indicated I should again resume my seat on her sofa. Hanging up, she said with a voice of relief, "Gosh, I've been on the phone constantly since lunch. I'm glad you're here—I need a break." Walking over and sitting next to me she asked, "Did you and Bill have a good talk?"

"Yeah. I like him. It sounds like he knows where he wants to take the company. What's the proper word to describe that in a CEO, vision?"

"The analysts call it that, I think, but the more I know the more I realize it's the ability to spew believable B.S. without cracking a smile." She grinned. I thought she was amazingly beautiful. I wanted to see her again—outside of this office.

"It's just after two," I said. "I hated that things got cut short last night. Any chance that you're free for dinner this evening?"

A look of disappointment swept across her face. "Oh, Matt, I'd give just about anything to be able to join you, but I am up to my eyeballs trying to set up this meeting on the west coast. Some things have come up about proposed new environmental regs in California, and Bill thought we needed to call an emergency Directors' meeting out there next week to firm up a stand on the company's position. I've got to coordinate the schedules of about thirty people, not to mention finding an available venue, arranging for the corporate jets to pick everyone up, and so on. I'm sure I'll be here until midnight. How about tomorrow night?"

"I really need to get back to Walkerville. But I'd love to see you again soon. Are you planning any trips down that way in the next week or so?"

"I can. I am absolutely certain there's *something* at our biofuel pilot plant that will need the personal attention of Mr. Gray's assistant. Why don't you call me in a few days? You've got my numbers." She reached out and placed her hand on top of mine. Glancing quickly at the door to be sure no one was watching, she gave me a quick peck on the lips.

Sandra offered to walk me out, but I said I could find my way. I said goodbye and walked to the door, leaving her sitting on the sofa. I nodded to Margaret who nodded back and had made it half way toward the public elevator lobby when I realized I'd forgotten something. I walked back past Margaret to Sandra's door. She was just starting to dial a number, but quickly put the receiver down with a smile when she saw me. "Back so soon?"

I leaned against the door frame and said, "Sorry. I forgot to ask you one thing. Did you ever have a chance to look and see if you had David Hargrove's address, or any information about a next of kin, or whatever? I think I should at least make an effort to find out a little bit about him and his relationship with Laura."

"Please don't apologize, Matt. I'm the one who should say I'm sorry. I forgot to tell you I looked in our personnel database the first thing this morning, and there's really nothing there. Like I said yesterday, with over twelve thousand employees nationwide, we have a huge staff turnover. When someone is terminated or resigns or—as in David's case—dies, their data are removed from our active files and archived somewhere, I'm not really sure. In fact the IT people update the databases nightly, so he's been out of the system for weeks. Let me do this. I'll call someone in Human Resources and get you everything that we have on file. It'll take a few days, but it will give me an excuse to call you. Will that be okay?" She flashed an impish grin.

"Of course. I'll wait by the phone," I said and turned again to leave.

I'd almost reached the door to the outer reception area when I heard Margaret call, "Mr. Rutherford?"

I turned around to see her walking toward me with some papers in her hand. "Yes?"

"I'm glad you came by to visit today. Ms. Williams said that Mr. Gray gave you an overview of the company, but I thought you might like to have a copy of our annual report. If you'll look carefully on the inside, you'll find quite a bit about our financial status and the various types of forest products we produce." She held up a thick, glossy booklet embossed with the company name in raised gold lettering. "I'll just slip it in this envelope for you." She put it in a large white mailing envelope and handed to me. "Do come back and see us soon."

I thanked her, tucked the envelope under my arm and headed for the elevators. She seemed rather strange, but probably didn't have much of a life otherwise. I was still thinking about Sandra.

It was nearly four by the time the cab dropped me off at the hotel. I considered driving home, but since I'd have to fight the afternoon rush and had already paid for the room for another night anyway, I decided to stay. I'd get a good night's sleep and leave about nine the next day, getting home before noon. I took off my coat and tie, kicked off my shoes, grabbed the TV remote and flopped on the bed.

After flipping through the channels half a dozen times and finding nothing of interest, I looked around for something to read. ATH's annual report was in the envelope on the desk. I took it out and studied the cover. It was an aerial photo of a vast expanse of timber, green in the foreground, blue-green in the intermediate distance, and fading into a bluish haze that hovered around a mountain range on the horizon. On one side, the sun was just peeking over the summit of a peak, painting the clouds from a palette of reds and golds.

I opened it to start reading, and a small booklet printed on white paper slid out on the desk. It didn't appear to be part of the annual report. I picked it up and read the title:

American Timber Holdings, Inc.
Personnel Directory
Atlanta Headquarters/ Southeastern Division
Confidential

A small red flag, the kind accountants use to indicate where to sign your tax forms, protruded from one side. I opened to the page to find one listing circled in blue ink:

Hargrove, David L.
Associate Research Scientist
Southeast District R & D Facility
Office: 770-625-7777
Home: 678-585-2197
Cell: 678-478-7541
Email: david.hargrove@americantimber.com

Someone wanted me to know about David Hargrove. More importantly, I wondered why someone else didn't.

CHAPTER Twenty

It took me less than ten minutes on the hotel's Business Center internet to connect David Hargrove's home phone number with an address in the metro Atlanta area. Pasting it into Google Maps, I came up with a location off Ponce de Leon in Decatur, less than five miles from the hotel and about the same distance from the ATH Tower downtown.

I was unsure how to approach things, but decided to try a phone call first. Using one of the Business Center's lines—in case they had Caller ID—I dialed the number and on the third ring got a cheery, "This is Will. I can't come to the phone right now, so leave a message." The machine beeped. I glanced at my watch—ten after five. I muttered, "Sorry, wrong number," and hung up.

It occurred to me that while I'd connected Hargrove's number with an address, I hadn't tried connecting it with a name. A few keystrokes on the computer brought up a "William Reich," at the same Decatur address. If I left right away, I could probably make it there by shortly after six. I had no idea who he was, what he did, or his relationship to David Hargrove, but I needed to find out. Assuming that he worked, I'd have a better chance of catching him at home now than during the day. I called valet parking and asked them to bring my truck around.

Named for the Spanish conquistador who "discovered" Florida while searching for the Fountain of Youth, Ponce de Leon Avenue, along with

Peachtree Street, was once one of Atlanta's great boulevards, lined with the stately homes of the wealthy. Time has not been kind to it. It runs in an east-west direction, connecting the central city's heart to the bedroom community of Decatur to the east. The two cities are indistinguishable, separated only by an artificial line demarking one tax district from the other.

Reich's address was on a small side street of assorted brick bungalows on tiny lots shaded by leafy hardwoods. I cruised past once, confirming the address before turning around and parking across the street. The neighborhood was one that had hit bottom and was back on the way up through gentrification and an influx of young professionals and first-time homebuyers. Most of the houses showed signs of recent renovation, with fresh coats of paint, new shingles and well-tended landscaping. The driveways were full of BMWs and Land Rovers.

If Reich's house had been covered with stucco, it would have fit nicely in an older Los Angeles neighborhood. The style was 1920s craftsman adopted for the southern vernacular, with brick siding and white-painted cast concrete accents. The grass was neatly trimmed and edged, and the boxwoods lining the walk smoothly pruned. A blue late-model Lexus was parked in the tiny driveway. A magnetic stick-on sign on the driver's door read, "Reich Interior Design" followed by a phone number.

I climbed the steps to the porch and rang the bell. Nothing. A minute passed. I rang the bell again to hear, "Just a sec. I'm coming," followed by the sound of footsteps on a hardwood floor. A slightly pudgy, bald-headed man opened the door. I guessed his age to be about thirty. He was wearing a starched pink twill shirt with the monogram "WR" on the sleeve, and dark blue trousers over penny loafers *sans* socks. His first reaction seemed one of surprise, then a smile and, "Well, hello. What brings *you* here this fine day?"

I smiled back, cautiously. "Mr. Reich?"

"Yes?"

I stuck my hand out and said, "I'm Matt Rutherford from Walkerville. I...."

He grabbed my hand with a lingering grasp and said, "Well, hello, Matt Rutherford from Walkerville. It's good to see you." He continued to smile.

"I...."

"Don't tell me. Just give me a minute and I'll remember." He opened the door wider. "We met at...., at..., I know..., The Pink Elephant two weeks ago, right?"

"No, I'm sorry. I don't believe we've met. I...."

"I know. Jon sent you by, didn't he? That sweet thing. He told me he had someone named Matt who he wanted me to meet. Well, come on in and sit down." He stepped back and waved me into a small living room furnished straight out of the 1950s.

"Mr. Reich, I don't...."

"I'm Will, you're Matt. That's all we need to know for the moment. I am just..."

This time I interrupted him. "I really think you have me mistaken for someone else. We've never met, and to be honest I don't know anything about you. I'm looking for some information, and I thought you might be able to help me."

Reich's smile darkened slightly. "But you knew my name. Why *did* you come to see me?"

"I want to find out about David Hargrove."

His face went blank, drained of color.

"David."

"Yes, David."

"He's dead. What more do you need to know? And why is it important to you?" I caught suspicion and some hostility in his voice.

"The girl who was killed in the crash with him, Laura McIntosh. Her parents asked me to find out more about the circumstances of her death."

"What are you, then? Some kind of investigator?" There was open hostility in his voice now.

"No, just a friend. I'm not a cop, and I'm not investigating anything. Just trying to find out what happened."

"So how did my name come up?" More curious now.

"You're listed as having the same telephone number as David Hargrove."

"So?"

"I presume you knew him?"

"Hmm!" Reich snorted. "Knew him? Of course I knew him, what do you think? We've been living here for four years."

I wasn't exactly sure how to phrase my next question. "You were roommates?"

"Yes, of course. And friends and partners and lovers. And if this damned state and its fucking Republican right-wing legislature weren't so backwards, we probably would have been a married couple one day."

"Oh." This caught me totally unprepared. I took a deep breath. I needed to take it very slowly.

"I'm so sorry about your loss."

Reich stared at me for a moment, then said, "You're serious, aren't you?"

"Yes. It's just that I had no idea you two were involved."

This time Reich took a deep breath. "Well, it's understandable." A pause, then, "Can I get you a drink? How about some champagne?"

"Sure, that'd be fine." Anything to keep him from throwing me out.

He got up and headed to the back of the house, returning shortly with a bottle of Spanish cava and two glass flutes. He poured them slowly in silence, letting the bubbles dissipate before filling them to the top. Raising a glass, he said, "To David." I responded in kind and we both took a sip. He set his glass on a small coaster and said, "What do you want to know?"

"I'm not sure, really. Of course you know the circumstances of Laura's and David's deaths?" Reich nodded, taking another sip of the wine. "There appears to be some evidence that Laura was on drugs..."

"That's a pile of horse crap!" Reich spit out. "I don't know what they were up to, and I really don't want to know. That *bitch*. She was probably trying to convert him or something. Who the hell knows? But drugs, no. Neither one of them. It was all I could ever do to get her to drink a second glass of champagne."

"Will, I know this may be a bit of a delicate question, but why would Laura and David be naked up in that stolen plane in the middle of the night?"

"At this point, I don't know and I *want* to tell you that I don't really care, but I do." He paused, gulping down the rest of his wine and pouring himself another glass. "I've really, really tried not to think about it, but I guess he was cheating on me. I mean, that seems to be the only logical explanation. But…, but…, I just can't understand it. It wasn't him. It wasn't his thing."

"How do you mean?"

"David was gay, for god's sake. He'd had sex with one woman in his life. When he was sixteen, in high school. He said it was disgusting. What happened to make him change?"

CHAPTER Twenty-One

"Let me tell you the truth," Reich began. "It doesn't really matter now, I guess." He topped off his glass and held the bottle up for me. I waved it off. "I met David about five and a half years ago, just after he went to work for that timber company. We dated for a while and one thing led to another. We got to be really close; it was just wonderful. He was smart and talented, and he just loved his job. There was one problem, though. David's never been out of the closet. He was so very much afraid if someone found out he was gay, it would hurt him—or hurt his chances of moving up at work.

"So we had this arrangement. We'd keep a very low profile as a couple, and as far as anyone at his job knew, David was another single guy into a lot of outdoorsy things. And it worked great, at least I thought it did. He was doing heavy research there—something about alternative fuels made from pine tree scraps or something like that—and they kept promoting him. As it turned out though, the more responsibility he got, the more he had to socialize with the people from work, you know, parties, corporate retreats and things like that. I mean, he couldn't just show up with *moi*, this queen of an interior designer hanging on his arm. It just wouldn't look right—or that was his excuse.

"Anyway, he was consulting with the technical people at Georgia Tech and got to know Laura when she was a graduate student. In fact, he was the one who talked her into working for the company. And since she'd met him outside of work, she knew he was gay and wanted to keep it a secret, which I think is pretty crazy, but that was David.

"So they had this arrangement. Whenever he absolutely needed to show up at some company function, he'd bring Laura. Lately, she'd gotten involved with a boyfriend back home, she said, a tradesman or air-conditioning person or somebody like that. She didn't want to stay home, but she was being loyal to this guy. It worked out perfect for both of them. David got cover and she got an escort. Otherwise people would be hitting on both of them."

"What about his family? I understand his parents are both dead."

"That's another pile of horse crap, another of David's cover stories. No, he was an army brat, his daddy was a colonel in the Air Force. He's the youngest of four kids. His parents are retired and live down on Lake Oconee near Greensboro. His old man hadn't spoken to him in years, ever since he found out David was gay. His mom would call every couple of weeks or so—about once a month she'd come up and we'd all go out to dinner. She's a nice lady."

"So nobody at work knew any of this?"

"No, not that I know of. I mean, he even had friends from work who were in his skydiving club, but they didn't know. No one knew. But he was doing well and moving up and we both figured once he really established himself we could make the great announcement and invite his whole fucking division to one big coming-out party."

"Did David ever mention a girl at work named Sandra Williams?"

"Yes! What an evil bitch. She was doing her best to get in his pants. In fact, that's when he and Laura really started making sure everyone at work knew they were 'dating.' Gave him a legit excuse to turn her down. Laura laughed about it—said she was doing him a favor. Little did I know she really wanted him for herself. They're all evil bitches, every one of 'em." He drained his glass again and splashed the remaining few ounces into the flute.

"So you think what started out as just a convenient 'arrangement' ended up leading to something else?"

Reich snorted, "Well, what else am I supposed to think? They weren't up in that plane playing tiddlywinks." There was anger in his voice. I thought I'd better calm him down if I were going to find out anything more.

"I know you must feel terrible," I said.

"How am I supposed to feel? Sad? Shocked? Betrayed?" He emptied the glass again. "How about all of the above?" He grabbed at the empty bottle and dripped the few remaining drops into his glass. "You know what I think? I think she was planning it all along. I think she just wanted to fuck him. I think this story of some 'boyfriend back home' was just as much a lie as David's carefully cultured image of the macho he-man he wanted everybody at work to think he was."

I didn't think continuing the conversation was going to get me anywhere. Reich was angry, and now having consumed most of a bottle of sparkling wine in a matter of minutes, he was getting drunk. I said, "Will, I know this has been hard on you, but I really do appreciate your help." He stared at the floor, not replying, his jaw muscles gripped tightly. "You wouldn't by any chance happen to have a photo of David that I could have?"

Reich looked up suddenly. "Photos? You want photos? Yeah, I've got fucking photos, a whole goddamned box of them." With that he leaped up, opened a small closet in the foyer and hefted a substantial cardboard box off a top shelf. Thrusting it at me, he said, "Take 'em. Take all of them. They're every photo I have of the bastard. I want 'em—no, I want *him*—out of my life completely." He jerked open the front door and stood waiting for me to leave.

Taking the box, I said, "I'm sorry for your loss," and headed toward my truck.

Reich stood in the door watching me as I walked down the steps. "And tell the bitch's parents they spawned a *fucking harpy*. Trying to take my David from me." He said more, but the slamming of the door muffled his words.

CHAPTER Twenty-Two

There was something that didn't quite fit, but I wasn't sure what it was. I took my time driving back to the Hyatt, turning things over in my mind. Mentally, I tried to arrange the facts in three piles. In the first group, everyone seemed to agree that Laura was both brilliant and beautiful. From what little contact I'd had with her more than a year earlier, I couldn't argue with that.

In the second group, there were things that seemed to be true, assuming no one I talked with had any reason to lie to me. She was apparently promiscuous, at least according to the one person—Sandra—who seemed to know her best. Theo Thigpen hadn't confirmed this, but then he admitted that he really didn't know a lot about Laura's personal life. She was probably a casual drug user, based on Sandra's suspicions, as well as the fact Thigpen had found cocaine in her apartment.

The third pile contained things I couldn't figure out. There were a strange assortment of "facts" that just didn't seem to mesh, like pieces of a jigsaw puzzle thrown in the wrong box. From all I could see, Laura did not appear to be a risk-taker, yet at the time of her death she was up in an airplane naked with a man. Anyway you cut it, the tabloids labeling this as a "Mile High Club" episode didn't seem far off track. But the guy she was with was gay and not into sex with women, at least according to Will Reich, his lover.

Perhaps this was a classic example of the blind men and the elephant. It could be that I was simply seeing different facets of a very complex personality. It was possible both Sandra and Reich were correct; Laura was a brilliant but sexually aggressive female who saw David Hargrove's rejection of women as a challenge. Reich may have been right; perhaps she did have some strange desire to "convert" him.

There was no way that I could report all this back to the McIntoshes. Sure, I could present some conveniently altered version of the facts, but in my own mind there were too many lingering questions. Was Sandra lying to me when she said she had trouble finding Hargrove's personnel data? And why was Margaret, her secretary, trying to make sure I got it? What about the boyfriend at home, Roger Barmore? How did he fit into the picture? Too many loose ends. I ate a quiet supper in the hotel restaurant, watched TV for a while and was asleep by ten.

I had packed and was just finishing my room service breakfast the next morning when my cell phone rang. I didn't recognize the number on the Caller ID. I answered it to be greeted by a soft, "Good morning, Matt. Did you sleep well last night?" Sandra.

"Hey, good morning to you," I said. "Where are you? I don't recognize the number."

"Well, I'm not sure, but I'd guess we just flew over Memphis. I'm calling you from the company jet. I'm on my way out to San Francisco to set up next week's meeting."

"That's a change of plans."

"That's part of what makes this job fun. You never know from one day to the next exactly what you'll be doing."

"Are you flying by yourself?"

"No, if it were just me, I'd still be sitting at the gate at the Atlanta airport. I'm with Bill and a couple of other directors. They're on a conference call in the back. I just wanted to call you and say hello. I'm sorry I had to work last night. Did you find something to do?"

"Yeah," I lied. "I watched a movie on HBO and went to bed early." No sense in telling her about Will Reich. Not yet, anyway.

"I hope we can get together soon," she said, promising before hanging up to call me when she got back in town. No mention of Laura or David Hargrove, but they didn't seem to be the focus of her interest. Her call gave me an idea.

I called the main number for American Timber Holdings and asked to be connected to Sandra Williams. A now-familiar voice answered, "Ms. William's office."

"Margaret?"

"Yes?" She didn't recognize my voice.

"This is Matt Rutherford." I heard a short sharp breath. "I want to thank you for giving me the envelope yesterday with the annual report."

A pause, then, "Yes, of course."

"I reached David Har...."

"I'm sorry, Mr. Knight," she butted in, "but Ms. Williams will be out of the office for the next few days. If you could give me your phone number I'll get back to you with that information as soon as possible."

She couldn't talk just then. I gave her my cell phone number and hung up. Ten minutes later it rang. "Mr. Rutherford?"

"Yes."

"This is Margaret Powell. Is this a good time to talk?"

"Thank you for calling me back. I...."

"Did you get the personnel directory?"

"Yes. I found David's number, and I tracked down his address." I wasn't sure where her loyalties lay, so I asked, "Why did Sandra have trouble finding it?"

Margaret hesitated, then said, "Knowing her, she probably didn't try. I don't think it was important to her. She's like that."

"I met Will Reich." Another sharp breath.

"Oh. I wasn't sure you'd be able to find him. Then you see the problem, don't you?"

"I'm not sure. Did Sandra know that David was gay?"

"It's possible, but I don't know. I do know that she was jealous of Laura."

"Why?"

"Laura was real. She earned what she had. Sandra will do whatever she has to do to come out on top."

"So, why...."

"I don't think I want to talk about it any more. The walls have ears."

"Please answer one question for me."

"If I can."

"Why did you want me to find out about David?"

"Mr. Rutherford, I've been married to a wonderful man for twenty-eight years. This is my second marriage. I had a son by my first. I lost custody of him when he was only eighteen months old—it's a long story. My first husband's last name was Reich. You figure it out." With a click the line went dead.

CHAPTER Twenty-Three

I was back in Walkerville by noon after driving through intermittent rain squalls that slowed traffic to a crawl. The house was dark. A note on the counter from Eula Mae said her sister from Wrightsville was in the hospital in Dublin with "dropsy"—whatever that meant—but might be transferred to Macon or Savannah and that she'd let me know as soon as she heard anything but she expected to be away for at least two or three days. She also said she'd made a casserole for me and left it in the freezer so I wouldn't have to eat "junk food" while she was gone. She really cares. I threw together a sandwich with some ham I found in the refrigerator and washed it down with sweet iced tea.

I made a quick trip to my office, opened bills and returned a few emails. I thought about calling my uncle to tell him I was back, but still hadn't decided what, if anything, I'd say to him at this point. Or to the McIntoshes for that matter.

By three, the front had blown through and white wispy clouds darted in front of the afternoon sun. I drove back to the house to find an Adams County Sheriff's Department patrol car parked in my back yard. The officer, seeing me pull in, got out and leaned against the driver's side door, his arms crossed. Muscular frame, short wiry brown hair. I recognized him as the man in the photo with Laura. I parked in the stables and walked over. Without smiling, he extended his hand and said, "I'm Roger Barmore."

"I'm Matt Rutherford," I said, to which he replied he was pleased to meet me, but really sad about the subject that had brought us together. "I thought you were in the heating and air-conditioning business," I asked.

"I am, but I work for the Sheriff's Department part-time. Neither one really pays that much, but between the two jobs I can make a pretty decent living." He paused, looking down, then said, "Mrs. McIntosh said you wanted to talk with me. About Laura."

"If it's okay, yeah, that would be helpful."

"She said they got you to go to Atlanta to try to find out what happened to her."

"I got talked into it. I didn't volunteer."

"They asked me to do it, did you know?"

"No, I didn't."

"I couldn't. I loved her. We were going to get married. I told them I didn't want to know what happened. I wanted to remember things like they were. Before she…." He didn't finish the sentence. "But I've been thinking a lot about it these past few weeks," he continued. "I believe," he said slowly, choosing his words carefully, "that if I don't know the truth, if I don't discover who she really was, my life will never be the same. I'll grow old wondering if I can ever trust anyone, anybody again. And I don't want to be that kind of person. So I've been sitting here waiting on you to tell you I want to help. I want to find out exactly what happened. I want to know if my loving, caring fiancée was nothing more than some kind of dime-store hooker the minute she got out of my sight." It must have been one of the most painful things he'd ever said.

"Are you sure?" I asked. "Sometimes it's better to remember the good things about a person."

Barmore had been staring at his shoes. He looked up and said, "I think, maybe, good and bad are relative terms. They're values that people place on actions and outcomes. I'm beyond that. I told Laura I loved her, and I meant it. I still do. When you love someone there's no good or bad. All I want is the truth, and I'll try to let time sort out the emotions."

"Okay," I said. "Then we'll do this together. Let's talk."

Barmore said he was on duty, but would be getting off at five and could come by sometime after that. We agreed on seven. I told him he could help me eat Eula Mae's casserole, to which he readily agreed. I didn't know him at all, and before I decided to share all the details of what I'd learned in Atlanta, it might be best to get a feel for him. The truth was going to hit him like a battering ram, and I wanted to be certain he could take it.

Barmore arrived at six-fifty. This time he was driving a white Ford pickup with a bright orange Trane logo on each door over the neatly lettered "Barmore and Son, Climate Control Specialists." I watched him through the kitchen window. He parked and sat in the truck for a moment, his hands gripped tightly on the wheel. Taking a deep breath, he got out and shut the door firmly. He brushed off his shirt, tucking it tightly in the front, then throwing back his shoulders marched deliberately up the back steps to ring the bell. This had to be difficult for him. I needed to calm him down.

I met him at the back door with a friendly smile and the offer of a beer, which he eagerly accepted. We sat in the kitchen waiting for the casserole to heat, talking about nothing in particular. I got the sense that he was feeling me out. Halfway through the second beer I said, "I'm glad you decided to come over. I know this has been eating at you. Maybe talking about it will help you get things straight in your mind."

Roger replied, "You seem like a nice guy, Matt. I guess I should say I really appreciate what you're doing to help out the McIntoshes. Sometimes I don't know how they make it from day to day."

"I didn't want to get involved at first, but I did. My Uncle Jack talked me into it."

"They've been friends for years. Laura always spoke so well of him." Something I didn't know.

"Tell me about you and Laura," I said.

"Where to start?" Roger said.

"How about the beginning?"

"There's not much of a story, really. We're the same age, in fact our birthdays are only a week apart. We were never that close until our junior year of high school. Laura was elected editor of the annual, and I got volunteered to do the sports section. We started spending a lot of time together. I guess you could say we were pretty serious in a teenage way.

"But we were very different people back then. I was the sports jock—football in the fall, baseball in the spring, that kind of thing—while she was the brainy one. She knew from the start she wanted to go to college and get a doctorate in something. Stupid me, I was always working out for the next game. It didn't matter much until we started applying to colleges. She had her choice of about anywhere she wanted to go, but the guidance counselor said that with my grades, I'd be lucky to get into a technical training program somewhere. That would have been fine with my dad; he wanted me to go into the heating and air-conditioning business with him. But the funny thing was," he laughed, "I had great plans to go to law school.

"Anyway, Laura ended up at Georgia Tech, and I managed to squeak in an acceptance to Georgia Military College as a day student. I did good on my SATs, but they told me if I really wanted to get a degree and go to a decent graduate school I'd have to prove I could cut it in college. GMC was the best I could do at the time.

"Laura and I kept in touch, but we drifted apart. She was into life in Atlanta and I was busting butt trying to prove I wasn't as dumb as I seemed, so we didn't see much of one another. I was majoring in Criminal Justice and after a couple of years I was pushing a three-eight average. Things were looking pretty good for me actually, but then my dad had his heart attack and was out of work for six months. I had to drop out and basically take over the business for him; otherwise he would have lost it. Even when he did come back, he couldn't work full time, so I gave up the idea of law school and starting taking night courses in HVAC at Walkerville Tech." He took a swig of his beer. "Another set of crashed dreams." There was irony in his tone.

"When did you two get back together?"

"Last fall, not long after I took the part-time deputy's job. In some sense, we'd never really been apart. We'd go six months or so without seeing one another, then she'd be home and call and we'd go out. It was so easy for both of us. Even though it may have been months, we could take up just like we'd seen each other yesterday.

"I'll tell you when things changed, it was last September. Laura was finishing up her dissertation and was home for a few days. We went out to the river and sat and talked for hours. I think she could finally see the end of school and wanted to start thinking seriously about the rest of her life—she was like that, always the planner. She said she'd been thinking about us, and how we'd known each other for all of our lives and how we had so much in common and wanted the same things. She didn't come right out and say it, but reading between the lines I think she was trying to tell me she thought maybe we had a future together. We sort of came to this informal agreement that we weren't going to date other people.

"Over the next few months we saw a lot of each other. Last Christmas I gave her a little pendant I had made, a gold pine tree with a diamond in the middle. We talked about getting engaged, but she wanted to wait to make the official announcement. She'd been promised a position here as head of ATH's research lab, and we thought we'd wait until it officially came through to tell everyone." Roger's voice cracked slightly. He got up, walked over to the sink and splashed his face with water.

Turning back to me he said, "You know, I never really knew what she saw in me. I mean, I don't even have a college degree. I've got to work two jobs to make ends meet. But she said she didn't care. She said that she loved me, and that was all that really mattered." He turned back to the sink and splashed his face with water again. I realized he was trying to hide his tears.

We were both silent for a moment, then I said, "Roger, I know you and Laura had talked about marriage, but honestly, how well did you know her?"

He forced a grim smile, answering my question with a question. "How well can you ever know anyone?" Then without waiting for my response continued, "I thought we were close. We talked on the phone almost every day. I saw her at least two or three weekends a month. There was nothing...."

"How often did you go to Atlanta?"

"That's just it, I couldn't. Not with my work schedule. I took the deputy's job originally just as a fill-in, but after we started talking about getting married, I saw it as a way to save up some money for the down payment on a house. I work mostly weekends, so it was hard for me to get away. The only reason I was working this afternoon was to fill in for one of the guys who's out sick. Normally I put in about six hours on Friday nights and then work ten or twelve hours during the day on Saturday and Sunday. When Laura was home on weekends, we'd see each other after work. I've probably been to her place in Atlanta only half a dozen times."

"Did you ever meet the roommate, Sandra Williams?"

"Just once. She went out a lot, according to what Laura said. Every now and then she'd answer the phone when I'd call." Roger looked away as if thinking about something, then said, "She was a hot one."

I didn't respond. There was one thing I needed to know, but I had no idea how he'd react to my asking. I said, "May I ask you a very personal question?"

He nodded.

"I don't know exactly how to put this, but were you and Laura ever intimate?"

He half laughed. "No, that's the funny part. For all her education, for all her years in the big city, she was still a small town girl. I tried, God knows I tried, but she said no, she wanted to save it for marriage. Matt, that's why I find everything so hard to take. I swear to you she had me believing that she was a virgin."

CHAPTER Twenty-Four

We talked for the next hour and a half. Or more correctly, I talked, Roger listened. I told him everything, omitting only the details of my semi-date with Sandra Williams. It had nothing to do with Laura, anyway, I reasoned. My words hit him like body blows, but he said little, revealing his emotions only with the occasional clenching of his jaw or a quick swipe to his eye. The casserole had gone cold on the stove top.

When I finished he said, "Well, shit." He got up, walked over to the refrigerator and grabbed another beer, twisting the top off as if he were strangling someone. "You know, either I'm the biggest sucker that's ever lived or there's something totally wrong with this whole story." He took a long pull on the bottle. "What do you think?"

"I don't know. There are a lot of things that don't fit neatly in the picture."

"Like this queer guy, David. I knew all about him, at least I thought I did. Laura told me they were just friends, and that he didn't want anyone to know he was gay. And all this shit about her going clubbing every night, hell, she worked a lot of nights. That's why she wasn't home. I know. She told me. A lot of times she'd call me at nine or ten o'clock and she'd still be at the lab working on something."

"How do you know she was at the lab, or wherever?"

"That's just it, I didn't. I trusted her. For all I know she could have been at some guy's apartment." He was getting angry now. "And the cocaine," he continued. "My god, I'm a part time cop! Did she think I wouldn't figure it out sooner or later?" He slammed the beer on the countertop with such force that I thought the bottle was going to break. He turned and stared out the window into the dim of the late spring twilight, alternately clenching his jaw and wiping his eyes.

After a moment I said, "So what do you want to do? I don't think we need to tell the McIntoshes the whole thing. We can just say that…."

Roger whirled around. "Hell, no! We're not going to tell them anything. Anything, that is, until we know the truth. I need proof. I'm going to flip over every rock until…."

"You can't bring Laura back."

"I know that. But I'm not doing it for her. I'm doing it for me, and I'm starting tomorrow morning. We can work together or I'll do it by myself." He stared at me, arms crossed, waiting for a reply.

"Let's do it," I said.

"Good! I'll be taking a few days off work. See you tomorrow afternoon." He finished his beer in one long swig and without waiting for my reply headed out the back door.

I scooped some of the cold casserole onto a plate, reheated it in the microwave and picked at it while I thought about Roger and Laura. For some reason I'd lost my appetite. I stuffed everything back in the refrigerator and went upstairs to read a book.

✈ ✈ ✈ ✈

The sound of a lawnmower in the neighbor's yard awakened me the next morning. The weather was balmy. I'd slept with the windows open. I lay in bed and wondered what Roger was going to do. I still hadn't completely sized him up. He was obviously intelligent, but I couldn't decide if his determination to discover what he called "the truth" was motivated more by anger or disbelief. I presumed I'd find out soon enough.

I ate a light breakfast and called my uncle to tell him I was back in town and still working on things. He asked for details, but I put him off explaining I needed to tie up some loose ends. I started to go by and see the McIntoshes, but ended up calling them instead to tell them more or less the same thing I'd said to Uncle Jack. I didn't want to risk a face-to-face meeting. It was easier to lie over the phone.

I spent most of the day looking over the logging operation on the tract where Laura's body had been discovered. The crew was just finishing up and readying their equipment to move to the next job. The foreman, Charlie, inquired about the investigation. "They ever figure out what happened with that dead girl?"

"I haven't heard anything new," I lied. "The coroner said she and the guy in the plane with her had been overcome by carbon monoxide. That's about all I know." I reasoned that much was public knowledge and I could plead ignorance otherwise.

"Well, I heard she was on dope. Cocaine is what they are saying. And that she was hooking on the side to support her habit."

My ears sat up. "Really? Where'd you come up with that?"

"I don't know. That's what they're saying. Being as how I was here when we found her, everybody wants to ask me about it, and that's just what they tell me."

"Yeah, but who are 'they'?"

"The guys at the woodyard. The guys at the mill. You know, you come by to pick up your load sheets and somebody says, 'The word is the McIntosh girl was on drugs.' That kind of thing."

No one had any reason to know that.

Shortly after five I heard the crunch of vehicle tires on gravel. I'd been home half an hour and was reading the newspaper on the sun porch. I watched as the now familiar white pickup with its Trane logo pulled to a halt in front of the stables. Roger Barmore emerged, this time dressed in his deputy's uniform and carrying two expandable file folders. He climbed the back steps and rang the bell.

Opening the door, I said, "I thought you were taking the day off."

"I am." His demeanor was muted.

"So why the uniform?"

"You do what you gotta do."

"Pardon? How do you mean?"

Without replying, he walked past me into the kitchen and laid the folders on the table. He plopped down in a chair, took a deep breath and said, "Matt, I'm sorry. I know I left in a rush last night. I didn't thank you for all you've done. This thing is…., I don't know…, driving me crazy. After what you said last night, I had this idea that if I just knew the truth, the *facts*, things would be okay. I could put it all in perspective and move on with my life. I mean, the truth is out there. You know it. I know it. Maybe you've already found it. I just don't know…." His voice trailed off and he took another deep breath. He wasn't making much sense.

"So," I asked cautiously, "why the uniform?"

"I had this idea…," he started again. "I had this idea that if we took a fresh look at the investigation, we—you and I—could sort it all out. Think about it. There are two dead people. The State asks, were their deaths the result of an accident or something else? See, basically the government is in charge of the investigation, and basically they really don't care. If it's an accident, it's a statistic. End of story. Case closed. That's all they want to know.

"Now me…, No, us, you and me, we're asking a different question. How did this happen? Why did this happen? To us, to her parents, Laura's not a statistic, she was a living, breathing person who we knew and cared about. So, last night, I had this idea. Get all the records from the Crime Lab and the GBI and the Feds who investigated the crash and take a look at them ourselves.

"You see, technically this is still an open case, and will be until the final results of the autopsies are released, not to mention the crash report from the NTSB. I'd asked around and they said that could take six months or more. But in reality, it's not an open case. Everybody thinks they 'know' what happened. And really, as far as the State and Feds are concerned, they've done all the investigating they're going to do. What they're waiting on now is paperwork.

"So this is what I did. I called the Crime Lab in Macon and the GBI office in Milledgeville and told them we still had some issues we wanted to look into here in Adams County, and that I wanted to pick up copies of the case files so we could proceed with our investigation."

"Who is we?" I asked.

"As far as they know, the Adams County Sheriff's Department. That's what I told them. I showed up in my uniform and signed for them."

"Uh..., are you going to get in trouble for this?"

"Probably not. I doubt if they'll find out. The worst thing they could do is fire me, anyway. It's not a criminal case. Technically the records would eventually be available under the Open Records Act. I just speeded things up. Oh, and I called the NTSB. They're sending copies of what they've got—should be here in a few days. "

"Okay...."

"So, I'm driving back to Walkerville and realize that in all probability the answer to every question I want to ask is inside these folders."

"How so?"

"The preliminary autopsy reports mainly. There'll be drug screens and...," his voice broke, "...specimens. You know."

"Yeah."

"And I don't have the guts to look." He stood up. "I'm not one to run from something, but I don't think I can do it."

"Do what?"

"Look at the reports, the photos, that sort of stuff. You do it, Matt. You look and just tell me what you think. I'm going home now. I'll be back tomorrow." Without another word he walked out the door.

CHAPTER Twenty-Five

I stared at the folders lying in front of me. This was not what I wanted. But in a sense, Roger was right. Directly or indirectly, the answers to his questions—and maybe to the McIntoshes's—were somewhere hidden in those files. I picked them up and moved them to the dining room table. Neither folder was labeled. The smaller of the two held documents from the Georgia Bureau of Investigation's files, the thicker was from the Regional State Crime Laboratory.

I decided to start with the GBI's report. A quick perusal confirmed Roger's take on the situation. As far as the state cops were concerned the case was closed, and they were just waiting on the final autopsy and NTSB reports to send it to the file room. The summary report was signed by Capt. Austin Moore, the cop who interviewed me at the scene. I scanned it quickly. The only thing new to me was the report on the plane crash in Hancock County.

Briefly, it appeared that the plane, a Cessna Stationair, had run out of fuel and crash-landed in a relatively smooth cattle pasture, snapping off the landing gear and skidding some three hundred forty-five yards before plunging into a dense stand of scrub oak and pines. Fifteen or so digital photos were printed on attachment sheets stapled to the report. The aircraft was surprisingly intact. According to the accompanying diagram that reconstructed the plane's path, the major damage was done when the starboard wing struck a tree, snapping it off and pivoting the fuselage to the right, which in turn smashed the left wing and tail section into other trees before coming to a halt. The impact seemed to have taken place at a fairly low speed, with most of the energy and velocity expended in the thousand-plus foot slide across the open grassland. David Hargrove's body hadn't fared so well. He had been thrown from the open side door with the initial impact, striking a large boulder face first. The plane was traveling in excess of a hundred miles an hour when it touched down. Judging from the pixilated images of his body attached to the report, I doubted that a visual identification would have been possible.

I turned my attention to the Crime Lab files. They were less well organized, and consisted mainly of autopsy reports and toxicology studies with pages of graphs that I guessed were immunoassay and gas chromatography printouts. A slim jewel case held a CD labeled "Autopsy Photographs" followed by a case number. I put it back in the folder, not wanting to look.

David Hargrove's report was on top. There was a brief one-paragraph summary labeled "Circumstances." It stated the decedent was the victim of an aircraft accident, and that no foul play was suspected. The next two paragraphs were headed "External Examination" and "Internal Examination," followed by a diagram of a body with hand-sketched annotations by the pathologist. I skimmed it rapidly, not wanting to focus on the details. The phrase *"massive blunt trauma to cranio-facial area"* caught my eye.

On the next page under "Additional Studies," the first sentence read, *"COHb level 47.6%."* COHb? Carboxyhemoglobin? I wasn't sure. Below it, *"Stomach contents, blood and urine screens negative for alcohol, THC, benzodiazepines, opiates (including synthetics), barbiturates and benzoylecgonine. Results attached."* High blood carbon monoxide levels with a negative drug screen? I made a mental note to ask someone if this included cocaine.

The final sheet of the report was headed "Provisional Anatomic Diagnosis," with a disclaimer under it stating that the examining pathologist reserved the right to make a "Final Anatomic Diagnosis" based on microscopic studies, etc. Two items were listed. *"Death secondary to carbon monoxide inhalation, presumed accidental."* Below it, *"Massive trauma to facio-cranium, with associated fracture of C-1, C-2 and C-4."*

Under a section labeled "Comments," the pathologist had dictated,

1. The preliminary identification of the subject as 'David Levin Hargrove' is based on information received from the Investigating Officer(s) and subject to confirmation based on additional investigation. The condition of the body does not allow visual identification.
2. Either of the above two PADs is sufficient in itself as a cause of death, but based on a lack of post-trauma exsanguination, it is presumed that the subject was deceased at the time of impact.

Hargrove was dead when he hit the ground.

Clipped to the back sheet of the autopsy report was a single sheet headed, "Results of DNA Comparison Testing." The top two-thirds was filled with technical jargon. Skipping to the last paragraph, I read, "*Summary: Based on genetic comparison material (hair from brush) provided by Col. and Mrs. Alfred S. Hargrove, the probability that the decedent is not in fact their biologic son, David L. Hargrove is less than 1 in 4 billion. This result can be considered a definitive biologic identification for all legal purposes.*" No doubt as to identity, I thought.

Laying Hargrove's autopsy report to one side I picked up Laura's and stared at the front sheet for a minute. I hadn't been as close as Roger, but I wasn't sure I wanted to do this either. I flipped over to the final sheet headed "Provisional Anatomic Diagnosis," with the same disclaimers as on Hargrove's. Again, two items were listed. The first read, "*Death due to massive trauma, including multiple penetrating wounds, sustained (by provided history) in fall from aircraft.*" The second, "*Carbon monoxide inhalation, non-fatal.*" She was alive when she fell from the plane. A cold shudder ran over me.

As in the other autopsy, the pathologist had also dictated a "Comments" section"

1. Based on perimortum exsanguination, the subject is presumed to have been alive when she struck the ground. The primary cause of death is multiple penetrating wounds from branches of loblolly pine.

2. Carboxyhemoglobin levels, while significant and possibly contributory, are not considered to be the primary cause of death.

3. There is evidence of recent sexual activity, however trauma sustained in fall from aircraft precludes comments on any premortum perivaginal and/or perianal trauma.

The question had been answered definitively.

I lay the report back on the table. I didn't know how I was going to break this to Roger. If I backed off and just thought about it, the findings weren't surprising. Maybe everything did fit after all. The late nights Roger thought Laura was working at the lab. Will Reich's accusation that she'd seen Hargrove's sexuality as a challenge. Sandra's assertion of her promiscuity and involvement with multiple men. Even the rumors Charlie had heard of her "hooking' to support a drug habit.

Drug habit? The summary hadn't mentioned drugs. If Laura had been using cocaine on the night she was killed, it should have shown up in the crime lab examination. I picked up the autopsy report and flipped to the "Additional Studies" section to read:

1. COHb Level 41.1%.

2. Stomach contents, blood and urine screens negative for alcohol, THC, benzodiazepines, opiates (including synthetics), barbiturates and benzoylecgonine. Results attached.

3. Vaginal and anal fluid specimens show numerous motile spermatozoa.

Suddenly I wasn't so sure.

CHAPTER Twenty-Six

I started to call Roger but thought better of it, instead punching in Wayne Guillard's home number. I interrupted him in the middle of the Evening News. He'd served as Adams County's Medical Examiner for years and should be able to help me interpret some of the autopsy results. Off the record, of course. We knew each other well enough for me to feel comfortable asking him for information but not telling him why I needed it.

"You want to know what?" he asked. He sounded a bit annoyed.

"I said can you tell me how long sperm stay motile?"

"Matt, that's kind of a crazy question. Exactly in what context are you talking about?"

"Sorry. Let's say that two people, a guy and his girlfriend, have sex, right?"

"Right...."

"If you examined her later, how long would you find motile sperm in her vagina?"

There was a pause. "Matt, are you in some kind of trouble?"

"No. No. It's a question that was put to me. By a friend. In Atlanta." I didn't think I was being a very convincing liar.

"Yeah. Like the fellows who come to see me in the medical office and say, 'I've got this *friend* who's really worried about having herpes and would like to know what it looks like.' That kind of friend?"

"No, Wayne, honestly, it's just something I'm working on. I need some information and thought you might know the answer."

He chuckled, "Only for you, Matt." Then, "It's not the sort of question I get asked every day, but I believe I'm correct in saying that you'll find motile sperm for a couple of days at the most. But there have been reports of much longer survival. Why do you need to know?"

"Trust me. I'll tell you later if I can."

"Okay. Do you want me to check on that? I can call the Crime Lab in Macon...."

"No. Definitely not. It's not a criminal matter." At least I hoped it wasn't.

"Can I do anything else for you?" Guillard asked.

"One more question. How is cocaine use detected in a person?"

"Matt, are you *sure* you're not in some kind of trouble? Be honest with me. I'll do what I can to help you."

"No, I'm fine. It's something I'm trying to find out for a friend."

"What's the quote from Shakespeare's Julius Caesar? *'A friend should bear his friend's infirmities.'*"

"Something like that, I think." I had no idea what he was talking about.

He chuckled again. "Then he—or she—must be a close friend. But, to answer your question, most screening for cocaine use is based on looking for metabolites of the drug in the urine. The one they commonly test for is benzoylecgonine. Now there are other ways of...."

"No, that's fine. That's all I needed to know." I thanked him and hung up. Both of the specimens from Hargrove and Laura were negative for benzoylecgonine. I tossed things back and forth in my mind before deciding I needed to take a long walk to get a breath of fresh air.

Roger appeared at my back door the next morning at eight, his presence announced by the ringing of the door bell heard over the gurgling hiss of Mr. Coffee as the last bit of boiling water dripped through the grounds. I said hello, invited him in and poured him a mug. We sat at the kitchen table. He didn't ask. He was waiting for me to tell him. Finally I said, "I looked over the reports last night."

His jaw clenched. "And ...?"

"There's evidence that Laura had been having sex with someone within a reasonably short period of time before she died." I didn't want to go into detail.

Roger sipped at his coffee, silent, eyes on the table.

"The reports showed…," I continued.

"No. That's enough," he said quietly.

"Let me finish," I said. "The reports showed no evidence of drug use."

After a bit of a pause he said, "Well, that's a plus." A hint of sarcasm.

I waited for him to say more. When he didn't I said, "I'm really sorry."

Again he was quiet. The ticking of the grandfather clock in the hall counted the seconds. A heavy truck passing by on the street gave a slight rattle to the windows. Eventually Roger looked up and said, "Matt, have you ever been in love? Really in love with someone?"

I thought about Lisa. "I think so. I'm not sure anymore."

"I'm a guy and I guess I'm not supposed to be sensitive, but somewhere deep inside of me is this person who once had this idea—no, this fantasy, if you will—that one day I'd find the perfect girl. That we'd fall in love and that we'd be truly honest with one another. That we could bare our souls and it would be all right. And that we'd get married and have kids and grow old together." He paused, sipped from his cup and looked at me. "You know, I thought that person was Laura. Now, well…, I've gotten that out of my system." Another pause, another sip. "So next time—if there is a next time—I won't be such a damned fool."

He stood up, carefully setting the cup on the table. Taking a deep breath and blowing it out slowly, he extended his hand and said, "Well, I guess that's over. Thanks for all you've done." He turned to leave.

"What about the McIntoshes?" I asked. "You want to go with me to talk with them?"

"I think not. I probably won't see much of them from now on. And they're old. They'll be gone, too, before long." A hint of bitterness this time.

"Okay. I'll talk with them."

Roger headed for the door. "Come by and have a beer sometime," I said, feeling stupid as soon as the words left my lips.

"Yeah, I'll do that," he replied over his shoulder as he disappeared down the steps.

I finished my coffee, dreading what I had to do next. I'd talk first to my uncle and then to the McIntoshes. I called Jack, and as with Roger, gave him the highlights while leaving out the details. There was silence at the other end of the line. Then he said, "Well, you just never know about kids these days."

"What should I say to Carl and Agnes?"

"I don't know. What can you say that won't destroy them? You never expect your children to…," he started, not finishing, then said, "Like Lance." Lance was my first cousin, Jack and Margie's son. He'd died violently in a drug related killing shortly after my return to Walkerville.

I caught his implication. "Laura's body was negative for drugs."

"Perhaps, but you said there was cocaine in her apartment."

"The manager found some. That's all I know."

"Still, it's sad," he said and hung up without saying goodbye.

The clock on the stove read nine forty-eight. I dialed the McIntoshes. Agnes answered. I asked her if I could come over. "Do you have some news for us?" she wanted to know.

"I've found out a few things," I said. She told me the front door would be unlocked and I could let myself in.

Carrying Laura's jewelry box in a sack, I walked slowly to their house, trying to compose my speech. I'd spare them the details, just hitting the high points. I wouldn't repeat what Sandra Williams had said, or mention the autopsy results. I'd paint the best picture I could.

Steeling myself, I opened the front door into the same dimly lit hall with its same familiar smell. Carl called from the rear of the house, "We're here. In the den. Come on back." I found them sitting in the dark-paneled room, waiting. The curtains were closed tightly, shutting out the bright daylight outside.

Agnes sat rigidly on the sofa, her legs close together, her hands tightly gripping a white handkerchief. Carl tried to get up from his recliner. I told him to keep his seat and walked over to shake his hand. Agnes nodded, not saying anything. "Sorry to have it so dark in here," Carl said. "Ever since I had cataract surgery I can't stand too much light." Agnes nodded.

Carl said, "That was a heavy rain we had the other day. My grass was getting dry. Kinda needed it." The exchange of pleasantries always has to come first.

"Yeah, the farmers are going to be happy. The spring's been a little dry," I replied.

"You still have that boxwood maze up there at Rutherford Hall? I remember your aunt buying fertilizer for it back when I owned the hardware store."

"It's still there. The yard service keeps it neat and trimmed."

"Better than you having to do it," Carl said. I wasn't sure if he was being sarcastic or not. Agnes sat silently, twisting the handkerchief in her hands.

"Yeah," I said, both of us avoiding the obvious.

"So what'd you find out?" Carl asked.

"About Laura." Agnes chimed in, as if there might be another reason for my visit.

"I spent three nights in Atlanta earlier this week," I started. " I talked with Theo Thigpen, Laura's apartment manager...,"

"Such a nice man," Agnes interjected.

"...Sandra Williams, who roomed with her for a few months, some people at American Timber Holdings who knew her, and to Will Reich, who was David Hargrove's roommate. Mr. Thigpen sent this back to you." I handed the jewelry box to Carl.

"Such a nice man," Agnes repeated.

"What'd you find out?" Carl repeated.

"I know all this is not easy for you, so let me just tell you my overall impression based on everyone I talked with."

"Okay," Carl said.

"To sum it up, Laura was everything you thought she was. She was a fine, loving Christian girl. I couldn't find a single person who had anything but the highest praise for her. They were all so shocked and saddened at her death. They..."

"No drugs?" Carl asked.

"None."

"What about this Hargrove boy?" Agnes asked.

"Everyone said she was in love with Roger Barmore and planned to marry him and they couldn't understand what was going on with Hargrove. The consensus is that he must have tricked her into going up in the airplane and was trying to take advantage of her. It just appears to have been a terrible accident."

"I knew it! I knew it!" Agnes said, clapping her hands. I thought I might have caught a fleeting smile on Carl's face.

I stayed for a few more minutes, fabricating quotes and mythical episodes detailing Laura's life in Atlanta. Carl and Agnes both walked me to the front door and again stood on the front stoop, waving goodbye as I walked away. He seemed stronger this time.

When I was sixteen, Uncle Jack had offered me a beer. I told him my mother would object. He'd said, "What she doesn't know won't hurt her." I thought about that on the way home.

CHAPTER Twenty-Seven

I called Jack to tell him what I'd done. He listened and then asked, "Why?" I told him I'd decided at the last second to lie, and reminded him of what he'd said to me years before. He mumbled something about "It's probably better this way," and hung up, again neglecting to say goodbye. I don't think he really approved, but would keep quiet just the same. I considered calling Roger Barmore, but decided against it. He was unlikely to talk to the McIntoshes anyway.

The problem now laid to rest, I set out on foot for the City Square and lunch at The Country Buffet. Rutherford Hall is only a few hundred yards up Main Street, and it was a pleasant day to walk. The temperature was in the mid-eighties, the sky blue, and the smell of freshly mown grass mingled with the perfume of purple wisteria that covered the trellis by the old stables. I felt like a weight had been lifted from my shoulders, and I was hungry.

The Square was crowded. Parking spots near the Court House were packed with Mercedes and BMWs, indicating the quarterly plague of tassel-shoed attorneys visited upon Walkerville during Superior Court sessions. The restaurant was nearly full, too, with families of the accused in their Sunday best interspersed among knots of blue and grey-suited lawyers chowing down on fried chicken and okra while avoiding excessive familiarity with their miscreant clients. I went through the line and found a small quiet table in a back corner near the kitchen.

I was still on my first glass of iced tea when I spotted Earnest Tookes, one of the County Commissioners, threading his way toward me across the dining room. Without waiting to be invited, he eased into the other chair and said, "Hiya doin' Matt?" sticking out his hand at the same time. Typical politician.

I swallowed, wiped my hands on my napkin and shook his, replying, "Good to see you. What's up? The next election is more than a year off."

He laughed, taking my cynicism as a joke and said, "No politics this time. I really just came over to see how you were doing. We haven't talked in a while." He was lying. He wanted something.

"I'm doing fine, thanks. Trying to keep busy." Now I was lying.

Tookes nodded. "Sad about the McIntosh girl, wasn't it?"

"Yeah, a tragedy." I tore into a piece of chicken, wondering where he was going.

"How's the timber business?"

"Fine, I guess. Prices have been pretty good. You've got a few trees, don't you?"

"A few hundred acres, yeah, but not like the Rutherfords."

"I inherited it," I said between mouthfuls, stating the obvious.

"You keep up with it though, don't you? I mean the overall business, the timber markets, and stuff like that?"

"As much as I need to." I forked down some turnip greens.

"Well, I was wondering if I could get a little advice from you, Matt? You know, I'm just a country boy at heart, and I've spent most of my life in the propane gas business. Now you, you've been out there in California in big business...."

"The computer industry, basically," I corrected him.

"Whatever, but you know about stocks and bonds and that kind of stuff, don't you?"

"I guess." What did he want?

Tookes looked around the room, then lowered his voice and hunched over slightly to say, "I've gotten a tip on a stock and I want to see what you think about it."

I put my fork down. "Look, Mr. Tookes, I honestly don't think I'm the one to be asking about...."

He held his hand up to silence me. "No, this is something you probably already know about and I just want to get your opinion." He paused, looking around again to be sure no one was listening, before saying, "You know this company, American Timber Holdings, right? Well, you know they own a bunch of land here in the county and they've been talking for a good while on opening a big plant down here to make gasoline from pine trees? You'd heard that hadn't you?"

"I think I heard they were going to try to make ethanol—it's a type of alcohol that can be used as a gasoline substitute—from wood products. There've been articles about it in the press." I thought about the article in the Georgia Tech alumni magazine.

Almost whispering now, Tookes continued, "I hear they made a big breakthrough, and their stock is going to go through the roof. You heard anything?"

"No," I said, again lying. "Who told you that?"

"Can't say exactly, but as you may know, we Commissioners have put together a pretty good tax incentive package to help these ATH folks get their plant construction off the ground. Just say I was talking with someone highly placed. Very highly placed."

"Bill Gray?" I asked, taking a stab in the dark.

Tookes jerked back as if pricked by a pin. "How'd you know?"

"Lucky guess." I smiled.

"What do you think? Bill says their stock is going to go way up. Think I should buy some?" I noticed that they were on a first name basis.

"When did he tell you about this?" I asked.

"Not long ago. We were finishing up the negotiations for the incentive package."

"In that case, I'd buy it," I said. It sounded like a bribe to me, but Tookes was probably too dense to realize it.

By the time I'd finished the last of my banana cream pie, the crowd had thinned to a few hard-core regulars who sat around drinking coffee and swapping tales. I paid my six dollars at the register, tossing a one into the basket labeled "Tips," and strolled out onto the sidewalk feeling well-fed and lazy.

The Court House clock chimed twice. I thought about Sandra Williams. It was eleven in San Francisco. Sitting down on one of the benches, I found her number in my wallet and called her on my cell phone. It rang once before going to voice mail. I said hello and gave her my home number before beginning my leisurely walk across the Square and back up Main Street.

I'd been home only fifteen minutes when Sandra called. She sounded both eager and apologetic. "Matt, I am so sorry," she began. "I have been in meetings almost constantly since we got out here, and I've barely had time to eat or sleep. You just can't imagine how complicated things are with these regulations and …"

"Hey, hold on," I said. "You don't need to explain. I just called to say hello."

"I know," she said, taking a deep breath, "but I've been thinking. I really want to see you and I'm stuck out here. It's like…."

"You don't need to explain," I said again.

"No, please let me. I want to," she continued. "I realize we hardly know each other, and I feel kinda silly acting this way. I mean, even if you pushed all the time we've spent together into one lump it would be just a few hours, but I can't help feeling like there's so much more that we haven't said. I guess I'm being pushy, but what I'm trying to say is that I want to get to know you better."

I wasn't about to object. "That's good. I'd like to see you, too."

"Look, I think it will take a few more days to wrap things up out here, then I'll be on my way back to Atlanta. I've been working pretty much twenty-four/seven, so I'm going to take a day or two off. I need to come down to Walkerville anyway, so why don't we plan on getting together?"

"I'd like that," I said, with visions of her long blond hair falling over her shoulders running through my mind. "Can you stay for a couple of days?"

"Sure, I don't see why not. Normally I'd drive back and forth but…"

"You can stay at my place," I said.

"Are you sure? I don't want to impose."

"Not at all. I'd like that. I've got a comfortable guest room," I replied, thinking she wouldn't need it if my plans worked out.

CHAPTER Twenty-Eight

The next morning, a Saturday, found the Square almost as deserted as it had been crowded only twenty-four hours earlier, the main attraction now being the informal weekly farmers' market. The usual collection of pickups was parked in front of the Court House, their tailgates loaded with stacks of June corn and early summer peas packed in thin wooden hampers. A couple of intrepid sellers had made the trek to south Georgia and back to have watermelon and cantaloupe to peddle before the local crop matured and prices plunged. A desultory group of buyers wandered from vendor to vendor, comparing prices and sizing up the merchandise. It seemed that most of Walkerville had found something else to do on this fine summer day.

As for me, it had been a rough week. The thing with Laura's parents now behind me, I found myself looking forward to seeing Sandra, and generally getting on with my life. Eula Mae called to say her sister had been transferred to the hospital in Savannah and she felt like she needed to be with her—"if you gonna let me off a day or two, that is." I told her that would be fine, and she promised to be back at work by the end of the coming week. I spent most of the day working on my project in the old stables behind the house, for a change generally feeling glad to be alive.

Early Sunday morning my uncle called and invited me to go to church with him and Aunt Margie. He said my mother was "doing better," a genteel way of saying she was sober, and that it would be nice to have another Rutherford in the family pew. I politely declined and spent most of the morning reading. The Court House clock was chiming ten when the phone rang. A familiar voice said, "Hi. Hope I didn't wake you." Sandra.

"Are you kidding? I've been up for hours."

"I know, but for some reason I was thinking about you in bed...." She didn't finish. "It's barely seven out here."

"What are you doing up so early?"

"We're just about to get on the company plane to fly back to Atlanta. I wanted to see if things were still good for next week."

"Of course. I have nothing else scheduled."

"Well, this is what's going on. The Board met and has decided to make the announcement about the new plant this coming Friday. I know it's short notice, but they want to get the word out as soon as possible—especially before the competition can come up with something similar. There will be a groundbreaking ceremony in Walkerville, and hopefully a lot of media coverage. I've got to be there most of the week to make sure things are running smoothly. Honestly, I don't think I'll have that much to do, but Bill—Mr. Gray—wants me on site to handle any last minute problems. He's going to make the big announcement and doesn't want to leave anything to chance."

"Great. My housekeeper's out of town with her sick sister, but I'll try to get the house cleaned up for you."

"Don't be silly, Matt." She hesitated a second, then said, "It'll be good to spend some time with you."

"I know," I replied, smiling.

Sandra said she'd need to be in the Atlanta office all day on Monday, but she hoped to leave early the next morning and be in Walkerville by ten. "I need to meet with the new lab director and see about a whole lot of little details to make sure things come off as planned on Friday. Why don't I pick you up? I'd love some company, and you'll get a VIP tour." I said I'd be waiting. I flew through the rest of the day.

On Monday I bounded out of bed at seven and began a systematic house cleaning. I will be the first to admit that I'm not especially domestic, and normally leave such things to Eula Mae, who takes great pride in her work.

On the other hand she was out of pocket, and the kitchen sink had somehow managed to accrete several days' worth of unwashed dishes. I didn't want Sandra's first impression to be a bad one.

I cleaned and straightened up, hauled out stacks of old newspapers and sacks of garbage, and checked the towels in the guest bathroom. Satisfied that I had adequately feathered the nest, I spent an hour in the gourmet section of the local grocery store stocking up on food, followed by a visit to the wine shop to replenish my meager selection of premium vintages.

By nine-thirty Tuesday morning I was excited, a feeling that I hadn't experienced in a long time. Somewhere deep inside of me I still missed Lisa, but I knew I had to move on. I read the morning paper and paced back and forth in the house, glancing out the window every few minutes hoping to see Sandra's BMW. By five past ten I began to worry. At ten past, I was considering calling her cell phone when mine rang. I recognized her number on Caller ID. "Matt," she said, "I am so sorry. I'm running just a little late— there was a bad wreck on I-20 that had things backed up for miles. I thought I could make it up but the cops are everywhere and I've already gotten two tickets this year. Anyway, I'll be there in about fifteen minutes."

"That's fine, I wasn't worried at all," I lied. "See you shortly."

As promised, she arrived a quarter hour later and already had her bag out of the car before I could make it down the steps to meet her. She looked incredible, dressed in a slim black skirt and a bright green silk blouse that accentuated her ample figure. She smiled, flicking her hair back with her hand as she reached out to hug me. "I've been *so* looking forward to this," she said as I grabbed her black leather Tumi bag. "San Francisco is great, but it was cold and drizzling rain. This is home. I feel like I belong here." She paused to look at the house. "You have quite a place."

"It's old, but comfortable," I said, following her eyes as they roamed over Rutherford Hall.

"But it's you," she replied. "You know, riding down here with nothing to do but listen to the radio, I was wondering what your house would look like." Looking at me she continued, "I think it suits you."

"How so?"

"I don't know. It's just…, just you." She looked at her watch and said, "I hate to rush, but I told them I'd be at the plant by eleven. I need to meet with Clay Wynne for a few minutes first to go over a few things."

"Who is Clay Wynne?"

"Oh, that's right, you haven't met him. He's just been appointed head of the new lab here—the position that was supposed to go to Laura. And I picked up some things for lunch from my favorite deli this morning on my way out of town. I thought maybe I could meet briefly with Clay, then we'll do the tour thing and then have lunch later in the afternoon."

"You really don't have to give me a tour."

"Oh, no, it's not for you. I think—or I *hope*—you'll enjoy it, but part of my reason for being here is to go through a dry run for the event on Friday. There will be a lot of reporters who're going to get the same dog and pony show. I'm supposed to be sure that things run smoothly. And, too, I'd like your suggestions. You said you've never seen the pilot plant, and that makes you a good guinea pig. Explaining the technology can be confusing, and I want to be sure we've got it right."

Apologizing for Eula Mae's absence, I showed Sandra to the guest room and left her alone to change. She bounced down the stairs ten minutes later in jeans and a khaki shirt embroidered with the ATH logo in bright shades of green and brown. Her hair was pulled back in a French braid. "Gotta dress for the part, as they say. The plant can be a little messy sometimes." I followed her out to her car and climbed in the passenger seat. She looked at her watch again. "I think we can just make it there on time if we push the speed. You know the local cops pretty well?"

I thought of Roger Barmore. "Some of them."

"Then let's go for a ride," she said and spun out of the yard heading north on Main Street.

Yeah, I thought.

CHAPTER Twenty-Nine

We left Walkerville on Highway 15 toward the hamlet of Warthen. Sandra ran through the six-speed gears like a pro, pushing past seventy as we cleared the city limits. Though I'd never seen it, I knew ATH owned several thousand acres in the northern part of the county not far from the old Lazard plantation. Part of it was flat and ideal for pine, but much of it was rolling hilly land interspersed with creeks and swamps that fed into the Opahatchee River along the county line.

After nearly ten minutes we turned off on a paved road traveling west. I noticed boundary markers with American Timber Holdings's logo every hundred yards or so. "We're almost there," Sandra said over the purr of the engine. She downshifted and made a sliding turn on to a smaller freshly paved road that disappeared into the forest, ignoring a sign reading, "Private Property: Admission by Permit Only."

"The facility here is fairly new," she said. "When Bill came on as CEO, all of ATH's research was being done in our Atlanta lab. This used to be just a small administrative office for our timberland in this area, but he thought we should expand our research down here, closer to our timber resources, and away from the prying eyes of our competitors. So a lot of what you see—this road, the buildings—has been built in the last five years."

After about a mile, the road curved to reveal another straight stretch, this time only a few hundred yards long and ending at a guardhouse and chain-link fence topped by three strands of barbed wire. The BMW slowed as a uniformed guard emerged to stand at the edge of the gate. Recognizing the car, he smiled and peered in the window, "Welcome back, Ms. Williams."

"Hi, Charles, how's it going? Ready for the big event this week?"

"I guess so. We've been putting in a lot of overtime fixing this place up. Who's your guest?"

"Matt Rutherford. He's not a spy—don't worry." The guard looked as if he wanted to say something, but thinking better of it waved us through.

"That's a lot of security for your average timber operation," I observed.

Sandra glanced over at me and smiled as she wheeled the BMW into a parking spot next to a large building. "I agree, but this is not your 'average timber operation,' as I think you'll see." She opened her door. "Would you mind waiting on me just a few minutes while I go and find Clay? I won't be long, promise. Get out and walk around if you'd like."

She swiped an ID card through a reader next to a door on one end of the building, tapped a code into a keypad, then disappeared inside. I got out, leaned against the car and surveyed my surroundings. The parking lot was huge and, like the road, recently paved. I estimated it could easily accommodate three to four hundred cars, better suited for a shopping center than an industrial plant miles from a major highway. A small forest of high intensity lights sprouted from the tops of regularly planted pylons. On the other side, half a dozen workmen were putting the finishing touches on what appeared to be a covered stage, evidently being built for the big announcement later in the week. Beyond them in the distance bulldozers and motor graders were flattening and leveling a wide expanse of red clay earth that had been freshly cleared out of dense forest.

Behind me, several buildings of varying sizes and uncertain function were clustered around an open work area. One of them had to be the biofuel pilot plant. I decided it was probably the one that Sandra was in at the moment, based mainly on the fact that I could see large mounds of wood chips stored under a covered shelter behind it. There were no windows visible, just plain sheet metal walls and several chimneys or vents protruding through the roof in an irregular pattern. Logging equipment was parked in front of one of the other buildings, apparently awaiting repair. A loading dock on another meant it was probably a warehouse.

Ten minutes later Sandra emerged followed by a tall muscular man wearing a stained white lab coat. They appeared to be having a heated discussion about something, but stopped the moment they sensed me looking in their direction. As they walked toward where I was standing, I noticed the man walked with a slight limp. Sandra said, "Matt, I'd like you to meet Clayton Wynne, the new head of our research facility here."

Wynne stuck out his hand. "Good to meet you, Matt. Sandra tells me she's going to force you to sit through our little press presentation and then give us a critique." He grinned and folded his arms across his chest. He looked familiar, but I couldn't decide why.

I shook his hand and said, "I'll do anything she wants as long as I don't have to write a report." Sandra winked at me and flashed a little smile.

"Well, let's get the show on the road," Wynne said and headed back toward the large building, speaking as he walked. "I hope by Friday we'll have this place gussied up some—if what I hear is right we'll be having a couple of hundred people down for the announcement. I guess you've gotten some hints about what we're going to say and all, right?"

"Actually, no," Sandra answered for me. "We've been on a need-to-know basis thus far, but at this point it probably doesn't matter. What we really want to achieve is the element of surprise with the press. The Board wants to make a big splash on Wall Street."

"Okay…," Wynne said as he swiped his card in the reader, punched in a code, and held the door for us to enter. "That actually makes it a little easier. I can just start at the top and give you a condensed version of the whole presentation."

Unlike its plain and austere exterior, the door opened to a wide and brightly lit hall leading to a carpeted reception area. Wynne ushered us into a large conference room with rows of chairs set up facing a small stage at one end. A wide-screen projection TV occupied the middle of the platform, with a lectern to one side. "Have a seat," he said, motioning toward the front row. Then to Sandra, "Want to start with the video?"

"No, just pretend we're reporters for the *Wall Street Journal* and you're making the announcement for the first time. We'll do it as planned. You speak first, then the video, followed by the plant tour."

Wynne raised his eyebrows as if most of this was unnecessary. "Gotcha," he said and took his place behind the lectern. "First of all, Matt, let me tell you the order of things. The official announcement and groundbreaking ceremony will take place at 1:00 p.m., but we've asked the press to try to get here two or three hours earlier, with the politicians and business types arriving around noon. We'll have tents set up with barbeque and an open bar, and there'll be a series of tours of the plant which will start here with a brief intro, followed by a video before they actually see where we work our chemical miracles. We'll be taking people through in groups, maybe twenty or twenty-five at a time."

"We're doing it like this because a lot of reporters and politicians think ethanol is mainly good for drinking, so part of the process becomes basic education," Sandra explained. "We'll have handouts and graphics on CDs. The marketing department has already written a lot of their copy for them, all they'll have to do is blend it into their own stories they submit for publication. So, hit it, Clay. Act like we're two business writers who know nothing about biofuels."

Wynne suppressed a frown and looked at his notes. "I'll have a more polished presentation by Friday, but let me go over the highlights of what I'm going to say." He consulted his notes again. "Basically I—no, we—want to make three points. The first is that the United States is totally dependent on foreign oil. If something were to happen, say another oil embargo like 1973, our entire economy could crash. The second point is that we have, right here and right now in this country, the potential resources to reduce our need for imported oil to nearly zero in less than ten years. Finally, and this is the big one," he looked up and grinned, "We're going to announce one of the biggest breakthroughs in biofuel technology in the last decade, maybe even in the last century."

He paused, waiting for our reaction. Sandra said, "Go on. Imagine you just heard a massive gasp from the audience, followed by a round of wild applause."

Wynne looked up, clearly annoyed, "Sandra, listen. I just really don't have time for this right now. If I'm going to get things ready by Friday, I've got a lot of other more important things to do." Then to me, "Matt, I'm sorry.

It's been really hectic around here, so if you don't mind, let me give you a quick five minute summary and save you having to sit through...."

"Clay...," Sandra began.

I interrupted her, "No, that's good with me. I'd rather hit the high points." The truth was, I was more interested in Sandra than what this guy had to say. She started to speak, but sat back and nodded.

"Okay, then," Wynne said and continued, consulting his notes, "Here's the meat of it. The US produces about 8 percent of the world's oil supply, a figure that's down about 18 percent over the last ten years. On the other hand, we consume about 25 percent of the total amount of oil used globally, and that's up by about 17 percent in the same time frame. And it's getting worse. The estimates are that the world's oil production is going to peak sometime in the next ten to fifteen years, not to mention you have countries like China and India whose economies and oil demands are growing like gangbusters.

"Ninety-eight percent of our transportation system is dependent on liquid fuel, essentially all of which is gasoline and diesel. And if that's not bad enough, thanks to the environmental lobby, this country is thirty years behind Europe and the rest of the world in nuclear power plants, while other practical alternative energies like hydrogen are still decades away. With me so far?"

I nodded. Sandra said, "I hope you're going to be more professional when you present this on Friday."

Wynne grimaced and continued. "Second point. Everyone is talking about ethanol as a readily available substitute for oil. They always cite Brazil, which has cut its petroleum usage by 40 percent1 by switching to ethanol as a gasoline substitute. It sounds good, but what they don't tell you is this. Much of Brazil sits right on the equator, and is ideal for growing sugarcane. A gallon of ethanol produced from sugarcane yields ten times—get that, *ten times*—the amount of energy it took to produce it. In this country, the politicians are pushing ethanol made from corn. Good for the farmers, good for agribusiness, good for votes..."

"Clay!" Sandra said.

"Okay, I'll tone that part down, but what I'm getting to is that a gallon of corn-based ethanol only produces something like 1.3 times the energy spent on its production. Most of the energy crap that's coming out of Washington these days is..."

"Clay, you cannot do this," Sandra sounded annoyed. "This is one of the most important...."

"Okay, okay," he said, clearly irritated. "I'll play the part. What I will try to get across in a very *polite*," he looked up from his notes at Sandra, "way is the fact that this country is headed for an energy train wreck with profound economic implications. Is that politically correct enough?" She nodded approval.

"At that point I'll say a few words about the energy potential locked up in what we now consider waste from timber and logging operations. There'll be a few slides on the screen to illustrate how wood is made up primarily of cellulose and supporting fibrous material, and how cellulose is nothing but a bunch of sugar molecules—specifically glucose—linked end to end. And sugar, as any good bootlegger knows, is what you need to make liquor."

I was beginning to like the guy. Sandra sat forward in her seat. "Clay, I am serious. This is ATH's future. Mr. Gray does not want any sarcasm to...."

"Gotcha," he said. I detected tension in his voice. He didn't like Sandra telling him what to do. "Anyway, that gets us to my third point, which is something I actually like to talk about. What I say will be pretty short, because most of it will be covered by the video the marketing people put together. I'll say thanks to a lot of hard work from our team, and especially based on a series of innovative ideas that grew out of research Laura McIntosh started when she was working on her doctorate at Tech, we've found a way to unlock the energy potential of cellulose at a cost that will make it comparable to ethanol produced from sugarcane." He folded his notes and looked up. "That's it, cut to video, which says about the same thing with pretty graphics, then the group goes on to the plant tour."

I turned to Sandra. "So that's the big announcement. Impressive, I guess."

"It should be. If things work out as planned, it'll increase ATH's bottom line by several billion dollars a year."

"Now, *that* is impressive. But if this is background for the reporters and media types, what is the big reviewing stand out in the parking lot for?" I asked.

"A photo op, mainly. And to give the politicians a chance to take credit. Part of what we're doing is funded by tax breaks and other incentives. We'll have a couple of congressmen up there and the governor's planning on coming in to do the ground-breaking ceremony."

"That'll get good press. What are you going to be doing while all this is going on?"

"Making sure Bill doesn't flub his lines. He's going to read a short version of what Clay just said, and make the announcement the plant is being named in memory of Laura McIntosh."

CHAPTER Thirty

"Now for the video," Sandra said.

I could read the look on Wynne's face. I said, "Why don't we just cut to the tour of the plant? I'm sure the video's great, but I know Clay has a lot to do."

"Okay," she agreed, sounding defeated. "I need to make some phone calls anyway." Turning to Wynne she said, "Why don't you two take a quick tour, then Matt and I can have lunch."

Wynne half smiled. "You can use my office. We'll wait for you in the break room when we finish." He led me back through the reception area toward a door at the end of the hall labeled "Laboratory—Authorized Access Only." Again he swiped his key card through a reader, then entered several digits on an adjacent keypad. The lock clicked and he pulled the door open for me to enter.

"I'm surprised you have such tight security here," I said.

"We do. It may look excessive, but this is big business. One of the main reasons for moving the biofuel research lab down here is to get a better handle on who sees what. Corporate secrets can be worth a lot of money."

The door led into another hallway, this time with a glass wall on one side, behind which was a large open area with counters and electronic instruments I didn't recognize. About a dozen workers in white coats huddled over keyboards or in front of the machines, absorbed in whatever they were doing.

A middle-aged woman looked up at me and smiled before resuming pipetting a yellow liquid into small glass test tubes. "This is our main workspace," Wynne explained. "Our focus here has been almost exclusively on making ethanol from cellulose. Most of the other research is going to stay in the Atlanta lab. It's all pretty technical, and I don't want to bore you with the details. I thought we'd make a quick walk-through of the pilot plant, then sit down and let me try to answer any questions you have."

He stopped just in front of a second door at the end of the hall, opening an adjacent cabinet to remove two yellow hardhats and two sets of clear plastic goggles. "OSHA requirements," he explained, handing me one of each. He tapped a code into another keypad next to the door before pulling it open.

We left the quiet bright coziness of the hallway and entered a cavernous space filled with tanks, vats and piping supported by a forest of welded scaffolding. Metal staircases disappeared up toward the high ceiling, ending in catwalks snaking between the vats. The atmosphere was noisy and the air hot and humid. A vague sweet musty odor pressed down on my nostrils. "Smell it?" Wynne yelled over the loud hum of hydraulic pumps. I nodded. "Recognize it?" I shook my head. "Fermentation. A combination of supercharged yeast and bacteria turning sugar into ethanol. That's a smell that got many a bootlegger busted back home in Tennessee where I grew up. Now it's the sweet smell of money."

"It's really hot in here," I yelled back.

"It's part of the process. Fermentation produces heat and carbon dioxide. That's why champagne's bubbly, remember? Here we recycle the heat and vent the CO_2." He pointed to a large vat near the rear of the building. "See that? That's the digester. We bring in chipped wood, or scraps, pine tops or whatever, mix them with water and genetically engineered bacteria, and hold them in that area for about twelve to fourteen hours. The cellulose is freed from its supporting matrix, then pumped over there," he said pointing to a row of tanks, "where we clean it up and process it further before pumping it to those vats back there where it's fermented. It's a pretty simple operation really. One of the best parts about it is that it's totally automated. It runs by itself twenty-four hours a day. All you need is one man to sit and watch the monitoring panel."

"What's so secret about it all?" I yelled.

"The combination of bioactive enzymes, and genetically modified yeast and bacteria. If Laura were here, you'd have to thank her for that. It's based on her research."

We spent the next twenty minutes climbing ladders, peering into tanks and vats, and inhaling the fumes of fermenting pine trees. Wynne proudly pointed out how wood chips came in one end and a clear liquid composed of water and alcohol came out the other. I smiled and nodded and looked appropriately amazed, but lost interest after a quick look into the first digester vat filled with a thick mixture that looked like vomit and smelled like week-old garbage in August.

The tour finally finished, Wynne led me back through the door and into the hall by the lab. He looked at his watch. "It's just past noon. Let's sit for a few minutes and talk while we wait on Sandra." I followed him into a small room with a table and chairs and row of vending machines against one wall. He fed a bill into one of the machines and got out two bottles of cool water.

"So what do you think?" he asked.

"It's quite a place," I said. I wondered how long Sandra was going to be tied up. I was ready to leave.

"It wouldn't have been possible without Laura's work. She was a genius, you know."

"So I've been told."

"Sandra said you knew her. That you'd been looking into her death."

"Her parents asked me to check on a few things, nothing more."

Wynne took a drink from his bottle. "Well, she's missed. And David, too. They were both good people." He took another drink. "It was kinda strange about how they died. What'd you find out?"

"Nothing, really. Lifestyle issues, if you want to put it politely."

"Oh." Another drink. "I never really could see her and David together, but you never know...."

"Did anyone in the lab know he was gay?" I regretted saying it as soon as the word flew off my tongue.

Wynne gave me a sharp look. "No. Well..., yes. We found out later. We were trying to schedule some kind of memorial service for both of them and..., uh, it came up. He and his father didn't get along and we ended up canning the idea. Mr. Gray decided to name the new facility after her. They thought that would be enough."

There was an awkward silence. I said, "How did you get in the research business?"

"An accident really." Wynne seemed relieved to be talking about something else. "I was born in Knoxville. My parents were both dirt-poor mill workers. I dropped out of high school when I was sixteen and by the time I was seventeen I was in and out of trouble with the law. A couple of buddies and me 'borrowed' a car one night and got caught by the cops. The judge gave me the choice of jail or enlisting in the military. I was still underage, and he said he'd wipe my record clean if I did.

"So I joined the Navy. Hell, I'd never even seen the ocean. I realized once I was in, the discipline and structure gave me what I needed to get my life in order. I did well in basic, then signed up for SEAL training, made the cut and went through the whole program.

"We were due to ship out to the Middle East and were doing a nighttime training mission. The chopper I was in went down. There were six of us. I was the only survivor. For a long time they didn't think I'd make it either, both my legs broken, internal injuries, that sort of thing. When they figured out I was going to live, they told me I'd never walk again. I spent three months in the hospital and a year in rehab. Of course I got a medical discharge. So I went back to school courtesy of Uncle Sam. Got my college degree, then a Master's and finally my doctorate. I've been with ATH about four years now. End of story."

"Did you work closely with Laura?"

"Very much so. Hell, I wanted to date her, but I thought she and David were an item. The next thing I heard was she had a boyfriend back home."

"I take it you're not married."

Wynne laughed. "Once. Right after I finished basic. Some girl I met in a bar. It lasted six months. I was at Fort Benning when I got a 'Dear John' letter. She'd moved out and filed for divorce. But it's a good thing I guess. It makes it easier for me to move down here to Walkerville. No strings attached. I guess you're not married either. I see how Sandra looks at you."

I smiled, "No, I…."

"Hey, guys," Sandra said from the doorway. "Have a good tour?"

"Very interesting," I lied. "Did you get everything done?"

"I hope so." Turning to Wynne, she said, "Clay, I talked with the tent rental people. They'll be here tomorrow, and the caterers…." She stopped in mid-sentence. "We don't need to go over this right now. I think Matt and I will go and have some lunch, then I'll take him back to town. We can meet today about four-thirty. That okay with you?"

"You work for the boss," Wynne replied with resignation.

"So do you," Sandra replied sharply.

CHAPTER Thirty-One

Leaving Wynne quietly fuming in the break room, we left the cool comfort of the building for the bright heat of the June midday. Sandra said, "Are you up for a picnic?"

"Sure."

"There's supposed to be a pretty spot not far from here. I talked with one of the logging foremen this morning and he told me how to get there. We've got to take the first little dirt road to the right off the paved road going out, then turn left at the first fork and follow it to the end. There's a lake and a table set up for the employees, but he said he'd pulled his crew to work back here getting things ready for Friday. I guess that means we'll have it all to ourselves."

I acted as spotter; she drove. We missed the road the first time we passed it, then turned around and found it on our second try. It was a dusty, rutted logging track, scraping the undercarriage of the car as we eased through the forest. A quarter mile into the woods, the road split. We veered left on an even smaller road and after a few hundred yards entered a large clearing. An open-sided equipment shed stood on a slight rise above a blackwater pond backing up into cypress-filled headwaters. Three pairs of wood ducks noisily departed as we crested the hill. At the water's edge just below us, a wooden picnic table nestled in the shade between two ancient oaks. "It's pretty," Sandra said, pulling the BMW under the shelter and parking it next to a row of logging equipment.

"It is," I agreed.

"They tell me this was a dairy farm at one time," she said as she pulled a wicker hamper and a small plastic cooler from the car's trunk. "I think that's why ATH bought it. They say planted pine does well in old fields, especially ones that have been fertilized for years by cattle. In this business a lot of it gets flung around. I'm glad they found a use for it." I laughed. She was in a good mood.

I picked up the hamper and followed her down the hill toward the pond. She opened it, unfolding a red and white checked cloth to spread on the table. "I hope you don't mind sandwiches," she said, laying out paper plates and several plastic boxes. A bottle of Chilean chardonnay emerged from the cooler with apologies for plastic cups. I didn't care, I was enthralled.

We ate quickly, talking about nothing in particular. She told a funny anecdote about bumping into one of the ATH's directors and his mistress at a restaurant in San Francisco the week before. Apparently he was someone famous in the business world who I was supposed to know, but I'd never heard of him. The combination of heat and wine gave me a little buzz.

Sandra looked up at the equipment shed and said, "You know, my father works for a lumber mill and I work for one of the country's biggest timber producers, and I don't even know how trees are harvested. I had this picture in my mind of sweaty men with chainsaws and mules hauling logs, but I imagine they use those machines, right?"

"Yeah, you want to see 'em?"

"Sure," she said and grabbed my hand to pull me up. We trudged up the hill slowly in the afternoon heat.

"That," I said pointing at a green and yellow John Deere next to Sandra's car, "is what they call a skidder. I guess you can say it replaced mules, or whatever they used to use to haul the trees out."

She walked up to it and peered at the massive machine looming over her. The thick-treaded tires were nearly as tall as her head. "What's that for?" she asked, pointing at a long hydraulic boom with a powerful pincer-like claw on its end.

"The operator grabs a bundle of trees and drags them out to a clearing, where the limbs and tops are cut off before they load them on trucks," I said.

"But how are the trees cut and put in bundles in the first place?"

"With that thing over there." I nodded my head toward a yellow Caterpillar machine with a jointed hydraulic arm and a massive cutting head on the end. "That's called a feller-buncher."

"A *what*?"

"A feller-buncher. I don't think there's any other name for it. It fells the trees—cuts them down—then picks them up and puts them in a pile—bunches them. Come here, let me show you." She followed me over to the machine. "See, the main part of it with the cab and motor looks pretty much like the skidder, but it's got this special boom on the front." Sandra looked at it, turning her head to one side. "These big claws at the top grab the tree about eight feet up and this hydraulic shear at the bottom cuts it off near the ground. The operator then just lifts it up and lays it in the pile that can be dragged out by the skidder."

Sandra studied it for a moment. "It looks like a big pair of scissors," she said. "How big a tree can you cut with that thing?"

"Close to two feet in diameter, I think. There are other kinds that have a saw for even bigger trees. This one just snips 'em right off. Like cutting flowers."

"Scary," she said, pausing to look at me. Then, "Come here. I was lying." She put her arms around me and snuggled her head against my chest. "I was just looking for an excuse to get close to you." I caught a faint whiff of floral perfume mixed with sweat. "I can't wait for tonight," she said.

I kissed her. "What's wrong with now?" I asked.

She nipped gently at my neck, sending chills down one side of my body. "Nothing, except I don't think I should go back to the lab looking like I've been…, well, in the woods."

"Tonight, then," I said as we walked hand-in-hand back down the hill.

Sandra drove me back to Rutherford Hall, sticking to the speed limit this time. Keeping her eyes on the road, she reached out to touch my hand and said, "I enjoyed that." She dropped me off at the back steps, saying she hoped to be back by six. "There are a lot of little things I need to do—like go over that presentation with Clay," she said, half apologizing. "A lot is riding on Friday's announcement, and I know I'll catch it from Bill if there are any screw-ups. I'll call if I'm going to be late."

I had considered taking her out to dinner, but decided it might work better if we stayed at home and did something less formal. Walkerville's restaurant selection is pretty limited anyway, so I'd lain in provisions for what I hoped would end up being a romantic meal.

I put a couple of bottles of California chardonnay in the refrigerator, and set out some Australian shiraz as a back-up in case she wanted red. I thought we'd start with wine, then move on to an Italian chicken salad the lady behind the deli counter told me was "sinful." For a finale, I'd bought an amandine and vanilla cheesecake which I intended to top with fresh strawberries. I spent half an hour carefully washing and cutting them into neat slices, then another fifteen minutes arranging them in an overlapping pattern on top of the dessert.

Satisfied with my handiwork, I managed to discover where Eula Mae kept the good china, crystal, and silver, and set the table for two in the dining room. It occurred to me that one of Aunt Lillie's sterling candelabra might be a nice touch, but after placing it on the table decided it was too much. I stuck it back in the closet and played with the dimmer trying to find the best lighting for the overhead crystal chandelier.

At a quarter to six I looked up to see Sandra pulling into the yard. She parked in front of the stables, got out and stretched before heading toward the house. I met her at the top of the back steps. "How'd it go?" I asked.

"Really good," she said, smiling. "I was worried about Clay. He can have an attitude sometimes, but we went over his presentation and I think he's going to do fine." She reached the top of the steps and greeted me with a quick kiss.

"Why not get someone in marketing to do it? Seems like that would be their job."

"You're right, it is, but the Board would rather have some PhD with a pocket protector talking about it instead of some slick guy in a three-piece suit. Lends more credibility."

"Is that a problem? The press won't take things at face value?"

"Matt, I don't think you realize how big this is. It's truly a major scientific breakthrough. ATH's future depends on it."

"Okay," I said, much more interested in watching her eyes.

"It's been a long day. I could really use a glass of wine, and a little down time," she said. "Let me go take a quick shower and change." She disappeared up the stairs.

Having given it significant thought, I'd decided we'd have drinks on the glassed-in dogtrot overlooking the boxwood maze. The afternoon sun was now below the tops of the elms lining Main Street and filtered light painted the privacy of the garden and yard in muted pastels of green and yellow. I opened the windows and turned on the overhead ceiling fan. A soft cross breeze carried a hint of a tea olive from one of Aunt Lillie's plants blooming just below the window. I put the open chardonnay in a sterling wine cooler I found in the silver closet and set out two glasses with a plate of cheese and crackers.

I heard Sandra calling my name from the direction of the house. "Out here," I said, and she appeared at the door dressed in a slim silk shift in a riot of bright colors, cinched loosely around her waist with a dark sash. Her hair was down now, and fell in golden curves over her shoulders. "I like your dress," I said, trying not to let my mouth hang open.

"Thanks," she smiled. "It's batik, from Indonesia. I bought it last week in San Francisco. It's pretty, isn't it? The girl at the shop said the design is all done by hand, with wax to keep the colors from running together." She could have told me it was woven by pygmies in Uganda. I didn't care. She was beautiful, and she was here with me.

"Wine?" I asked.

"Of course," she said, flipping her hair back with her hand.

CHAPTER Thirty-Two

We sat on the dogtrot, Sandra with her legs tucked under her on the overstuffed sofa, me in one of the wingchairs. We talked and laughed and were well into the second bottle of wine by the time both of us realized we were hungry.

We moved to the dining room. She sat; I served the salad. We finished the chardonnay and opened the Australian red. I watched her move in the soft light, now smiling, now laughing, sometimes serious. I dusted off silly stories I hadn't thought of in years. It seemed I could say nothing wrong.

By now half-drunk, I served the cheesecake, managing to cut us each generous slices without dropping it on the table. Sandra ate hers slowly, carefully slicing, savoring each bite as she stroked her foot against my leg under the table. "This is so good," she said.

"The cheesecake?"

"That, too," she said, licking a bit of strawberry from her fork, "but I was thinking about…, well, this. You know, being here with you."

"I get points for my cooking, right?"

She picked up a bit of crust and popped it in her mouth. "Let's just say you get points for being you." Pushing her plate to one side she reached out and took my hand. "Why don't we go and find a comfortable place to sit down? I think I need to relax after this feast. Didn't I see a bench out in your garden? It's a nice night to be out, so different from Atlanta or San

Francisco. You can actually see the stars in the sky down here."

We took the back steps from the dogtrot and sat on a weathered cast-iron bench overlooking a small area of finely groomed grass behind the maze. It was just after nine, and the last glow of the fading day brought out a riot of fireflies, their flicking green bioluminescence signaling others of their readiness to mate. "They're beautiful, aren't they?" I said.

Sandra snuggled next to me and replied, "Did you arrange this show especially for me?"

"But of course."

"If I remember correctly, they're beautiful but deadly, at least to other lightning bugs. They're meat eaters, you know?"

"You're kidding?"

"No, I did a science project on them in high school. We actually made it to the state finals. Sometimes the females use their signals to attract males of other species and then eat them. Apparently that's common in the insect world. The praying mantis, the black widow—but I guess spiders are not insects."

"No, and neither are we," I said turning to kiss her.

Ten minutes later she said, "Why don't we go inside. It might be more comfortable." My arm around her, we stumbled up the back steps, through the dogtrot and had just reached the stairs when the doorbell rang, followed by a sharp rapping on the back door.

I looked at my watch. Nine twenty-five. "Who the hell is that?" I said.

Sandra flashed a half-frown and leaned against the massive carved newel post. "Just get rid of them. We've got more important things to do."

Through the glass of the back door I could make out a male figure standing on the stoop. I flipped on the porch light to see an agitated-looking Roger Barmore, his hands thrust deep in his pockets and a large envelope tucked under one arm. I eased the door open and stuck my head out. "Roger, how are you? It's…, uh…, kinda late. What's up?"

"Something big. Something really big," he said, nearly knocking me over as he pushed the door open and barged past me into the vestibule.

"Uh…, look, Roger, I'm a little busy right now. Maybe this could wait until…."

"Matt, this is important. I've got to talk with you."

"Well, it's past nine and...."

"Now. I need to talk with you now."

"Honestly. I'm really..., kind of..., in the middle of something right now..."

Ignoring me, Roger stepped into the hall. Sandra was sitting on the bottom stairstep, her chin on her hands and her long hair falling over the bright colors of her silk dress. She looked up. "You're Laura's boyfriend, aren't you?"

Roger stared at her for a moment, then, "Yeah. You're Sandra. We met once." Neither made more of an effort to acknowledge the other's presence.

I said, "Roger. Sandra and I were..., having dinner. Why don't you and I talk in the morning? I've been drinking a little wine and really, I'm kinda plowed. If you could just...."

"I need to talk with you now. It's important. Something I just discovered." He made no effort to move.

"About...?" I waited for his reply.

Roger looked at Sandra, who looked back, both showing signs of annoyance at the other's presence. "It's, like, private, you know. I need to show something to you."

I looked at Sandra. She raised her eyebrows and shrugged. I said, "Okay, but let's keep this quick. We can...."

"You got a computer, right?"

"In the study." I pointed to the door across the hall. He followed me in, shutting it behind us. I caught a glimpse of frustration in Sandra's expression as it closed. I moved the mouse and the computer sprang to life. "Okay, it's on. Now what?"

"I want to show you something," he said, looking in the large envelope to find a slim jewel case with a CD inside. "This," he said, holding up the envelope, "is what I got today from the NTSB. Their final report won't be out for months, but I'd called the investigator last week and asked him to send me—or rather the Sheriff's Department—what he had. I got a preliminary report, which is pretty much the same as the stuff in the GBI's report. That was nothing new. But this," he said, waving the CD case, "is. It's digital photos of the plane crash site." He reached over and pressed a button on the computer. The CD tray slid out and he dropped the disc into it.

Sitting down in front of the computer, Roger made a few clicks with the mouse, then studied a long file list before selecting and double-clicking one he'd highlighted. The screen filled with a close-up shot of what appeared to be the interior of the crashed Cessna. "Okay, here it is," he said. "There are about two hundred pics on this disc, and several of them show it, but this is the best one. This was taken from the back of the passenger cabin of the plane, looking forward toward the instrument panel, see?"

In my opinion, there wasn't much to see, at least nothing new. The shot was not too different from one or two that were part of the GBI report. In the background I could make out an instrument panel and two seats. Above the instrument panel a smashed windshield appeared to be pushed against a leafy tree branch. In the foreground, a crumpled blanket lay to one side. On top of it I could make out a man's shoe, and what appeared to be part of a woman's bra. "I see," I said. "It's kinda like the ones in the GBI report."

"Right," Roger replied, "but look at this." Highlighting the magnifying glass on the toolbar below the screen, he dragged the small icon to focus on an area just below the passenger's seat on the right. The area filled the screen. "See. See that?" He pointed at a small slender green object on the cabin floor that seemed to be wedged under the seat support.

I really was just about drunk. I wanted to check on Sandra behind the closed door in the hall. Moving close to the screen I tried to focus my eyes on the object. "Okay, I see it. What is it?"

"Don't you recognize it?"

"No. Should I?" Sitting down and taking the mouse myself, I blew up the area even further. The camera must have had a much higher resolution than the GBI's, but even at extreme magnification, whatever it was that had caught Roger's interest seemed to be just a small green generic thing, and nothing that I could make into a familiar object. "I give up," I said.

"It's a type of valve wrench," he said confidently. "The kind you use to open valves on compressed air cylinders." I looked up at him. He stood with his arms crossed, his legs spread and with a look of vindication on his face.

"Uh..., so? What is a valve wrench?" I asked.

"It looks like this." Snatching a piece of paper from the printer he sketched a crude object and held it up for me to see.

"Okay...," I said. "So, what's that got...."

"Don't you see, Matt," he said. "That is exactly the kind of wrench you'd use to open a tank of compressed carbon monoxide. Somebody could have...."

"Hold on," I said, waving my hand for him to be quiet. I leaned close to the screen to study the green object. With the mouse, I enlarged the image until it became lost in irregular splotches of pixels. Turning back to Roger, I started, "Are you trying to say that...."

"Yep."

I didn't know whether to hit him or try to physically toss him out. I was probably too drunk to fight, and had other plans, anyway. Biting my tongue I said, "Roger, I know this is really important, and I know you felt like it couldn't wait, but why don't we talk about it in the morning, okay?" I handed him the CD, flipped the off switch on the computer and got up to hold the study door open.

"Good. I'm glad you agree," he said, heading for the back door. "I'm taking a few days off work next week so we can work on it. I'll call you in the morning."

"Right," I said, shutting and locking the door behind him.

I turned to look for Sandra. The bottom step was empty. I bounded up the stairs to find the door to the guest room shut tightly, and no light peeking through the crack under it. I dragged myself to bed, silently cursing the day I met Roger Barmore.

CHAPTER Thirty-Three

In the summertime, I sleep with the windows open. My bedroom is upstairs on the corner of the old house, and usually a breeze keeps things cool, even in August. The downside of this is that I can hear cars on the street, dogs barking at strange shadows, and a persistent rooster somewhere in the distance who usually alerts me to the imminent arrival of dawn. He had just finished his morning serenade when I heard a creak, followed by a click and felt—more than saw—the silk-gowned figure that slipped quietly beneath the sheets with me. "I hate that guy," was all she said, the rest being non-verbal communication.

Sandra left for the lab and pilot plant about nine. Her goals for the day, she stated, were to double-check things with the caterers, and to make sure the tent people had everything in place. Also, she had to be certain the company out of Atlanta that was setting up the microphones, public address system, and temporary wireless internet for the press had tested and retested their equipment. As for me, I had no plans. The first two hours of my day had worn me out, and I was drifting somewhere in the stratosphere.

At nine-fifteen Roger called, sort of apologizing for the night before and rambling on about how he'd thought all along that "something just isn't right," and how he had to look into some things "before we get together next week." I was not in a mood to argue with him, so I just half-listened, saying "Uh-huh," occasionally before hanging up. He was becoming an annoyance.

I drank coffee and read the paper until about ten, then walked down to my office on the Square to check my business mail and sign checks. Beverly, my part-time secretary, was busily entering bills into the computer. "Where have you been lately?" she asked. "I got some credit card charges from Atlanta so I know you were there, but I haven't seen you in a couple of weeks."

"Oh, I got talked into going up there to check on some things for Laura McIntosh's parents. Kind of a waste of time, really."

"Yes, that was so sad. I still think about her a lot. She was such a cute child. I taught her in Sunday school when she was about ten. She had pigtails and…."

"Uh, yeah." I cut her off. "Any important mail that I need to take care of?"

"Not really. Some brokerage statements, and the usual. I see where the guy who handles your accounts in Atlanta bought a bunch of American Timber Holdings stock. Wasn't that the company Laura worked for?" She wouldn't let me change the subject.

"Yes. She did research for them. Apparently they've made some advances on producing ethanol from cellulose based on some ideas she was working on. I don't know the details." Beverly nodded. I suspected I'd lost her on the word "ethanol." She's not terribly bright, but works cheap and does a good job.

She looked at me over her half-frame glasses and said, "My husband bought some, too."

"Really?" I said, sifting through a pile of envelopes.

"Yes. We don't normally have much money to spend on stocks, but he heard from a reliable source that this was a sure thing, so he put our IRA money into it."

I looked up, interested this time. "Really?" I repeated. "Where'd he hear that?"

"I'm not supposed to say." She looked sheepish and turned back to the computer.

"Oh, come on, Beverly."

"You won't tell, will you?"

"Of course not."

Lowering her voice for no good reason she whispered, "From one of the

County Commissioners."

"Ernest Tookes?"

"No, one of the others. Inman Greene." Then, "I shouldn't have told you."

"Don't worry," I replied. "Your secret is safe." It would appear someone at ATH made sure the Adams County commissioners would be well rewarded for their tax breaks and whatever other "incentives" they offered.

Curious, I sat down at the desk in my office and booted up the computer. With a few clicks I brought up a graph of ATH's stock price over the past ten years. It had been a high flyer back in the 1990s, falling sharply with the market in 2000 and 2001. About five years ago, it took a sharp turn upward. I estimated that would be about the time Bill Gray was appointed CEO. It stayed in the same range, up and down perhaps twenty percent one way or the other until about a month earlier when it began a steady upward trend. If things continued, it could easily reach an all-time high with the public announcement on Friday.

I signed a stack of checks and left Beverly busily stuffing them into envelopes before heading to El Gordo's. I took my time, savoring my spinach and chicken quesadilla washed down with a Dos Equis Especial. I was still just a shade hung over from last night's wine. Sandra called on my cell to say she'd be finished a little early, "maybe around four." I said I'd be home, a certain stirring disturbing my otherwise leisurely meal.

I was waiting for her as she drove into the yard at four-twenty. By a quarter to five, we were upstairs in my bedroom. I was glad Eula Mae was out of town. Sandra had a perfect body, honed to a silky hardness on her health club's machines, and exquisitely maintained by someone who realized it was one of her finest assets. Later, exhausted, she lay beside me in the bed, the sheet half pulled to her waist, her hair flowing off the pillow next to my head. "Sandra…," I started.

Placing two fingers on my lips, she said, "Sssh. Don't talk. Just be there."

I traced my index finger lazily over her breast, circling her nipple and watching it respond. As I worked my way down toward her belly, I detected a slight thickening and noted a small short scar under each breast. "You found my secret," she said.

"I like them."

"The best plastic surgeon in Atlanta," she replied, slipping on top of me.

By eight, after a nap and a shower, we were hungry again and settled on the Mexican restaurant where I'd had lunch. The waiter brought tortilla chips and salsa. Sandra ordered a frozen marguerita which arrived in a huge glass, its rim encrusted with salt. I settled for another beer. "Why did Roger barge in like that last night?" she asked. Other than her comment in bed that morning, it was the first time she'd mentioned him.

"Oh, he's got this crazy idea about Laura. You could beat him on the head with the truth and he still wouldn't believe it. I think he's hatching some theory that the plane crash wasn't an accident, that maybe somebody poisoned them or something. I don't know. He wants to talk about it next week."

Sandra frowned. "I thought her parents were the ones behind wanting to look into her death. When did Roger get in on this?"

"They had originally asked him to go to Atlanta. He turned it down. I can't blame him. He said he was too close to things, and it was a stupid waste of time anyway. So I got volunteered. Then Roger decided he had to know 'the truth,' whatever it is, and said he wanted to help me investigate. He got his hands on the GBI and Crime Lab reports but they both confirmed what everyone suspected. Both David and Sandra were overcome by carbon monoxide, and her autopsy showed evidence of recent sexual activity."

"Mine would, too, at the moment," Sandra whispered, a sly grin on her face.

I laughed. "Anyway, he requested some photos from the feds, the NTSB...."

"Who's that?"

"The National Transportation Safety Board, the guys who investigate all the plane crashes in the country." She nodded. "What was I saying? Oh, yeah, he thinks he saw something in one photo that made him suspicious. That's what he wants to see me about next week."

"Are you going to meet with him?"

"The guy's pitiful," I said. "He can't seem to accept the fact that his fiancée was screwing around on him. I guess I owe it to him out of human kindness."

"Hmm!" Sandra snorted. "Pushy guy, isn't he? How about the parents? Have they accepted things?"

"I lied to them. Told them Laura was something between Mother Teresa and the Virgin Mary. They're old. Let them go to their graves in peace."

"Probably a good idea." She scooped some salsa on a chip and eased it between her lips, trying to avoid dripping it on the table. "But, you know, maybe I should go by and pay them a courtesy call before the announcement on Friday."

"I would have thought you'd want them there at the ceremony. After all, you're naming the new plant in memory of their daughter."

"That actually came up at one of the Board meetings. Someone suggested we invite them, but then considering the way she died...." Sandra didn't finish, instead scooping up more salsa on another chip and examining it before putting it in her mouth. She chewed a moment then said, "The consensus was that her personal life could be an embarrassment to the company, so technically the plant is being named in honor of her research. It's a subtlety, I know, but Bill Gray keeps saying, in business, perception becomes reality."

"So you're just going to let them read about it in the paper? Isn't that a little..., what, cold?"

"No, they should be getting a letter in the mail tomorrow. It'll be signed by the Chairman of the Board of Directors, and have a ten thousand dollar check enclosed. The company will be showing its appreciation, but at the same time keeping its distance." She ate another chip. "But, you know, I really should go by and meet them."

"Okay. Want me to set it up?"

"Tomorrow afternoon would be good...," she started, then stopped as she looked over my shoulder. "I think that's somebody I know," she said as a guy in his late twenties, beer in hand, sauntered over to our booth.

"Sandra? Is that you?"

She smiled and got up to hug his neck. "Rob, how are you? You look great! It's been a long time."

He stepped back and looked at her. "It has. A long time. What seven years? Eight years?"

"Something like that. You haven't changed a bit." Then turning to me she said, "Do you know Matt Rutherford? Matt, this is Rob Howell, from Valdosta. We were in college together our freshman year." I rose and shook his hand.

"I know the Rutherford name, but we've never met. I'm up here working on a construction project." I sized him up. He was dressed in a khaki shirt, jeans and work boots. I thought he looked a little on the rough side. Running his eyes over Sandra he continued, "I'm out with guys on the crew, so I'll be going. Good to see you, Sandra. Nice to meet you, Mr. Rutherford." He turned and walked away.

"Old friend?" I asked.

"Just somebody I used to know," she said and sipped her drink in silence for a moment. She seemed lost in her thoughts. "Back to what we were talking about, though. I think everyone should just leave them alone."

"Who?"

"Laura and David. They're dead, aren't they?" I had no idea what she meant.

CHAPTER Thirty-Four

Sandra announced over cereal the next morning she needed to return to Atlanta at the end of the day. "I really hate to leave, Matt, but I've got to. I need to check in at the office tonight and then tomorrow morning Bill wants me to drive back down here with him and a couple of the directors who're flying in from New York. I guess I'm supposed to be the entertainment. I know them—they're a couple of old gazillionaires. I hate being around them. They're real leches, constantly hitting on me."

"So why do you do it? Tell your Mr. Gray you're driving alone or something. You can spend the weekend here."

"I wish, but it's just part of the job. I know it and everybody else does, too. For tomorrow, I'm the CEO's arm candy." She reached out and laid her hand on top of mine. "But you're going with me to see Laura's parents, right? And you'll be at the ceremony tomorrow."

"Laura's parents, sure. But I really wasn't planning on going to the groundbreaking."

Sandra looked hurt. "Why not?"

"It's just not anything I'm involved with."

"Hello…? How about me? Don't you think maybe I want you there? You can at least give me an excuse to fend off the old men. I'll tell them you're my boyfriend." She laughed.

"If you want me there, I'll go, then," thinking that it hadn't occurred to me exactly what I was to her. I said I'd check in with the McIntoshes and give her a call on her cell phone with the details. She was planning on having a working lunch with Clayton Wynne, but thought she'd be finished by one. I told her we'd aim for two to give her a chance to come by the house and change.

I called the McIntosh house shortly after ten. Agnes answered the phone with a cheery "Hello" and said she'd love to finally meet Laura's old roommate. "I know she's a sweet girl," she said. Everyone seemed to be "sweet" or "nice" in Agnes's world, but even knowing this she seemed in a particularly ebullient mood. "Guess what we just got in the mail this morning."

"I can't imagine," I lied, presuming that the letter from ATH had arrived.

"A wonderful letter signed by the Chairman of the Board of American Timber Holdings telling us they are going to name their new plant in honor of what our Laura did for them. They are going to announce it tomorrow."

"That's fantastic," I said, trying to sound surprised.

"But there's more," she continued. "A check. A very, very nice check. They said they wanted to show their appreciation."

Nice checks from nice people, I thought, and wondered how she'd feel if she knew the truth. I said we'd see her around two in the afternoon.

Sandra called to say she was running late, then screeched into the drive at Rutherford Hall at a quarter 'til two. She gave me a quick air kiss on her way upstairs to change out of her khakis. The courthouse clock was just striking two as she descended, her hair down and dressed in a conservative blue linen jacket-skirt combination. She was as beautiful as ever. If we'd had more time I'd have taken her back upstairs. "This look okay?" she asked.

"Stunning."

"You gotta dress the part. I guess I'm sort of an official representative of ATH."

"Yeah," I said, watching her as she walked down the steps in front of me. That was not what was on my mind.

Agnes McIntosh greeted us at the front door with a broad smile. I introduced Sandra and she hugged her as if she were a long lost child. We sat in the small front parlor this time, Carl and Agnes on matching fabric-covered armchairs, Sandra and I on the settee. A plate of cookies, four cups and saucers, and a porcelain tea pot with matching cream and sugar dishes occupied the coffee table in front of us. Carl smiled and once again commented on the weather. Agnes insisted on our having coffee and busied herself pouring and passing the cups, then the cream and sugar. I felt awkward, to say the least.

Delicately balancing her cup on her knee, Sandra said, "Laura was a wonderful person. We were all so saddened by the accident." Carl and Agnes both said, "Thank you," seemingly approving of Sandra's choice of words.

"Well, it's good to meet one of her Atlanta friends," Carl said. "She was establishing her new life up there. We kind of felt like we were losing touch there toward the end."

"She was a fine person," Sandra said. "She reached out to help me when I needed it. I'll never forget her."

Agnes nodded, smiling. There was a moment of uncomfortable silence, then she said, "Would you like to see some of Laura's photos? From when she was living at home? I've got them in an album."

"I'd love that," Sandra replied. We'd been there less than ten minutes and I felt like the room was closing in on me. I sipped my coffee, not in a position to say anything. Agnes bustled off toward the rear of the house. Carl commented on the weather again, this time saying he hoped it would be sunny for the big shindig planned up at the ATH plant the next day. Sandra, consummately comfortable in what to me was a painful situation, smiled and began talking about how much Laura's research had meant to the company. She was good, no doubt about it.

Agnes returned with a large photo album, gaudily bound in faux red leather. She slid the coffee service to one side and laid it in front of us, opened so we could see the photos. Kneeling on the carpet on the other side of the table, she began to go through the pages. "Now this was Laura in kindergarten...."

Fifteen minutes later I was ready to scream. Sandra gave the appearance of genuine interest, making positive comments and asking questions on every page as we followed Laura's life in faded photographs through elementary school, into middle school and on to junior high. I had pretty much zoned out when Sandra said, "Now where was that one taken?"

Agnes replied, "Which one, dear?"

"That one, there," Sandra said, reaching out to point at one of two photographs at the top of the page.

I just happened to have my eyes on Agnes at the moment when I saw her stiffen and draw back with a little gasp, saying "Oh!" She clenched her jaw and placed her hand over her chest.

"Are you all right, honey?" Carl asked.

"Uh…, yes. Yes…, of course." She appeared suddenly pale, and struggled to push her ample frame up to a standing position. A dark look came over her face. "I…, I'm not feeling well all of a sudden. Perhaps you should go."

Carl leaned forward in his chair, looking puzzled. He tried to push himself out of the chair. "Agnes, are you…?"

"I'm fine," she said, still holding her hand over her chest.

Sandra stood up and reached out to steady her. Agnes backed away. "I'm fine," she said again, some strength in her voice now. Turning toward her husband she said, "Please show our guests out, Carl. I'm going to lie down." Without another glance in our direction she bolted through the door toward the dining room.

Having gained his feet, Carl said, "I'm sorry…, uh…, I don't know what's gotten into her. She's been…, uh…, well, kinda…, acting…."

"You don't need to apologize, Mr. McIntosh," Sandra said. "Why don't you go check on her. We can show ourselves out."

Carl looked at her, then me. "Are you sure?"

"Of course," I said. "But call us if we can do anything. I hope Mrs. McIntosh is going to be all right."

"Thanks," he said, and headed through the dining room door.

We were silent until we reached the sidewalk. I said, "What the hell was that all about?"

Sandra frowned. "I have no idea." She paused, "But that look. Did you see the look in her eyes?"

"No, not really. She looked like she might be having a heart attack or something."

"No, it was something else."

"What are you talking about?"

"It was that expression on her face. Like she suddenly hated me."

"But why?"

"I don't know, and I don't think I want to find out. Let's leave. Now."

I wasn't sure what I'd just missed, but I knew there was something.

CHAPTER Thirty-Five

To my surprise, Eula Mae was in the kitchen hunched over the sink rinsing dishes when we got back to the house. She turned, a big smile on her face and said, "I's back." Spying Sandra, she said, "Now who is this here young lady, Mr. Matt?"

I said, "Eula Mae, what are you doing here? I thought you were in Savannah with your sister."

"Oh, they gon' send her home tomorrow. She be fine, now. I needed to get back up here and make sure you ain't got yo' self in no trouble. And I see you done got you a new friend." I could see her sizing Sandra up as she dried her hands on a dish cloth. Folding it carefully and laying it over the edge of the sink, she walked over, extended her hand and said, "I'm Eula Mae Miller. I works for Mr. Matt. Now who might you be?"

Sandra seemed a bit taken off guard. Brushing her hair out of her face, she took Eula Mae's hand and said, "I'm Sandra Williams."

"Where you from?" Eula Mae asked, a bit suspicious.

"Atlanta."

"You live there all yo' life?"

"No, I'm originally from Jesup, in south Georgia."

"Well, I guess that's okay then. Pleased to meet you." Turning to me she continued, "I thought I'd just come in and straighten up some, and then tomorrow morning I'm gon' give this house a good cleanin'. It needs it what with me being gone and all." She turned back to Sandra and said, "I 'pologize for this messy place, but I been out of town with my sick sister and Mr. Matt here ain't one to keep a place clean like it ought to be."

"Oh, it's fine. It's good to meet you, but I'm leaving in just a moment— as soon as I can get my things."

Eula Mae shot me a quick look, her eyes slightly squinted. "Oh, you been stayin' here then? Well, let me help you. That's my job." And with that, she followed Sandra up the stairs. She clearly wanted to size up this intruder. "So tell me about yo'self…," she began.

Fifteen minutes later I helped Sandra load her bags in the trunk and gave her a hug before she climbed in the BMW and sped out of the yard. Eula Mae was waiting for me just inside the doorway. I started, "Eula Mae, you didn't have to come in today to…."

"Well, I'm glad I did. I wasn't 'spectin' to see you had no woman here, though. All I gotta do is leave town for a day or so and you be gettin' yo'self into some trouble again."

"Hey, Sandra's a nice girl."

"No, she ain't." Eula Mae squinted again and crossed her arms across her chest.

"How can you say that? You just met her. You can't get to know somebody in ten minutes."

"How long you known her?"

"A few weeks."

"Well, I don't know, but I thinks that woman is after somethin'. I ain't 'actly sure what, but you better watch yo' step around her."

"Don't be silly."

"I ain't, but that's all I'm gon' say." She headed back into the kitchen, saying over her shoulder, "For now, anyways."

On Friday I left for the ATH ceremony shortly after noon. The main event was due to start at one; I figured fifteen minutes to get there, half an hour to fill up on free food and another fifteen minutes to find Sandra and say hello. She'd probably be busy anyway and not have much time for me.

Actually, I was glad to get out of the house. Eula Mae had arrived as usual about eight-thirty, evidently still upset about Sandra. I'd expected to hear a long monologue detailing her stay in Savannah; instead she nodded a "good morning," and disappeared upstairs to gather the laundry and change the sheets. I think she still held out some hope Lisa might come back and resented any woman who represented a potential threat to that possibility. She'd spent the morning scurrying about in her usual efficient way, keeping whatever thoughts she had to herself. I'd tried to make conversation, but she'd informed me curtly that she was "kinda busy," adding as a total *non sequitur,* "You is a grown man, anyway."

I turned off the main road toward ATH's plant along with a dozen other vehicles all heading for the same destination. The plain unmarked entrance of a few days earlier now displayed a huge banner strung over the road announcing the groundbreaking for American Timber Holding's Adams County Energy Facility. The grass along the road had been freshly trimmed with a neatness that resembled a golf course fairway, and the guardhouse seemed to have acquired a fresh coat of paint. Charles, the guard who'd stopped Sandra and me at the gate on our earlier visit, was waving people through with a big smile, sweat brought on by the summer heat soaking the underarms of his double-breasted blue blazer.

The parking lot was, for the most part, full. I drove around trying to find a slot to fit my big truck, noticing that most of the cars bore out-of-county tags, mainly from Atlanta. The reviewing stand the workers had been building was now complete, painted in ATH's logo colors of green and brown and incongruously hung with clashing buntings of red, white and blue that could have been left over from some Fourth of July celebration.

On the far side of the lot one of the tents set up next to an industrial barbeque grill was spewing out sport-shirted men and women carrying plastic plates laden with thick slabs of pork and beef ribs. Next to it, knots of others holding cups of beer and mixed drinks clustered around what had to be the bar tent. The sweet smell of honey and mustard-based barbeque sauce floated in the air.

Next to the pilot plant building an enclosed white tent with a guard by its entrance bore a sign reading "Press Only." A large portable air conditioner powered by a diesel generator pumped cool air inside through oversized hoses. Whoever planned this event knew how their bread was buttered. The whole thing reminded me of a county fair.

I threaded my way through the throng toward the food tent, seeing a number of familiar faces of prominent local citizens. Several politicians anticipating the upcoming July primary were busily working the crowd. After a brief stand in line I hauled my plate piled with chopped pork, brunswick stew, coleslaw and white bread into the sunlight and sidled up to grab a cup of beer from the uniformed bartender.

I was looking around trying to find a spot to prop my plate and eat when I heard someone calling my name. I turned to see Inman Greene, the County Commission Chairman, bearing down on me. He wasn't smiling.

"Hi, Inman," I said. "How ya' doing?"

"Pretty good. How you doing, Matt?" He squirmed uncomfortably in his wide-lapelled polyester knit sport coat, looking for all the world like a fashion refugee from the late 1970s. He wanted something.

"Big event, isn't it?" I said. "You tried the barbeque yet?"

Glancing around, he said, "I need to talk with you."

"Okay. Let me find a place to put down this plate and we can talk while I eat."

He still wasn't smiling. A bead of sweat trickled down his forehead. Lowering his voice and moving closer, he said, "What I got to say won't take but a minute, but you better listen to it and listen to it good. What's this I hear about you poking around into Laura McIntosh's background?"

He caught me off guard. "I don't know what you're talking about."

"The hell you don't. A little bird told me you've been asking all sorts of questions, trying to dredge up things that might be embarrassing to ATH."

My gut reaction was to back up, or barring that assume some sort of defensive stance, but I couldn't. I had a plate of barbeque in one hand and a full cup of beer in the other. Greene inched in, his face now close to mine as if we were having some private conversation. I said, "Back off, Inman. Laura's parents asked me to check on a few things in Atlanta, that's all."

Greene moved back a hair and said in a softer voice, "Look, Matt, put things in perspective. This company—this event—can be the economic salvation of this county. You know the story. We're not like the big city. We don't have the bright lights and shopping malls and subdivisions it takes to attract companies with good paying jobs. This plant here, once it's built, is going to bring several hundred of 'em—new jobs—right here to Walkerville. That means more people making more money they'll spend in local stores. That means an increase in our tax base. We've got to look to our future, Matt. There are lots of other places in this state they could have chosen to build this plant, but we got 'em here. And I for one don't want to see anything screwed up."

"I don't see how anything...."

He cut me off. "I didn't ask you for a discussion, Matt. I'm just giving you a message. You better take it to heart and back off."

"A message from who?"

"You can say it's from me. I've heard about all the crap this McIntosh girl was in to. We don't need it thrown back up in anyone's face, got it? They're going to name the plant in her memory. If you have some crazy idea about digging up some dirt on her, you want to forget about it. Is that clear?"

"Clear as a bell, Inman," I said and dumped my beer on his shoe.

CHAPTER Thirty-Six

I left the Chairman of the Adams County Commissioners sputtering, cursing and stamping his feet all at the same time. I thought for a minute he might try to jump me. He had twenty years on me, but even then I wouldn't want to take him on in a fight. I quickly said, "Sorry," and disappeared into the crowd.

The exchange had a strange way of killing my appetite. I ate a couple of mouthfuls of barbeque and dumped the plate in a trash can before going back to the bar tent to get another beer. I had just taken a sip when I felt a tap on my shoulder and turned around to see Sandra's smiling face.

"You're here!" she said, reaching up to give me a hug. "I'd about given up on you. I've been looking all over for you. I saw your truck and knew you had to be somewhere in the crowd."

"I was just about to start looking for you. It looks like you've got a great turnout."

"I think so. I checked in at the gate about fifteen minutes ago, and they'd already counted more than five hundred people coming in." She glanced at her watch. "The governor's supposed to arrive any minute."

"He'll have trouble finding a place to park."

"No, silly, he's flying in. His helicopter will land over there behind the main podium."

"Everything okay with the execs?"

"I hope so. Bill and a couple of the directors are giving some private interviews to a few of the more important journalists. I think they are almost finished. He sent me out to make sure there were no problems." She looked up toward the distance behind me. "There he is now. Gotta go. Wait for me by the podium right before the ceremony starts." She reached out, squeezed my hand and plunged into the crowd heading toward the press tent.

I downed the beer in a few swallows and headed back for a refill. The exchange with Inman Greene had upset me. Whatever I'd done trying to help the McIntoshes had nothing to do with ATH, or this damned plant. And I couldn't imagine who'd told him I was trying to—what were his words?— "dig up some dirt" on Laura. There appeared to be plenty to dig up, but at this point, it didn't really matter. Like Sandra had said, she was dead. I decided Greene was just a compulsive asshole and was probably worried that anything negative might have an adverse effect on the price of his newly purchased ATH stock. I needed to forget the whole thing.

A low thumping in the distance announced the arrival of a Georgia State Patrol helicopter. It landed in a cloud of dust in the cleared area just beyond the podium. The governor, heavy-set and bald headed, scrambled out, followed by a uniformed officer and several over-dressed hangers-on. His dark charcoal suit would have been more appropriate in a corporate boardroom than in the middle of an industrial plant site, but I remembered what Sandra had said about dressing the part.

The pilot killed the engine. Bill Gray, followed by three other men I didn't recognize, moved in to greet the governor. After a moment of hand-shaking and back-slapping they headed toward the crowd who by this time had lined up to greet the state's head politician. I glanced at my watch. Ten minutes before the ceremony was scheduled to start. I found a spot of shade next to the food tent and sipped on my beer while I watched the crowd. Sandra came over and stood beside me, slipping her arm around my waist. A hint of floral perfume wedged its way past the scent of barbeque.

The ceremony went quickly. The podium was populated by a diverse group of self-interested individuals, most of whom could count as their crowning success in life the fact that they'd won a position to an elected office. In addition to the governor and all five of the county commissioners,

I counted three state representatives and two state senators. The half-dozen middle-aged men in suits I presumed to be ATH directors.

Bill Gray acted as the master of ceremonies. There were the usual series of mutually laudatory comments by several of the politicians, followed by a few words from the governor. Gray seemed to be the main speaker. He gave a brief but rather inspiring address on the dangers of America's dependence on "foreign oil," then announced what he described as a "major scientific breakthrough" in the ability to efficiently produce ethanol from the otherwise useless byproducts of timber harvesting. He said because of this American Timber Holdings was years ahead of others in the field, and was positioned to be "a dominant force in alternative energy solutions" in the coming decades.

From my vantage point I had a good view of both the podium and the throng in front of it. As Gray spoke, dozens of cell phones were suddenly glued to the ears of the crowd. I caught Sandra's attention and nodded at the scene. "I'd imagine they're calling their brokers," she said, and turned her attention back to the stage. It crossed my mind that most of the podium party had already locked in their shares.

Gray was winding up. "If you look back over the great scientific advances made over the last hundred years, most of the time they were the result of a team effort. While many here at ATH have contributed to this success, I believe we all can agree the research of one single individual provided our team with the tools necessary to make this breakthrough. Sadly, that person is not with us today, having perished tragically in an accident earlier this year. Laura Anne McIntosh had one of the most brilliant scientific minds I have ever encountered. And she was born and raised here in Adams County." Gray paused and looked up from his notes as a soft murmur swept over the crowd followed by the sound of clapping, first a few hands, then dozens, then hundreds until the whole assemblage broke into spontaneous applause.

Gray waited a moment, smiling grimly as the crowd settled down. "Accordingly, we at American Timber Holdings want to honor her today and in the future by naming this new facility the McIntosh Energy Facility in memory of Laura's invaluable scientific contribution to this company's success." As he spoke, two men carried a large cloth-covered object on the stage and placed it on an easel. "And now I'm going to ask the governor to help me unveil this portrait which will hang in our corporate offices in Atlanta."

Gray stepped to one side of the easel while the governor stood on the other. Gray nodded and they both lifted up the cloth to reveal a full length oil painting of Laura McIntosh. She stood, looking at the audience, dressed in a green blouse and slim black skirt, her long hair falling over her shoulders. The artist had placed her outdoors on an overlook with a pine forest in the background illuminated by a rising—or was it setting?—sun. "Like it?" Sandra whispered. "I stood in for the portrait. The artist did her face and head from photographs. You recognize the outfit? That's the one I was wearing last week. It was kind of a rush job, but I think it turned out great."

It was a good likeness, I thought, but decided the body—and breasts in particular—far more resembled Sandra than they did Laura. Another thought flashed through my mind, too. I wondered where they got the photographs.

CHAPTER Thirty-Seven

The ceremony ended with the governor, Bill Gray, and Inman Greene stepping down from the podium to turn symbolic spades of dirt while posing for photographers. I could still see the beer stain on the bottom of Greene's pants leg. He picked me out of the crowd and pointed at me with a mean smile, his hand making the shape of a pistol. I smiled back at him and acknowledged his gesture with a wave.

Sandra said, "I've got to get back to work. I think we're going to leave for Atlanta shortly. Will you call me?"

"Of course. Tonight okay?"

"Probably tomorrow afternoon. I know Bill's planning on entertaining the directors tonight and I'm sure I'll need to be involved with that."

"Good. Tomorrow then," I said. She hugged me and headed toward the knot of well-wishers surrounding Gray and the governor. I thought I'd better leave while I had a chance. I didn't want to have to deal with Inman Greene, who at the moment was basking in the reflected glory of his transient association with the state's governor and the head of a multi-billion dollar corporation. He really needed to get a life.

Eula Mae was polishing the dining room table when I arrived back at Rutherford Hall. She seemed to be in a better mood. "That Sandra woman gone yet?"

"She's probably on her way back to Atlanta as we speak."

"Good," Eula Mae replied, intensely rubbing her chamois over a barely discernable spot on the table. "I s'pose I oughta say I'm sorry," she continued without looking up. In all the years I've known her, I've never heard Eula Mae apologize.

"Why?"

"'Bout what I said."

"What you said?" I repeated.

"'Bout that Sandra woman."

"Eula Mae, you don't ever need to apologize to me."

"No, I do. I jes' spoke too quick-like. I wasn't thinkin'. You is a man, and I knows how mens are. I jes' don't want to see you get in with the wrong kind o' woman."

"Why do you say that? What's wrong with Sandra?"

"Ain't nothing wrong with her, dependin' on what you wantin' her fo'. If you's lookin' for some entertainment, she be fine. If you's lookin' fo' sumthin' more, she ain't the one."

"But why do you…?"

"That's all I'm gon' say. We ain't gon' talk 'bout it no more. You is a grown man." She'd said that before. She bent over her polishing, the conversation ended. As I was walking out the door she said, "Oh, Roger Barmore come by to see you. I told him you's gone, so he left you a paper there in the kitchen."

I found a note scribbled on a Barmore & Son notepad sheet folded on the table. It read

Matt,

I need to talk with you. I'm on duty with the Sheriff until midnight tonight, and I'm working the 8 AM to 8 PM shift tomorrow. Can you meet me at Gordo's at about 8:30 tomorrow night? It's important and I don't want to wait till next week. Call me if you can't make it.

Roger

He apparently planned for me to be there. He didn't leave his phone number.

I slept late on Saturday, and then spent the latter part of the morning back at work on remodeling the stables. I figured another couple of months, and I'd have things done. Then I'd have to find a new project.

I called Sandra half a dozen times starting at about two in the afternoon. She didn't answer her home phone and her cell went directly to voice mail. Probably still having to help entertain the out-of-town directors, I thought. I left a message and told her I'd call on Sunday. I wasn't especially interested in meeting with Roger, but was glad he'd chosen the Mexican restaurant for our rendezvous. I reasoned that I'd drink a couple of beers, listen to him let off steam, then look at my watch and say I had to go. It would be a hell of a lot easier than getting him out of my house.

I quit work about six-thirty, and spent half an hour putting up my tools. By the time I'd taken a shower and eaten some cold fried chicken Eula Mae left for me in the refrigerator, it was a quarter past eight. I set out on foot for the Square, enjoying the June weather and the waning light of the afternoon sun. The Square was full of pickups and SUVs. The pickup drivers were most likely to be found tossing back tequila shots at El Gordo's bar, while those arriving in SUVs were mainly families out for The Country Buffet's Saturday night $16.95 all-you-can-eat "seafood feast."

El Gordo's was crowded. A few brave souls, most of them teenagers on dates, were trying to choke down fajitas and tacos over the din of Columbian pop tunes blasting from the speakers in the bar. Roger was waiting for me in a booth near the rear, a half-empty Tecate dark in front of him. I sat down, waved the waitress over and ordered the same. "What's up?" I said.

"Matt, there's something going on here. I know there is. I just can't get it out of my mind. And the worst part is I don't know who's behind it."

"Okay...." I said. He was beginning to sound paranoid. "I thought we were going to get together next week. Did something new come up?"

"Well, yes and no. I haven't found anything definite, but I'm having the crime lab run the DNA on the..., the specimens..., you know..., from Laura's body."

"The ones that showed semen, right?"

"Yeah." He took a long draw on his beer.

"Why?"

"Why? Don't you see, this guy Hargrove was supposed to be gay? Laura's autopsy proved she'd recently had sex with somebody. You said his roommate—or partner, or whatever the hell he was—said Hargrove didn't have sex with women. Now, you couple that with the compressed gas valve wrench in the wreckage and you begin...."

I held up my hands. "Roger, just back off for a minute. I think you're trying to find a conspiracy...."

"No, I'm not! I'm just trying to turn over every stone. Look, it's no big deal to get the DNA done. They've already done Hargrove's. If it matches with the specimen from Laura, I'll back off. If not, then it's a whole new ballgame." He slammed his fist on the table for emphasis.

I saw there was no arguing with him. And when the results came back as expected, maybe he'd be convinced. "Sounds like a plan," I said, "but doesn't it take weeks to get DNA results?"

"Months is more like it," Roger said, "at least for the crime lab. Actually with the new instruments you can have the testing done in less than twenty-four hours, but they have a backlog of thousands of specimens."

"So I guess it'll be a while before you know anything."

"A couple of days. By Monday at the latest."

"But you just said...."

Roger finished his beer in one swallow. "One of the crime lab techs has a bad compressor in her air conditioning unit. It gets awful hot this time of year."

"You didn't?!"

"You do what ya' gotta do," he replied, waving at the waitress for another beer. I told her to make it two.

The beer arrived promptly with a basket of tortilla chips and bowls of salsa and guacamole. "So why'd you want to meet with me tonight instead of next week?"

"I want you to go somewhere with me on Tuesday. I know you've got the time."

"Where?"

"Up south of Atlanta, near Griffin. A company named Recovery Systems, Inc. has a junkyard. There's something I need to look at, and I don't want to go by myself."

"A junkyard? What the hell do you need to look at in a junkyard?"

"They specialize in salvaging aircraft. Everything from crashes to planes damaged by wind or hail. They've got the wreckage of the Cessna."

I couldn't believe what he was saying. "You're not planning on actually....?"

I was interrupted by someone calling my name. "Matt." I looked up to see Sandra's friend Rob sauntering over from the bar area, a beer grasped firmly in one fist. He stuck out his hand and said, "Good to see ya,' Matt. How's it going?" He was obviously very drunk. "Mind if I sit down?" he said and without waiting for a reply slid in the booth next to Roger. He introduced himself with, "I'm Rob Howell. Old Matt and I have a mutual friend in common."

Roger looked annoyed but slipped over to give him room. I shrugged and raised my eyebrows. Roger said, "Pleased to meet you."

Turning back to me Howell continued, "So you and Sandra are an item, eh? She's pretty hot. I haven't seen her, like, since my second year of college—'course that was my last year 'cause they flunked me out. 'Too much partying, Mr. Howell,' is what they said. But shit, I have fun and make a hell of a lot more money doing what I do now than most of those smartasses in their coats and ties." He took another hit on his beer. "Yeah, old Sandra looks good, but it looks to me like she's bought herself a new set of tits. Back when I was doing her, they were nice—just the kind you could get in your mouth...."

"Hey, Rob! That's enough, okay?"

"Yeah, man, I know. She's got you all wrapped around her little finger. That's the way she works, I tell you right now. Like in college—that girl fucked her way to a straight-A average—caused two of the professors to lose their jobs, even." He finished his beer and looked for the waitress to order another.

I was getting angry. Trying to sound calm I said, "Rob, you're pretty drunk. Roger and I need to talk. Why don't you go back over to the bar? We can talk in private later."

He gave me a puzzled look. "Hey, man, I'm trying to do you a favor. She's bad news, I'm telling you. Maybe she's changed—shit, I don't know—but if I were you, I'd watch my back." With a quick "Catch you later," he pushed himself out of the booth and headed back toward the bar.

"Drunk son of a bitch," I said, half under my breath.

"He may be right, Matt. You need to be careful."

Roger's tone annoyed me. "How would you know? You've only seen her—what? Twice? And the second time was just the other day at my house."

"Yeah, but the other time was when she was rooming with Laura. I got to the apartment a little early. Laura called to say she was hung up in traffic and would be late getting in. She was hitting on me, Matt. Sandra was hitting on me, knowing that I was engaged to Laura. Kinda makes you wonder."

"Kinda," I said, feeling like I'd been kicked in the gut. "Why didn't you tell me about all that?"

"Why should I?" Roger replied. "It looked like you two were fixing to get it on. I didn't want to spoil the special moment." His voice reeked of sarcasm.

"So that accounts for the dirty looks the other night?"

"I guess you could say that." He dug a chip into the guacamole and stuffed it in his mouth. "So, you gonna go with me Tuesday?"

If he'd asked me just five minutes earlier, I'd have said no. Now I wasn't so sure. My mind was somewhere else. "Let me check my schedule. I'll call you tomorrow or the next day." It would be easier to say no over the phone anyway.

CHAPTER Thirty-Eight

I drank a couple more beers to ease my nerves and walked home feeling like a total fool. Or was I? There was no doubt Sandra had been around the block once or twice; she never tried to deny it. But first Eula Mae, then the old boyfriend and now Roger, all waving red flags in my face.

I suppose I hadn't really thought about the relationship. I liked Sandra. I liked her a lot. I wasn't in love with her by any stretch of the imagination, but I did care about her. It had been one of those things that just happened. And was it fair to try to draw any conclusions based on what she did in college, or when she was living with Laura just after she broke up with her boyfriend? I stuffed the thoughts in the back of my mind. The reality was there was no need to do anything. As far as I could tell, neither of us had an agenda. We were—as they say—just "seeing" each other. Things would work out one way or the other. They always do.

The house was dark. I turned on one of the lamps in the hall. Through the kitchen door I could see the red message light blinking on the answering machine. I pressed the button to hear an unfamiliar male voice say, *"You don't know me and I'm not going to tell you my name. The word is you want to find out the truth about Laura McIntosh. I know what really happened. If you want to find out, meet me tomorrow night and I'll tell you. Take Highway 15 north up to Kitrell Creek Road and turn right. Go about three-quarters of a mile and turn right again down a logging road into the woods. I'll mark it with yellow flagging tape. Follow it about a quarter mile until you come to a clearing—there'll be a bunch of equipment parked there. Get there about 7:30—it'll still be light—and come alone. Don't tell anyone about this call. If you don't show up I won't call again."*

Despite the calming effect of the beer, a cold chill ran over my body. The voice had a rough edge about it. It sounded like he was reading from a script, as if he wanted to keep the conversation short and succinct. I pressed the button and listened to it again. The accent was non-specific, probably local, which would go along with his wanting to meet me in an isolated part of the county most outsiders wouldn't know.

I picked up the phone and checked caller ID. There had been only one call since I left to meet Roger. It showed up as "Restricted." No luck there. I looked at my watch. Roger left the bar at the same time I did. He'd probably be home by now. I started to call him but thought better of it. It would just stir the pot. I had no idea what the anonymous caller would have to say, but I figured it would be better if I heard it before Roger did. He was paranoid enough, and his knowing about the call would just add fuel to the fire.

The sound of the phone ringing awoke me Sunday morning. I looked at the number before I answered. Sandra. A cheery voice said, "Wake up!"

Half-asleep, I replied, "You're up early."

"I know. I was at the gym at six this morning working out. I am *so* glad to be finished with this plant kick-off thing. I'm sorry I couldn't talk yesterday. Bill ended up inviting everyone up to his place at Lake Burton. I was probably out on the boat when you called. I think I may have gotten a sunburn."

"I'm sorry...."

"Anyway, the nasty old men are all gone and I can get back into my routine. I thought the best way to start would be back in the gym." She paused. "So how are you?"

"Fine, I think. Still waking up." I stretched and rubbed my eyes. "What time is it?"

"Seven-fifteen. I wish I were there in bed with you."

"That would be nice," I said, trying not to think about the conversation of the night before.

"So, when am I going to see you again?"

"Soon, I hope. I got some things to do the first part of the week, but maybe next weekend? Why don't I call you later today after I wake up?"

"Could you call me tonight? I'm meeting a couple of girlfriends for brunch, and then we're going shopping this afternoon. I should be home by six."

I thought of the meeting scheduled for seven-thirty. "I've got to meet with someone tonight on business. I'll be back by nine. I'll call you then if that's okay."

"Great. Have a good day. I'll talk with you tonight."

The day passed rapidly. Jack and Margie dropped by after church to check on me. Jack asked if I'd heard any news about Laura. I told him I hadn't and he let it drop. They invited me to lunch, but I made an excuse that I had some paperwork to do. Jack knew I was lying.

As the afternoon wore on, I became more and more apprehensive about meeting with the unknown caller. There were apparently a number of people who knew that I, and later Roger, had been looking into Laura's background. I had no idea what to expect, and the idea of going alone to meet him looked less and less inviting. I shuffled through my dresser drawer and found the Beretta .25 caliber pistol I'd inherited from my father. It was small and would fit in my back pocket nicely with a bulge not much bigger than a wallet. I cleaned and oiled it, making sure the clip was full. I didn't think I'd need it, but I didn't want to take any chances.

I pulled out of the driveway at seven. Assuming I didn't get lost, it would take me about twenty minutes to reach the turnoff. The day had started with soft wispy clouds, but a mass of cool air had blown in from the northwest covering the sun and rendering the sky in shades of grey and white. The forecast called for thunderstorms, followed by clearing for the remainder of the week.

I turned off the paved highway onto Kitrell Creek, a heavily rutted dirt road that wandered aimlessly through miles of planted pines before emerging near the county line to the east. At one time all of this had been open farm land, with a few hardy souls managing to scratch out a living from cotton and cattle. Those days were long gone, with most of the big tracts now owned by timber companies or absentee landlords.

I found the logging road without a problem. Half a dozen ribbons of yellow flagging tape tied to an open gate whipped back and forth in the wind. Brightly colored ATH boundary markers were nailed to both gate posts with a warning that read "Posted—Keep Out." Apparently this tract was part of their Adams County holdings. I pulled in, stopped and looked for tire tracks. Even though the sky was threatening at the moment, no rain had fallen in several days so I couldn't be sure if the marks I was seeing were old or new. I slipped the truck into 4-wheel drive and proceeded cautiously up the narrow road between rows of freshly thinned pines.

Per the caller's description, the road ended in a clearing bulldozed out of the forest for use as a loading yard, now deserted on this Sunday evening. A half-loaded log truck was parked next to a machine that limbed the trees and cut them to length, its massive saws still and quiet. On the other side three skidders and two feller-bunchers sat next to a dilapidated fuel truck with its dented tank painted a shade of deep red that matched the rust spots on the crumpled fenders. Otherwise the clearing was empty. No sign of the mystery man.

I looked at the clock on the dash. Seven twenty-five. I was early. I switched the truck off and settled in to wait, rolling down the windows so I could hear the sound of an approaching vehicle. There was still a good hour of daylight, but the heavy cloud cover darkened the forest as the wind whipped through the trees. A flash of lightning lit the sky followed by a throaty roll of thunder some fifteen seconds later. The storm was about three miles away. A smattering of wind-driven raindrops hit the hood of the truck and rolled off, creating little islands of moisture in the layer of dust laid down from the dirt road.

Seven thirty. The sky was darker now and the rain began to fall in earnest. I rolled up the windows and watched as horizontal sheets of wind-blown water whipped across the clearing. Near constant lightning flashes followed by peals of thunder illuminated the trees like strobe lights. The truck rocked back and forth in the gale. A tall skinny pine just beyond the log truck snapped off with a sudden crack and thudded harmlessly on the ground. And suddenly, as quickly as it had begun, it ended. The wind died rapidly, and the buckets of rain slowed to a fine drizzle before stopping completely.

Seven forty-five. I was still alone in the clearing. A few spots of blue sky began to peek through the overcast. I reasoned that the caller had probably been caught by the storm and decided to give him another fifteen minutes before leaving. I rolled down the windows again to be overwhelmed by a blast of warm, humid air.

Seven fifty. I was getting antsy sitting in the truck. The loggers had spread a thin layer of gravel over the loading yard to keep the heavy equipment from bogging down in the muck. Even with the rain, it wasn't so muddy that I couldn't walk around. I got out and walked over to the edge of the forest, having nothing in mind other than stretching my legs.

I was about fifty yards from my truck when I heard the sound of a diesel motor starting up. Although multiple tracks led off in all directions through the pines, the road I'd followed in was the only way in or out for a conventional vehicle. But the sound was coming from the opposite direction and was immediately followed by a rumble, then roar, of a second engine. I turned to see puffs of black smoke emerging from the exhausts of a skidder and a feller-buncher parked on the edge of the clearing. I could just make out a figure inside the cab of each machine, but the heavy black-painted protective wire mesh obscured anything more in the dim light.

I wasn't sure what to do. I stood frozen with indecision as the driver of the feller-buncher raised the boom that held its massive cutting head and slipped the machine in gear. The skidder driver did the same, raising his articulated grappling hook while opening and closing its pincer-like arms. Together, like two giant mechanical insects, they advanced toward me.

I bolted toward the truck, but the skidder driver was quicker. Waving his boom with its deadly claws, he positioned himself between me and safety. As he did so the feller-buncher circled behind me, forcing me to flee toward the parked equipment. I made a quick lateral move in that direction, but the recently toppled pine blocked my path. With a running leap I tried to jump over it, only to catch my foot on a branch and send myself sprawling in the mud.

Both machines closed in on me, blocking any forward path of escape and trapping me with the log truck to my back. I scrambled up as the hydraulic blades of the cutting head reached out and snapped the downed pine like a matchstick, grabbing it and tossing it to one side in a single motion. The skidder leaped through the breach, its hook reaching out for me just as I slid under the truck and freedom in the forest beyond.

My escape was short-lived. I set out running down an open row of planted pines. The heavy machines, designed for rapid movement under rugged off-road conditions, followed, paralleling my track and passing me before I'd covered a hundred yards. The driver of the feller-buncher took the lead, snipping off trees that blocked his path and tracking my every move while the skidder operator covered his flanks, herding me back toward the clearing. If I could get to my truck ahead of them, I'd have a chance of making it out alive.

I'd almost made it when my foot caught on a root, sending me sprawling a second time into the mud. The cutting head of the feller-buncher snipped off an eighteen-inch pine and, tossing it to the side, moved toward me as I lay on the ground. The pincers of the skidder reached out to be in on the kill.

I tried scrambling up, but slipped and fell again, slamming my butt against a tree in the process and landing face up on my back. It was then that I remembered the gun. Reaching behind me I could feel it in my back pocket. With muddy hands I grabbed for it just as the hydraulic shears of the cutting head poised to descend on me.

I could see the drivers of the machines now. Both were wearing ski masks, revealing only their eyes. The driver of the feller-buncher, spotting the gun, pulled back his boom and put the machine in reverse. Holding the pistol in my right hand, I racked a round into the chamber with my left and began firing wildly toward the machines, first the feller-buncher, then the skidder. As rapidly as they'd advanced on me, they backed off a few dozen yards, my shots apparently doing no damage.

I don't remember how many times I fired; I just kept pulling the trigger until nothing happened. The Beretta .25 has a very short barrel. It's somewhat accurate at close range, but a hit beyond ten or fifteen yards is more luck than skill. The drivers must have realized that. They waited for me to run out of ammo, then came at me once again.

I was about fifty yards from my truck and they were the same distance from me in the opposite direction. I think I'm a pretty good sprinter, but the mud-slicked pine straw made me feel like I was running on ice. They were closing in as I made it to the edge of the clearing. I wouldn't have a chance if they caught me out in the open, so I made a sudden swerve and headed toward the log truck. I reasoned if I could get it or some of the other equipment between me and them, I could make it make it back to my truck and a have a chance of escape.

The sudden change in direction threw my pursuers off, opening a little gap in the distance between us. I circled around on the forest side of the log truck, ducking under the logs protruding over the end of the cradle in the back. I stood still for a moment, pretending to be winded, hoping to lure them into position. It was working. First the feller-buncher, then the skidder slid around the back of the truck and slowed to move in on me like attack dogs against a trapped fox. They eased forward. I backed up slowly, planning to hit the ground, roll under the truck and make a run for my pickup.

The cutting head reached toward me like a snake preparing to strike its victim. I took a step back. Then another. Then a third, when my foot caught on a branch sending me pitching backward against the steel framework of the truck. I felt a sharp pain in the back of my head, then darkness as I collapsed in the mud.

CHAPTER Thirty-Nine

The first thing I remember feeling was a splitting pain in my head, followed rapidly by a sensation of cold and wet. There was no sound. I opened my eyes and looked up, trying to remember where I was and how I got there. I stared up at the bark of a pine log. I tried moving my right hand and felt slippery mush. Then it came back to me and I sat up with a start. The last things I recalled seeing before I tripped were the hydraulic blades of the cutting head reaching out toward me. Now there was nothing in front of me but open forest. Both machines were gone. I was lying under the half-loaded log truck in the mud, apparently just where I'd fallen.

I fumbled for my watch, scraping the dirt off the face to make out the time. Eight thirty-two. I must have been out—what?—twenty or twenty-five minutes. The back of my head throbbed. I touched it with a muddy hand and came back with a sticky mass of blood. Reaching up for support from the frame of the truck, I pulled myself to a standing position and waited a moment for the dizziness to pass. Stumbling around the log truck I saw my green pickup exactly where I'd left it, and the logging machines parked where they'd been when I arrived. For a moment I thought I'd dreamed the whole thing, but the fallen pine was there as I remembered, snipped in two by the powerful blades of the feller-buncher.

I walked back around to where I'd fallen. I could make out two sets of boot prints around the spot where I'd lain. My assailants must have come over to check me out after I hit my head. Maybe they thought I was dead. Maybe they didn't intend to kill me in the first place. I had no way of knowing. I thought about the Beretta. I remembered dropping it after I ran out of shells, and to my surprise found it easily in the dim light lying on top of the pine straw where it landed.

I tried to remember where I'd left the truck keys. They weren't in my pockets. Moving as fast as I could, I ran to the truck and pulled open the door to hear the familiar pinging signal warning me I'd left them in the ignition. Something else caught my eye, a folded sheet of typing paper in the middle of the driver's seat. I picked it up to read a simple message printed in block letters: "THAT WAS YOUR FINAL WARNING."

Half an hour later I was home, standing in the shower as layers of dried mud mixed with blood peeled off me and washed down the drain. I'd taken off my clothes in the middle of the tile-floored laundry room, throwing them directly in the washer with a cup of laundry detergent.

Now standing naked in front of the sink, I used a hand mirror to try to see the cut on the back of my head. The scrubbing had opened up the wound, and a fine trickle of blood soaked my hair and dripped down my neck. I didn't want to have to explain it to anyone, but judging from what I could see, it needed sutures. That meant a trip to the emergency room. I found a pack of gauze pads and bandages in the closet and bound them over the cut as well as I could before getting dressed. Grabbing a large towel to lay over my mud-covered driver's seat, I started formulating a plausible excuse for my injury as I headed for the hospital.

By the time I parked my truck in the ER patients' area and made it inside, the bandages wrapped around my head were soaked with blood. The emergency room was nearly deserted. A latina mother was trying vainly in broken English to explain to the triage nurse that her child had a fever and was throwing up. A disheveled-looking black man snored loudly on one of the couches as he waited for some friend or relative who was seeing the doctor. Apparently I gave the appearance of a serious enough injury to warrant immediate passage to one of the trauma rooms and the attention of a nurse to check my vital signs. I gave her the necessary information, creating a story of having fallen down some stairs and bumping my head. She seemed to believe me, and was more interested in whether or not I had any allergies or chronic medical conditions than she was in how I actually injured myself. Another routine case.

The ER doctor appeared, said hello, and examined the wound intently under a bright light. "How'd you say you did this again? Looks like you packed your cut with mud to stop the bleeding."

"I slipped down in the mud after I fell down the steps."

He glanced at my clean shirt. "Oh, I see. Glad you got cleaned up before you left for the ER." He was suspicious. "We don't need to notify the police about this, do we? It's the law, you know. We're required to notify the cops for anything that might be...."

"No need for that, Doctor." The voice came from Roger Barmore, dressed in his deputy's uniform and standing in the trauma room door. "I know Mr. Rutherford quite well and I'm sure someone in his situation wouldn't get himself tangled in anything involving the law. Isn't that right, Matt?"

I nodded. The doctor shrugged and left while the nurse went off in search of a wash basin to clean my wound. "What are you doing here?" I asked.

"It looks like I might be about to pull your ass out of trouble. What's this crap? You fell down the steps?" Clearly he didn't believe me either.

"Did someone call you?"

"No. I was sent up here to the ER to take a statement from a guy involved in a fender-bender out in the county and I saw your truck in the ER patients' lot, parked right under one of the halogen lights. I took a look in the window. The driver's side seat is covered with mud and there is something that looks a lot like blood on the headrest. You want to explain all that?"

"Do I have to?"

"Matt, look, I don't know what's going on with you—and maybe you don't want me to know. But if it's something you need some help with, I'm here, okay?"

I was torn between telling him the truth, which would feed his paranoia about Laura, or making up some convenient lie to cover up the whole thing. On the other hand, someone had just tried to kill me, or at least make me think they could have if they wanted to. I didn't have a choice. He needed to know what happened. I said, "We'll talk, but not here. But as far as anyone has to know, I got this cut when I fell down some steps."

"Gotcha," he said, and headed off to clear things with the doctor. The nurse returned wheeling in a large stainless basin filled with hot water. "Ready?" she asked. "This may sting a little bit."

✈ ✈ ✈ ✈

The courthouse clock was striking eleven as I finished telling Roger the details of the assault. "What kind of a fool are you, Matt? You knew about this last night and didn't call me? You could have been killed. You almost were."

"So what does it all mean?" My head was pounding as the local anesthetic wore off.

"I don't know. Obviously, someone doesn't want you—or probably anybody—looking into Laura's death. I just think it goes along with what I've been saying. There's been a cover-up. I don't think it was an accident. I think she was murdered." That was the first time he'd used the word.

I didn't know how to react. I still thought Roger's conspiracy theory was farfetched, but I wasn't as sure of it as I'd been a few hours earlier. He continued, "You said Inman Greene had sort of threatened you at the groundbreaking on Friday. You think he might be behind it?"

"Anything's possible, but I don't know. I mean, someone had to tell him I was looking into the circumstances surrounding Laura's death. I guess he could have heard it on the street, but other than you, the McIntoshes and my uncle Jack, I haven't told anyone."

"How about Sandra? Or the CEO guy, what's his name? Gray?"

"I just can't see it, not from either one of them."

"How about this guy Wynne, out at the pilot plant?"

"Why would he care?"

"I don't know? What's the motive? That's Criminal Procedure 101. When you investigate a crime you look for two things, motive and opportunity."

"Okay, let's forget the motive for a minute and look at opportunity. Whoever jumped me tonight was on ATH property, and driving ATH machines. I'd think the gate would be locked, especially with all the equipment left out there in the middle of nowhere. Somebody had to have a key to get in, and they had to know that nobody would be likely to show up there and discover what was going on."

"So who does that point to?"

"Somebody at ATH." Now I was beginning to sound like I was becoming a conspiracy theorist.

"And...?"

"I don't know. That's it. I don't know what to do next."

"Why don't you start by coming with me to have a look at what's left of the plane?"

I nodded, thinking I really needed something for a headache.

CHAPTER Forty

"You didn't call me last night." Sandra sounded hurt. The bedside clock flashed seven twenty-four.

"I had a little accident and ended up in the emergency room."

"No! What happened? Are you all right?" Surprise and concern.

"I slipped down the steps and hit the back of my head. The doc put a few staples in it. It still hurts, but I'm fine."

"Matt, are you sure? Do you need anything? Do you want me to come down there? I can take a day off…"

"No, no, I'm fine. It was just one of those things."

"That's terrible! I know it must be painful, but I guess it could have been worse." Totally sincere. She couldn't have known about what happened. Scratch her off the suspect list. We talked a few minutes before hanging up. I promised I'd call later to let her know how I was doing. The pounding had degenerated to a steady dull ache. I got up, swallowed a couple of naproxen tabs and went back to bed.

Roger called at ten to check on me. I had just gotten out of the shower and was trying to examine my wound with the hand mirror. I counted seven staples holding together an ugly cut at least two inches long. "You okay?" he asked.

"I'll live."

"The sheriff's office got a call this morning about some vandals taking a couple of pieces of logging equipment for a joy-ride off Kitrell Creek Road. Said there wasn't much damage. They sent a deputy up to take a report. The foreman said he thought it was probably a bunch of teenagers. I didn't say anything about what happened to you."

"Good."

"We still on for tomorrow?"

"Yeah."

"I'll pick you up at eight."

✈ ✈ ✈ ✈

The "office" of Recovery Systems, Inc. was a dilapidated single-wide mobile home located in a sparsely populated area of farmland some forty miles south of Atlanta. Behind it, a ten-foot high chain-link fence topped with barbed wire surrounded a series of steel-frame buildings that looked like warehouses. Two heavy-lift cranes and a couple of large flat-bed tractor-trailers were parked to one side. The manager, a short, intense-looking man in his mid-thirties with close-cropped hair examined Roger's badge and ID before asking, "So what are you guys looking for? The word we got on this crash was that the pilot and passenger were overcome by carbon monoxide."

"That's correct, but there are some other issues we're examining. It's part of a wider investigation."

"Drugs?"

"I can't say. It's an ongoing case."

"Sure, I understand," the manager replied. "Now you know technically the wreckage is the property of the insurance company—you don't need a search warrant do you?"

"No. We're just following up on some loose ends."

The manager led us through a gate and past the steel buildings into what could only be described as an airplane graveyard. "We make most of our income from two sources," he explained. "We recover wrecked planes—or what's left of them—and charge to store them here until the insurance and legal issues are settled. Most of the time we end up paying the insurance company a nominal fee for what's left, and we try to make the rest of our profit by stripping out the avionics, engines and other usable parts, then selling the metals for what we can get on the open market. What remains of most of the 'routine' crashes gets stored out here in the open. For your high profile crashes, the ones that have big insurance dollars riding on them or where they may want to do a reconstruction of the air-frame, we keep them in one of these climate-controlled warehouses." We were walking down a wide gravel road now, the ruined carcasses of once-sleek aircraft corroding in weed-covered plots to either side of us.

The manager stopped to consult a clipboard. "Let's see, the one you want to look at is over here, number M-382." He pointed in the direction of a battered fuselage with the designation "M-382" spray-painted in fluorescent orange on the side. "If you fellows need anything I'll be back in the office."

Roger and I stared at the wreck for a moment. The cowling was missing and the engine had been snapped from the firewall. The smashed windscreen framed a jagged view of the pilot's and passenger's seats. Both wings were torn off near their origin, leaving only short stubs protruding above the cabin. The pilot's side door was missing and the yawning opening that had been used as a jump door exposed the rear of the interior to the elements. "You ready?" I asked.

He swallowed and said, "I guess so." Stepping over the shattered wings and other debris that had been piled next to the fuselage, we worked our way around to the jump door and peered in. The tan carpet was stained with mud and reeked of mildew from the rain that poured in through the windows and doors.

Roger produced a small flashlight from his pocket, lowered himself to his knees and crawled into the cabin. After a moment, he said, "Got it," and backed his way out, holding up a small green object for me to see. "Look, it's what I thought it was, a compressed air valve wrench." There was a sense of vindication in his voice. He handed it to me and said, "Hang on to this. I want to look around some more."

"What are you looking for?"

"I'm not sure, but I'll know it when I find it."

I waited while he crawled around in the interior of the wreckage. We were surrounded by death. To my left I recognized the remains of a half-burned Learjet, and beyond it what appeared to be the smashed tail assembly from a 737, the airline logo painted over as a gesture to avoid frightening current ticket holders. The fuselage rocked back and forth as Roger contorted himself to peer in every nook and cranny of the wrecked plane. After a moment he yelled, "Oh, ho!" and scrambled out of the plane holding up a small, thin plastic object. "Recognize this?" he asked.

I took it and turned it over in my hand. "It looks like a plastic cable tie."

"Exactly! It goes along with what I've been saying. Laura was brought here against her will. She was kidnapped."

"But cable ties are everywhere." I kneeled down and pointed at the broken instrument panel. "See there—behind the yoke—the wiring is bundled up with plastic ties, like these."

"Not exactly. These are the kind we use in law enforcement as temporary handcuffs." Roger said. "Look at it. It's been pulled tight then cut open with a sharp edge. If you put the cut edges together they form a circle that's a good four or five inches in diameter, just the right size to bind someone's hands. Much too big for wires. And the edge that's pulled out beyond the plastic catch is still in place. If it had been used to bind wiring or cables, they would have trimmed it up neatly like those behind the instrument panel." He did have a point.

"Okay, but of all the things that cable ties can be used for, what makes you think someone used this particular one for handcuffs?"

"Because it fits. Everything fits."

"No it doesn't, dammit!" I was angry. "Face it, Roger. Laura's dead. She was up in this damned plane screwing some guy she worked with. It may be kinky, and it may be strange, but you keep grabbing at straws, trying to change the facts to fit your preconceived notion of what really happened. You're talking about canisters of compressed carbon monoxide, cable ties, god knows what. Back off and look at the big picture. Hargrove was a pilot. He was the only one who could fly the plane. There's no evidence anyone else was with them when they took off—remember what you said about the airport video? Just accept things for what they are. Let the dead rest in peace."

Roger stood mutely, looking like he'd been slapped. Maybe he had, verbally at least. He said, "Okay. Let's go home." We trudged out, the only sound being our footfalls crunching on gravel and echoing off the ruined hulks along the path.

We were nearly ten miles down the road when he spoke. "The tech from the crime lab called. She said she was late in getting the specimens done. She should have the results by tomorrow."

CHAPTER Forty-One

We rode most of the way home in silence. Roger drove; I slumped down in the passenger's seat thinking maybe I'd been too harsh on him. I had to give him credit for blind faith and loyalty. He wasn't exactly delusional, but he was veering in that direction. On the other hand, the cut on the back of my head was very real. There was something about Laura or the circumstances of her death that someone didn't want the world to know. Maybe I'd stumbled onto it and didn't recognize it. Or maybe not.

About fifteen minutes before we reached home Roger said, "There was something else I found." He was looking straight ahead, his eyes misty and fixed on the road. Reaching in his shirt pocket he pulled out a thin gold chain and handed it to me. The clasp was shut; one of the links had been pulled apart. A small gold pine tree with a single diamond set in the middle was still on the chain. "I found it in a crack under the seat. I gave it to Laura last Christmas. She promised me she'd never take it off."

I looked at it and then gently handed it back to him. "I know this is hard on you, Roger," I said. "Maybe it's a sign you should...."

"You're right. It *is* a sign. It's a sign I don't need to stop looking until I find the answer." He was quiet for a minute, then said. "We didn't see the video from the airport the night they took the plane. They kept it in a hangar at the Winder airport, just outside of Atlanta. We just took the word of the police up there that it confirmed what everyone thought. I need to look at it myself. And I need to call the NTSB and get more information on the radar plots of the flight path. I'll do that tomorrow."

At this point I wasn't going to try to stop him. He was a nice guy, and maybe he was going to need a friend when the whole thing was over. I resolved to stay around to help him pick up the pieces.

It was after five by the time we arrived back in Walkerville. Eula Mae had come and gone, leaving a note on the table saying there were some fresh-cooked butterbeans in the refrigerator and that "Sandra" had called. I noted she deleted the usual honorific of "Miss." I wasn't in a mood to call her back. I had some thinking I needed to do. I'd leave it to Roger to pursue whatever quixotic ideas he might have about Laura's death. I needed to figure out what I'd done to earn the staples that were holding together part of my scalp. I grabbed a beer, legal pad and pen and settled in on the dogtrot sofa.

I made three columns on the pad: First, people who knew or might have known I'd been in Atlanta looking into Laura's background. Second, negative things that might happen if some terrible secret about her were made public. Third, people—or companies?—who had the access and local knowledge to set up the ambush Sunday night. Anyone in the first column who I couldn't connect to at least one of the listings in both the second and third columns could probably be ruled out as a suspect.

The first column filled rapidly with more than a dozen names, ranging from Bill Gray to the McIntoshes, to Roger and even my uncle and aunt. But then there was Inman Greene. I couldn't directly connect him to anyone on the list. There could be, and probably were, others. I ended up with a series of question marks at the bottom representing a person or persons unknown.

The second column was equally problematic. Greene was ranting about my—what did he say?—"dredging up things that might be embarrassing to ATH." It was hard to see how the actions of a single middle-level employee could have some negative effect on a huge publicly-traded company. Could Laura have been involved with Bill Gray or one of the other Directors? Possibly, but in the world of big business such peccadilloes were hardly unusual.

How about her research? Everyone seemed to agree she'd been responsible for a huge advance in the science of biofuels. If Laura's personal life was a mess, would that have any bearing on the products of her research? Not likely. On the other hand, the process was still secret. Were there as yet unrevealed toxic byproducts, or some other major problem someone was trying to cover up? Not likely either, especially since ATH had broken ground for a new plant costing several hundred million dollars.

Or did Laura have some other secret? Something she knew that could hurt someone, or the company for that matter? There was still no good explanation for the drugs the manager found in her apartment. Like the first, I finished the second column with a series of question marks.

The third column was easier, but no more helpful. In terms of having the wherewithal to try to intimidate me, I could safely rule out most of the names in the first column. Someone from ATH was probably involved, but that someone could be one of the question marks. Greene, or perhaps one of the other county commissioners, could have set it up, but why? Greene was concerned about "embarrassing" ATH. I suspected all of them were more worried about something that might have an effect on the price of their newly purchased ATH stock. Again, I added question marks to the bottom of the column.

It was probably all an exercise in futility. If there were an obvious connection Roger would have thought of it, even if he did seem obsessed at the moment with Laura's death and the plane crash.

Maybe I didn't have enough information. Maybe there was something in the corporate or business structure of ATH that would make the stock price vulnerable to some negative news or rumor. I had little or no interest in the stock market, but between what I'd inherited from my Aunt Lillie and my father, I seemed to have a hefty portfolio. I usually left the management of it to my broker in Atlanta, taking only a minimal interest in the statements that arrived like clockwork on the tenth of every month. I dug through the desk drawer in the study until I found his card. His name was Scott Averbush, and like the portfolio, I'd inherited him from Aunt Lillie. We'd met just once, when he drove down to Walkerville to meet me a few months after her death.

It was eight forty-five. I figured he wouldn't mind my calling him at home, and if he did, too bad. He'd printed his number on the card. Scott greeted me like an old friend. "Matt! How are things down there in Walkerville?"

"There're good. I need a little favor from you, though."

"You name it."

"You're familiar with American Timber Holdings, right?"

"Of course. Who isn't? It's about the hottest stock out there at the moment. If you're calling to ask me to buy some for you, I'm one jump ahead. I picked up a couple of thousand shares for you about six weeks ago."

"How's it doing?"

"Through the roof, as they say. You bought at about eight and a half. It closed today at twenty-two and a fraction. You're way to the good."

"Fine. How much do you know about the company?"

"Our analysts say it's poised for a long uphill run. You've heard about their biofuel plant project?"

"Of course, they're building it here in Adams County. But that's not what I want to know. Can you find out what's been driving the stock price up, and if there's anything that might send it plunging?"

"Well, I'll tell you right now what's driving it—the market. Investors want it and they're buying it so the price goes up. What more do you need to know?"

"I want to know if the run-up is justified, or if it's speculation. I want to know if there are any problems on the horizon."

"Matt, who cares as long as you're making money? It's the old buy low, sell high. When the stock peaks, we'll dump it and buy the next one."

If I'd been standing in the same room with him I think I'd have thrown something at him. I tried to sound calm. "Scott, I have a fairly large account with you, don't I?"

"Absolutely. I won't say you're my biggest client, but you rate on up there. You get your statements every month. Why do you want to know?"

"Again, I want you to do me a favor...," I paused for emphasis, "...and in exchange for that I'm going to let you to continue to manage my account."

His tone immediately became serious. "Uh..., right. What can I do for you?"

"I want you to do an in-depth analysis of American Timber Holdings. I want you to pull the annual report, the thing they have to file with the SEC, the K-1...."

"You mean the 10-K?"

"Yeah, that. And aren't officers and directors supposed to file reports when they buy or sell company shares?"

"Yes, the reporting requirements are pretty strict now. Under Sarbanes-Oxley they have ten days to…."

"Good. Do it. Call whoever you need to find out all there is to know about ATH."

"Got it." A clumsy silence, then, "Why are you so interested? We're making money and…."

"Just do it."

"Right. Give me a few days."

"I'll be waiting," I said and hung up without saying goodbye.

CHAPTER Forty-Two

I half-expected to hear from Roger the following morning, but didn't. Sandra called again, still concerned about my injury. Once I'd reassured her I was healing nicely, she launched into a long account of how well the company was doing as word of the new biofuel plant reverberated through the investment community. I pretended to listen but for the most part tuned her out, dropping an occasional "Really?" or "That's great," as I tried to decide what to do about our relationship. I wanted to see her, but couldn't shake a nagging and nonspecific uncertainty that floated somewhere in the back of my thoughts. She jolted me back to reality with, "Well, do you? Are you listening to me, Matt?"

"Yes, I'm sorry. I was just thinking…"

"Well, do you?" I hadn't been paying attention and had no idea what she was talking about.

"Sure, but I need to…." I had to think of something to say.

She saved me with, "Like I said, it's going to be two weeks from Friday at the Piedmont Driving Club. Black tie. It'll be the ATH directors, the division heads and their spouses. Bill Gray told me not to worry about the cost. I can't show up without some great-looking guy to make all the old men jealous. That's why I want you…."

"Arm candy." I tried not to sound sarcastic.

She laughed. "Oh, come on, Matt. It'll be fun."

"Okay, I'm in," I said, thinking that would buy some time until I could figure things out. She apologized, saying she had to get back to work, and hung up. I had no idea what I was going to do.

The rest of the day passed quietly. Eula Mae came and went, busying herself around the house without a lot to say. She was still in a mood. The cut on the back of my head ached less, but the staples were beginning to itch. I tried to do some work on the stables, but quickly lost interest and headed back to the house for a beer.

Shortly after five Roger pulled in the back yard driving the Barmore and Son pickup. It was covered with dust and could have used a good wash. I watched him, unseen, from my perch on the dogtrot sofa. He eased the truck to a halt at the foot of the back steps and sat for a moment, his hands locked on the wheel, his eyes staring straight ahead. Then, leaning over to the passenger's seat, he picked up a manila envelope and pulled out a document which he studied intently, clenching his jaw and pursing his lips as he read. Tossing it back on the seat, he reached toward the ignition, started the motor, and almost immediately shut it off. He grabbed the envelope again, took a deep breath and opened the door to trudge up the steps. I greeted him at the top, stuck a beer in his hand and pointed him toward the kitchen table.

Roger sat down, took a long draw on his beer and said, "I got the report from the crime lab, and, uh…, it was, uh…, positive." His voice cracked.

"Yeah. But I guess we knew that, didn't we?"

He nodded. "We did, but this was the DNA report. The one on…, you know, the specimen."

"Right."

"But it didn't really show what I thought it would show. They…, she, I mean the lady who did it for me, she…, she…." He was having to pry out every word.

He took another drink and said, "You know the specimen they tested was the…, uh…."

"The vaginal swab."

He nodded. "Yeah. And well, the results were not exactly what I expected. Laura…, she…, apparently hadn't had sex with…." He stopped in mid-sentence and slid the envelope across the table to me. "Oh, hell! You read it."

I folded back the clasps and extracted a thin sheaf of stapled pages. A fax cover sheet from the State Crime Lab was on top. I flipped past tables of numbers, graphs and immunoelectrophoresis patterns and found the summary on the last page. As I scanned it, the words leapt off the paper:

....can be said with certainty that this specimen, which was originally observed to contain motile sperm, does <u>not</u> contain genetic material from the decedent David L. Hargrove (CL#21-8107). Two distinct and genetically unrelated patterns of male DNA are defined, however, and further testing of specific surface antigens indicate that these correlate with two separate intermingled populations of spermatozoa. While no conclusions can be...

It took a moment for the technical jargon to sink in. She'd had sex with two men shortly before she died, neither of whom was David Hargrove. I looked up at Roger. "I can see why you're upset. I'm really sorry."

He took a deep breath and walked over to the refrigerator to find another beer. "What can I say? Maybe you're right. Maybe it *is* time I faced reality."

"That might be good. You keep grabbing at straws. The little wrench thing you found in the plane, or that piece of plastic.... You keep hearing hoof beats outside the window and think it's a herd of zebras. Everything I've seen or heard points in just one direction."

"They do, but new things keep popping into my mind. I thought about something today. Do you remember they found Laura's driver's license in the plane wreckage?" I nodded. "It was in a purse. She never carried a purse. I mean, she had purses, but she said the only people she knew who carried purses were old women. She usually had her driver's license, a couple of credit cards and a few dollars in a little clip she'd stick in her pocket. The only time I ever saw her carrying a purse was at church, or a wedding, or something like that." He still hadn't given up.

I didn't say anything, thinking I should just let him vent. Instead of talking, though, Roger finished his beer in silence before saying "I guess I need to get on home." He picked up the envelope and rose to head toward the door.

"If you need to talk...," I started.

Turning back, he said, "Oh, I did forget one thing." He reached in the envelope and brought out a slim plastic case with a DVD inside. "This came in the mail this morning. It's a copy of the surveillance tapes from the Winder airport. The ones that are supposed to show David and Laura taking the plane. I talked with the airport manager on the phone. He said no one from law enforcement has even looked at them. Someone from the GBI called up right after the crash and asked him if he could confirm it was Hargrove who drove to the airport that night. He reviewed the videos, and recognized Hargrove, and could see a girl in the background he supposed was Laura, but didn't know because he'd never met her. I don't think I want to see her—especially like that. You suppose you could look at them for me? You can play the DVD on your computer."

"Roger, do you really think I need to? When are we going to say we've learned everything we need to know?"

He looked at the floor for a moment, then said, "I made a promise to chase down every lead. I can ask someone else if you want me to."

"No, that's fine. Just wanted to be sure."

He handed me the envelope with the DNA report and DVD. "If you don't see anything, just trash those. I don't think I need to keep them." With a brief, grim smile, he turned and walked out the door.

CHAPTER Forty-Three

I stood on the back stoop and watched Roger drive out of the yard. Maybe he'd given up, maybe not. Time would tell. I looked down at the envelope in my hand, thinking the best option would be to shred it and forget the whole thing. But I couldn't do that with a clear conscience. I'd promised him I'd look at the airport videos.

Grabbing another beer, I settled down at my desk in the study and examined the DVD. It was a standard-format recordable disc, labeled in indelible black ink "Winder Airport" followed by the date. I slipped it into the computer and reviewed a list of files on the screen. There were seven in all, with names evidently describing the location of the cameras: "Gate 1" and "Gate 2," "Keypad," and "Field 1" through "Field 4." I double-clicked "Gate 1" and was rewarded with a screen view of a driveway blocked by chain-link gate and what appeared to be an entry keypad on one side. The scene was mostly in shadow, with partial light from an unseen street lamp nearby. A time stamp on the bottom of the screen ticked off the seconds in real time.

At 31 seconds past 11:32 p.m. the gate was illuminated by headlights, followed by a silver C-class Mercedes pulling up slowly and stopping next to the keypad. The overhead camera seemed to be positioned primarily to record the tag number of the vehicle and not its driver or occupants. The window slid down smoothly. In the dim light I could barely discern a male hand reaching out and punching a code into the pad, followed by the gate winching back, then closing automatically some 15 seconds later. The video ticked off another 30 seconds before the screen went dark.

I clicked the restart button and watched the scene again, this time focusing on the time stamp at the bottom. The video recorder was programmed to save data only when it sensed motion or changes in light, capturing the scene from 30 seconds before until 30 seconds after all motion had ceased. I clicked the "Gate 2" file and watched the same scene from a camera positioned above the inside of the gate, apparently designed to record the license plates of departing vehicles. The angle was not ideal, but I could see enough through the windshield to make out a man in the driver's seat and a long-haired woman next to him.

The "Keypad" video was far more interesting. It must have been taken from a hidden pinhole camera just above the entry keypad, triggered to record by the first press of a button. The lens was not of the best quality, producing a wide-angle view that seemed to distort everything at the periphery of the field. A magnified, outstretched hand disappeared off the bottom of the screen, and led back toward the face of a ruggedly handsome man with a close-cropped dark mustache. Beyond him in the shadow of the car, I could recognize Laura. The hand moved, then withdrew as the man's head swiveled to his right, apparently looking at the gate. He then turned back toward the camera and said something while peering straight into the lens. The video did not have a sound track, so I had no idea what he was saying. Laura stared straight ahead the entire time, either not hearing or not acknowledging the man's words. The window slid shut and the car pulled ahead. The video continued for another thirty seconds before going dark.

I played it again several times, looking for something I might have missed. I could see Laura clearly; there was no doubt as to her identity. As for the driver, he had to be David Hargrove, but I wasn't sure. The only photos I'd seen of him were those of his body from the GBI's and NTSB's files taken after the crash. He'd required DNA for a positive ID. I'd asked his friend Reich for a photo, and got a box full, which I hadn't opened. They were still where I'd left them weeks before on the back seat of my truck.

I played the video a couple more times. As the car pulled forward, I got a transient look at the back seat through the rear driver's side window. The light was dim and the reflection from the glass prevented seeing anything. I magnified the screen shot, focusing on Hargrove's lips, trying to understand what he was saying as he looked at the camera. I got nowhere.

My beer had gotten warm and I'd lost interest in drinking it. I dumped it down the kitchen sink and went out to the truck to get the box of Hargrove's photos. The one on top was all I needed to see. It was an eight-by-ten close-up color shot of his face, apparently taken at a mountain resort. He was wearing a wool cap with goggles pulled up on his head, grinning into the camera with the ruddy-faced flush of a downhill skier. There was no doubt that the man in the photo and the man in the video were one and the same. I put the box on the dining room table, thinking perhaps I should send the photos to his parents.

The other four videos were taken from cameras mounted to record events near the hangars and on the runways. "Field 3" and "Field 4" were shots of the Cessna taxiing and taking off in the dim light. It appeared to be the same aircraft whose remains now lay rusting in the aircraft graveyard. "Field 1" caught a view of the Mercedes turning down a driveway toward what appeared to be aircraft hangars and disappearing out of sight behind a building.

"Field 2" took over where "Field 1" left off, showing the car turning onto a long paved drive with hangars on one side and a taxiway on the other. The headlights at first blinded the camera, then, as the automatic iris adjusted for the bright lights it showed the car turn and park between two buildings with only its rear third still in view. It was at least a hundred yards distant. The entry door to the hangar must have been on the side. The interior light in the Mercedes came on, then went off a minute later. Thirty seconds thereafter, the screen went dark, then reappeared after a thirty-two minute gap as the hangar door opened, flooding the taxiway with light. A figure emerged from the hangar door, opened the trunk of the Mercedes and lifted something out before closing it and reentering. Shadows from the interior played back and forth in the light on the taxiway. A couple of minutes later the Cessna eased out, engine running. It made a sharp turn and rapidly taxied toward the runway. I played the scene over and over, magnifying it to try to see more of the man in the light of the open trunk. All I could make out were shadows, but there was something strange about the way the man walked. I wasn't sure what, but it just wasn't right.

The airport videos had shown nothing. Or at least nothing I could put my finger on. But still, what was Hargrove saying to the camera? What was it that gave me a strange feeling about the figure in the video? I lifted the DVD out of the computer tray and looked at it. The shredder sat ready next to my desk. I reached to drop it in, then changed my mind, slipped it back into the case, and slid the case back into the envelope.

CHAPTER Forty-Four

I walked out into the yard and through the boxwood maze, settling on the bench where Sandra and I had watched the fireflies. The sun was below the horizon now, and the pink reflection from a few clouds floating high overhead bathed the garden in a soft light. I thought about Roger and his apparent paranoia. He kept hinting at conspiracies, yet he'd never voiced any believable scenario as an alternative explanation for Laura's death. He just kept casting bits and pieces, little shreds of doubt. Perhaps they were in fact small articles of faith in someone he'd loved. I didn't know.

But now I wasn't so sure either. However crazy some of Roger's ideas might have sounded, they didn't earn me the cut on the back of my head. I stared off into the dusk, turning things over in my mind. I closed my eyes and mentally played back scenes from the airport video. I could see Laura's face. She was looking straight ahead, expressionless. A guy and a girl out for a night of kinky fun? It was all wrong. And what was Hargrove saying as he punched in the code to open the gate?

I pulled out my cell phone and dialed Wayne Guillard's home number. I told him what I wanted and was answered by a deep-throated belly laugh. "Oh, come on, Matt. I know you're joking now. First you call me up and want to know the survival time of sperm, and now you're looking for someone who can read lips. You gotta be kidding."

"I'm serious, Wayne."

He caught the tone of my voice. "You are, aren't you?" Then, "Well, there was something in the paper last week about the school system hiring a new speech therapist. They gave a little reception for her down at the school board office. She could probably help you—or at least would know who might. You said you wanted someone who could look at a video without a soundtrack and try to read someone's lips, right?"

"Right."

"Weird," he said, and promised to call me the next morning with her phone number.

✈ ✈ ✈ ✈

Were it not for the initials "B. S., M.S" after her name, and the title "Speech-Language Pathologist" under it, I could have mistaken Krista Nielsen for a high school sophomore on her summer break. She was small-framed, with snow-blond hair and intense blue eyes. "So how did you get my name?" she asked.

"I called one of the local physicians who'd seen it in the paper, who in turn called the school board to get your home phone number which he passed on to me."

"Oh," she said, a slightly amused look on her face. "You know, this is my first job out of school—and my first time in the South. It's not much different from home."

"Which is...?"

"Lac de Fourchette. You've never heard of it. It's a little village in northern Minnesota, about like Walkerville. I guess small towns are the same everywhere." We were sitting on the sofa in her apartment surrounded by hills of packing boxes. "Tell me again exactly what you wanted me to do."

"I want to know if you can help me figure out what someone is saying on a video. You can see his lips moving, so you know he's talking, but there's no sound recording."

"Uh..., should I ask what's this all about?"

"It's a long story. I'm trying to help out a friend."

She shrugged. "Let's see it."

I set up my laptop on top of a large box labeled "Kitchen Stuff" and pulled up the "Keypad" video. "This was taken from a camera in a keypad that's used to open a gate," I explained. "You'll see what I'm talking about in a minute." David Hargrove's face appeared on the screen. Krista studied it intently, then rewound and played it a couple more times.

"Who are these people?" she asked.

"One of them was a friend," I said.

"Was?" She gave me a puzzled look. "Well, I hope it wasn't the girl. She's not a happy camper. Look at the expression on her face. Lips fixed, slightly pursed. Eyes narrowed." She pointed at the screen. "See there, how she's clenching her jaw? She's either very angry, or very afraid—I don't know which. Maybe both."

"But how about the guy? Can you tell what he's saying?"

"I don't think he's saying anything. His lips are moving but I don't think he's speaking."

"What do you mean?"

Krista backed up the video to just before the point where Hargrove started talking. "Look here, see how he exaggerates his lip movements. He's over-articulating, like…"

"What?"

"Over-articulating. Like an actor might do when he's looking into a camera." She paused. "I take it he knew he was looking at a camera, right?"

I hadn't thought of that. "I guess so."

"See here," she reversed the video and played it again, "his lip movements are far in excess of what is necessary to generate the words he's trying to say. And, too, look at the girl in the background there. She doesn't react or respond to him. Maybe she's mad or upset about something, but a more likely explanation is that the guy's miming for the camera and she's not hearing anything."

I studied the screen. She appeared to be right. "But can you tell what he's saying?"

Krista took a deep breath and said, "Give me a minute." She ran the video back and forth, silently mimicking the movement of Hargrove's lips with her own. I watched her in silence. After a moment she said, "I'm not sure."

"Any guesses?"

"Well, I think—and I'm not sure about this—that I can pick out the phrase 'help us' in the first part." She pointed at the screen again. "See here how his lips move. He's emphasizing the 'h.' The 'u' sound in 'us' is throwing me off, though. It's guttural, from way back in the throat. That's really about all I can say."

"Nothing else? There's more after that."

"I know, but like I said, he's over-articulating—acting for the camera, I'd guess. It actually makes reading his lips harder."

"But can you pick out anything? A word, a name, maybe?"

"Not really. I thought for a minute I could read something into what he's saying, but it just doesn't make sense. And it's only one word, anyway."

"It might make sense to me. What was it?"

She ran the video forward to just before Hargrove stopped speaking. "See here, how he's pressing his tongue against his lower teeth? That's associated with a 'k' sound, as in 'key.' And it's a long word. I know it's crazy, but it looks like he's saying 'kidnapped.'"

CHAPTER Forty-Five

Krista Nielsen had joined ranks with Roger, tossing another morsel of doubt into the mix. I thanked her and offered to pay for her time, which she accepted in the form of my lifting a heavy TV up to a shelf in an entertainment center she was setting up in her living room. I still couldn't decide whether or not to call Roger. I knew I'd have to eventually, but given his Procrustean propensity to adjust the facts to fit whatever theory he must be harboring in his mind, I decided to wait until my own thoughts were a little clearer on the subject. I drove back to the house and put the DVD in the safe.

It was nearly noon. Eula Mae had set out a bowl of rewarmed butterbeans, fresh local corn, and some pork chops she'd smother-fried in thick gravy. She was evidently in a better mood. "You havin' a good day?" she asked, a bit more formally than usual. "Seems like you been studyin' 'bout something."

"Yeah," I said, digging into the butterbeans. "I'm still thinking about this thing with Laura McIntosh."

"Why you worryin' 'bout that? Ain't nothin' you can do now. You hoped them old folks—her mama and daddy. You done yo' piece."

"Still, there're a few things that…."

I was interrupted by the ringing of the phone. Eula Mae picked it up, announcing, "Rutherford residence," then placing her hand over the receiver and asking, "Does you wanna talk to somebody from Atlanta, says his name is Scott somethin'? Says he buys stocks for you."

"Yes, I'll get it in the study." I put my fork down under Eula Mae's disapproving look, questioning how anything could be more important than country-fried pork chops and vegetables.

I sat down at my desk and picked up the phone. "Scott, how's it going? Got anything for me?"

"Yeah, and I want you to know that since you and I talked I've spent about six hours on-line and talking with our New York office about American Timber Holdings." He paused. "Maybe I didn't make myself clear the other day. You really are an important customer to me and I didn't want you to think...."

"Yeah, yeah. Just cut to the bottom line. Is anything going on with ATH that may not be evident to the general public?"

"Well, yes and no. In fact it's hard to even begin to answer that question. There's no doubt ATH stock is one of the hottest things around at the moment. Hell, it's up another four and a half bucks a share since we talked the other day. Our guys still have a firm 'Buy' recommendation out on it, and given what looks to be their future with this cellulosic ethanol thing, they're probably going to come out with a 'Buy/Hold' recommendation, which means a lot of people out there will add it to their IRAs.

"But see, here's the problem. A lot of times the price of a stock doesn't necessarily reflect what's actually happening at the moment; it reflects what the market thinks is *going to happen* in the future. I mean, for example, you take a big oil company. They may be rocking along just fine, and then they announce they've found a big field of high grade crude somewhere in the Gulf of Mexico. Well, it may take them two or three years to get the wells drilled and the pipelines in place, but the stock price will zoom up overnight. Same thing here with ATH. My guys tell me it's going to be twelve to eighteen months at best before they can start producing ethanol in quantity, but the market has already pressed the top button on the elevator. When it comes right down to it, in terms of the company's ability to make money not a hell of a lot has changed in the last couple of years. And won't until they get some of their new plants built."

"So, what does that mean?"

"I'm not sure, so I tried looking at it another way. I pretended for a moment that ATH hadn't done any biofuel research, and started examining them just for what they are—a very big timber company with huge land holdings, a number of mills, and lots of employees. In other words, a lot of assets. You with me?"

"I think so. You wanted to assess the underlying fundamentals of the company?"

"Exactly. The most basic form of accounting. Assets are on one side of the balance sheet, and liabilities on the other. When you start looking at just those two things—assets and liabilities—a whole different picture emerges. Matt, they're up to their eyeballs in debt. Most of the other big forest products companies unloaded a lot of their timberland years ago and cut way back on their debt load. ATH apparently looked at that route, and then rejected it, instead bringing in a new CEO, Cranston Gray, to turn things around. Gray's baby has been the alternative fuels-ethanol thing, and it looks like he's hit a hole-in-one. He just better hope things work out as planned. If not, he'll be in deep doo-doo."

Scott paused a moment, taking a deep breath. "But there's something else, too. You don't happen to have a copy of their annual report there at your house, do you?"

I thought of the one Margaret had given me as cover for slipping me the personnel directory. "As a matter of fact, I do," I said, and put him on hold while I found it in my briefcase.

Scott continued, "Open it up, and look toward the back on page 45, at the top, under the heading 'Other Compensation Paid to Officers and Directors.' If you scan that section, it's pretty much legalese gobbledygook, but what it says is that the Directors and the CEO all got hefty stock options which are based on 'certain performance goals.' It's one of those things most people would just look at and skip over. What's there in the annual report doesn't—by itself, at least—raise any red flags.

"But Matt, I saw that and got to thinking about it. I said there's got to be something more on those 'performance goals' somewhere, so I went back and pulled all the annual reports, 10-Ks and every other SEC filing I could find on ATH for the past seven years. That's when I began to worry. You know about stock options, right?"

"Pretty much. I had a few myself at one time."

"They got to be pretty popular back in the 1990s. CEOs were demanding multimillion dollar salaries, but if the company's stock tanked, the shareholders would stage a revolt and fire the Directors. So, in the best spirit of insider trading, compensation committees began to grant their executives options to buy the company's stock at a certain fixed price at a later date. If the stock went up, the execs could unload it on the open market, and it wouldn't appear as salary on the annual report balance sheets."

"I know all that. So?"

"Well, with Gray, they cut quite a deal. I had trouble finding all this—it's out there, but not all pulled together in one place. And even then, I had to get some inside stuff from a contact of mine who used to be on ATH's Board of Directors.

"About five or six years ago when American Timber Holdings was looking for a new CEO, the Directors' biggest concern was finding someone who could turn the company around. They interviewed quite a few candidates, but ended up picking Cranston Gray, based on an unusual promise. He told them this. Give me six months to figure out the problems, and five years to fix them. He said grant me some stock options as a signing bonus, then give me an equal amount at the end of each anniversary I stay with the company. Fix the strike price—that's the price he can buy the options for—at whatever the price of ATH's stock is the day I sign on. Make them all expire at the end of five years and six months—in other words, the time frame in which he promised to turn the company around. In exchange, he took a low salary—I think it's only a couple of million bucks a year—and put all his chips on his ability to make ATH's stock soar."

Scott paused, waiting for my response. "Looks like his gamble paid off," I said.

"You're right, and guess when his options expire."

"Shortly?"

"In thirteen days. He's already started exercising and unloading them."

"How much is he due to make?"

"I can't be exactly sure, but I know that he got options for a quarter million shares as a signing bonus, then another quarter million on each anniversary during the five years he's been there. That makes a total of a million and a half shares. Again, I'm not certain, but I think his strike price would be around four bucks a share. As of today, ATH is trading at thirty-two and a quarter—so that's, what?—twenty-eight times…," I could hear the sound of a desktop calculator chattering in the background, "…one-point-five million, equals…, Hey, looks like the guy's gonna get a forty-two million dollar payday this year. Not bad for five years' work."

"Not bad at all," I echoed, thinking any number with six or so zeros behind it might drive someone to commit rash deeds.

"Oh, and one more thing," Scott said. "You may call me a fool later, but I dumped your ATH stock. You've made a hell of a profit anyway, and I think it's time to let someone else ride the rollercoaster to the top."

CHAPTER Forty-Six

I thanked Scott and hung up. It was probably just another episode in the great world of American business. There was no direct connection to Laura, of course, but if I believed Scott, her research had almost single-handedly created millions in wealth for a select group of insiders, including Bill Gray.

But then, that argument alone would be the best reason in the world to want Laura alive and actively working for the company. I pushed the thought to the back of my mind and headed into the kitchen to finish my lunch. I found my plate and the dishes of meat and vegetables in the oven where Eula Mae had put them to keep them warm. I could hear her in the adjacent dining room, humming softly to herself while she straightened up.

I finished eating and was moving my dishes to the sink when I heard the thud of a heavy object on the kitchen table behind me. Eula Mae was standing over the box of Hargrove's photos. "What you gon' do with these here things? They in the way o' my dustin'."

"Those are photographs…,"

"Well, I can see that!" Eula Mae sounded a bit offended.

"…of a dead man." She stepped back, taking her hands off the box.

"What you doin' with dead folks' pictures in the house? You know if they ain't relatives that be bad luck."

"They're of the guy who was killed in the plane crash with Laura. His…, uh, friend gave them to me." Eula Mae took another step back.

"Well, I thinks you need to get them outta here. Ain't no sense in takin' chances with yo' luck."

"You're right. I need to. Why don't you just leave them there on the table? I want to send them to his parents, but I think I'd better sort through them first." Eula Mae nodded and headed back to her cleaning. What I didn't say was that I wanted to get rid of anything that might be embarrassing. Let the dead rest in peace.

I went back in the study to try to decide what I needed to do next. Assuming for the moment Krista Nielsen was right—that Hargrove did say "help us," or "kidnapped" or both, then who might want them dead? And how could they have pulled it off? A plane can't take off by itself. And why were they naked?

Maybe I'd been wrong all along. I'd been focusing on Laura and ignoring the possibility Hargrove could have been the target and she an innocent person who happened to be in the wrong place at the wrong time. Still more questions than answers. I needed to know more about Hargrove, and I needed to know more about what was going on at ATH. The one person who might know something about both was Margaret Powell, William Reich's mother.

The American Timber Holdings Annual Report was on the desk in front of me. I flipped it open and found the main number for the corporate offices on the front page. I asked the switchboard to connect me to Margaret Powell in Sandra William's office. A familiar voice answered, "This is Mrs. Powell. How may I help you?"

"This is Matt Rutherford."

There was a pause, then, "Yes?"

"I need to talk with you."

"Are you sure that's necessary? I'm not at all certain there is anything more I can do to be of assistance to you." She was being excessively formal. Someone was standing nearby.

I said, "Do you still have my cell phone number?"

"Yes." I told her to call me when she could talk. "I'll be glad to do that for you. Thanks for calling." The line went dead.

Five minutes later my cell phone rang. "Mr. Rutherford, I don't think I should be talking with you. I..., I need my job. I don't want anything...."

"Margaret, no one is going to know we've talked. There are some things that have come up—some new things—and I need to get your perspective. I need to see what you think. I swear to you, we'll keep this totally off the record."

There was a moment of silence. "The police are not involved, are they?" I wondered why she'd ask.

"No. So far as I know there's no evidence a crime has been committed." I heard what sounded like a sigh.

"What do you want to talk about?"

"Why don't I tell you when I see you?"

"Tell me now. It may be that I don't want to see *you*."

"About David Hargrove, and who might want to hurt him." I paused. "And about the company."

"I can't tell you any corporate secrets."

"I don't want you to. I just need perspective. Just facts, as you see them."

Another long silence. I heard traffic passing in the background. She must have been standing on the sidewalk. "I'll call in sick tomorrow. Meet me at ten at the Waffle House at the Evans Mill Road exit off I-20. It's just past the Stonecrest Mall exit if you're coming into town. There shouldn't be many people there that time of day. If anything happens, and I can't make it, can I call you at this number?"

"Of course."

"Okay. Let me give you my cell phone number in case you're running late or can't make it. I don't want to wait too long."

"Sure," I said, fumbling on the desk for a pen and something to write on. I flipped open the back inside cover of the ATH Annual Report and scribbled her number on the blank page before hanging up.

I don't know if you call it serendipity, or fate or what, but for some reason my eyes drifted to the other page on the inside of the back cover, a listing in small type of the printer's name and various photographic credits. The sentence leaped out at me: "Cover photograph and photos on pages 4, 16, 33(top), 34 and 37 © by Anthony M. Rizzoli and Rizzoli Media Services."

CHAPTER Forty-Seven

There could be only one Anthony M. Rizzoli. The "nicest man," by Agnes McIntosh's description. The man behind "The Mile High Club" articles. I had no idea who he was but I needed to find out. Atlanta's a big city, but Rizzoli's connection to both the McIntoshes and American Timber Holdings had to be more than simple coincidence.

What I wanted from Margaret wouldn't take me that long. I'd probably be free by eleven. I'd have plenty of time to drop by and pay a visit to the mysterious Mr. Rizzoli. I remembered his card gave an address somewhere in Atlanta's midtown. He shouldn't be too difficult to track down for an unannounced visit.

And Sandra. I didn't know what to do about her. Admittedly, my attraction to her was at first a physical one, but now I wasn't so sure. I had this uneasy sense that my feelings for her were beginning to change into something more, and I found the prospect unsettling. I still hadn't gotten over Lisa, and didn't think I needed to be so deeply involved with anyone for a while. But if I had to be in Atlanta to see Margaret Powell, I could spend some time with Sandra, maybe try to sort things out. I looked at my watch. She'd probably still be in her office. I dialed her cell phone.

"That's wonderful!" she said when I told her I was going to be in town. "I was hoping you'd call. I have absolutely nothing planned for the weekend— Actually, I turned down a couple of things just in case you wanted to get together.

You can stay at my place, of course? And dinner. We have to go out to dinner. I'll get reservations at this great little Peruvian restaurant over near...."

"Whoa," I said, slowing her down for a moment. "I've just got to be in town on business. We don't need to do anything special."

"But we do," she protested. "I've been wanting to call you, to see you, but I didn't want to make a pest of myself." She hesitated, then, "Matt, I'm not really sure how to say this, but I like you a lot. A whole lot. I'm not trying to become a part of your life, but I want us to spend some time together. I want us to get to know one another. I...."

"Shhh," I said, hushing her. "I want to see you, too. We can talk about all this later." She gave me the address of her condo and I said I'd meet her there at six the next afternoon. I hung up thinking it had been a long time since I felt butterflies in my stomach.

✈ ✈ ✈ ✈

If Margaret Powell were looking for somewhere we'd be unlikely to be recognized, she couldn't have picked a better place than a Waffle House just off the expressway east of Atlanta. It was familiar in a generic way. I'd spent plenty of hung-over Sunday mornings in Waffle Houses during my college years. I've often imagined one would be relatively cheap to build. They use the same basic plan over and over, a narrow box of a restaurant that can be shoehorned onto whatever leftover sliver of land has good visibility from the nearest major highway. They're the sort of places that serve greasy food ordered from plastic-laminated menus, attracting the type of diners who slather ketchup on their hash-browns and mop the last drop of gravy from their plates with butter-soaked slabs of white bread.

I'd decided to arrive early to scope the place out. This particular franchise was located in an area dotted with low-end housing and cookie-cutter apartment complexes, mainly catering to a transient blue-collar population making ends meet while hoping for something better. As Margaret predicted, traffic seemed slow, with only half a dozen vehicles in the parking lot. I backed my truck into a spot at the far end and waited, watching the customers come and go.

At 9:55, a dark blue Honda Civic turned in and parked carefully several spaces away. I thought I recognized Margaret as the driver, but wasn't sure. She was wearing a head scarf and dark glasses that looked straight out of some 1950s spy movie. She stared at the entry drive for a moment and, satisfying herself that she hadn't been followed, scurried across the parking lot and into the restaurant. I waited a couple of minutes, then followed her.

The interiors of Waffle Houses are all variations on the same basic layout: a long counter with stools facing an industrial-sized skillet-stove, a couple of semi-private booths toward the back next to the restrooms, and a line of smaller booths against the windows on the side and front. Margaret had settled in one of the more private booths, her back to the entrance. She'd slipped off her scarf and glasses and buried her face in the menu.

She looked up nervously as I slid in the booth opposite her and ordered a cup of coffee. "I almost didn't come. I really shouldn't be here," she said, glancing furtively over her shoulder. "Are you sure you weren't followed?"

"Why would I be?" I replied.

"You don't have any idea, do you?"

"About what?"

"About what's going on."

"Going on where? At ATH?" She glanced over her shoulder again, then nodded. I said, "Do you?" I had no idea what she was talking about.

"Not really. I just..., I just have my suspicions."

"Look, Margaret, I didn't ask you here to talk about the company. There are just some things..., some things that have come up about Laura and David's deaths. Everyone, including the authorities, think it was all a terrible accident. But I want to be certain nothing's been missed."

"Why?"

I wasn't sure how to answer her. "I don't know. Just a feeling." I spontaneously rubbed the cut on the back of my head. "And I think I'm safe in saying you worry things are not right, too."

She nodded. "So what do you want to know? I won't tell you anything, but if you ask the right questions, I'll try to answer them."

"Tell me about David Hargrove. Do you know of any reason someone might want him out of the picture?"

"Oh, no. Not David. He was the one person who didn't seem to have any enemies. From what I know, he was deathly afraid someone would discover that he was gay, so he tried to be everyone's friend. From what I knew of him through William, he was easy-going and just rolled with the punches. And I think I'd know, too, because part of my job is acting as liaison between the Human Resources group and the CEO. You pick up a lot of little things. I heard nothing but good about David. Everyone was shocked to hear about his death."

"So no one else knew he was gay?"

"Just Laura, so far as I know. Now, of course, I think a lot of people know. It came out later."

My theory had been shot down. I decided to head in another direction. "How about Laura? From all I've heard she was the one responsible for the breakthrough in the lab. Did she have any enemies—people at work she'd crossed? Were there any problems that hadn't been made public?"

The harsh glare of fluorescent lights has a way of paling a person's complexion. Despite this, I thought I saw the color drain from Margaret's face as she turned to stare out into the parking lot. After a moment she said, apropos of nothing, "You know, I used to live not far from here, just down the road there, really. I married young; I was just past twenty. His name was Rod. I still don't know why I married him. He was a truck driver—older than me. He stayed on the road most of the time and when he was home he liked to drink. He was a mean drunk, too. He'd yell at me, say the house wasn't clean enough, or that I was a lousy cook. He'd slap me around, make me feel lower than dirt. I guess I should have had the sense to leave him, but I got pregnant and thought maybe once he became a dad, he'd change.

"Well, he didn't. The baby came, and all he could talk about was the smell of diapers and how the crying at night kept him awake. He started spending more time on the road. I'd be by myself, just me and the baby, for a week or two at a time, and when he finally did come home, all he'd want to do was get drunk and demand sex.

"So I had an affair. He was a neighbor, not married, worked the night shift at the mill that used to be up the road there. He was kind and gentle, and would hug my baby like he was his own son. Then Rod showed up one afternoon, unexpectedly. He caught us in the act. There's no other way to put it. He beat both of us nearly to death. I was in the hospital for a week—I told them I'd fallen down some stairs. And my friend—I don't know what happened to him. I never saw him again, never heard from him. They told me he moved out of his place, but I don't know...." She paused and dabbed a tear from her eye.

"Anyway, after I got out of the hospital I moved in with my sister. Rod sued for divorce on the grounds of adultery. His family had some money and knew some people. They had me declared an unfit mother and took my child away. The court terminated my parental rights and banned me from seeing my precious baby.

"So, since I'd failed at marriage and motherhood, I went back to school, got my college degree and married Mr. Powell. He was nearly twenty-five years older than me. He didn't want any more kids, so we didn't have any. And now he's had a stroke and is in the nursing home. It's all I can do to pay his bills and keep up the house. Like I said, Mr. Rutherford, I need my job."

My question about Laura had started Margaret on her soliloquy. I said, "I'm sorry for all you've been through," and asked again, "Was something going on with Laura that no one knows about?"

Margaret sniffed and said, "I'm not sure. But there was something—I think it was a problem with the research—it came up about a month before her death. I don't know the details. I just overheard some of what was going on."

"Tell me about it."

"It was a Monday, if I remember correctly. Sandra usually handles Mr. Gray's appointments, but she was out that day—I think he'd sent her to the Denver office for something—so I was taking over her duties. Anyway, I got a call from Laura first thing, shortly after nine. She said she 'had to'—I remember those words, 'had to'—meet with Mr. Gray as soon as possible. I checked with him, and we cancelled a couple of appointments so he could meet with her about eleven.

"Laura arrived a little early. Clayton Wynne was with her. They had to wait a few minutes, and I could tell they were arguing between themselves about something. I don't know what; I couldn't hear what they were saying. Mr. Gray's earlier appointment left, and he told me he'd meet with Ms. McIntosh and Mr. Wynne in the conference room and that they were not to be disturbed for *anything*. He was real firm about it.

"Well, they'd been shut up in there for only about ten minutes when I heard some yelling. I could hear Laura saying, 'It's not going to work, dammit. We need more time.' And then Mr. Wynne said something like, 'We can do it. I know we can if we…' do something. I couldn't hear the rest. So I moved over close to the door pretending to look through a file cabinet so I could hear what was going on, but I couldn't. They'd lowered their voices, but you could tell they were still arguing.

"After about five minutes more, the door flies open and Laura is storming out. She turns back to them and says something like, 'One month. Thirty days. That's it. Either we do it or we make the announcement. And if you don't, I will.' Then she walked out and left the door to the conference room open. The next thing I know, I hear Mr. Gray saying something like 'That idealistic bitch,' and then he slams the door and he and Mr. Wynne stay shut up for another half an hour."

I waited for her to continue, but apparently she'd finished. I asked, "Was there anything more?"

Looking me straight in the eye, she said, "Mr. Rutherford, that was the last time I saw Laura McIntosh alive."

CHAPTER Forty-Eight

Margaret cautiously peeked over her shoulder again as if she half-expected a squad of goons armed with billy clubs to come rushing through the door. "But you didn't hear or see anything more?" I asked. "No threats? Nothing to suggest that anyone might want Laura out of the way?"

"No, but you've got to understand how it is. I just work there. I handle papers and reports. I do the administrative type of things that make the office run smoothly. I see people coming in and out all the time. Big people. Famous people. Rich people. Mr. Gray is a very powerful man. What they do—what they decide behind those doors—is what he likes to call 'corporate strategy.' Decisions are never written down, or if they are, they come from some division head or regional manager, or someone like that. This time with Laura and Clayton Wynne was different though. I just don't know…. I just had a feeling like things were not going as planned."

"But again, you have no knowledge that there was any direct threat to Laura or David from anyone inside the company."

"No," she said quietly, biting at her lip, and looking down. Then, raising her head, she continued, "I do know how things work, though. I've been there a long time. I've seen things happen—happen to people who didn't play the game, who thought they could do things their way. Reputations ruined, marriages destroyed, and worse. It's possible, Mr. Rutherford. When some little minor thing could send share prices plummeting, anything is possible."

I wasn't sure where to go in my questioning. "Okay, if that's the...."

She cut me off. "That's all I'm going to say. I need to go." She reached out to grab her scarf and sunglasses.

I laid my hand on her arm. She tensed her muscles. "Margaret, please. Just a few minutes more?" She was hinting at something, but I didn't know what I needed to ask her. I decided to try to buy some time by changing the subject. "Do you know a man named Anthony Rizzoli? He did some of the photos for ATH's last annual report." I could feel her relax.

"Mr. Rizzoli? Sure, I know him. He does photography and some freelance PR stuff for us sometimes. He's not the sort of person we normally use, though. He's..., he's..., how do I put it? He's too rough."

"So why do you hire him?"

"He's one of Mr. Gray's buddies. He moved down here to Atlanta shortly after Mr. Gray became the CEO. I think they knew each other up north, or something like that. Mr. Rizzoli—everybody calls him 'Tony'—called up and made an appointment. I sort of think Mr. Gray was surprised to hear from him. They slapped each other on the back and laughed and went out for drinks and all, and since then, we've been instructed to give him some of our business." She paused. "I really shouldn't be so negative. He does a good job." Another pause. "But why do you ask about Tony?"

"I don't know," I lied. "I'd seen his name in the list of credits in the corporate report. I thought it sounded familiar."

"Well, he doesn't just work for us—in fact, I'd say we're one of his smaller accounts. You may have seen his name in any number of places. He's not very polished, but I think he's pretty bright. Writes articles, does some paparazzi stuff when celebrities are in town—that kind of thing."

"No connection between him and Laura that you know of? Or David Hargrove?"

She looked at me strangely. "I don't know why you'd ask. No, none that I know of." A pause, then, "Oh, yes there is. He took some PR shots of her six or eight months ago for an article in the Georgia Tech alumni magazine. But as far as I know, that's it."

No help there, I thought. Margaret eased toward the edge of the booth, still grasping her scarf and glasses. There was one more thing I needed to know. "Let me ask you one more question."

She rolled her wrist over to see her watch. "I need to go. I can't have anyone see me talking with you. I'll give you three minutes."

"Tell me about Sandra."

A fleeting scowl crossed her face. "What do you want to know? And why?"

"Curiosity."

She stared into my eyes for a moment, then said, "She's a ruthless bitch. She'll do whatever it takes to make it to the top."

I returned her stare. "Why do you say that?"

"How do you think she got her job, Mr. Rutherford? She was a secretary in the research lab. One little smile at Mr. Gray, and suddenly she's his personal assistant. She's only been at ATH a few years. That's a big leap up the corporate ladder. You don't honestly think she got where she is because of her job skills?" There was anger in her voice. I'd asked the wrong question.

"I don't know. I thought you might tell me."

"It's her long blond hair and her short dresses," Margaret hissed, tying the scarf around her head as she edged out of the booth. "A woman like that is dangerous, Mr. Rutherford. I'd remember that if your question was prompted by anything other than simple curiosity." She slipped on the dark glasses and hurried off toward her car, head down as if she was avoiding a hailstorm.

I paid for my coffee and walked slowly back to my truck. I cranked up the air conditioning to full blast, eased the seat back and stared at the ceiling. I'd blown it with Margaret. I'd missed something, but didn't know what. And I'd made the mistake of asking about Sandra. Fool that I was, I should have realized that from Margaret's viewpoint, Sandra had probably stolen what she considered her rightful promotion. "Long blond hair and short dresses." That said it all. Sandra was everything Margaret was not.

But there was more. She must have wanted to tell me something—or at the least have me "discover" it. And it was secret and important, otherwise why did she keep looking over her shoulder, as if discovery might bring some bad consequence. I mentally kicked myself. I might have gotten somewhere if I hadn't asked about Sandra. The spite, the jealousy were all too obvious.

I eased the truck into gear and drove slowly down the frontage road searching for a pay phone with a directory, a rare commodity in these days of cell phones. After a couple of miles with no success I pulled into a seedy-looking convenience store and talked the dark-eyed latina behind the counter into letting me look at her copy of the greater Atlanta Yellow Pages.

Finding Rizzoli's address was no problem. His ad was displayed prominently under "Photographers, Commercial" with cute little icons of a camera on one side and a quill pen on the other. The copy read "Anthony M. Rizzoli" in bold font over "Rizzoli Media Services" in smaller type. A bulleted listing of his offerings included "Commercial Photography," "Public Relations," "Media Coordination," etc. He seemed to be a veritable jack of all trades, and master of at least one, I thought, given his success with the "Mile High" articles. I scribbled down his address and phone number.

Margaret hadn't been very helpful about Rizzoli. She hadn't reacted negatively to my asking about him, and she did say he worked independently. The idea of ATH being behind the smearing of Laura's reputation seemed disingenuous. After all, it was her work, and the company's belief in it, that had sent the stock price soaring. No, Rizzoli was probably just a guy who saw a chance to make a buck by capitalizing on a sordid tale of a beautiful girl and kinky sex. I wasn't sure he fit into the picture at all, but I felt like I needed to pay him a visit, just to be sure.

I looked at my watch. Eleven twenty-five. I punched his number into my cell phone and was greeted on the third ring by a recorded message in a male voice, Boston accent, that Mr. Rizzoli was "out on assignment," but all calls would be returned promptly. I left my cell phone number and the name Joseph M. Turner, thinking it would be unlikely he would be familiar with early nineteenth century English landscape painters. The chances were slim, but I wanted to be sure that he wouldn't recognize me, and I didn't want him to connect my name in any way with Laura McIntosh or American Timber Holdings.

I got back on I-20 headed toward Atlanta, exiting when I spotted an office supply store in one of the malls that surrounded a sea of asphalt near the off-ramp. Finding the instant-print section, I had a hundred business cards printed in the name of Joseph M. Turner, Vice President for Sales with the Forest King Manufacturing Company of Macon, Georgia, a name I made up on the fly. I used my cell phone number and a fictitious post office box address embossed on high-quality white linen stock.

While the cards were being printed I went next door to a sandwich shop and settled in with a Philly cheese steak and a Coke. The phone rang just as I was finishing; I recognized the number on caller ID as Rizzoli's. I answered "Joe Turner."

The same Boston-accented male voice said, "Mr. Turner. This is Tony Rizzoli. I'm returning your call."

"Oh, yes, thank you so much for calling me back. I'm with the Forest King Manufacturing Company and we're looking for someone to do some photography for our next sales catalogue. I'd heard your name and...."

"That's right down my alley, Mr. Turner. I'm sorry I was out of my studio when you called earlier, but I'll be glad to meet with you and go over my portfolio."

"That's what I had in mind. I live near Macon, but I'm up here today in Atlanta on some business and was hoping I could drop by and talk with you this afternoon."

There was a slight hesitation. "I am so sorry, but I'm in north Georgia at the moment talking with a client. I'd called in to check my messages and got yours. It'll be late when I get back tonight. Any chance of meeting with you tomorrow? Or one day next week?"

I thought quickly. I'd planned to spend the next day with Sandra, but reasoned I could break away for an hour or so to talk with Rizzoli. "Sure, that'd be fine. I'm spending the night in town. Could we meet tomorrow morning?"

"I'm free all day. How about ten?"

I agreed and he gave me directions to his studio, located in midtown south of Piedmont Park. He continued, "If I'm going to show you some of my work, it'd be helpful if I knew what you manufacture. I can pull some stuff from my portfolio from similar projects."

"We manufacture custom logging equipment, mainly for smaller timber operations. Skidders, loaders that kind of thing."

"Well, that's a coincidence. I've done lots of work in that area." He lowered his voice slightly. "In fact, right now I'm visiting with the CEO of one of the largest timber companies in the US. He's a personal friend."

A cold chill swept over me. Too many coincidences.

CHAPTER Forty-Nine

I drove toward Atlanta somewhat aimlessly, trying to make some sense of things, flipping the brief conversation with Rizzoli back and forth in my mind. I was probably overreacting and needed to see him in person before trying to reach any conclusion. But he was unavailable, and I had several hours to kill before I was scheduled to meet Sandra. I veered north on the downtown connector, exited at 10th Street, and spent the next two hours in the fantasy world of the latest James Bond flick.

The movie was over shortly after five. It would take me fifteen minutes at most to make it to Sandra's condo. I plunged into the Peachtree traffic, relieved for the moment by the distraction. The butterflies were back. I wanted to see her, but I didn't know what I wanted to say. I don't think I've ever been rational about relationships. They just happen. You spend enough time around someone and things work out—or they don't. I'd always assumed there was some sort of occult natural selection process that guided it all. What's supposed to be will be, but overall, my track record has been one miserable string of losses. I had an idea about where Sandra wanted things between us to go. I was almost afraid to try to define what I wanted. But again, things work out, or they don't. I tend to wait for some sign. Maybe by tomorrow I'd know.

The address she'd given me was in the Peachtree Battle area of Buckhead. The neighborhood was an upscale mixture of stately homes and high-end condos less than a mile from Laura's old apartment, but on the other side of Peachtree Road. The jump across Peachtree raised house prices by a couple of hundred thousand, at the least. This was old Atlanta, with Mercedes in driveways and white-uniformed maids at bus stops.

Sandra's condo was located in what city planners euphemistically refer to as infill housing. The massive brick pillars and ornate iron gate at the entrance couldn't disguise the fact that the plot had been sliced from the original multi-acre back yard of a 1940s white-columned colonial mansion next door. A polished brass plaque announced one was entering Aldwych Place, the name no doubt adding a few tens of thousands to the selling price. The architect had done a good job. The units were townhouse style, each with its own unique design in brick or stone, with slate roofs and tasteful plantings. Short driveways disappeared into ground-floor three-car garages, with second floor entrances off raised porches. Copper gutters and downspouts, aged nicely to a brownish-green patina, added a finishing touch of quiet wealth.

Sandra's was No. 12 Aldwych Place, the next to the last on the right, she'd said. I cruised slowly, my big green pickup drawing a suspicious stare from a blue-haired matron watering the ferns that erupted from cast-iron urns at the base of her steps. I parked in a spot marked "Guest" and waved back at her smiling, hoping to avoid the hassle of explaining my presence to one of the private security services I'd seen cruising the neighborhood.

Sandra must have been watching from the window. She emerged from the front door and rushed down the stairs to give me a hug, much to the obvious dismay of her neighbor. "I'm so glad you're here," she said. "I was worried. I hadn't heard from you all day. I was kind of hoping you'd call."

"I'm sorry. I had a few things going on in Walkerville and was a little late getting out of town," I lied. I didn't want to mention Margaret Powell and Tony Rizzoli.

"Well, come on in," she said, putting her arm around my waist. "You sounded like you didn't want to go out tonight, so I picked up a few things at Fresh Market. We can graze and talk." She sounded genuinely excited to see me.

We trudged up the ornate brick stairs, their custom-molded treads ending in a herringbone pattern of stone pavers on the entry porch. Whoever built the condos had spared no expense. The fine mahogany door, its tight-grained pattern shining under layers of clear varnish, was flanked by fluted pilasters supporting a cast stone pediment in a matching shade of alabaster. The foyer was floored in a diagonal pattern of white and green marble, with columns on either side marking the entry into other formal rooms.

Sandra took my hand and led me to the back, past a stairway and into a sitting room that spanned the entire width of the house. French doors opened onto a balcony that looked down onto an intimate stone-walled courtyard. A gentle stream of water from a wall-mounted fountain trickled musically into a pool below. A ray of afternoon sunlight reflected briefly a glint of bright crimson as a koi broke the surface and descended again to hide below a small mat of dark green lilypads.

"You have a nice place," I said, trying to hide the understatement.

Sandra laughed. "It's not mine, of course. You know I could never afford this. It comes with the job."

"How so?"

"This condo is like the roof garden at the ATH Tower. It was one of those crazy things the previous CEO bought. Thought the company needed a private place to entertain, some place to put up big investors, pension fund managers, that sort. Of course now, the Feds have cracked down on all that, and it's sort of lost its purpose. But as Bill said, it's paid for and if we hold on to it long enough the company can probably sell it for a good profit. So I get to stay here, in exchange for paying the utilities and hosting an occasional private dinner party for whatever visiting dignitary Bill is trying to impress."

"Not a bad deal," I opined.

"No, it isn't. But..." She started to say something and apparently thought better of it, continuing, "In a company the size of ATH that owns thousands of properties worth billions of dollars, a little asset like this condo tends to get lost. It has its purpose, I guess." I didn't ask what she meant.

Sandra smiled and gave me another hug. "Look, I know you're tired after your drive up here. Why don't you relax out on the patio for a minute while I finish up a few things?" She led me through the French doors onto the balcony and down a cast-iron spiral staircase to the courtyard below. Pointing to a fabric covered chaise, she commanded, "You sit there and I'll bring you a drink."

"But...," I started to protest.

She placed her finger over my mouth and whispered, "Shhh.... I'm the hostess, remember? You have to do what I say." With that she disappeared through a door into the house.

I sat back and surveyed my surroundings. The condo's designer had created an oasis of tranquility in the middle of the city. The stone walls of the enclosed courtyard made this a private space. The fountain and the koi pond on one side were balanced on the other by towering green leaves of a banana tree, surrounded by the bright plumage of bird-of-paradise plants and bromeliads in half the colors of the rainbow. It was in a word, incredible, and no doubt very expensive.

The door opened and Sandra appeared with a silver tray holding two champagne flutes and a bottle of Dom Perignon. Setting it carefully on a small table she said, "Why don't you pour us something to drink while I finish up? It'll take me less than five minutes, promise."

She disappeared back into the house while I peeled the foil off the familiar squat green bottle, untwisted the wire and eased the cork out with two thumbs. It launched itself skyward with a sharp pop, tracing a high arc that ended in the koi pond. I scooped it out, poured both glasses half full and sat back to wait on Sandra. I don't know what I'd expected, but it hadn't been this. She was a talented and complex woman to be sure, but I had no idea she was living rent-free in a corporate condo. Was it simply a perk of the job or...? My thoughts were interrupted by her emergence with another large silver tray, this time laden with nearly a dozen small plates, each holding a different morsel. She held it up and smiled, "Are you up for tapas, Georgia style? I've got mushrooms stuffed with crab, some prosciutto and aged parmesan, seared tuna tartare with sesame seeds,...."

"Sandra, you really didn't have to do all this. We could have just sent out for pizza and beer."

She put the tray down and gave me a serious look, softened only by a slight smile on her face. "Matt, we can do pizza and beer anytime. I'd like that. But I want tonight to be very special."

"But why?"

"Because I've been thinking."

"About what?"

Without answering she picked up the champagne flutes, handing one to me and holding the other up for a toast. "Just enjoy yourself. We can talk later." She gently touched her glass to mine, and took a long sip.

CHAPTER Fifty

An hour and a half later and three-quarters way through the second bottle of champagne, I said, "You told me you'd been thinking. You said that we'd talk later. Is now the right time?" We'd moved to the upstairs sitting room, abandoning the remains of the feast in the courtyard below. I was half-sprawled on one of two matching sofas covered in soft cream leather, Sandra across from me on its twin, the bottle of Dom Perignon on a low table between us.

"I don't know, Matt," she replied softly. "Maybe I shouldn't have said that. I just want us to be together tonight, to enjoy each other's company. I don't want you to think I have an agenda."

"I don't," I replied, "and I like being with you. You're an incredible cook."

"Well, I hope there's more to it than *that*," she said with mock indignation. "No, I don't really know what I want to say...." Her voice trailed off.

"You'll never find out if you don't try."

"Will you forgive me if I say the wrong thing? I'm so afraid of..., of scaring you. Of running you off. Of making you think that...." She stopped.

"You won't say the wrong thing. I promise."

"Okay. I don't really know how to start. Ever since you told me you'd be here this weekend I've been trying to think of what to say. I've lain in bed at night with the lights out searching for the right words—but they won't come."

She sat up, pouring the last of the champagne in our glasses. She took a sip and said, "Let me try to start at the beginning." I settled back to listen.

"Matt, we haven't known each other that long, but you need to understand that the person I've become is not the person I want to be. And I need to be honest with you. When I first talked with you on the phone, I was just trying to find out who you were, and what you wanted. I was doing my job. I was doing what Bill Gray told me to do—to check you out, to be sure you weren't planning to sue the company or make trouble because of Laura's death. But when I met you in person it didn't take me long to realize you had nothing but good intentions. You only wanted to help out a couple of old people who'd lost their daughter. And that first night when we were alone, away from the office at The Pearl, there was something about you that was…, was different. And then I got the phone call and had to leave. I hardly knew you, but what I really wanted was to sit there and talk with you all night. It was so strange. It was like I was back in high school…." She stopped to take another sip of champagne.

"I think deep down we have a lot in common, and maybe you can understand what I want to say. I grew up in Jesup. You've been there, you've seen it. It's a small little town with a railroad and a couple of paved roads running through it, but that's it. There's nothing there unless you want to work at the mill or teach school or stay at home and have babies. When I was a kid I read books and magazines and watched television. There was so much in the outside world to see, so much to do, and all I wanted was to get as far away as possible from south Georgia, to get a job in the big city. My parents didn't object, really. They knew I wanted bigger things. They did what they could to help, but in the end it was up to me. All I had were my looks and my brains, and I used them both. In less than ten years, I've gone from being the Homecoming Queen to the executive suite of a multi-billion dollar corporation. It's like I went to sleep and woke up in a world of private jets, million dollar condos, Dom Perignon by the case—in other words, every thing I ever thought I wanted. Everything that is, until I met you.

"Matt, I'm not saying that I want you, or that I could ever have you even if I did. I just want to say that in these few weeks we've been together you've made me realize these goals I've been chasing are all wrong for me.

This is not something new. It's been eating at me for months. After being with you I know that deep in my soul I simply want to settle down and lead an average life, hopefully with someone who can care about me as much as I care about him.

"I know we've been naked together and made love, but I don't think I really know you, and I don't think you really know me. And that's not right. This whole relationship has started off wrong. I said I didn't want anything from you. I was lying. I do. I want you to know who I am, the real me, the small town girl who is capable of giving and receiving love and so much more. And in return I want to try to learn who you are, too. And in asking for this one thing, I'm taking a risk. You may discover I'm not someone you want to be with. Or perhaps I might discover the same about you. But in the end, we will have tried and if we fail, we can part as friends. Is that too much to ask?" She finished her champagne in one long drink.

I didn't know how to reply, but I had the uneasy feeling that if I could have found the words to do so, they might have mimicked Sandra's. Instead, I smiled and said, "Come here." She lay down next to me on the sofa, her arms around me and her head buried on my chest. After a moment, I raised her face to kiss her and saw tears trickling down her cheeks.

She started to speak, "Matt, I...."

This time I placed my finger over her lips to silence her. "There's plenty of time to talk later. I don't think we need words right now."

"No, let me say this, please. I'm quitting my job at ATH. I've already written my letter of resignation and am going to turn it in on Monday morning. I've been looking into a job in Savannah. It doesn't pay very well—I'll probably have to sell my car and make some other changes, but it will get me away from here. I'll have my freedom. I want to make a break. I want to start over while I still can. And—if you can find the time—Savannah's not that far a drive from Walkerville."

There are some things you never talk about. I will always remember the night that followed, but I haven't spoken of it since.

CHAPTER Fifty-One

I left Sandra asleep in the bed the next morning. We'd stayed up late, woken up early and then drifted back into a peaceful sleep. Sunlight streaming through the window aroused me with a start. Through foggy eyes I peered at the clock. It was a quarter past nine, and I'd told Rizzoli I'd meet him at ten. I slipped quietly out of bed, showered in the downstairs bathroom so as not to awaken her, and left a note on the kitchen table that I'd be back by noon. I copied the number of a neighborhood florist from the Yellow Pages and called from my truck to order two dozen red roses be delivered to the condo within the next hour. I thought it would be a pleasant way to wake her up.

Rizzoli had given me an address on Myrtle Street in midtown Atlanta. I had thought the area was mainly residential, but it was a part of the city I didn't know well. Myrtle is a short shady street lined with hundred-year old oaks and old-fashioned homes with generous front porches and manicured lawns. I drove slowly trying to read the house numbers. A smiling same-sex couple with matching vandykes walked hand-in-hand, each holding a Scottish terrier straining at the end of short leashes. A couple of houses had brightly colored rainbow banners flying from the front porch. William Reich would feel at home here, I thought.

I'd been looking for a business sign, and almost missed it. At what I thought should be Rizzoli's address I could barely make out a small black plaque with white letters on one of the porch support posts of a neatly painted

1920s frame house. He had probably gotten a zoning variance to operate a home business, or maybe was doing so illegally. I didn't really care. I parked in a sunny spot a couple of blocks down the street and walked back to the house. The grass was trimmed and edged and a bright bed of golden daylilies bordered the porch and walkway.

I rang the bell and waited. I was curious about Rizzoli. The McIntoshes described him as polite and well-mannered. Margaret Powell said he was "rough," whatever that meant. He had a Boston accent and an Italian name. I'd come up with a mental picture of a bald, disheveled little fellow with a huge mustache—a sort of Super Mario with a camera. I couldn't have been more off the mark. The man who answered the door was at least six-one, with a shaved head and gym-honed muscles rippling under a tight-fitting tee shirt. A tattoo on his right biceps peeked out from under the sleeve. He extended his hand with a friendly smile. "Mr. Turner? I'm Tony Rizzoli."

"Call me Joe," I said, smiling back and handing him one of my newly minted Forest King business cards.

"Well, it's good to meet you, Joe. Sorry that I was out of town yesterday. I've pulled together a few things for you to look at—you did say you were wanting to rework some of your sales materials, right? Come on in and let me show you what I've got."

He ushered me in the door, continuing, "I hope you'll pardon the mess. In case you haven't figured it out, I use this floor of the house as a studio, and live in an apartment in the basement." I followed him down the central hall to what appeared to be a former bedroom, now converted to an office and work space. Through open doors I could see that both the living and dining rooms had become portrait studios, with light reflectors, pull-down backdrops, and assorted furniture props pushed against the walls.

"I do a fairly varied business," Rizzoli explained. "Professional photographers are a dime-a-dozen here in Atlanta, so in this town you do what you gotta do to make it. I do my portrait work up front—you know, business photos and the like, plus a few glamour shot portfolios for the ladies. Those pay great, by the way. The bulk of my corporate stuff is done on location, wherever they need me." We were in the work room now, and he waved his hand about explaining, "This is where I put it all together, do my editing, some retouching, that kind of thing. When I was doing film stuff, I spent a lot of time in here. Now, almost everything is digital, so I spend most of my time downstairs in front of a computer screen."

He swept a stack of prints to one side on his work table and motioned for me to sit down, plopping three thick portfolios in front of me. "I was thinking that before we got around to talking about what you needed, you might want to get a feel for my style and what I can do. This one here on the top has mainly corporate and advertising shots, the one below it has business portraits and a few studio pieces toward the back. And the third folio is miscellaneous stuff—some weddings, informal portraits, glamour shots, celebrity photos, whatever. So, just take your time. I'm going to fix me a cup of coffee. Can I get you one?"

"Thanks, I could use some. Make it black." He returned a few minutes later with a large mug, placing it at my elbow and instructing me to take my time and "give a yell" when I'd looked things over. He left me alone, and a moment later I heard him creaking down the stairs to the basement.

I untied the ribbon on the first folder and slowly flipped through the images. There was no doubt about it, the guy was good. He had a feel for composition and balance. Many of his outdoor shots were done early in the morning or late in the afternoon, using the soft reddish light to its fullest advantage. I recognized one of the shots from ATH's annual report, but saw none of Laura.

The second portfolio was, as Rizzoli described, business portraits and product photos. Again, his talent was evident, imbuing the most ordinary balding accountant with an aura of corporate wisdom and business savvy, while softening the frown lines on the faces of battle-scarred old crones garbed in masculine office wear.

The third portfolio was interesting. There were the usual formal wedding portraits, but Rizzoli's other forte seemed to be his ability to capture his subjects in the most telling of informal moments. A shy smile on a nervous bride, the look of pride on a father holding his newborn child, and graphic desire radiant from the moist lips of his glamour shot subjects. He seemed to have a knack for being in the right place at the right time to capture unsuspecting celebrities. In one shot, bright lights of a theatre marquee reflected off Elton John's oversized glasses; in another, an aging Mick Jagger flashed a crooked smile at a beautiful young female fan. If I had actually been in the market for a professional photographer, I'd have hired him in a minute.

But that was not why I was here. The glamour shots made me think of Sandra, and I wanted to finish up and get back to her. I stepped out in the hall and called, to which he immediately responded by bounding up the stairs. "What do you think?" he asked.

"You do good work—I think it's what we're looking for." We sat at the work table while I rambled for the next fifteen minutes about our proposed advertising campaign, making it up as I went along. Rizzoli listened intently, scribbling down a few notes on the back of my business card and occasionally interrupting with a question. I needed to get to the heart of the matter. "Now you said you'd done some work for one of the larger timber companies, did I hear that right?"

"Yeah, ATH—that's American Timber Holdings. The guy who's the CEO now, Bill Gray, I knew him way back when in Minnesota, before he made it to the big time. He gave me my first real break after…," he paused, seeming to have misspoken, "…after I got in the photography business." I decided to let it pass, thinking I'd get back to it later.

"What sorts of things have you done for them? Advertising, product photos, or what?"

"A little bit of everything, to be honest. Bill and I have gotten to be friends. In fact, that's where I was yesterday, up at his place on Lake Burton. He throws me a good bit of work, probably more than I deserve." In contrast to his über-macho look, Rizzoli came across as calm, polite and well mannered. I could see how he could have fooled the McIntoshes.

"You do public relations work, too. Is that right?"

"Well, I sort of backed into it. As I said, you gotta make a living, and if someone'll pay me for it, I'll do it—or at least try. Companies like ATH, they've got their own marketing departments, but a lot of small businesses need somebody to put together print ads, send out a few press releases, plant a few 'news stories' in the papers, that sort of thing. I really got into it by doing celebrity shots. The photos were great, but I discovered the tabloids wanted stories to go along with them. I sent a few in and found out they pay pretty good. From that I moved on to doing the press release stuff. It's not a big part of what I do, but it tides me over. Your company got a marketing department or public relations department?"

"You're looking at them," I lied again.

"Well, maybe I can work with you on that, too," Rizzoli said, sounding eager for the business.

Preliminaries out of the way, I needed to see how he'd respond to a proposal for a little less conventional work. Pretending to hesitate a moment, I lowered my voice slightly and said, "We…, we, uh, did have a little problem last year that cost us a lot of business. I was just wondering how you would have handled it."

"Talk to me."

"Well, we had just come out with a new design for a debarker—that's a machine that strips the bark off timber in the field. It can save a bunch in hauling costs and cut down on processing time at the mill. Anyway, one of our engineers who'd worked on the project got mad about something, quit and went to work for one of our competitors. He put out the story that our new machine had some defects, and that he'd quit because we wouldn't correct them. It was all a pack of lies, but it helped the sales of his new employer and hurt ours. We tossed about the idea of trying to discredit him, because basically he was out there trying to get back at us. Some of us—and I was one of 'em—said that if we could let folks know what a sonofabitch the guy truly was, people would think twice before they'd listen to what he had to say. As it turned out, he got fired anyway from his new job, so we ended up doing nothing, but it got me to thinking. If I find myself in that kind of fix again, I want to be prepared. What would you do in a situation like that?"

Rizzoli's eyes narrowed and he seemed to be studying me for a moment before replying, "Like I said, I try my best to do what the client wants done."

"Say the guy hadn't gotten fired, and was still giving us trouble. What could we do?"

Almost reflexly, Rizzoli looked around as if he were afraid someone might overhear. "The first rule in that situation is to be certain that whatever's done can't be traced back to the company. You hire outside help and pay 'em indirectly so if there are any problems later, things can't be connected to you. Then you decide what you need to do. Some people just need to be talked to—you know—a friendly conversation from a stranger in a bar, or in the grocery store, or wherever. Sometimes they need something more public, maybe an accident or something. You get the idea." He leaned back slightly in his chair and continued, "But you wouldn't want to do anything illegal or unethical, of course." I caught a hint of sarcasm.

"No," I replied, trying to sound equally sarcastic. "You ever run into any similar situations?" I asked.

"Not that I'd admit to," he said smiling, "but as I said, I try to do what the customer wants." I realized I was beginning to see the real Tony Rizzoli.

CHAPTER Fifty-Two

"Now, getting back to your experience with companies in the timber industry," I continued, "could you show me some of the work you've done for ATH?"

"I'll be glad to," Rizzoli said, getting up from his chair. "Let me pull some things from my file room." He headed toward the back of the house. I needed to find a way to get him talking more about ATH and his "friend" Bill Gray.

Momentarily he returned with a thick folder, from which he removed a dozen or so smaller photos. "I'm sorry, Joe, these are all the prints I've got, and they were some extras I'd sent over for approval. Like I said, pretty much everything we do these days is digital. If you'll forgive the mess, I'd like to take you downstairs to see what I've got on discs. That'll give you a much better look at what I can do for you."

"Sure," I said, and followed him down a narrow stairway accessed by a door off the hall. The basement was dim, and it took my eyes a moment to adjust to the light. We crossed a cluttered living room dominated by a threadbare cloth sofa and a large-screen TV against the opposite wall. A couple of beer cans and four or five empty containers for Chinese takeout littered a coffee table. The sink in a small adjacent kitchenette was piled high with unwashed dishes.

"I know you think I'm a slob," Rizzoli said, half apologizing. "I'm not, honest. My girlfriend moved out on me a few months ago, and I just ain't into housecleaning like she was. But I guess you can see that."

"Hey, no problem. Mine did the same thing and I know how it is," I replied, telling the truth for a change. "But you seem to have a lot going on. How do you keep up with everything?"

Turning back to look at me, he said, "Oh, I couldn't do all this by myself. I've got an assistant who works half-days to help with the studio stuff, and a part-time bookkeeper who comes in once a week. Plus, I get student interns every now and then from some of the trade schools here in town."

I followed him into another dim room where the glow of two large-format flat panel monitors provided the only illumination. "This used to be my spare bedroom, but I've taken it over. Sit down and let me show you some things." Rizzoli shuffled through a stack of DVDs before finding one and inserting it into his computer. The twin screens filled with thumbnail images. "So let me show you what I can do with pine trees and logging equipment...." I sat quietly for the next five minutes, occasionally complimenting him, but generally marveling at the quality of his work.

I was ready to get back to Sandra. I said, "I've seen enough, Tony. Let me do this—I'll present some things to my boss first thing next week and get back with you shortly thereafter. You do some of the best work I've seen in a while. Tell, me, how'd you get into photography in the first place?"

Tony was staring at the monitor. I saw his eyes narrow briefly and his jaw muscles clench. "I, uh, went to trade school for it."

"Really? They must have taught you well. But I remember you said something about the CEO—what's his name, Bill Gray?—giving you a break. From what I've seen here, it looks like you wouldn't need much help."

Rizzoli swiveled his chair around to face me. The pale light from the monitors cast a blue glow on his face. "Uh, Joe..., I gotta be honest with you. Usually the subject doesn't come up, but I guess this time I brought it up, so you might as well know. I didn't start out to be a photographer. I was raised in Boston and signed up for the military just after high school. I did real well, got some advanced training—even got the tattoo." He pushed up his shirt sleeve and flexed his massive biceps to show an eagle perched on an anchor grasping a trident and pistol. "But I got in some trouble. I'll spare you the details, but it happened on the base. I was given a dishonorable discharge, after which I was tried in Federal Court and sent to prison in Minnesota. And I was guilty, too, no doubt about it. Well, when you're in the pen, you can make the time go faster by taking trade school courses. I signed up for photography school, and found out I was good at it. Toward the end of my sentence, I got put in a work-release program. Bill Gray was one of the VPs at the company I was assigned to. He liked my output, and we got to know each other. He wrote a letter to the parole board that got me out a few months early. I worked for a while in Minnesota, then moved down here to Atlanta not long after Bill took the job at ATH. End of story."

"So you two must get along pretty good, if he's having you up visiting at his vacation house...."

Rizzoli half-scowled. "Put it this way. We've each done the other a lot of favors. We had a pretty big falling out last year, though. But, shit, we've gotten over it and moved on. It's water under the bridge now. We're back on good terms—not best bro's—but we get along. But enough about that. I don't like to talk about it."

I didn't think there was much more to be learned from Rizzoli. He was an ex-con, a good photographer, and probably the kind of guy who'd do pretty much anything to make a buck. I didn't know what to make of his relationship with Bill Gray, but I couldn't tie it in specifically to anything else. I looked at my watch. "I need to be getting back to Macon. If you'll give me your card, I'll get in touch with you."

"Better yet, I've got a little presentation folder I send out to prospective clients. It's got a list of services, rates, that sort of thing. Let me get you one." He arose from his chair, flipped on an overhead light and began digging through a cluttered filing cabinet against the far wall.

While he searched, I looked around the room. A large corkboard mounted next to the door caught my eye. It was covered with a haphazard collection of what appeared to be informal photos. Curious, I walked over to look at them. Most were mounted with thumbtacks, a few with pushpins, others with odd scraps of tape. A photo of Rizzoli in a tank top holding a huge barbell above his head dominated the center. Next to it, Rizzoli and a petit redhead with huge breasts grinned at the camera from two lounges on a Caribbean beach. Below it, in a faded Polaroid, a younger and thinner Rizzoli with shoulder length hair leaned against a vintage Corvette. From behind me he said, "It's my scrapbook. Kinda ironic, ain't it? The photographer who's too lazy to put his shots in an album."

"At least this way you see them. Most people I know don't ever open photo albums once they've filled them."

"Yeah," Rizzoli said, sounding a bit nostalgic. "I'm not close to my family, and I guess this is as much of my past as I want to remember."

A small snapshot in the lower corner attracted my attention. The edges were worn, and the colors dulled with age. It was of two men in military fatigues, sitting with two women at a table in a bar or restaurant, I wasn't sure. I recognized Rizzoli easily. His current shaved head was not too different from his GI buzz cut in the photo. The other man looked familiar, but I couldn't place him. "When was this taken?"

Rizzoli leaned over to look at the photo. "Uh, that was a few years ago. We'd just finished our scuba training and had a two day pass. We picked up these chicks and...." He stopped, then said, "Yeah, that was a long time ago."

I peered at the other soldier. "Who's that with you?"

"A friend of mine. In fact, he's still my friend. About the only one who's stuck with me over the years." He seemed lost in thought for a brief moment, then continued, "Yeah, a good guy. He was living here in Atlanta, but he's moved south of here with his job. In fact, he works for ATH, too. Name's Clay Wynne."

CHAPTER Fifty-Three

"You all right?" Rizzoli asked. I'd made a noise that sounded like a gasp.

"Yeah, I think so," I said, trying to think quickly. "We did a little too much partying last night. I'm kinda hung over."

"Tell me," he said, slapping me on the back. "I've been there. You need some hair of the dog? Sometimes a shot of vodka'll do you good."

"No, thanks. I'll be okay." My mind was racing and I felt like I'd been kicked in the gut. Clay Wynne. Laura's co-worker and head of the new research lab. Everything seemed to connect to everything else. I needed to talk with Sandra—but should I? I didn't know where she fit in the picture. She'd worked in the lab at one time sure, but...?

"I really need to get on the road," I said.

"You look a little pale. At least lemme get you some Gatorade. There's some in the fridge."

"Uh, yeah, thanks. That'd be good." I said, wanting to get out of there as soon as possible. I followed him back through the cluttered living area into the kitchenette. He flipped on an overhead fluorescent and opened the refrigerator, pushing the beer bottles to one side searching in the back for the Gatorade. Finding it, he twisted the top off in one motion and stuck the bottle out toward me.

"Dehydration. That's it. You load up with this stuff when you get home from the bar, and then drink a liter or two when you wake up. It'll kill a hangover every time."

I leaned back against the counter and downed half the bottle in one long drink. My mouth was dry. Rizzoli leaned against the opposite counter, his arms crossed. "Better?" he asked.

"I'll get there," I said, setting the bottle on the counter and glancing around the cramped kitchen. A glamour shot of a girl with long blond hair in a pink negligee was affixed to the refrigerator door with four small magnets in the shape of pineapples. She was half-propped on pillows and turned to one side, her hair falling over and covering her face, one of her breasts exposed to the camera's lens. I nodded toward it and said, "Nice," wanting to change the subject. "Did you take that?"

"Yeah. What a cunt." There was a tinge of bitterness in his voice.

"How so?"

"That's my ex live-in. I did a series for her right after we met. But she moved out."

"Yeah," I said, finishing the last of the Gatorade. "It hurts sometimes."

"The worst part of it all, though, is that we were getting along fine. She met another guy, high class type, decided she wanted him. She figured out she couldn't have him as long as she was living with me, so she just leaves, walks out—just like that. No excuses, nothing. If you want to know the truth, she thought she was trading up."

"Yeah," I said again for lack of anything else to say.

"That's an old print anyway," he continued. "She's had a boob job since then. Her new guy paid for it." Rizzoli continued to stare at the photo, then said, "It's a funny thing, though. I thought the guy was kind of a friend. When I found out what was going on, I got in his face about it. He said she was the one put the moves on him, so I said screw it—I'll just get over it and move on to the next one." A sly grin eased across his face. "But, hey, little does he know. She couldn't stay away. I've been sneaking over to her place when he's out of town and getting a little. She likes it kinda rough, you know the type."

I didn't, I thought, but said, "Yeah," for the third time.

"Shit, I may be an ex-con, but I coulda made it with the girl. We got along, you know. But I couldn't compete with the guy. He bought her a fancy car, and has got her put up in some ritzy condo up in Buckhead. I say fuck 'em both."

A wave of nausea swept over me. I asked, "What did you say her name was."

"I didn't. But it's Sandra. Sandra Williams. Why? You know her?"

I vomited in the sink.

Rizzoli said, "Man, you got a bad hangover."

CHAPTER Fifty-Four

I stumbled out of Rizzoli's studio, my guts churning and my head spinning. I'd been a complete and total fool. I thought about Sandra and the last thing she'd said to me only hours before as we drifted back into sleep. I remembered her soft touch as she ran her hand across my chest, and the soft vanilla smell of her hair. Her words pounded in my brain, "I think I could fall in love with you...."

I'd left my cell phone in the truck. I hadn't been expecting any calls, but I didn't want to have to explain why I wasn't answering it while I was with Rizzoli. The morning sun had turned the interior into an oven. I lowered the windows, turned the AC to full blast and retrieved my phone from the console. There were four missed calls, all from Sandra. The voice mail icon was blinking. I flipped it open, pressed the message key and entered my PIN code. There were two messages. The first began, "Darling, the roses came. They're beautiful! You are so...." I hit the erase message key. The electronic voice said, "Next message, sent today at eleven thirty-two a.m.," followed by, "Matt, I've been thinking about you—about us—and I want so much...." I pressed the erase message button a second time. The electronic voice said, "End of messages." End of everything, I thought.

I rammed the truck in gear and headed for the expressway. I was a dozen miles past the city limits when the phone rang again. I turned it over, looking at the number on the display. Sandra. I picked it up wanting to hurl it out the widow, but instead opened it and said, "Hello."

A soft voice said, "Matt, hey, are you okay? I hadn't heard from you. The roses are so beautiful. I…."

"Sandra, something's come up. An emergency. I need to get back to Walkerville."

There was alarm in her voice. "What's happened? Are you sure you're okay? "Can I do…?"

I cut her off a second time. "I'll call you when I know something," I said, and flipped the phone shut. Ten seconds later it rang again, Sandra's number on the display. I cut the ringer off and stuffed the phone in my pocket.

I was thirty miles past the Perimeter before I could push enough of the crap out of my thoughts to start considering what I should do. I drew a picture in my mind, a box with Gray, Wynne, Sandra and Rizzoli at each corner. Rizzoli was Gray and Wynne's friend and Sandra's ex—and current?—lover. Wynne worked with Gray and Sandra and was friends with Rizzoli. Rizzoli, Wynne and Sandra were employed in one role or another by Gray. And Sandra. Wynne's co-worker, Gray's mistress and Rizzoli's…, what? I didn't want to think about it. What was it that she'd said? *I want to make a break. I want to start over while I still can.* It was all suddenly clear.

But this was not about Rizzoli or Gray or Wynne or Sandra, it was about Laura McIntosh and David Hargrove. Where were they in this web of deceit? Any way you cut it, they were squarely in the middle of the box. In one way or another, both of them were connected to all of the others. And they were both dead. But why? And how?

I flipped open my phone and dialed Roger Barmore's cell phone number. He answered immediately. I spent the next half hour telling him everything I knew, everything I'd discovered. He listened quietly, asking an occasional question, but not reacting, especially when I told him about Sandra. When I'd finished, he said, "We need to talk. How long before you'll be home?"

I looked at my watch. "Another hour."

"I'll meet you at your place. I'll be there when you get in."

I hung up and tried to think of what I should be doing. In the end, I decided there was nothing I could do. I didn't have any hard evidence that could connect Laura and David's death to anyone associated with ATH. But still…. I tried to call Roger back, but my cell phone battery was weak. I looked at the missed calls and realized why. Sandra had been calling every ten minutes. The ringer was off and I hadn't heard it. I cut the phone off and tossed it in the console.

To go from Walkerville to Atlanta I usually take Highway 15 north until I reach Interstate 20, then turn west for the quick 80 mph run into the city. On the return trip, I leave I-20 on Exit 138 at the village of Siloam. The run-up to the exit is a long three-mile stretch of straight expressway, starting at the top of one hill and ending with the exit ramp at the top of the next one in the distance. I'd seen a column of dark smoke billowing up in the sky as I approached, but thought little of it; in Georgia farmers burn off fields in mid-summer to prepare for their fall crops. As soon as I topped the hill, I knew it was something else. The plume of smoke was dead ahead in my lane, and at its base I could make out flashing red and blue lights, plus a two-mile traffic jam pointing back in my direction. I eased the truck to a stop at the end of it, and was soon blocked in by a line of cars stretching miles behind me toward Atlanta.

I needed to tell Roger I'd be late. I tried turning on my cell phone, but it beeped twice, flashed a "Low Battery" warning, then died. I thought about cutting over to the other side, making a U-turn, and heading back to the last exit I'd passed, four miles in the opposite direction. But I was trapped at the top of a steep fill, blocked on my left by a tractor-trailer rig and on my right by a guard rail. I had no choice but to sit and wait.

Forty-five minutes later the line began to move, inching our way forward past the hulk of a burned-out Suburban. A sobbing mother with two young children sat on suitcases at the roadside while the father seemed to be arguing with the wrecker driver about the cost of towing his ruined car.

I exited the expressway and pulled in at a convenience store with a pay phone. I dialed Roger's cell number again, paying for the call with a credit card. I should have been arriving home at that very minute. "Don't worry about it," he said. "I got here a few minutes ago, and Eula Mae let me in. It's cool inside. I'll just wait for you."

"What's Eula Mae doing there?"

"I asked her the same thing. She pulled in about the same time I did. Somebody gave her a bushel of summer corn and she wanted to bring it over and put it in the freezer before it went bad. I helped her haul it in the house."

"Well, that's good. Make yourself at home and I'll see you in just under an hour."

Fifty minutes later I pulled in the driveway at Rutherford Hall. A tattered twenty-year old Chevy pickup sat in front of the stables. I recognized it as belonging to Eula Mae's cousin. She borrows it occasionally when she needs to haul something. Roger's truck was nowhere to be seen. I bounded up the back steps to find Eula Mae in the kitchen, humming quietly to herself while she shucked and detasseled the corn. She looked up, smiling. "Looka here what I done got you. My cousin, he got this garden and...."

"Where's Roger?" I asked sharply.

She gave me a slight disapproving frown and said, "He ran outta here like a man on fire, not too long after you called him."

"What do you mean?"

"I mean, ain't you glad somebody done sent you a mess o' corn?"

"Yes, of course, but Roger—where'd he go?"

"I don't know. He didn't say nothin' to me. Says he was gonna call you."

"He couldn't have. My cell phone battery is dead."

Eula Mae shrugged and focused on pulling a long strand of dark fiber from an ear of light yellow corn. She held it up. "Ain't that jes' the prettiest corn you ever...."

"Eula Mae. This is important. Why did he leave?"

"I told you, I don't know."

"Well, what did he say?"

"Nothin' to me, I told you that."

"Just tell me everything that happened before he left, then."

"Okay, well...," she paused to chop off the top end of a green husk and began pulling at the leaves, tossing them in a brown paper bag she'd propped up on the counter, "him and me come in the driveway just 'bout the same time, 'bout an hour ago. He says, 'Hello,' and I say, 'Hello,' and we both 'greed that it was kinda hot and that we needed some rain. Then he seen I got this here corn and he hoped me carry it in. So he sot it here on the counter, and then I offers him some tea, and he says thank you and I gets him a glass of it.

"And then you calls and y'all talk for a minute, and then he says to me that iffin I don't mind he's gonna sit and wait 'cause it be kinda hot outside like we'd talked about and I says to him that suits me jes' fine, causin he seems like a nice young fella.

"And so he sits there for a minute or so at the kitchen table and notices that there box with them pictures of dead folk in 'em, and he says to me does I think it would be okay if he jes' looks at them, 'cause that be what y'all been talkin' about anyways. And I says I ain't payin' no mind to that 'cause them bes dead folks and I told him what I'd said to you about that and bad luck."

Eula Mae paused again, this time selecting another large green ear from the basket, examining it carefully, then chopping the end off so as to preserve the maximum number of kernels on the cob. She continued, "So he sits there, takin' 'em out one by one, and studyin' 'em and laying 'em in a pile right there." She pointed at the table. "And then he gets down toward the bottom of the box where the pictures ain't in no frame, just laying out loose there, and he picks one up and he gets to studyin' it and then he turns it over and looks at the back and then he says somethin' like, 'holy…,' well, I ain't gon' say that word, and he throws 'em back in the box, and asks me iffin I gots a phone book.

"So I gets him a phone book and he calls somebody on the phone and is all polite-like, but kinda business-like at the same time and says he wants to meet him and talk 'bout somethin'. And then I think he calls you, but I didn't hear what he was talking 'bout 'cause I was runnin' water in the sink. And then…."

"Eula Mae, he didn't talk with me. He couldn't have. My cell phone battery was dead."

She gave me a disgusted look. "Don't you folks have what they calls 'voice mail?'"

I leaped up from the table and ran to the truck to retrieve my phone. Springing back up the stairs, I rushed into the library and grabbed the spare battery I keep in the charger. I popped the back off, switched the dead battery for the freshly charged one and pressed the "On" button. The display came to life and the antenna indicator showed four bars. The voice mail icon was blinking. I pressed the retrieval key, entered my PIN, and was told that I had twelve messages. I deleted the first eight—all from Sandra—without listening to them. Finally, I heard Roger's voice. "Matt, I know what happened, and I'm going to arrest the son of a bitch myself. I'm not going to leave that pleasure to anyone else. I'll call you when I get back." The line clicked, with the voice saying, "End of message." I quickly skimmed and erased the remaining three, again, all from Sandra.

I ran back into the kitchen. Eula Mae was finishing up with the corn. "Do you have any idea who Roger called?"

She gave me another disgusted look as if the question were not necessary. "You."

"No, I mean before me."

"No, he used that little cell phone."

"What did he do after he called me?"

"I don' told you. He ran outta here like a man on fire. I thinks he was in a hurry to get somewhere."

CHAPTER Fifty-Five

Eula Mae can be obtuse at times. I don't think she means to be; she's quite intelligent in her own way. It's just that sometimes her perception of what's important doesn't coincide with everyone else's. I needed to find out where Roger had gone. I tried his cell phone first, immediately getting his voice mail. I left him a message to call me. I called the Sheriff's office, but they said he was not on duty and they hadn't heard from him. I called his home phone and his parents, only to be greeted by an answering machine at both numbers.

Turning back to Eula Mae I said, "Tell me again what Roger was doing before he asked you for the phone book."

"He was looking at them pictures," she said, nodding toward the box on the table.

"Which one, do you know?"

"Like I said, I ain't gon' have nothin' to do with no pictures of dead folk."

"He didn't take one with him, did he?"

"No. After he sees the one he got all excited 'bout, he put 'em back in the box."

"And you don't have any idea which one that was?"

"You done axed me that. I said no." She was getting tired of my questioning, as evidenced by the forceful use of the butcher knife in whacking off the end of the ear she'd pulled from the basket. "Only thing I knows was that it didn't have no frame on it."

I sat down at the kitchen table and began pulling the photos out of the box. There were two dozen or so in all, most in frames. All of them were of David Hargrove, a few—like the one I'd looked at earlier—were shots of him alone, but most had more than one person in the shot. About half were of Hargrove and Reich, either as a couple or with a few other young men. In one, they grinned at the camera from the front of a raft, a dangerous looking river and steep cliff in the background. On the back of the frame, someone had taped a scrap of paper that read "Colorado, June 2005." In another, Hargrove and three other men stood on a golf course green holding putters and posing for the camera.

At the bottom of the box I found six loose photos. Several had tape marks or pin holes on the upper corners, as if they'd been stuck up somewhere, perhaps on a bulletin board like Rizzoli's. Eula Mae said Roger had been looking at one of the unframed photos when he got excited about something. Four of the six were of Hargrove and Reich in various social settings. A fifth was of Hargrove alone, dressed in leather and chaps atop a vintage Harley, looking like a cross between James Dean and a member of The Village People. The final one was a group shot, with about twenty-five people posed in front of a Cessna Caravan. All were wearing helmets, goggles and parachutes, as if they were about to go skydiving. A banner held up by those on the front row read, "Atlanta Sky Masters—2006."

I studied the photo in detail, trying to identify Hargrove. I reasoned Reich wouldn't have given me the photo if he weren't in it. I narrowed him down to one of three men, but with the diving garb I wasn't sure which one he was. I flipped it over on the back to find a typed label reading "Atlanta Sky Masters Diving Club—Annual Columbus Day Formation Dive, 2006" followed by a list of names, starting "Top Row Lt. to Rt: McQuigg. J.; Staton, C.; Connelly, J.;...," etc. A smeared stamp at the bottom read "Photo Courtesy of Rizzoli Media Services." My palms began to sweat.

I studied the list of names in more detail. On the front row, to left of center, two names flew off the paper at me "...*Wynne, C.; Rizzoli, A.;*...." Suddenly it all fell into place. Wynne and Rizzoli were both members of Hargrove's skydiving club. The surveillance video from the airport. The figure that emerged from the hangar and opened the trunk of the car had a strange walk. He was limping. It had to be Wynne. I didn't know the why yet, but thought I knew the how.

I looked up. "Eula Mae, this is very important. When Roger called someone and said that he wanted to meet him," assuming he was talking with Wynne, I thought, "did you hear *anything*? Anything at all?"

She continued to focus on the corn. "Well, I weren't payin' it no mind."

"You told me that, but can you remember anything they said?"

She looked up at me, still slightly annoyed, then took a deep breath and stared at the ceiling for a moment as if she were replaying the scene in her mind. "He said…," she paused, maddeningly, "…somethin' like, 'Where?' then the other fella must o' said somethin' and he—Mr. Roger—comes back with "It'll take me fifteen or so minutes to get up there," and then the other fella musta said somethin' and he says "Okay." Then he puts his phone in his pocket and runs outta here."

Fifteen minutes or so to get up there. He had to be talking about the lab and pilot plant north up Highway 15. I didn't know who, if anyone would be working on a Saturday, but I needed to get there as soon as possible. Whether or not Roger thought he had enough evidence to make a summary arrest without a warrant based on a presumed felony charge, his obsession had no doubt overcome his better judgment.

I turned back to Eula Mae. "I'm going to the American Timber Holdings research lab up near Warthen. If I haven't called you here at the house in an hour, I want you to call the Sheriff, and tell him to send somebody there to check on me. You got that?"

"I's probably gon' be don' here 'fore an hour."

"Just wait for me, please?"

She raised her eyebrows, nodded and went back to the corn. I was partially out the door when I heard her call, "Oh, Mr. Matt?"

"Yeah?"

"I remembered one mo' thin' Mr. Roger said 'fore he left."

"What's that?

"He said he 'preciated my hospitality and he thanked me for the tea." Even Eula Mae can rise to sarcasm when she deems it appropriate.

CHAPTER Fifty-Six

I made the fifteen minute drive in something under eleven minutes, thinking if I happened to run into a cop, a police escort might not be a bad idea. I didn't know what I'd find. I was sure the lab operated Monday through Friday, but didn't know about the pilot plant, or the construction work on the new facility that had gotten underway before the groundbreaking. When I toured the plant with Wynne, I remembered his saying something about it being an automated twenty-four-hour-a-day process. Even then, there'd have to be a security guard and people to watch it in case something went wrong. Halfway there it occurred to me I should have picked up my pistol before I left, but I didn't want to waste time by going back to get it.

I made a gravel-spewing turn on to the private road leading to the plant, slowing down only as I made the final turn approaching the guardhouse and gate. To my surprise, the gate was open, the guardhouse unoccupied, and the parking lot empty except for Roger's truck and a Chevy Tahoe I assumed was Wynne's. I parked next to them, got out of my truck and looked around. In the distance beyond the vast asphalt stretch of the parking lot, a construction trailer had replaced the reviewing stand built for the groundbreaking. A row of dusty yellow earth-moving machines was lined up next to it, construction apparently on hold for the weekend.

Except for a low steady hum from the direction of the pilot plant building adjacent to the lab, there was silence, broken only by the caw of a crow perched in a distant pine tree. I caught a whiff of the musty-sweet odor of fermentation. A wisp of steam emerged from a small chimney on the plant building only to disappear almost immediately in the hot summer air.

I followed the walkway to the door leading to the lab, remembering that an ID card and keycode were necessary to get in. I found it slightly ajar, propped open by a rolled up copy of *American Forests* magazine. Cracking it open a few inches, I peered inside. A rush of cool air pushed back the afternoon heat. Opening the door wider, I slipped in, being careful to put the magazine back in its spot to keep it from latching shut. The lights were on and the hallway brilliantly lit. Somewhere in the distance the building creaked, but otherwise I heard only the soft hum of machinery.

I tried to remember the configuration of the interior. The hallway led to a reception area, and off that was the large conference room where Wynne hosted the press briefings at the groundbreaking ceremony. I hadn't paid much attention to the hall on my earlier visit. Now I was looking at several doors opening off each side. The one to my immediate right displayed a black and white reading, "Security and Monitoring." On my left, the first door read, "Facility Administration," and the one beyond it, "Document Center." I gingerly tried the handles on all three doors. They were locked. Two more doors further down on the right side were restrooms, one for men, the other for women. I peered in each, finding them empty.

At the end of the hall I could see the door marked "Laboratory—Authorized Access Only" with its adjacent card reader and keypad. I reasoned that Roger and Wynne were likely beyond it, but it was shut tightly and I had no way of getting in. More confident, I moved ahead to find the reception area deserted. The remaining doors, including the conference room and what appeared to be offices, were all locked. Considering the options—or more properly, the lack thereof—I decided the best thing would be to call for help. I pulled my cell phone out of my pocket, only to discover that the steel building prevented me from getting a signal.

Just as I was turning to head for the entry door, I heard a soft click, followed by the sound of a door shutting and latching into place. I rounded the corner to see a large-framed figure blocking the hall and my only means of escape. "Hello, Matt," Clay Wynne said. "I was expecting you." I could see he'd come out of the room labeled "Security and Monitoring," and that above him, unknown to me, was a video camera that had allowed him to watch my every move.

Wynne was holding a large caliber automatic pistol pointed at my chest. "I don't think I should let you make any phone calls," he said calmly. "If you'd be so kind as to put your phone on the floor and kick it over to me, I'd appreciate it." I lay my cell phone on the floor and gave it a shove with my shoe. It slid across the carpet and stopped six inches in front of the tip of Wynne's boots. Not taking his eyes—or the gun—off me, he calmly stepped forward and crushed it under his heel, kicking the detritus to one side.

Again, I tried to consider my options. There were only two ways out: through locked doors or past the man who stood in front of me holding a gun. Neither appeared to be a viable alternative. I said, "Where is Roger? I came looking for him when he wouldn't answer his cell phone."

Wynne smiled, "He couldn't answer it, because I have it." With his free hand he reached into his pocket and held up a cell phone. That's how I knew you were coming. He's got your name programmed into his contact list, and it popped right up when you called. Since he seems to have gotten some of his information from you, I figured it wouldn't be long before you showed up. I'm just glad you came alone—I've been watching your every move on the video monitors in there. They're really quite sophisticated." He paused. "But to answer your question, he's back in the lab, behind you through that door."

"I...."

"No talking," Wynne said harshly. "Move." He waved his gun in the direction of the laboratory door. I turned and walked. He stayed far enough away to prevent me from surprising him with a sudden lunge, but close enough to be sure he couldn't miss hitting me with a quick shot if I tried.

I reached the locked door leading to the laboratory. "Against the wall, there," he said, shoving me face-first into it. He held the pistol against the back of my head while he used his other hand to swipe his ID card and punch a code into the keypad. The lock clicked open. He pulled the door back and pushed me in. The lab to my right was dark behind its glass wall. With the overhead illumination dimmed, red, green and blue LED monitoring lights twinkled like stars in a Technicolor sky. The door leading to the pilot plant was at the end of the hall, and ahead to my left, the break room with its vending machines where we'd sat after our plant tour.

"Ahead, through the door on your left," Wynne instructed.

"Where's Roger?" I repeated. He responded by giving me a shove forward with his boot. I stumbled into the break room to find the answer to my question. Roger was bound hand and foot to a heavy wooden chair, which was itself tied to a table. A roughly torn piece of grey duct tape covered his mouth. His head was slumped forward, but I could make out a nascent black eye and a trickle of blood draining from his nose, dripping across the duct tape and falling in an irregular dark blotch on his jeans.

I whirled around to Wynne, "You son of a bi...."

I didn't get to finish my sentence. Never moving the gun he held in his right hand, his left came out of nowhere and slapped me across the face, knocking me back into a drink machine with such force that it whirred and dropped several coins into the change slot. I sank to the floor. Wynne laughed and said, "Shit, I shoulda tried that with the slots in Vegas." Then to me, "You forget I was trained as a Navy SEAL. One of our specialties is hand-to-hand combat. I may be rusty, but I wouldn't try anything if I were you." At Wynne's command I picked myself up and stumbled to a chair. Instructing me to put my hands behind me, he looped two plastic ties tightly around my arms, one at my wrists and another just above the elbows, pulling my shoulders back in a painful position.

Roger stirred with a moan and raised his head. Seeing me, he tried to say something, but the tape muffled his words, and another backhand from Wynne silenced him. "Well, now that we're all here, I think we need to take a little walk," he said. He pulled a knife out of his pocket and cut the ties binding Roger to the chair but leaving in place those holding his arms behind his back. "Up we go," he said and grabbed the one just above the elbow, hyperextending Roger's arms backwards. Roger's face contorted as he let out a scream, again muffled by the duct tape.

"What do you...," I started, but didn't finish as Wynne raised his hand to strike me again.

"I told you, no talking." To be sure, he ripped a long piece of the grey tape from a roll sitting on the table, slapping it over my mouth and looping it around my head and back on itself so I would not be able to easily remove it. He stepped out in the hall, blocking any exit back toward the reception area and freedom beyond. Waving his gun he said, "Let's go."

We walked out in the hall. Wynne nodded toward the door to the pilot plant saying, "That way." A wave of horror swept over me. I knew what he was planning to do.

CHAPTER Fifty-Seven

Shoving us both against the wall and holding the gun close to our heads, Wynne used the same technique to open the door into the pilot plant and push us through. The heat was worse than it had been when I'd toured the plant before, the noise louder and the smell nearly overwhelming. "Sorry, Matt. No hardhats or goggles this time," he said in a sarcastic tone. Roger shot me a puzzled look. Yelling instructions over the whine of pumps and grinding of gears, he directed us to climb a set of metal stairs. We headed toward the rear of the plant, toward the hopper and conveyor belt that fed the initial fermenting vats.

Wynne's plan was all too obvious. The fermenting process, powered by—what had he called them?—"supercharged yeast and bacteria," would quickly destroy any organic material thrown into the mix, including our bodies. And even if it didn't, the foul smell would cover up any strange odors. He would be far away by the time anyone figured it out, if they did at all.

We were walking single-file down a perforated metal catwalk now, high above the machinery. Roger trudged in a half-daze in front, with me next and Wynne behind prodding me with his gun. "I guess you know where all this is leading, eh, Matt?" he yelled over the noise. I turned and glared at him. "Sorry, but you stuck your nose into somebody else's business. But I'll make it quick, you won't suffer." I didn't think Roger could hear us. He had no idea what was about to happen.

The catwalk dead-ended in a "T" with the cross arm paralleling a long trough-like conveyor chute, the top of which was a few inches below the walkway's perforated metal floor. A waist-high guardrail protected its outside edge. Maintenance openings every ten feet or so were blocked by chains hooked across them and hung with fluorescent orange signs reading "DANGER" in six-inch high letters. Wynne herded us toward one end of the cross arm. He raised his gun.

Behind me there was a whirring of gears. Wynne hesitated, then lowered the gun. With a clanging sound, the conveyor began to move slowly in the direction of the fermenting vats. At the other end a rhythmic thumping rose in volume as a steel panel on a huge hopper folded up toward the roof. I looked around to see a screw auger pouring wood chips from the hopper into the conveyor trough. Another section of the mechanical symphony struck up as a three-foot high set of blades resembling an oversized paper shredder began to spin and hum at the base of a large chute where the conveyor ended over the fermenting vats. I could read the terror on Roger's face as he realized what Wynne was about to do. To the conveyor belt, we'd be no more than a couple of logs. And when our bodies—or what was left of them—fell from the shredder into fermenting vats, we'd be finely chopped food for Laura's microorganisms.

Wynne reached over to unhook one of the chains blocking access to the slowly moving chute. I was nearest to him. He raised his gun once again, then suddenly swiveled and pointed it past me, firing off two quick shots in what had been Roger's direction. Out of the corner of my eye I saw Roger leaping into the moving pile of chips then jerk and fall forward, his head making a metallic clank as it struck the side of the conveyor.

Wynne focused on Roger's motionless body, his pistol held pointed in a two-fisted stance. Seeing my chance I ducked down and leaped toward him just as he swiveled and fired. The shot went wide as I hit him in the solar plexus with my head. He pitched back, trying to hold his aim with his right hand while reaching out for the railing behind him with his left. He missed and the steel top rail hit him in the small of his back. His right hand flew up, losing grip of the gun. For an instant time seemed to slow as the pistol floated lazily toward the end of the conveyor, landing less than a yard from where it dumped into the shredder.

Wynne lashed out with his right foot, striking a glancing blow to my shoulder but with enough force to knock me back on the catwalk. He leaped on the conveyor belt and like a man running through sand, slogged across the mounds of chips toward his weapon. With a lunge he grabbed it just before it fell into the shredder. He stood up, pointed it in my direction and walked toward me, progressing in slow motion like a man walking the wrong way on a moving sidewalk. "I'm not going to miss this time. I won the gold in competition pistol shooting." He stood still and carefully raised his gun in a two-handed stance. He hadn't noticed me easing in front of the oversized bright red "Emergency Conveyor Stop" button on the handrail. With my hands still tied behind my back, all I could do was slam it down with my fist.

The conveyor jerked to a sudden halt, just as Wynne pulled the trigger. His feet firmly planted, the momentum carried the top of his body back. His shot went wild, striking somewhere over my head. Trying desperately to maintain his balance, he reached back, in the process accidentally hurling the gun into the maw of the shredder which accepted it greedily with a staccato riff punctuated by the sound of exploding ammunition.

Wynne pitched over the side of the conveyor trough, half-on, half-off, his right knee hooked over the edge and holding on with his right hand while the rest of his body dangled over the plant floor sixty feet below. While he struggled to right himself, I looked around for some sharp edge that I could use to cut through the plastic ties binding my hands. Hooking my wrist restraints under the edge of the metal "Emergency Conveyor Stop" sign, I sawed through them in less than thirty seconds. I could see Wynne struggling not to fall.

My wrists free, I was still severely hampered by the ligature above my elbows that forced my shoulders back into an odd and painful position. The sign with its sharp edge was too low for me to try to cut them standing up, and too high for me to attempt to do so sitting down. I worked myself into an uncomfortable half-stooped position and tried rocking back and forth on my haunches, tensing the quadriceps muscles of my legs to maintain cutting force.

I was making slow progress. Wynne's left hand reached up and grabbed the far side of the conveyor. He unhooked his right leg and did a sort of chin-up maneuver, his face snarling at me from twenty feet away. I thought about running over and stomping on his hands to make him lose his grip, but with my arms useless for balance it was likely I'd be the one to plummet over the side. His head disappeared below the edge and I watched as he inched hand-over-hand down the side toward my direction. Frantically, I sawed at the plastic tie.

Wynne was now less than a dozen feet away. The only thing between us was the stalled conveyor and the guardrail edging the catwalk. With a sudden push, he flung his left leg over the edge and rolled into the chips in the conveyor trough. I kept sawing, the muscles in my legs burning with the awkward position. He stood up slowly, dusting himself off just as the plastic broke. I pulled my arms in front of me, shaking them to restore the circulation while I backed down the catwalk toward the way we'd originally come. I painfully peeled the duct tape off my head, taking large chunks of hair with it as I pulled it free.

"One down, one to go," Wynne said, apparently none the worse for his exertion.

Behind him, Roger moaned, rolled over and raised his head. The tape over his mouth had come loose and dangled from one cheek. "He did it, Matt," he yelled, his voice hoarse. "He confessed. Don't let him get away."

Wynne shrugged and backed up, stopping in front of a short grey metal locker that appeared to be an electrical junction box. Keeping his eyes on me, he reached in his pocket and pulled out a set of keys. Glancing at it, he selected one, inserted it in a keyway on the locker and turned the handle. The hinge was on my side, so as the door opened, it blocked my view. Cautious not to take his eyes off me for more than a second, he reached in, appeared to turn something, then closed the box and relocked it, putting the keys back in his pocket.

Raising his hand, he said, "Just give me a second if you will, Matt, then we'll get back to the matter at hand." He backed up toward the red emergency conveyor stop button and with a sharp blow from his hand snapped it off. With a slight smile, he placed one finger on the adjacent green reset button and pressed it. The clanging sound resumed, and the conveyor belt began to move again in the direction of the whirling jaws of the shredder.

But instead of inching along as before, it sped up. Wynne had increased the speed. Roger rolled back and forth trying to get to his feet. It was evident he wasn't going to make it. Wynne said, "Like I said, one down, one to go." He rolled his shoulders like a prize fighter and headed toward me.

CHAPTER Fifty-Eight

Wynne was no more than eight feet away when Roger wailed a weak, "Help me." At the rate the conveyor was moving, I figured I had about two minutes to do something, otherwise Wynne's "one down" count would be correct. If I turned and made a run for it, it was possible that I could outdistance him, especially if I could beat him out of the building to open ground. I didn't know the extent or details of his old military injuries, but I suspected they'd slow him up in a flat-out foot race. But I couldn't abandon Roger.

Wynne must have been reading my thoughts. He could keep his advantage as long as the confrontation was in close quarters. He stopped, looked over his shoulder for a brief instant and then began to back up, moving to the end of the crosswalk nearest the shredder and fermentation vat. "Hey, Matt, come watch while your friend gets osterized. Maybe we can lay a bet on how long it'll take." Roger was wallowing in the wood chips, struggling without success to roll over.

I hesitated, then began to approach him cautiously. His plan was obvious. All he needed to do was hurl me over the railing to a certain death. Or if he got lucky, he could just toss me directly into the shredder. Stopping at one of the maintenance openings, I unhooked both ends of a guard chain and ripped off the orange "DANGER" sign, sailing it like a sharp-edged Frisbee toward Wynne. He ducked and it landed with a clanging sound in the shredder chute, disappearing into the blades with a slight metallic burp. I grasped the two free ends of the chain in my hand, giving me about two feet of flexible steel to swing at him.

The conveyor carried the squirming Roger toward the shredder. Wynne stood his ground, grinning as I approached him. "You really think you're going to save your buddy, don't you?" I didn't answer, instead banging the chain against the guard rail with a decisive clang.

I yelled to Roger, "See if you can catch your legs on one of the guard rail posts." He continued to flop about like a fish in the bottom of a boat, carried ever nearer to a horrific death. Wynne didn't move. He didn't need to.

I closed the gap between us to six feet. I could see the beads of sweat on Wynne's forehead and his knuckles whiten as he clenched his fists. I had to make a move. I lunged at him, swinging the chain. He deftly stepped to one side and it clanged harmlessly against the rail. "I see you've never had personal combat training," he said calmly. Roger was now a dozen feet from the shredder.

"No, but what I lack in training I make up for in hard work," I replied, swinging again and this time catching the tip of Wynne's left shoulder. He involuntarily flinched and rubbed the spot.

"Hey, that hurt. Forget what I said a few minutes ago about making this quick and painless. I may just have to dangle you over those blades and feed you in slowly." This time he lunged at me, but I caught him across the face with the chain, knocking him back against the rail and opening a cut on his left temple that began to pour thick rivulets of red down the side of his face. He reached up and touched the spot, drawing his hand away and looking at the blood. "Now, you've made me mad." He sprang toward me, knocking me to the floor as he grabbed the chain and threw it over the side. The sound of it hitting the concrete floor below echoed before being lost in the din of machinery.

I tried to sit up, but he leaned over and punched me in the stomach. I gasped for breath, unable to move. He bent over, picked me up in a fireman's carry and slung me over his shoulder. I tried to resist, but couldn't. As he straightened up I was vaguely aware of Roger screaming, "You murderer." Wynne seemed to stumble forward and then fall, throwing me ahead of him in the direction of the wood chip hopper. I'd recovered enough to see that

Roger had managed to get his legs over the side of the conveyor and trip Wynne, the added weight of my body making him an unstable target.

Wynne seemed to be stunned. A fresh cut had appeared in his mid forehead, apparently from where he'd struck the guard rail in his fall. Roger had wrapped his legs around one of the support posts, but the motion of the conveyor had carried his body around such that his head was hanging over the chute that ended in the jaws of the powerful shredder. As I watched, his legs began to slip off the post. He moved forward with a jerk, catching it only with his ankles, which he tried again to lock around the post. But to do so he had to bend his knees, and every time he did that the conveyor moved him forward, forcing him to straighten them. He wouldn't be able to hold on long.

Wynne, still groggy, rolled over onto his knees and tried to stand up by pulling himself up on the guard rail. If I attacked him now, I'd lose Roger. If I stopped to help Roger, he might get the jump on me. There was only one thing to do. I crawled over on my hands and knees, reached out and grabbed Roger's belt, tugging him out of the conveyor trough and onto the catwalk.

I heard Wynne stirring behind me and felt the vibration of footfalls on the suspended metal surface. I whirled, holding up my fists to fend off the expected attack. But Wynne was gone. I caught a glimpse of him as he headed in the direction of the laboratory and disappeared behind some machinery. Roger croaked, "He's running. Get him!"

I said, "Do you have a knife on you?"

"Left pocket," he said. I fished it out of his jeans and cut the ties binding his arms. He tried to get up. "We gotta stop him."

I pushed him back down on the walkway. "Roger, you've been shot. We need to get you to a doctor."

He shook his arms and sat up. "Hell, no. I'm fine. The bastard missed. If I hadn't tripped and hit my head I was going to try to shimmy down the scaffolding and go for help. I didn't think he'd hurt you as long as one of us was alive to tell about it." I had my doubts, but held my tongue. He pulled up to a standing position, waving his arms and rubbing his wrists. "Come on. We gotta go."

I put my hand on his arm. "You're not going anywhere, unless it's to the emergency room. Let Wynne run. They'll catch him."

Roger was dusting off the wood chips. "Yeah. I was a stupid fool to come out here in the first place. After I talked with you and found the photo, it just all fell into place. He's a fucking peon, a henchman. I should have called the sheriff and let them arrest him." The stress hormones had kicked in and Roger appeared to have recovered.

"That's the first sensible thing I've heard you say in a long time."

"You're goddamned right. Somebody'll get those bastards. I want the guy behind it all. Let's go." Without waiting for my reply, he began to limp back toward the exit.

"Roger, what the hell are you talking about?"

"I'm going to arrest the man who had Laura killed." He had a maniacal look in his eyes.

"Who?"

"Come on and I'll show you." He paused. "But don't make the mistake of trying to stop me."

"Where are you going?"

"To north Georgia. Lake Burton. I'm going to be the one who clips the cuffs on Bill Gray's wrists."

CHAPTER Fifty-Nine

I looked at my watch. Only forty-five minutes had passed since I left Eula Mae with instructions to call the Sheriff if she hadn't heard from me in an hour. "Roger, this is crazy. Call the cops. You don't need to be trying to make an arrest..."

"I *am* 'the cops,' remember? I'm a fully deputized member of the Adams County Sheriff's Department." He was bounding down the stairs now, talking to me over his shoulder. "Hell, you know that's just an excuse." He stopped, turning to look straight at me. "I want to see the look in Gray's eyes when he knows he's been caught."

"Leave it to somebody else. We can call the GBI and..."

"And what? Spend two or three days presenting mostly circumstantial evidence to a bunch of laid-back desk jockeys, while Gray seeks shelter behind his lawyers? Try to convince a judge that a hearsay accusation with no supporting evidence is sufficient grounds for a warrant? Forget it, Matt. This is personal. Like I said, if you're not with me, don't try to stop me."

We reached the door to the lab building. I was worried about Wynne ambushing us. Pushing Roger to one side, I eased it open and looked in the hall. Nothing. Quietly, we advanced to the reception area, cracked the door and peered in. Again, nothing. In the distance I could see the exterior door was shut, the magazine no longer propping it open. I sprinted down the hall, pushed open the door and looked out into the parking lot. Wynne's

Tahoe was gone. Roger looked over my shoulder. "He's making a run for it. Probably going to alert Rizzoli and Gray."

"What do you think they'll do?" I asked.

"How should I know? If I were Rizzoli, I'd hit the road. Gray…, he's not going to run."

"What makes you say that?"

"He'd lose everything he's worked for. No, he'll build a stone wall of lawyers around him and blame it all on the other two. From what Wynne said, I'm not sure there is enough direct evidence to implicate him, but I know he's behind it. It was his idea. Come on…" He began a slow run toward his truck.

I hesitated. Roger stopped and looked back. "Are you coming?"

"Like I said, I think we should call the cops."

"Okay. See you later, then. It'll take me about two and a half hours to get to Gray's place. Wait three hours and call 'em." He jumped in the truck, cranked it and put it in reverse. I stood watching from the sidewalk. He backed out and paused to look in my direction. Leaning over, he opened the passenger's side door and yelled, "Get your ass in this truck. You've already saved my life once today. You may come in handy." I climbed in and slammed the door as Roger sped out of the parking lot.

"Do you have any idea where you're going?" I asked.

"Pretty much," he replied. "There's a folder under your seat there. Get it out if you would." I reached under me and struggled to drag out a thick expandable file held shut with an elastic band. It was scuffed and worn, as if it had seen a lot of usage. A tattered paper label affixed to the front read, "Laura—Investigation."

"Open it up and pull out the folder labeled 'Gray,'" Roger directed. I slid the elastic off and folded back the top. Packed tightly inside were two dozen or so individual sub-files, each labeled with a neatly printed tag. I scanned them quickly: "GBI Report," "NTSB Report," "ATH—Background," and so forth. There were individual files for each person whose name had cropped up in the course of the investigation, including one labeled "David Hargrove," and another simply, "Laura." I found Gray's together with a group of others associated with American Timber Holdings including Clay

Wynne, Tony Rizzoli, and Sandra Williams.

I slid out the one on Bill Gray and opened it on my lap. On the right side under a folding clip, individual sheets contained notes on every conversation or scrap of evidence that seemed in any way to tie Gray to Laura or the investigation in general. On the left side, again held in place by a clip, were Roger's written records of his interpretation as to how the subject—in this case Gray—might be viewed as a possible suspect or source of additional information. I flipped through it quickly. Every time I'd talked with him he'd duly documented and annotated the conversation. "Roger, what is all…?" I began.

He cut me off, pushing the truck past eighty as he spoke without taking his eyes off the road. "On the left side there, in the back, you'll find some baseline information on Gray—home address, phone numbers, that sort of thing. There's a sheet on his lake house and a location map. I think we take Highway 15 north to Athens, then 441 to Clarksville, then 197 to the cutoff toward his place. I believe it's called Laurel Lodge Road. That right?"

I studied the map for a moment. "That's right. But, Roger, again, what is all this? Why have you been accumulating all this…, this information?" I couldn't think of the right word.

He shot me a quick annoyed glance. "It's a case file, what the hell do you think it is? I know you've got a college degree, but evidently it didn't include a course in Criminal Investigation 101. It's the most basic thing you do when you run an investigation."

"Dammit, that's a job for the police, or the GBI or somebody. Not you."

"Yeah, and if we'd left it up to them, where would we be right now? Laura was my life, my future. It's the least I could do." He had a point.

We rode in silence for some minutes. My body ached from Wynne's beating. Roger continued to keep his eyes fixed on the road, lost in his own thoughts. I said, "Tell me what happened with Wynne."

He didn't reply at first, then said, "You need to know, don't you?" Without waiting for me to answer, he continued, "I called him, told him who I was, and that I wanted to meet with him. I didn't tell him what I wanted. He knew I was Laura's fiancé, I'm not sure why he would know that. Anyway, he sounded calm and agreeable and said he was just going out the door to do some work up at the pilot plant, and was it all right if we met there. I said it was and we agreed to meet about half an hour later.

"When I got there, I was surprised the gate open and the only vehicle in the parking lot was Wynne's SUV. He was standing outside the door, hands in his pockets and smiling when I drove up. We said hello and went inside. I asked him where all the workers were, and he said the plant was highly automated and designed to run with just one man listening out for any alarm. As a cost-saving measure, only one guy—a security guard—oversees the entire operation on nights and weekends, but there are people on call if any serious problems develop. Wynne said he gave the guard the rest of the afternoon off. The guy was working a 6-to-6 shift, and Wynne told him he'd cover for him until his replacement came in. Wynne is the head guy anyway, so I guess he could do that.

"I started to have second thoughts about trying to arrest Wynne—I mean I really thought there'd be people there. He took me back to the break room and we sat down at one of the tables. He asked me what he could do for me. Hell, Matt, I don't know what it was. Maybe it was the look in his eyes, or the fact I realized I'm sitting there making nice with the animal that killed the person I loved. I just freaked—kinda lost it.

"I got all in his face and told him I knew he was one of Laura's murderers and I was here to arrest him. He seemed a little surprised at first, and I think maybe he even thought I wasn't serious until I showed him my badge and told him to turn around, spread his arms and legs and face the wall so I could frisk him. He said, 'You gotta be kidding me,' and I said, 'No,' and...."

"Did you have a gun?" I asked.

"No," he said quietly. "I didn't want to take the time and go home to get it." Stupid, I thought.

"Anyhow," he continued, "Wynne makes like he's going to cooperate, and leans up against the wall and 'assumes the position.' I started to frisk him. When I bent down to check his ankles, he comes back at me with a mule kick that sends me flying across the room and into a table. 'Course, that's when I realized I was in deep shit." He rubbed his eye, which now sported a crescent of deep purple beneath it. "I tried to get up, but the bastard was all over me. I remember him punching me, and the next thing I knew I woke up tied to the chair with a gun pointed at my chest.

"He was calm at first. Said he knew 'you and Rutherford have been poking around'—those were his words—but he didn't think we'd found anything, because he had 'an inside track on that.' I told him I knew you, but I didn't know anything about what you'd been doing. Then he backhanded me and said I was lying, 'cause your girlfriend had passed on everything you two had said. I guess he was talking about Sandra. Then...."

"Okay, okay." I didn't want to hear the details. "You said he confessed. What did he say?"

"Well, he tried to get everything he could out of me, and when he realized I wasn't going to talk, he decided to beat it out of me. Then you called, and he backed off. I guess he realized you were on your way. He just sat down and said, 'Well, you know some of it—so let me give you the whole ugly truth. It won't matter anyway.' And then he started...."

For the next fifty miles, Roger talked, I listened.

CHAPTER Sixty

It had begun with a problem, a minor glitch early in the production process. Laura's alchemy worked like a dream in the lab, transforming otherwise useless forest byproducts into seemingly unlimited quantities of ethanol. The energy yield vastly exceeded the energy costs, a near-perfect antidote for an oil-addicted twenty-first century America. But somewhere between the Pyrex columns of the laboratory and the fuming, clanking machinery of the pilot plant, something changed. What worked well in theory was not nearly so efficient in actual practice, a fact unfortunately discovered long after Wall Street analysts were briefed and the future of American Timber Holdings stock price firmly hitched to the rising sun of a new dawn of independence from foreign oil.

The discovery of this fact, known only to those directly involved, precipitated a crisis in the executive offices of ATH. Under the hovering oversight of Bill Gray, frantic attempts were made to find a quick fix, some work-around that could transform the magic of the test tube into hard dollars on the bottom line. It would work eventually; everyone was confident of that. But no one could predict with any precision how long that would be. Days turned into weeks. The deadline for the announcement had been set. The Board of Directors was getting antsy. Weeks could not be allowed to turn into months.

The whole issue came to a head at a meeting between Gray, Wynne and Laura in the CEO's office, apparently the one described to me by Margaret

Powell. Wynne, the confident one, assured Gray the problem could be overcome in plenty of time to make the appropriate changes to the final design of the production plant. He told Gray to go public with the announcement and groundbreaking, that there was no need to mention more work needed to be done.

Laura was adamant that he should not. She argued it would be scientific fraud, and if a permanent solution could not be found, her reputation would be ruined. "She kept running on about honesty," Wynne laughed. "Bill Gray told her in big business, honesty is reality, and reality is perception. He told her he was moving ahead as planned." She said if the problem wasn't solved in thirty more days, she was going public with it on her own. She stormed out of the meeting, leaving Gray and Wynne to talk.

Wynne wasn't sure what happened next behind the scenes. Laura, fresh out of graduate school, had been brought in as his equal and was soon scheduled to take over as head research scientist. Relations were cordial, but strained, as they both continued to work long hours on retooling the process. They didn't make much progress. About three weeks later he was approached by his friend, Tony Rizzoli. Rizzoli said Bill Gray needed a job done, and was willing to pay well for it.

They discussed it over a few beers and a couple of lines of coke. "The plan was, we'd pay Laura a little visit, put the fear of God in her," Wynne said. "All I had to do was act as driver and lookout. Tony'd gotten a key to her apartment from Laura's ex-roomie, Sandra. He was going to rush her—home invasion style—and deliver a message, maybe rough her up a little, then leave. She'd never recognize him; he was going to wear a mask and gloves and said he'd be in and out in no time. It was going to be an easy ten grand for less than an hour's work. I said I was up for it—Laura was getting to be a pain in the ass anyway. Somebody needed to bring her down a notch or two."

Things couldn't have gone more wrong. They chose a weeknight, and waited until just after dark. "We were both pretty stoked on coke," Wynne admitted. They cruised through the parking lot of her apartment complex, making sure her car was there and the lights were on inside. With no one watching, they both approached the door. Wynne stood guard outside while Rizzoli pulled on his mask, quietly turned the key and burst in. Wynne said he heard Laura give a short scream, followed by silence for about thirty seconds. He then heard a man's voice followed by a crash and the sound of fighting. He rushed in to find Laura cowering in the corner and Rizzoli rolling on the floor grappling with David Hargrove. Rizzoli said later he'd burst in and found Laura alone, not knowing Hargrove had just stepped into the bathroom.

Rizzoli's mask had been pulled off in the fight. Laura and Hargrove recognized both him and Wynne immediately. They subdued them quickly, binding them with plastic ties and stuffing kitchen towels in their mouths to keep them quiet. They had a big problem with no good solution. Wynne said, "We sat down and discussed our options. There weren't many good ones. We'd been seen, and if we let them go, we'd both be looking at prison." Especially Rizzoli, the ex-con.

Rizzoli used his cell phone to call Gray, who went ballistic. They went back and forth, with Gray finally telling him to "solve the problem permanently." Rizzoli told him it would be expensive, but Gray replied the alternatives would be even more so. He instructed Rizzoli to "make it look like an accident, and make sure no one can trace it back to any of us."

They locked their bound victims in one of the back rooms while they tried to decide their fate. "Maybe it was because we were high, maybe it was because we were desperate, I don't know," Wynne said. "We decided a plane crash would be perfect." They were all members of the skydiving club and knew Hargrove was an instrument-rated pilot who had access to the hangar and planes. Rizzoli and Wynne were both experienced in nighttime parachute jumps from their days as Navy SEALS. "All we'd need was a brightly lit parking lot that we could see from 5,000 feet," Wynne said. As crazy as it might sound, they decided to go for it.

Initially, they thought they'd force Hargrove to steal the plane and take off, telling him they were planning to skip town and that he was to fly them to Florida, then refuel and on to the Bahamas. They would kill the two somewhere in route, skydive out and let the plane go down where it would, thinking that the crash would destroy most of the evidence. They soon realized it wasn't a good plan, as a stolen plane that crashes without a distress call from the pilot would raise suspicion and a detailed investigation.

"Then it hit me," Wynne said. "What if the pilot were out of it, and couldn't call in an SOS? Like those guys who get knocked out by carbon monoxide from a leaking exhaust manifold." It all began to fall into place. The lab routinely used carbon monoxide. It would be easy enough to borrow a small cylinder. If there were enough left of any bodies to do an autopsy, the blood levels of carbon monoxide would be in a fatal range, explaining the lack of radio contact as the plane went down. "We realized we were about to commit the perfect crime."

The next thing they had to decide was where they could safely bail out of the plane and land unseen in the middle of the night. It didn't take them long to remember that the near-deserted parking lot of the pilot plant in Walkerville would be the perfect spot. They'd just need someone to distract the security guard for a few minutes, then pick them up and bring them back to Atlanta. Rizzoli said Gray could figure that part out.

Rizzoli called Gray and talked with him while standing guard over the captives. Meanwhile, Wynne drove to the research lab to pick up a tank of carbon monoxide and some masks that could be rigged to fit over David and Laura's faces. When he returned he found Rizzoli had gone through Laura's files on Gray's instructions, stealing her laptop to make it appear there'd been a robbery. "Gray wanted to be sure she didn't have anything in her private files that might alert the cops about what was going on at the lab," Roger said. "And just to be certain they could discredit her, they planted the cocaine the apartment manager found."

Assuring Laura and David that they wouldn't be harmed, they drove to the airport in Winder, about half an hour outside Atlanta. David drove, with Laura in the passenger's seat and Wynne and Rizzoli in the back with pistols pointed at their victims' heads. They hunkered down as David punched his entry code into the gate and drove to the skydiving club's hangar.

Roger spoke without inflection, almost mechanically recounting Wynne's spontaneous confession. But I sensed the tension building in his voice as he replayed the scenes in his mind's eye. As the tale progressed he gripped the wheel ever tighter as if to avoid being sucked into a vortex of rage and sorrow.

I said, "Hey, why don't we talk about this later? We've got plenty of time. I don't need to hear all the details right now."

"No. I want to tell you. I am going to have to tell this story again—several times. This first time is the hardest, and if I break down and make a fool of myself, at least it will be in front of someone who'll cut me some slack."

"Roger, it's okay...." I started.

He said, "Let me finish," and resumed speaking.

Once at the hangar, getting the parachutes was no problem. Each member kept his own gear in a locker. Wynne and Rizzoli threw in theirs plus their reserve chutes, plus one each for David and Laura so as not to alert them as to what was going on.

I noticed Roger breathing more rapidly, his knuckles white as he gripped the wheel. I said, "Really, I think we should talk about this later."

"No, dammit, I am going to finish what I started to say." I could see tears welling up in his eyes. He swallowed, swiped at his cheeks, then said, "And then they raped her. Both of them, Matt. Wynne said it was a shame for such a fine piece of ass to go to waste. He laughed about it. He said she begged and pleaded and when they didn't stop, she squealed like a pig." He stopped, and the only sound was the soft roar of tires on the asphalt. I didn't know what to say. Then Roger said, "He laughed about it. If I ever see him again I'm going to kill him."

CHAPTER Sixty-One

We rode in silence the rest of the way. There was more to what Wynne had said, but Roger didn't want to talk, and I had heard enough. We skirted Athens, trading the turnpike for a two-lane byway near the foothills town of Demorest. Traveling north and west beyond Clarksville, we passed through green summer pastures set in broad valleys between the low mountains that mark the southernmost border of the Appalachians. At one time this was farming country, the sort of place where a man could make a halfway decent living for his family on a hundred or so acres. Now it was rapidly becoming a playground for Atlanta's huddled masses, a place of weekend respite from their gated subdivisions and high-rise prisons. We fell in line behind SUVs and luxury mini-vans with Fulton County tags, Roger's pickup looking strangely out of place in the Saturday afternoon parade.

A few miles north of the tiny settlement known as Batesville we turned off the highway into the rabbit warren of secondary roads that ring Lake Burton. It's an artificial lake, completed just after World War I to supply Atlanta's growing demand for electric power. The new dam flooded a ten-mile section of the Tallulah River, inundating the early nineteenth century gold-mining town of Burton, from which it drew its name. In return for the sacrifice, Atlanta's wealth propelled the area from a quaint backwater of dirt roads and fishing cabins to a showcase for multimillion-dollar weekend McMansions populated by the same folks who rub shoulders at the Capital

City or Piedmont Driving Clubs during the week.

We pulled over to study the map. Gray's place sat on the tip of a small peninsula on the west side of the lake. Roger's file included a printout of the local tax assessor's data; I noted it had three stories, five bedrooms, six baths and was valued at $2.34 million. We had no idea what to expect and I didn't want to risk a rerun of what had happened at the pilot plant. I said, "We don't even know if Gray is at home, and if he is, there's a good probability that he's talked to Wynne. He may be expecting us."

"Yeah, I'd thought of that," Roger said. "I'm not sure, but I think we might be able to get a look at the place from across the next cove, here." He stabbed at the map with a pencil. "I've got some binoculars behind the seat." He took a deep breath. "You were right, Matt, I was a fool to try to collar Wynne without backup. If his Tahoe's parked at Gray's place, I'm ready to call the cops. But like I said, I don't think there's enough evidence to talk them into issuing a warrant. I can do it—I'm an officer of the law acting on a spontaneous confession from one of his co-conspirators." Roger seemed to have recovered somewhat, dropping back into cop-ese.

We drove past Gray's driveway, a blacktop-covered lane flanked by two stacked granite columns, one of which bore a brass plaque reading "Graywood." I tried peering down it but could only see snatches of a slate roof and a massive stone chimney. We skirted around a cove until we were approximately opposite the peninsula some quarter mile across open water. I got my first full view of the house. It was a tall structure of wood and dressed stone, set on a steep lot and commanding a 270-degree view of the lake and the mountains to the north. It was just after eight in the evening, and most of the house was in shadow, protected from the heat of the setting sun by the forested slope behind it.

Roger studied it a moment through the binoculars, then handed them to me. The entrance appeared to be on the top floor through a small courtyard-like area. Beyond it, the roof of a four-bay carport was set on hewn timbers supported by stacked granite columns matching those by the entrance gate. Through a gap in the trees I could make out a 500-series Mercedes parked near the front door, and could just see the hood of what appeared to be an older model brown vehicle in front of the carport. Wynne's Tahoe was nowhere to be seen. "What do you think?" I asked.

"Two vehicles, neither of them Wynne's, unless he's changed cars. The other one looks like it's got some mileage on it—probably belongs to the housekeeper. What do *you* think?"

"I think we should call the house, see who answers," I said, slapping at my pocket for my cell phone before remembering that it lay in a heap on the floor of the ATH lab building back in Walkerville.

Roger said, "He got mine, too. Rule that out." He thought for a minute. "Screw it. Wynne was a hands-on killer. Gray's the CEO of a multibillion-dollar corporation. He hires his work done. We can handle him."

We backed the truck in a nearby driveway and turned around. My palms were sweating as we turned between the pillars marking the entrance to Graywood and eased down the driveway. The brown car was visible now, a faded decade-old Buick. I saw Roger's eyes widen, then watched him make a fist and slam the steering wheel. "Shit!" he spat vehemently.

"What?" His reaction caught me off guard.

"Look!" he said, gesturing toward the Buick.

"Look at what?" I said, just as I realized that it carried an Adams County tag. And then it hit me. I'd seen the car before. In a carport in Walkerville, parked next to an old pickup. "That's not...? It couldn't be...," I started.

"It is," Roger said, his voice lowered. "It belongs to Laura's mother, Agnes." He stopped the pickup in the middle of the driveway. "Look, Matt, I don't know what the hell this means." He cut his eyes back and forth rapidly, thinking. "It may be Wynne. He knew his car would be recognized, so he stole hers. If he's hurt her or Carl...." He didn't finish his sentence, instead putting the truck in reverse and backing up to the head of the driveway. He switched off the ignition and tossed the keys under the seat. "Okay, if it's Wynne, there's no way he's getting out of this driveway unless he can fly over this truck."

We got out, easing the doors shut to keep down noise. Cautiously, we approached the Buick. It was unlocked, the keys lying in plain view on the console. Roger touched the hood and said, "Still warm. It hasn't been sitting here long."

We crouched down behind the car, out of sight of the house. There was something wrong about this situation. I said, "We drove straight here and never got below ten miles over the speed limit. There's no way Wynne could have made it into town, found the McIntoshes' house, stolen the car and gotten here before us." I looked Roger in the eye. "Did you talk with Carl or Agnes after I called you from Atlanta today?"

Roger, angry as he was, looked a little embarrassed. "Yeah, of course. I've been talking with them pretty much every day. Mainly Agnes, sometimes Carl."

"But I thought you said...?"

"Yeah, you don't have to remind me. So I changed my mind. They were going to be family. I had to...."

"Have you told them any details?"

"Everything. Why not? Don't they have a right to know?"

"Did you talk with them today?

"Yes. Twice to Agnes."

"When?"

"The first time after you called me from Atlanta to tell me what you'd found out at Rizzoli's. Then again when I was on my way to arrest Wynne."

"So she knows everything you know."

"Up to a point, yeah."

I took a deep breath. "Roger, I have an idea it's Agnes in that house, not Wynne."

"No way. She's afraid to drive out of town. Says she'd get lost."

"Then we need to be very careful," I said.

Roger nodded and ran, half crouched, into the carport out of direct view of the windows on the front of the house. I followed and we took shelter out of sight behind a low stone wall. "Did you get a look at the front door?" he asked in a whisper.

"No. Did you?"

"Yeah, it looked like it was partially open. That's strange." Without waiting for me to reply he ran, again half-crouched, toward the house, reaching the front stoop and flattening himself against the stonework next to the entry door. He peered around the door jam, then turned toward me and held up his hands about six inches apart to show that the door was open. Following his signal, I ran across the courtyard and flattened myself against the wall on the other side of the door.

Making a sign for me to stay put, Roger reached around the door jam and gave it a little shove. With a creak, the thick oak swung back. A wave of cool air pushed out into the heaviness of the summer afternoon. We both peered around the corner.

The interior of the house was dark, but it appeared the foyer opened into a great room lined on the far side by floor-to-ceiling windows with an expansive view of the lake and the far shore beyond. The only sounds were the soft humming of the cooling system and the ticking of a grandfather clock just inside the door. Roger said, "Hello?" There was no reply. Cautiously, he slipped inside, keeping his body flattened against one wall. He advanced, flounder-like, toward the great room, then stopped, seemed to relax and stepped away from his protected stance. I heard him say, "Hello."

From out of the darkness, a soft voice replied, "Oh, is that you, Roger?"

CHAPTER Sixty-Two

Roger said, "It's okay," and waved for me to come in. I stepped into the richly furnished foyer, following an antique Shiraz runner toward the great room. Roger was speaking softly to someone sitting just out of sight behind the corner. It took a moment for my eyes to adjust to the darkness. I couldn't quite make out the figure in the shadows, but I heard a familiar, "Hello, Matt. I didn't expect to see both of you."

Agnes McIntosh was sitting primly in a straight-backed Windsor chair pushed against the wall next to an antique walnut hunt board. Her hair was neatly coiffed on top of her head in her usual beehive. She was wearing a faded cotton house dress and sensible lace-up brown shoes with stockings. She balanced an oversized purse on her knees, gripping the handle tightly with white-gloved hands. There was a look of calm on her face. "I was just sitting here, trying to decide what to do. I have a bad tendency to plan things only so far, and then I have to stop and think about what to do next."

"Agnes, are you all right?" I asked.

She smiled, "Why, yes, I am now, but thank you so much for asking." She hesitated, then, "I guess it's a good thing that you two came."

"Where is Gray?" Roger asked.

"Over there," Agnes said, nodding with her head and continuing to grip her purse tightly. We both looked in the direction of the window-wall. I noticed one of the panes was shattered. Gray was nowhere to be seen.

"Where?" we both said at the same time.

"Behind the sofa. I don't think he moved." In two bounds we were across the huge room. William "Bill" Cranston Gray, CEO of American Timber Holdings, Inc., lay on the floor in front of a multimillion dollar view of Lake Burton, a dark crimson hole in the middle of his chest while a deep red puddle under him spread and lapped at the silk fringe of a Isfahan prayer rug.

"I shot him, of course," Agnes volunteered from across the room.

"Agnes, why? Why?" There was anguish in Roger's voice.

"Well, you might say, 'Why not?' He was guilty. You know that— otherwise you wouldn't be here. I'm presuming you came to arrest him."

"Yes, but...."

"But, what?" Agnes spoke calmly. "Roger, you've been so good to keep me up to date on every single little thing, and when you called today about Mr. Rizzoli and Mr. Wynne, it all fell into place. Mr. Gray and his cursed stock options. He was the one that stood to profit the most from Laura's death. He had to be the ultimate one behind it all."

"He was. Wynne said...," Roger started.

"Did you arrest Mr. Wynne?"

"No, he got away."

"That's a shame," Agnes said, "But not without a fight, I see, judging from your black eye."

"Yeah."

"Well, what I was saying is that Mr. Gray would have hired the very best lawyers his blood money could buy, and in the end, he'd probably get away with it. Sure he might lose his job and spend millions on legal fees, but why should he care? He'd become so rich it didn't matter anymore." I noticed that she was speaking of him in the past tense.

"So I did a very bad thing," Agnes said. "I took justice into my own hands. I just said hello to him and killed him. It was really very easy." She took a deep breath. "You know, I was just sitting here wondering if I should call 911, or look up the local police number. Someone will need to arrest me. But now that you're here, Roger, maybe you can do that. You can arrest me, can't you?"

Roger ignored her question. "Agnes, how did you get here? I've never seen you drive outside of the Walkerville city limits."

"Oh, that was going to change. Laura, right before the accident, gave me one of those little GPS thingies that you sit up on the dash of your car. I'd been trying it out some at home. It's really quite easy, you just type in the address you want to go to and press 'Navigate.' There is a sweet voice that talks to you and tells you when to turn, or how far it is to the next intersection. In fact, the voice sounds a lot like Laura's. You don't suppose she had it programmed that way, do you?" She seemed to suppress a little giggle.

"Anyway," Agnes continued, "I called directory assistance and got Mr. Gray's phone number here and then asked them to confirm the address. I put it in the GPS and got here in just over two hours. It was no problem at all."

"So you shot him, just like that? No discussion, nothing?" Roger asked.

"I'd made up my mind it was the best thing to do."

"Where's the gun?"

"Here," she said, unsnapping her purse and withdrawing a long-barreled .357 magnum.

"My god," Roger said. "Where did you get that? I thought Carl hated guns. I remember him telling me about Korea, and how he swore that if he made it home alive he'd never touch a firearm again."

She slipped it back in her purse and said quietly, "I got it from Laura's father years ago."

"But I didn't think he kept a gun," Roger repeated.

Agnes shot him a sharp look. "I said I got it from Laura's father."

"But…."

"Oh, dear, she didn't tell you, did she?" Agnes seemed distressed.

"Tell me what?"

"You were going to get married. She promised me she'd tell you. I think you need to know that sort of thing."

"Agnes, what are you talking about?" Now Roger seemed distressed.

She looked at me and said, "Matt, this involves you in a peripheral sort of way. And since I have no secrets any more, I might as well confess everything. But I would ask that you not tell Carl, unless of course you absolutely have to. Will you both promise me that?"

We nodded.

"I want you to know that I love Carl. I have always loved him—there's never been a shade of doubt about that. But the one thing that hurt our marriage was the fact he couldn't father children. It was definitely his problem—maybe from something that happened in the war—I don't know. So we had resigned ourselves to be happy alone, just the two of us, to build a life and a future.

"Of course you two didn't know me in those days. You were scarcely toddlers, if that. I'm a dowdy old woman now, I know, but I like to imagine that back then I was what the kids today call 'hot.' I was slim and exercised and took care of myself. I did all the right things, but for whom? Without a child to care for there was something missing in my life."

Turning to me she said, "Matt, what I am going to say may be a shock, but I think at this point I owe everyone an explanation." She paused, "Do you remember last summer when you and Laura went out a couple of times?" I nodded. "And you called, but she made up some excuse not to see you and broke it off rather suddenly? Didn't you think that was a little strange?" I didn't, but I said nothing.

Agnes continued, "She thought you were great—of course that's before she and Roger got serious. But she refused to go out with you again because I told her not to."

"Why?" I was curious.

"Because she's your first cousin…"

"What?!" Both Roger and I spoke simultaneously.

"And now there are three people in the world who know that fact," Agnes said quietly. "You see, Carl and I have always been friends with your Uncle Jack and Aunt Margie. Just friends, nothing more. It was one of those times when I was so desperate, so yearnful for a baby. And it was one of those times when Jack and Margie were going through a rough patch in their marriage—everybody has them. It was wrong—I knew it was wrong at the time. Carl was out of town at a hardware convention. I made some excuse about the hot water heater suddenly flooding the basement and called Jack and told him it was an emergency and begged him to come over and help me get it stopped. He didn't have a chance. I seduced him. I put him in a position where he couldn't say no. And it worked. I got—we got—a beautiful baby girl."

I'd been watching Roger as Agnes spoke, his face drained of color and his jaw hanging open as if he wanted to say something but didn't have the strength to make his lips move.

"I was planning to tell her one day, if and when she decided to get married. I think it's important for you know your genetic heritage. You don't want to get involved with someone and find out later he's a close relative. When you two went out, it sort of forced my hand. I had to tell her. And she was supposed to tell you, too, Roger, but I guess she hadn't gotten around to it."

"You didn't tell Jack?" I asked.

"Oh, no," Agnes said. "It wouldn't have been fair to him, to let him know he'd been used like that. He was worried when he found out I was pregnant, but I told him the timing was wrong and that I was sure Carl was the father. That was in the days before DNA, of course, but when Laura was born, I told him the blood type proved that she couldn't have been his child. In fact, it proved that she couldn't have been Carl's, but he was none the wiser. As far as the world must ever know, Laura was Carl's child."

Roger and I were both speechless. Agnes sat up, thrusting her shoulders back and taking a deep breath. "So now you need to arrest me, I guess? I've just admitted to breaking at least two of the Ten Commandments, maybe three if you count my wanting a baby as coveting."

I looked at Roger. He looked back at me. I nodded. Roger said, "Agnes, can your GPS get you home?"

She seemed a little taken off guard. "Well, I guess so. It got me here."

"It's getting dark outside. Will you be all right to drive at night?"

"I think so…."

"Then why don't you go on home? Just be careful and don't have an accident. Don't say anything to anyone about where you've been. We'll talk next week." With that he took her by her arm and gently walked her out to her car, then walked up the driveway to move the truck. We watched in silence as she cautiously steered her way up the driveway and into the dusk.

When she'd gone, I said, "How do you want to handle this?"

He looked at his watch. "Give her fifteen minutes head start, then we'll call 911. We'll tell them that Gray was dead when we got here. That's the truth."

"Yeah," I said. We walked back in the house and sat silently in the darkened great room. Outside a few fireflies flickered past the window.

The phone rang. I looked at Roger and he shook his head. "They'll hang up."

On the tenth ring, there was a click, followed by the sound of an answering machine picking up. Bill Gray's voice spoke from beyond the grave, "Hi, you've reached Graywood, the Gray residence at Lake Burton. Sorry we missed your call. Please leave a message and we'll get back to you."

There was a slight pause, then another familiar voice said, "Bill, this is Sandra. I've tried to call you a couple of times today but you won't answer. I don't know why—maybe you've talked with someone, maybe you're mad. I hate to say this in a phone message; I wanted to say it in person, but I think you're avoiding me.

"I'm quitting. I'm leaving. I want to thank you for everything you've done for me, but I've gotten involved with someone else. Someone I care about. Someone who I hope cares about me. I want out. I want to change. I'm sorry but...." The machine abruptly clicked followed by the sound of a dial tone, then silence.

Roger looked at me, trying to read my expression in the near-darkness. Fortunately, he couldn't. I said, "It's been long enough. Let's dial 911."

Epilogue

Word of the murder of the CEO of one of Atlanta's major companies reached the newswires too late to make the Sunday papers, but was the topic of banner headlines on Monday and the remainder of the week. The delay was not wasted, however, as it gave reporters an opportunity to include the news of a second murder, that of one Anthony M. ("Tony") Rizzoli, an ex-con and a freelance photographer who sometimes did contract work for American Timber Holdings, Inc. Police were tight-lipped about how the two murders were connected, simply saying they were both "part of an ongoing investigation."

Roger and I spent most of the night talking with officers of the Rabun County Sheriff's Department, and later, investigators from the Georgia Bureau of Investigation. Their initial reaction was to arrest us on suspicion of murder, but a few phone calls and assurances from the sheriff of Adams County kept us out of handcuffs long enough to convince everyone we were operating on the same side of the law.

Based on what they learned from us, a squad from the Atlanta police descended on the Myrtle Street home and studio of Tony Rizzoli shortly after daylight and an hour after identifying Clayton Wynne's Tahoe parked two streets over. They found the lights on, the radio blaring and the handle of an eight-inch butcher knife extending from the middle of Rizzoli's sternum. There were signs of a struggle, and subsequent investigation revealed

Wynne's fingerprints on the knife handle. Rizzoli's Subaru station wagon was missing, together with an undetermined amount of cash his bookkeeper said he kept hidden in a cubbyhole behind one of the filing cabinets. Investigators recovered several pistols, all stolen, plus a significant quantity of cocaine in powder form and half a dozen vials of injectable steroids of the type favored by weight lifters. (It was later suggested that some of Rizzoli's and Wynne's bizarre behavior might have been a result of the abuse of steroids and cocaine, but few people paid much attention to the idea.)

A phone call at home Sunday night alerted me to the fact that they planned to arrest Sandra Williams on Monday morning. This was turning out to be a big case, and with two of the major suspects dead and the third on the run, the District Attorney was being deprived of his vote-getting televised perp walks. I was advised to tune in to WSB-TV at 8 a.m. The police cars and video vans arrived at Sandra's condo a few minutes after eight. They led Sandra out in handcuffs, followed by a tall man with a ponytail and business suit who was identified as her lawyer. Apparently she'd known the arrest was coming and had offered to surrender downtown, an offer that was denied in favor of the publicized arrest ritual. Her hair was perfect, her silk blouse shimmering in the sun, and she held her head high as she was placed in the back seat of the police cruiser.

The District Attorney himself executed the warrant. Sandra was charged as an Accessory to Murder, a fact vehemently denied by her attorney in the quasi-impromptu photo op that followed, complete with rebuttal from the DA accompanied by a few general words on how the city was safer under his administration. Hovering in the background I saw the same blue-haired neighbor, a smug smile of self-satisfaction on her face.

A detailed search of Sandra's condo turned up several pieces of jewelry that had belonged to Laura and had apparently been stolen at the time of the murder. She denied she was aware they were Laura's and stated they were gifts from Rizzoli, who must have taken them on the night of the murder. As it turned out later, Agnes's strange reaction to Sandra was the result of her recognizing the bracelet Sandra was wearing as one that had belonged to her daughter. For some reason, she had chosen not to mention it, thinking at the time that perhaps Laura had given it to her.

Threatened with having the charges against her elevated to First Degree Murder, Sandra elected to fire her attorney and began cooperating with the police. On Wednesday, her new attorney, a meek little bald fellow with thick glasses, managed to have them reduced to Accessory After the Fact, securing her release on a hundred-thousand dollar property bond signed by her parents. Her passport was confiscated and she was required to wear an ankle bracelet to monitor her whereabouts.

On Friday afternoon the multiple law enforcement agencies involved held a joint news conference to update the public on the status of the investigation. Based on the outline that Roger and I provided, plus what appeared to be copious quantities of corroborating evidence gleaned from five days of intense investigation, they described a series of events that eventually ended in the felony murder of Laura Anne McIntosh and David L. Hargrove as well as the nearly successful effort to make this appear as a tragic accident.

Roger and I watched the news conference live on CNN over a few beers at my house. They'd done a good job in tying up loose ends, Roger commented with some professional esteem. He was given credit (as "a deputy sheriff from Adams County") for cracking the case. According to the investigators, it was theorized that after escaping from Roger's attempt to arrest him, Wynne fled to Atlanta seeking protection or money from Rizzoli. They apparently argued and fought, with Wynne killing Rizzoli and taking both his vehicle and cash.

They also theorized that some hours earlier, Rizzoli had gone to Lake Burton to confront Bill Gray about his relationship with Sandra Williams, a showdown that resulted in Gray's murder. Rizzoli's fingerprints were found on numerous surfaces, with the telephone message from Sandra confirming the cause of the dispute. The single fatal bullet had passed first through Gray's body, then the window and out into the lake, so unfortunately ballistic evidence was not available. The investigators agreed that the facts in this case were sufficient to charge Rizzoli with murder, with his death rendering such an accusation moot. Both Roger and I felt they couldn't have arrived at that conclusion without some encouragement from Sandra, but were uncertain of her motivations.

The most shocking revelations concerned the details of Laura's and David's kidnapping and murder. DNA evidence confirmed that Laura had been raped by both Rizzoli and Wynne. Video evidence from the Walkerville lab and pilot plant security system cameras clearly captured them landing by parachute in the parking lot and being picked up by Bill Gray. "So he was in it up to his eyeballs," Roger commented.

There were other consequences. American Timber Holdings stock went into freefall, wiping out in one trading session all of its recent gains and closing by the end of the day at an all-time low. The SEC and other state and federal agencies launched investigations, one of which eventually snared three of Adams County's Commissioners on charges of insider trading. The hardest hit was Inman Greene, the Chairman. He'd gotten greedy and tied up nearly a hundred thousand shares, most of which he bought on margin in his own name and that of half a dozen other family members. He was unable to meet the first margin call, ending up bankrupt and facing both massive fines and jail time. He is currently serving forty-two months in a federal prison in Florida.

It turned out that Greene had been behind the attempt to scare me out of looking into Laura's death. I presume that Gray had said something to him, and he in turn paid his two sons-in-law—both in the logging business—to "put the fear of God in me." When the feds began investigating Greene, they chose confession as the better part of valor. I chose not to press charges.

I was one of only two people I knew who actually made money on ATH stock. My broker's decision to unload it was sheer luck, nothing more. The other person was my secretary, Beverly. While doing her routine filing she'd noticed on my brokerage statement that I'd sold my stock. Thinking perhaps I knew something she didn't, she sold hers, too.

The ironic thing was that in the weeks after Laura's murder, Wynne and his team had actually achieved the breakthrough they'd been searching for. The production plant, if it's ever completed, will help fulfill the dream of low cost energy. It's unlikely that it will be owned by American Timber Holdings, however. As Gray had so aptly observed, in business "reality is perception." No amount of positive publicity could offset the fact that the company's CEO ordered and was intimately involved in a bizarre double murder, and was himself killed by a rival for the mistress whom he kept in a company-owned condo. ATH was forced to put hundreds of thousands of acres of timberland on the market; I used my profits from their stock to buy a large tract next to some land I already owned.

Wynne was eventually caught trying to cross the border into Mexico near Laredo. He was extradited, and when faced with the overwhelming evidence against him, plead guilty to the murders of Laura, David and Rizzoli. I suppose he hoped that by doing so and throwing himself on the mercy of the court, he might avoid a death sentence. He didn't. He's now on death row working his way through the mandatory appeals, but no one sees much chance of his having any success.

The McIntoshes returned to their quiet life. It was rumored but never confirmed that they were paid a huge settlement by American Timber Holdings. I do know that the First Baptist Church has begun work on the new Laura McIntosh Sunday School Building, and that Georgia Tech announced the funding of ten annual Laura McIntosh Scholarships in Applied Biochemistry, but the source of the funds behind these projects has never been identified. With the exception of a new Buick in a shade of brown similar to the old one and a small satellite TV dish that has sprouted in their yard, not much seems to have changed in their world. I see them every now and then, strolling arm in arm down Main Street, appearing very much in love.

I never heard any more from Sandra. I don't know what she told the investigators, but she seemed to have kept my name out of it. It never became public as to what she knew and when she knew it. If she didn't know all the details, she certainly had to be aware at some point that a crime had been committed. Her main offense seems to have been that she maintained her loyalty to Bill Gray until the very end. She was sentenced to ten years in prison and will probably be out in six or seven, I'm told. She'll still be young, and may yet get her chance to start over.

Roger seems to be getting on with his life. He hasn't said anything to me directly, but the other day I saw him riding down Main Street with a young blond who looked a lot like Krista Nielsen sitting next to him on the front seat of his truck. He'll make it.

As for me, I've been back at work on the stables, still waiting for my life to take some positive direction. ∎

AUTHOR'S NOTE AND ACKNOWLEDGMENTS

For those readers not familiar with the timber industry—most of you, I assume—the details in *The Mile High Club* are for the most part true. American Timber Holdings could have been any one of a number of large wood products companies, and the descriptions of the business, logging operations, etc. are routine to those of us who live in "rural" areas of the American South. The concept of efficiently producing ethanol from cellulose has been the Holy Grail of those interested in alternative fuels, and biofuel plants like the one described in this book are more of a question of "when" rather than "if." I like to write believable fiction. As in my previous novels, if it didn't happen exactly as I said it did, I want to believe it could have.

I am most appreciative to those many persons who were kind enough to provide input, review and technical assistance. They include, in no particular order, Clyde Wright, Mimi Langenderfer, Sherrill Jones, Anne Nevin, Carol Gray, Marianne Santos, Sarah Arnett, Lisa McDonald, Dr. Roger K. Thomas, Dan Roper and Jackie Cooper. I apologize to any whose names I may have inadvertently omitted. My sincere appreciation is extended to the staff of Indigo Press, and especially to Scott Baber for his design work for the cover. My wife, Beth, and daughters, Elizabeth and Sarah, have been wonderful sounding boards for my creative efforts. As always, the greatest inspiration comes from my muse, Laura Ashley, who materially assisted me with so many scenes in this book.

I welcome feedback and comments from readers, both positive and negative. Feel free to contact me via email at rawlings@pascuamanagement. com or through my website at www.williamrawlings.com.

William Rawlings
Sandersville, Georgia

ABOUT THE AUTHOR

William Rawlings lives in Sandersville, Georgia where he practices medicine, raises pine trees and generally enjoys life far from the urban sprawl of Atlanta. He and his wife, the former Beth Dunwody of Macon, have two children. Besides writing novels, Rawlings is a frequent contributor to newspapers and magazines, an avid world traveler and an accomplished photographer. Please visit his website at www.williamrawlings.com.

Other Novels by William Rawlings

The Lazard Legacy

The Rutherford Cipher

The Tate Revenge

Crossword